Winter of Discontent

A Novel

Cover images and Northern Ireland map courtesy of Shutterstock.

This is a work of fiction. The characters, places, events, and dialog portrayed in this novel are the product of the author's imagination and are either fictitious or used factiously. Any resemblance to actual people living or dead, events, or locales is entirely coincidental.

"Winter of Discontent," by Douglas Clark. ISBN 978-1-63868-225-7 (softcover); 978-1-63868-226-4 (hardcover); 9 78-1-63868-227-1 (electronic).

Published 2025 by Virtualbookworm.com Publishing Inc., P.O. Box 9949, College Station, TX 77842, US.

By Douglas Clark

Belfast
Take Five
Shell Game
Evermore
Critical Mass
Fault Lines
Provoke the Devil
The Irish Spy
Endgame
Hunting Odessa
The American Spy
Havana
Moscow Winter
Southland Noir
Fire in the Hole
For God & Gold
Winter of Discontent

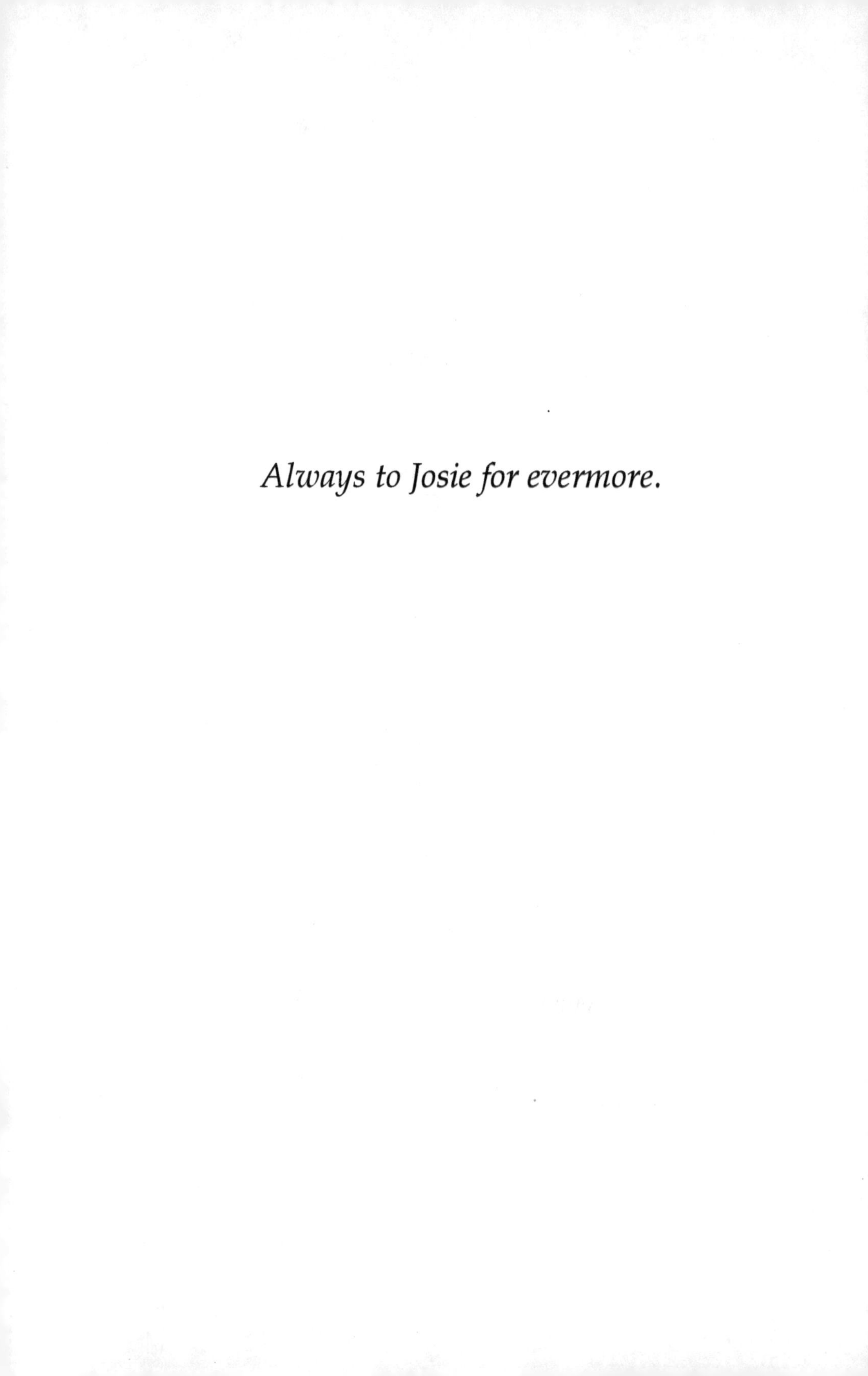

Always to Josie for evermore.

Winter of Discontent

A Novel

Douglas Clark

Kintyre
Campbeltown
Arran
North Channel
Inishowen
Pen.
Moville
Buncrana
L. Foyle
Coleraine
Portstewart
Portrush
Limavady
Ballymoney
Ballycastle
Cushendall
Mts of Antrim
ANTRIM
Letterkenny
DONEGAL
Lifford
Stranorlar
Londonderry
LONDONDERRY
Strabane
Sion Mills
Sawel Mt.
Sperrin
Newtownstewart
Magherafelt
Ballymena
NORTHERN
Randalstown
Ballyclare
Carncastle
Larne
Donegal
Castlederg
TYRONE
Moneymore
Lough
Antrim
Carrickfergus
Ulster
Omagh
Cookstown
Newtownabbey
Belfast L.
Bangor
Neagh
Belfast
Coalisland
Donaghadee
Lower
L. Erne
Irvinestown
Dromore
Dungannon
IRELAND
Comber
Newtownards
Ballygawley
Craigavon
Lisburn
Saintfield
Strangford L.
Ards Pen.
Enniskillen
Aughnacloy
Lurgan
FERMANAGH
Armagh
Portadown
Lagan
DOWN
Upper
Erne
Monaghan
ARMAGH
Tandragee
Banbridge
Ballynahinch
Portaferry
Middletown
Downpatrick
Keady
Dundrum
Clones
Ardglass
St. John's Pt.
MONAGHAN
Newry
Mourne
Mts.
Newcastle
Dundrum B.
Belturbet
Annalee
Castleblaney
Slieve Gullion
Slieve
Donard
LEITRIM
L. Oughter
Cavan
Cootehill
Warrenpoint
Dundalk
Greenore
Kilkeel
CAVAN
Carrickmacross
Carlingford L.
L. Gowna
Kingscourt
Louth
LOUTH
Dundalk Bay
L. Sheelin
Granard
Ardee

CHAPTER 1

Boston, Massachusetts | January 2025

Late in the late afternoon of an overcast frigid winter day, Terence Kelly sat in the living room of his second-floor apartment in South Boston in front of a fire in the fireplace. A well-appointed apartment in a stylish brick walkup row house a mile south of the Charles River. Two hours earlier he left his doctor's office. Following his medical appointment the previous day, he received a summons to return to the office. The receptionist told him only that the doctor wanted to review his recent test results in person.

Expecting a troubling prognosis, the doctor's pronouncement still came as a shock. Fourth stage small cell lung cancer. Needed further testing to confirm and provide more detail, but there was little doubt about the diagnosis. This was a fast-growing more aggressive form of lung cancer that tended to metastasize to other organs. Terminal. Inoperable. Depending upon chemotherapy effectiveness, he had only 6 to 12 months to live. To the doctor's consternation, Kelly spent considerable time asking about the symptoms approaching the end-stage period rather than discussing the recommended therapy regimen.

A couple of whiskeys and the warmth of the fire moved Kelly past the immediate shock of the unsettling news. For the last fifty years, living was an emotional ordeal. Events experienced in the early 1970s transformed an otherwise promising life into something quite different. Although professionally successful as an engineer, Terence Kelly became self-absorbed. Antisocial to the point of reclusive. Perhaps clinically suffering depression, yet in his situation he understood all too well the cause. Disgust and guilt for crimes committed in his youth remained a constant source for self-judgement. That and failure to have ever exercised the courage necessary to make any form of change that might be considered atonement.

This terminal diagnosis might now offer that opportunity. Admittedly since now revealing his secret could no longer replace his barren life with one of likely worse emotional distress. For several hours he sat without moving as the fire died away. From an immediate thought growing since the doctor delivered his diagnosis, Terence Kelly began earnestly examining an idea. As he sat in silence, the idea began taking shape into a rough plan. A technical problem with which to absorb his attention. Perhaps something that he could at least consider as a measure of atonement.

"This is Father Connor O'Brien. How can help you?"

The faculty secretary for the graduate school of the Morrissey College of Arts and Sciences at Boston College told Professor O'Brien this persistent caller would say only he had some material that might prove of historical interest. The material related to the period of the *Troubles* of Northern Ireland.

Terence Kelly replied, "Thank you for taking my call, Father. My name is Terence Kelly. Do you prefer to be addressed as father or professor?"

"Either is appropriate. Depends on the circumstances and what you wish to discuss."

"Perhaps both titles are then appropriate. However, my call will likely be of greater interest for its historical value to an academic scholar of Irish history. I have read your work. Your nonfiction scholarly historical works on twentieth century Ireland as well as your historical fiction novels. *Birth of the Irish Nation* and especially *Thirty Years of War in Northern Ireland* are among the best works on twentieth century Irish history I have read. The novels *The Paladin of Cork* and *Belfast Requiem* set against these same periods offer authenticity and insights. For a fellow Catholic Irishman, I very much admire your objectivity. By that I mean your views critical of various aspects of all the players in Ireland's troubled history regardless of which side they occupied during those conflicts. Among the heroes and villains are a much greater assortment of characters falling somewhere in between.

"I am one such character. Best characterized among the villains. You of course do not know my name. For good reason. I went to great lengths to remain unknown. Let me be more specific. I am seventy-six years old. I was born in Derry, Northern Ireland in 1948. Family emigrated to Boston in 1950. When I was in my twenties I returned to Northern Ireland for the first time in 1971. Remained in Belfast through 1973. The beginning years of the three decades of the *Troubles*. It is about those years that I have come to you."

"And what is the reason for coming to me, Mr. Kelly?"

"To tell you my story. What I did during those years. My name has never appeared in any accounts, but I assure you that I was intimately involved. What I did was make detonators used in untold numbers of IRA bombings. Reliable radio control detonators that probably saved many IRA fighters from prematurely blowing themselves up. However, the blood of countless innocent bombing victims is on my hands, Father. Most were noncombatant civilians rarely those serving with government security forces."

"Are you also looking to me for spiritual guidance?"

"Not exactly. For what I have done, there can be no redemption. I'm also not religious. I wish only to relate my story that includes never before revealed details. I need someone of your background to make sense of my conflicted experience in Northern Ireland. All your published works speak to the reader of emotion and personal motivation without appearing judgmental. You explain history in its contextual importance. Something far more than a collection of factual details.

"Why exactly do you want your story made public?" O'Brien asked.

"Nothing about my contributions to the violence in Northern Ireland is defensible as justified by ideology. Simply a deluded terrorist, not a freedom fighter. Publicly confessing by terrible deeds is my poor solution for making the only atonement possible given my circumstances. Call it an inexplicable obsession. Impending death has a tendency to greatly focus your thoughts. You see, Father, I am dying of end-stage lung cancer."

O'Brien was silent for a moment before asking, "Are you undergoing treatment?"

"No. I have opted against aggressive treatment. It's not possible to forestall the inevitable. Treatment side effects will adversely impair what remaining time I have left. Untreated, I have only six to twelve months remaining. That means I only have an indeterminate amount of time until the disease progresses to a debilitating condition preventing normal functioning in its end-stage. Time therefore is critical. Is my story of interest to you as a historian, Father?"

"As both a priest as well as a historian. Enough at least to meet with you face to face to discuss the matter further."

"Thank you. A question before I embark on purging my soul as it were. Is what I am going to tell you protected by the seal of confession, Father? My interest of course only applies until my passing. After that, I wish my story widely disseminated."

"I understand. Yes, what you will tell me comes under the sacramental confessional seal requiring my duty as a priest to maintain complete secrecy. Since you expressly wish your confession made public following your death, why is that of concern?"

Kelly laughed, interrupted by his now developing cough. "Because I'm a coward, Father. Although I have no remaining family or friends to be hurt by my revelations, I cannot abide the thought of becoming a publicly vilified person. Selfish enough to want to live out my remaining time quietly. Not much different an explanation than my confession falling short of meaningful atonement."

"Very well, Mr. Kelly. Do you live in the Boston area?"

"South Boston."

"How about we meet at my office at Boston College in Chestnut Hill?"

"Certainly. Any time of your choosing, Father."

"Let's make it this Thursday at 1:30."

Terence Kelly knocked on Father O'Brien's office door at the Morrissey College of Arts and Sciences at Boston College. O'Brien answered the door. "Mr. Kelly?"

"Thank you for seeing me, Father."

"Could not very well deny either of us the opportunity of taking our conversation further. Please come in and sit down. Are you in much discomfort from your condition?"

"Only modest annoyance from the chronic cough. Some shortness of breath. No pain yet."

Once seated in comfortable chairs, O'Brien said. "Before we begin, can you enlighten me by explaining in more detail exactly the circumstances that cause you to believe you have blood on your hands to use your own words?"

"Of course, Father. Far more than belief, certainty. I was in Northen Ireland from 1971 to the end of 1973. Beginning with *Bloody Friday* in July 1972 through December 1974 when the IRA announced a Christmas ceasefire, IRA bombs killed 75-80 people and injured another 750 by exploding approximately 60 bombs. I did not make or set those bombs. I only produced radio command detonators. More reliable than the ad hoc random jury-rigged timer detonators before my detonators became available. Safer for the bombmaker. Less inadvertent detonations killing the perpetrator. The effective range of my detonators allowed the perpetrator to remain at a safe distance for escape and detonate bombs on command rather than by a preset timer.

"I produced 52 of these radio command detonators during that period. You can do the math. Not all of these bombs were triggered by my detonators. However, some of my detonators were undoubtedly used after I had left Northern Ireland in late 1973. Regardless, it is not a stretch to estimate my detonators probably caused something like fifty percent of those deaths and a far greater number of those surviving with injuries. Fair to say I have a great deal of blood on my hands. Impossible to atone for such a monstrous past. The only true justice would be my execution. Too late now for that."

O'Brien nodded. Not yet convinced of Kelly's story. "And how is it that you stayed undetected? In all my research of records for the three decades of the *Troubles*, your name never appears. For that matter, no reporting I can ever recall made reference to a radio command detonation system being adopted as a standard weapon used by the IRA."

Kelly replied, "Did your research not show IRA bombings prior to 1972 were notoriously dangerous to the bomber? Subject to premature detonation resulting in death to many of those inexperienced and poorly trained in handling high explosives."

"True."

Kelly added, "I attribute that to the immergence of my improved radio detonators. I can only suggest that reports probably focused on the aftermath not forensic details associated with examining small fragments to determine the ignition mechanism of the bomb. More attention given to the probable type and quantity of explosives used. Fifty years ago, crime scene forensics were less rigorous. After all, there was rarely any question about who was behind the bombings during the *Troubles.* Either IRA or loyalist paramilitaries. Methods of detonation likely varied. My radio-command detonators did not necessarily replace various timing devices.

"As to how I remained unknown is a long story. Rest assured, mine is not one of those false confessions to crimes I did not commit wanting only notoriety. I will provide you with enough information to convince you once we get into the details."

O'Brien nodded. "Very well, Mr. Kelly. I have the afternoon free. If you're up to it, should we begin the interview process now?"

"Absolutely. Sooner the better."

"Do you mind if I record our sessions?"

"Not at all, Father. This entire exercise leads to publishing my story. As you will write it of course. Much of how you write it will come from your impressions during our conversations. My feelings, my emotions, my rationalizations, my expressions of guilt. Explaining how I discovered the folly of blindly following an ideology. Laudable ideals distorted by actions. The end never justified by immoral actions. Very few heroes immerged from the decades of the *Troubles* regardless of political point of view. Mostly fanatics expressing righteous ideological fervor, true villains exercising brutality, those following a herd mentality, and the occasional martyr."

"Let me begin by making this a true confession, Father O'Brien." Kelly then made the sign of the cross. "Bless me, Father, for I have sinned. My last confession was made when I was only a child. I have repeatedly committed the mortal sin of murder. A misguided pact with the devil that I wish to remedy by seeking atonement, however inadequate, and receive absolution so I may die in peace. "Shall I start with how I came to America?"

Father O'Brien replied, "This is your confession. You seem very well organized in your thoughts, Mr. Kelly. Therefore, you should be the one to direct the arch of your narrative. I shall ask questions along the way which may divert us down different paths, but this is your story. Obviously you're keen on explaining your deepest feelings.

"True. More than that I wish to explain how I came to accept certain circumstances that I eventually found conflicting, eventually leading to disillusionment. Therefore, I shall begin by explaining that like so many people, my strongest views were shaped by my family from an early age. I am no exception. For me the strongest influence was my paternal grandfather who I never actually met until 1971.

"Liam Kelly was larger than life in his native Derry. A veteran of the Easter Rising of 1916 followed by the Irish War of Independence of 1919-1922. More than that, he was a former member of Michael Collins' secretive assassination and counterintelligence unit the *Squad* known also as the *Twelve Apostles* operating in Dublin."

O'Brien sat forward at the mention of Liam Kelly. "Liam Kelly was your grandfather?"

"That's correct. Heard countless stories of Granda's exploits growing up."

O'Brien said, "Yes, I know the name Liam Kelly. Imprisoned in 1916 after the failed uprising. Obviously that did not break his spirit of rebellion. Becoming one of Michael's *Apostles* attested to his abilities."

"Granda was a larger-than-life character. From my earliest years to even now in my final days, Granda has played a significant role in my life. A fearsome IRA gunman back a hundred years ago. His presence dominates a good deal of my story. His son Eoin, my father, was born years after the Anglo-Irish Treaty of 1922 that established the Irish Free State of the southern twenty-six counties. Granda returned north to Derry. Partitioned Ireland with the northern six counties becoming Northern Ireland and still part of the British United Kingdom. Same status as Scotland and Wales yet by the 1970s still more like the last colony of the former British Empire. Granda was destined to resume the struggle in his later years."

"Doing research for my writing, your grandfather's name resurfaced again during the *Troubles.* A victim of a car bombing as I recall. He must have been pushing eighty years old. Did his death have anything to do with his past? Was his death a loyalist paramilitary bombing?"

"Perhaps. That's what the newspapers reported. That's what my father believed happened. Later in my story I'll relate circumstances that might suggest something different. You can then draw your own conclusions.

"But let me return first to relating my beginnings by explaining how I wound up in Northern Ireland at the beginning of the *Troubles*. My father Eoin was born in Derry in 1926. Lost his job at Harlan & Wolff Shipbuilding in 1948. The same year I was born. He always said it was because he was Catholic. Only because of the Second World War were any Catholics even employed by the shipyard. Yet he married my mother who came from a Belfast Protestant background. Her brother David also lost his job at the shipyard at the same time. I later came to believe the circumstances were nothing more than the economic downturn following the war hitting Britain and particularly Belfast shipbuilding very hard. Mother's brother emigrated to Boston and found work at the Boston Naval Shipyard. Two years later Uncle David enticed my father and mother to come to Boston where there was work for skilled welders in the shipyards.

"Now here is where events of my earliest years played a significant part in my story during the nineteen-seventies. In 1948, my parents had just moved from Belfast after my father lost his job at the Harland & Wolff Shipyard. They settled in with my paternal grandparents Liam and Agnes Kelly in the Catholic sector of Derry known as the Bogside on the west bank of the River Foyle. Bear in mind that my parents were from mixed religious backgrounds. Eoin Kelly was Catholic, and my mother Francis, family name Stewart, was Protestant. That was less of a sectarian issue at that time, however, once relocated in predominately Catholic Derry, mother felt uncomfortable after leaving Belfast. Partition of Ireland with the Anglo-Irish Treaty left pronounced legacy antagonisms in Northern Ireland.

"I was born in Belfast in my maternal grandparents' house with the aid of a midwife, typical for the time. Although neither of my parents were practicing churchgoers, I was baptized as Catholic under the name Terence Stewart Kelly. Born at home required my mother to register my birth with the Northern Ireland government. Fearing possible association with her famous father-in-law Liam Kelly, my mother had the forethought to preserve her Protestant heritage. In Northern Ireland government records, I appear as Terence Brendan Stewart rather than using my father's surname Kelly. The middle name derived from my maternal grandfather Brendan Stewart. On the birth registry my mother also identified the father as David Stewart using her brother's name thereby establishing a multi-generational Protestant heritage.

"The significance of that came when my parents decided to emigrate to Boston. Mother's brother David having emigrated two years earlier enticed my father to come to Boston where he could find employment with his skills as a journeyman shipbuilding welder. Fearing the Kelly name when filling out immigration documents possibly connecting him with the notorious IRA gunman Liam Kelly, my mother circumvented that possibility. She instead chose to ensure my entry into America with a British passport secured in Belfast using my official birth registration as Terence Brendan Stewart. I grew up in America of course as Terence Kelly. The idea of using Terence Stewart came about only when I sought to make my first journey to Northern Ireland in 1971.

"By 1971 sectarian strife had fully erupted in Northern Ireland. I already had a plan for spending an indeterminate duration getting to know my paternal grandfather better. By this time Granda had secretly become involved with the newly organized Provisional IRA. The old warrior still had more to contribute. I therefore understood the charged political landscape I was about to enter. Having dual American and British citizenship, I obtained a U.S. passport in the name Terence Stewart Kelly using church baptismal records while renewing my British passport from infancy in the name of Terence Brendan Stewart as registered with the government. Traveling to Northern Ireland I used my U.S. passport as Kelly. My British passport as Stewart only became useful if I intended to stay in Northern Ireland for an extended period of. At the time I only planned to spend the summer of '71. Unexpected circumstances changed those plans making my official British citizenship identity useful.

"Ultimately that dual citizenship under different names will later answer much of your questions of how I remained unknown during my time in Northern Ireland. In 1971 the benefit of using my British citizenship also allowed for receiving preferential entry and reduced tuition to apply for enrollment to pursue a post-graduate degree at Queen's University Belfast.

"Having received my undergraduate degree in engineering in Boston in 1970 opened me up to possible conscription in the U.S. military draft with the war in Vietnam still active. What better reason to visit Northern Ireland. Experience my heritage. Spend time with my famous grandfather. Pursuing a post-graduate degree provided the perfect reason for extending my time outside the United States and avoiding Vietnam."

O'Brien asked, "How did you link your undergraduate degree in the name of Kelly while applying to Queen's University under the name Stewart?"

"Not as difficult as you might imagine. I explained in a letter to Queen's University, and later my future employer in the United States that I was born in Belfast in 1948 with the surname Stewart. Birth registration as proof. Mother later remarried. My stepfather named Kelly adopted me at an early age and I grew up in the United States with the surname Kelly. Involving my British citizenship meant reverting to Stewart. No different than a woman changing her last name when marrying. Educational background documents inherently become affected. For my situation using an alternative identity supported by a British passport in the name of Stewart would afford an entirely more important benefit. Something integral to my story as you will see, Father O'Brien."

Although taping the interview, O'Brien jotted notes of key points on a legal pad. Listening to Kelly's narrative, he stopped writing. Looking up with an expression suggesting incredulity, "This alternative identity obviously plays a central part in what transpired during your time in Northern Ireland. A remarkable circumstance that originated at your time of birth."

"Thought that might provoke understandable skepticism, Father. I brought these along in support of my story." Kelly extracted his decades-old expired United States passport issued as Terence Stewart Kelly and his United Kingdom passport issued in the name Terence Brendan Stewart. Both passports indicated an issuing date of February 1971 with matching photographs.

CHAPTER 2

Derry, Northern Ireland | May 1971

Terence Kelly arrived at Dublin Airport on a direct flight from John F. Kennedy international Airport in New York. Before continuing to Northern Ireland by train he would spend a week in Dublin. Visiting locations, he only read about and heard first-hand details from his grandfather, fortified his feelings of Irish heritage. Walking Dublin he reimagined events from the Easter Rising of 1916 and the Anglo-Irish War of 1919-1921, better known as the Irish War of Independence.

Kelly had just completed his final year for a degree in electrical engineering from Benjamin Franklin Cummings Institute of Technology in Boston. Growing up in heavily Irish South Boston, he was steeped in Irish history. Many his age were first- or second-generation immigrants from Ireland.

The treaty signed in December of 1921 between Irish rebels and Great Britain did not win Irish independence from Britian, achieving only self-governing dominion status. The treaty also partitioned the Island of Ireland with the southern twenty-six counties becoming the Irish Free State and the northern six counties becoming Northern Ireland while remaining part of the British United Kingdom. Thus, the Irish Free State acquired the same status as Canada at the time, and Northern Ireland the same as Scotland. Terence Kelly's family came from Northern Ireland.

The result of the Anglo-Irish Treaty was not universally popular among the Irish population. The result became a civil war in the southern counties. Diehard committed dissident IRA precipitated in an unpopular conflict against former IRA comrades that now comprised the newly formed Irish National Army commanded my Michael Collins. The rebels that did not accept the treaty did not enjoy widespread popular support as was the situation throughout the war with the British. The civil war lasted ten months resulting in the spilling of much blood and lasting antagonisms for those that all fought for Irish freedom from Britain.

Terence Kelly's grandfather Liam Kelly chose not to take part in the civil war. He instead returned to his home in the predominately Catholic sector of Londonderry, called by Derry by its Catholic residents, now part of British controlled Northen Ireland.

When drawing the boundaries for the Government of Ireland Act British negotiators selected only six of the original nine counties of historic Ulster province to ensure an overall majority of British loyalists, in effect predominantly those of Protestant heritage. This resulted in a favorable loyalist majority vote on the referendum to remain part of the British United Kingdom. The industrial wealth of Ireland disproportionately located in the eastern counties of Antrim and Down of Northern Ireland was of economic interest to Britain. Civil war did not come to Northern Ireland. Yet sectarian strife increased over the proceeding decades. The 1920s even resulted in pogroms against Catholics not unlike those experienced by Jews in Eastern Europe.

The Irish Free State became fully independent in 1949 with the establishment of the Republic of Ireland while Northern Ireland firmly remained part of the United Kingdom. That continued partition of the Emerald Isle did not extinguish the centuries-old antagonisms of rule by Great Britian that lives on today. Those antagonisms would explode by 1969 beginning three decades of violent sectarian-political strife.

For Terence Kelly, his interest in Dublin was visiting the locations described by his grandfather from his participation in the

1916 Easter Rising and the Anglo-Irish War, the Irish War of Independence that began in 1919. Small enough to walk the entire city, he spent a week in Dublin before taking the train to Belfast. Stopping over for two days to visit Queen's University and getting acquainted with that area of Belfast.

Checking in with the administration office since not yet received a response to his enrollment application, he was delighted to learn of his acceptance. The official letter sent by mail to Boston did not arrive before his departure. Tuition payment was due the first of August. Time enough to make arrangements with his mother including airmailing her a personal check. She would then obtain a cashier's check made out to Terence Stewart and mail it to his grandfather's address in Derry but addressed to Terence Kelly. He was not yet ready to explain his reasons for applying to the university in Belfast, nor using his British citizenship, nor the reason why it was issued in another name. Until investing in the tuition cost there were still many weeks in which to change his mind.

For the time being, he was satisfied with his plans to settle into his studies in Belfast come August. He could now enjoy getting to know his grandparents over the summer. A special occasion having never seen them face-to-face. An opportunity to become acquainted with Northern Ireland. Understand what was going on. What was Granda up to risking his freedom by possible involvement with the newly organized Provisional IRA? Terence's father, himself a fervent supporter of the IRA, hinted with pride that Granda had not given up the fight.

Grandma Agnes answered his telephone call from Belfast with delight. "Been making arrangements for having you with us for the summer. You'll bring us such joy amid all the terrible things going on around us. Your Granda will meet your train and bring you straight away to the pub. The *Black Goat Pub* on Great James Street. Been in the Kelly family since your great-grandfather's time. From our street you can see the ancient walls surrounding old Derry just a short way down the street. Love you dearly for coming over the water to be seein' us, Terry."

While the Irish Free State gained full independence becoming the Republic of Ireland in 1949, the hostilities in Northern Ireland had deteriorated in the intervening five decades since the British left the southern Irish counties. The IRA that brought the British to the negotiating table had long since ceased having political relevance. However, the sectarian divide had dramatically worsened.

The strife that became apparent in the 1960s was a sectarian civil rights issue. A democracy that was anything but representative of the Northern Ireland population demographic. All governmental institutions were overwhelmingly dominated by Protes-tant British-loyalists that included all important business interests. The Catholic population comprised a significant minority of 35%. However, Protestant loyalist rule was rigorously maintained through gerrymandering. With the right to equal political representation denied those of lower income became disenfranchised. Combined with employment and housing discrimination against Catholics, Catholics overwhelming represented the strata of lower income families.

Terence understood the background described by his father and grandfather. It was starkly equivalent to the racial discrimination of African Americans driving the civil rights movement and race-violence in the United States. He therefore understood the resurgence of the IRA from its moribund throes to those advocating a return to militaristic activism in Northern Ireland. The ideological schism caused militants to break with the current IRA by creating the Provisional IRA. They applied the term *provisional* derived by the term used in the original 1916 declaration of independence to denote a temporary governing body. However, this was clearly becoming a civil rights struggle. Forcing the British United Kingdom to give up Northern Ireland was never realistic yet introducing the cause of Irish nationalism became convenient propaganda used by both sides as justification for violence.

Liam Kelly was waiting on the Derry train platform when Terence stepped down from the train carriage. They embraced both unabashedly shedding tears of joy.

"You're a handsome lad, Terry my boy! Breakin' the hearts of many a pretty girl I should image."

"Wonderful to be here, Granda. You look good and fit."

"Doin' well enough for an old man. Arthritis is a curse that I hold in check with the occasional whiskey. That's what we'll be doin right away. Havin' a serious drink with my grandson. Your grandmother is minding the pub. She can't wait to see you. Agnus makes the best Irish stew around that we'll be havin' for our dinner. Bloody grand your being here with us for the summer, Terry!"

With that, Liam took one of Terence's suitcases then led the way to a nine-year-old ADO16 Austin-Morris 1100 sedan. As much as they spoke on the telephone and corresponded, it intrigued Terence that his grandfather at the age of seventy-three became motivated to return to participating in rebellion. In what form neither his father nor grandfather would say. Both said details were on a need-to-know basis for security. That included even family members.

The train station was on the east side of the River Foyle that bisected Derry, properly named Londonderry. "Liam said, "We're standing on what's called the Waterside district. More Protestant." As he turned to get on the Craigavon Bridge, "Crossing over the river we're entering the Bogside district. Catholic country. Eighty percent of Derry is Catholic and most of us live in the Bogside."

The *Black Goat Pub* sported a large wooden sign with the black head of a goat with horns that looked to Terence like some satanic representation. Opening the door revealed an interior of dark wood with a matching heavy bar and a modest number of tables. A couple of patrons sat at the bar enjoying afternoon pints of Guinness. Liam announced loudly, "Listen up, lads. Let me introduce this young man. My grandson Terence is from America. He'll be spending the summer with us."

Both men stood up from their bar stools to come over and shake hands with Terence.

"And that pretty young woman behind the bar is Maureen Lynch," Liam said.

Maureen definitely caught Terence's eye. Not only a pretty face but wearing a form-fitting knit blouse that nicely displayed her full breasts and showed a bit of cleavage. She and Terence exchanged warm smiles as Agnes Kelly came out from the kitchen to rush over diverting his attention. Terence opened his arms to accept his grandmother's embrace, "Hello, Grandma."

That night became a grand celebration for the Kelly clan. Liam served pints on the house to all the patrons that night. "My grandson from America was born here in Northern Ireland. He's coming back to visit for the first time. An engineer no less. Just graduated from a university in Boston. He'll be spending the summer with us here in Derry."

For Terence, the attentions of Maureen Lynch added to the festivities that evening. Coming from behind the bar to greet him wearing a miniskirt with calf-high boots brought a grin to his face. As she later helped Agnes serve them dinner, she flirted with Terence, occasionally laying a hand on his shoulder. His thoughts immediately turned to the prospects of a delightful summer.

Anxious to spend some alone time with his grandson, Liam said to Agnes, "Going to show our boy his room. All grown up and ready for the world. I want to share a whiskey with him in the quiet of the parlor, just the two of us."

The Kellys lived in a spacious two-bedroom apartment above the pub. Settled in the parlor overlooking Great James Street, Liam poured each a glass of Irish whiskey. "Bushmills. Comes from the small village of that name on the north coast of County Antrim. Claim to have been making whiskey since 1608. That's years before the Battle of the Boyne. That terrible event so long ago that put Protestants and Catholics against one another."

"I know that history, Granda. 1690. The beginning of British rule over Ireland," Terence remarked. "Protestant King William of Orange III defeated deposed Catholic King James II."

"Seems you studied about the troubled history of our people with the British since that time, Terry."

"A fair understanding. Know more about the events during this century. Your era fighting for Irish freedom, Granda. From when I was a kid, my father educated me in that history and the part you played. You were among the famous IRA responsible for kicking the British out of the southern counties fifty years ago. My god, you knew Michael Collins! Worked directly for him."

Liam Kelly smiled, "That I did. Tough times. A brutal fight. Regrettably, not enough to free all of Ireland from British rule."

"Read a lot about that, Granda. Must have been particularly hard on you being from Derry."

"That it was. Once the Free State was established in the southern twenty-six counties, most of the old province of Ulster was left to our own fate. The problems here have always been different. In 1922 when the Anglo-Irish Treaty came into effect, over ninety percent of the population in the southern counties were Catholic. In Northen Ireland today, only about a third of the population are Catholic."

"According to my Da, the problem isn't the British but the Protestant loyalists. Is that how you see it, Granda?"

"More complicated than that. London props up the Northern Ireland provincial government. The Irish Protestant loyalists have taken total control of Northern Ireland government. Long standing discrimination against Catholics goes back to the colonization of Ulster centuries ago with Protestant settlers from Great Britain. In later times, British colonial corruption denying one-man one vote along with gerrymandering undermined the rights of Catholics by preventing representation in local government. A civil rights issue with discrimination in housing and employment becoming an unending hardship."

"Who's this Reverand Ian Paisley we hear so much about even in America?" Terence asks.

"Ah, that bloody sonofabitch Paisley. A right piece of feckin' work. Professing to be a man of God he does the devil's work by inciting loyalist violence. Years ago, he institutionalized loyalist opposition to the Catholic civil rights movement. He's a member of Parliament. Leader of the Democratic Unionist Party he founded this year. It's his fiery speeches that sets about stirring loyalists to violence against Catholics."

"Where does London stand on this?" Terence asked.

"Largely hands off. Wring their hands while declaring this is a local provincial problem. A police problem no less. The RUC consists predominantly of Protestant loyalists. Violence against Catholics breaks out and the RUC beats and arrests only Catholics. Something like Hitler's Brown Shirts beating up Jews before the Nazis came to power in Germany then turned to killing them in earnest."

Terence nodded and sipped his whiskey. He was more interested in what his grandfather was up to currently. Couldn't see the old warrior just standing aside. "Father admitted to me he was doing something to help you. Wouldn't say anything more than that. Never told Mother either that I know of."

"Good for Eoin. He understands the need for secrecy. But he also understands family. Eoin wanted to join the IRA when he became an adult. Wasn't old enough to be called up early to fight in the Second World War. Learned the welding trade as a teenager in Derry. At age eighteen he found a welding job at Harlan & Wolff that may have been more vital to the war effort in 1944 in the final year of the war. When he lost his job a few years later he and your mother came to Derry to live with us."

Terence said, "Father told me about those years. Tough economic times for all of you. Said Mother's brother David also lost his job at the shipyard and was already living in Boston."

"David is a good lad. May have been a Protestant but not a loyalist. At least not someone hating Catholics. It was because of David Stewart that Eoin met up with your mother. Never any bad blood between the families being from different backgrounds."

"Uncle David has always been good to us in Boston. Religious background doesn't cause the same kind of problems for Boston Irish."

Liam reverted back to Terence's question. "You asked how your father was helping me. If I tell you it must remain a secret. From everyone, including your mother. She's always feared that I was still secretly involved somehow with the IRA. Afraid I would drag your father into continuing the rebellion and the risk that involved."

"Yes I know, Granda. Let me show you something." He left his chair to go to a duffle bag deposited in the bedroom. Returning, he handed his grandfather a British passport. "This was Mother's doing when I was born."

Liam Kelly opened the passport to the photograph page. For several moments he starred at Terence's photograph and the name Terence Brendan Stewart. "What's this about?"

Terence produced his U.S. passport from his pocket and handed it to his grandfather. "This is my American passport, Granda. I am a naturalized citizen of the United States. Note that it reads with my real name, Terence Stewart Kelly. I have dual citizenship."

A confused and none too happy, Liam Kelly said, "Explain what this means, Terry."

"Mother's doing. This is what she told me only recently when I began talking of visiting you and Grandma. Seems she was afraid of you still being secretly involved with the IRA when I was born. She wanted to protect me."

"Protect you? From what? How does this protect you?" Liam said clearly angrily.

"Fearful of being arrested. She didn't know what you were doing. Or for that matter what my own father might be doing. With the decision to emigrate to America, she feared being refused entry by U.S. immigration if we were on some undesirable list. Said the failed IRA *Northern Campaign* in the early years of the Second World War left a lot of bad feeling for the IRA. Not only from the British but Americans fighting the Nazis. Called the IRA nothing but terrorists. Not that farfetched according to her."

"How did that make you become Terence Stewart?" Liam said holding up the passport.

"When we emigrated to America in 1950, she obtained a passport using her family name Stewart and one for me, her infant son using her family name. Said she used my birth registry that she filed since I was delivered by a midwife rather than at a hospital."

"Why are you traveling under the name Stewart rather than a Kelly?"

"Granda, don't be angry at Mother for what happened over twenty years ago. Anyway, that is no longer the reason I am carrying two passports in different names. Haven't told anyone but you that I'm planning staying on in Northern Ireland for more than just the summer. Not even my parents know yet. You see, I applied and was accepted for graduate school at Queen's University in Belfast starting in the fall."

Liam Kelly sat back in his chair with a look of surprise, remaining silent for a moment to gather his thoughts. "Why would you want to do that with all that's goin' on right now?"

"Because of that, Granda. Because of what's going on. Since what happened here in Derry during the summer two years ago. Father as much as said you had reverted to things you thought left behind fifty years ago. I wanted to see for myself. Experience what I've grown up with my family history. The cause of Irish freedom. What you risked your life for fifty years ago and maybe again doing now."

Tears started running down Terence's cheeks. Unsuccessfully trying to wipe them away with his hands he wanted to appear tougher. Afterall, his grandfather had been a feared IRA assassin. One of Michael Collins' *Squad* known as the *Twelve Apostles* responsible for assassinating British intelligence operatives in Dublin during the Anglo-Irish War.

Liam Kelly sat forward in his chair and placed a hand on his grandson's knee. "I shouldn't be holding that against your mother. That was a long time ago. She had reason to fear backlash for anyone involved with the IRA. Why is it though you saw the need to obtain a British passport?"

Terence composed himself for a few moments before saying, "Because I wanted to stay for an indefinite time. Couldn't find a job without getting a work visa as a foreigner. When Mother told me about my birth registration that led her to getting me a British passport as an infant when we came to America, I hit on a better idea to make my way in Northern Ireland. Go back to school and get an advanced engineering degree. Being a British citizen and born here, I applied to Queen's University in Belfast. Gives me preferential enrollment and lower cost for tuition. With Mother's Protestant heritage, figured I'd experience less problems than advertising that I'm a Catholic. I'll be starting classes the end of summer."

Liam registered surprise. "Your father and mother know nothing about these plans?"

Terence smiled. "Not yet. I'll be telling them soon. Need Mother to arrange sending a cashier's check from by bank account in Boston to the university since I'm registering as Terence Brendan Stewart. They accepted my undergraduate degree from Boston in the name of Terence Stewart Kelly as nothing more than the adopted surname when my mother married again."

Liam shook his head. "Can't say I like anything about using different names, Terry, but I'm touched that you want to experience your heritage."

"It's worthwhile for furthering my education. Couldn't expect to stay with you and Grandma without doing something meaningful. There's another reason for coming here more than just for a summer visit. Maybe I can contribute in some way to what you are secretly doing, Granda. If my father is also involved, then it must have something to do with smuggling. Most of Boston's Irish are Catholic. Lots of talk about supporting Catholics in the north with the RUC and those thugs the Ulster Special Constabulary violently preying on the Catholics."

Liam again shook his head and let out a sigh. "You have your life ahead of you, my boy. Too great a risk for you to get mixed up in this new fight."

"You risked everything when you took up the gun as a young man, Granda."

"That I did. This is a different struggle."

"How's that? Isn't it about uniting all of Ireland into the Republic?"

"Some might talk of that. Times are different now. Northern Ireland is on its own. Back when we fought to push the British out of Ireland the majority of the population supported the IRA military effort. Those in the Republic now have their independence. Since the Irish Free State became the fully independent Republic of Ireland, the IRA of long ago failed to accomplish anything for northern unification."

"You mean what my Da spoke about. The *Border Campaign*?"

"That and another earlier foolish effort called the *Northern Campaign* during the Second World War. The efforts focused only on Northern Ireland with any cross-border activity from the Republic suppressed by the threat of internment even from Dublin. Catholics represent a minority in Northern Ireland where a Protestant loyalist opposition majority population has always existed. That ensures failure of any Catholic rebellion backed by the military might of Britain."

"Were you not still involved with the IRA during those times, Granda?"

"No, I was not. Had my fill of lost causes when I became part of the Easter Rising of 1916. The War of Independence was another matter. The Irish population overwhelmingly sided with our cause. Sinn Féin swept the election of 1918. Made our military prospects seem possible."

"What about this Provisional IRA my Da speaks of?"

Liam took a sip of his whiskey before answering. "That's a different matter. The IRA that existed after the Second World War became more interested in politics rather than military action. Not my kind of politics. Marxist. Bloody Communists. A couple of years ago traditionalists like me broke away and created the Provisional Irish Republican Army. Not interested in politics. It's about pushing the bloody British off our island by the gun."

"Are you involved with the Provisional IRA, Granda?"

"In manner of speaking. Don't think we can ever force Britain to give up Northern Ireland, but the Catholic population needs an armed force for protection against a corrupt police state."

"How is my father involved?"

"The Irish in America have long since been the most important source of money and weapons going back fifty years. Your father is an important conduit with the sympathetic Irish American community that is helpful to the struggle. Can't go into details because security relies on having a need to know."

"I understand, Granda. Also understand that you do not wish me to become involved. Yet I have this need to do something. The same feelings you had at my age. The same feelings you apparently still have. Not sure how I can be of service. I didn't come to Northen Ireland to carry a gun but maybe there's some other service I can render without getting into trouble."

"Very good, Terry. I'll keep that in mind. Unfortunately, circumstances are deteriorating. Violence will undoubtedly worsen. Best that nobody else other than your parents, Agnes and I know you are staying on in Northern Ireland after spending your summer vacation with us in Derry. When you relocate to Belfast, we will tell everyone here you returned to America. Having a different identity in Belfast actually makes for added security. Avoids becoming associated with me should anything unfortunate happen. Your mother was right about the danger in that when you were a child. Maybe more important with what's happening now in Northern Ireland. We can still see each other occasionally in some neutral place reachable by train or bus."

CHAPTER 3

Derry, Northern Ireland | Spring 1971

The following day was spent with Liam Kelly showing Terence around Derry. At least the Catholic Bogside sector of Derry on the west bank of the River Foyle. They started first by walking east from the pub toward the ancient walls of Derry near the river. Erected in the early part of the 17th century the walls stood twenty-six feet in height.

Liam said, "That tall spire appearing above the walls is Saint Columb's Cathedral. The first Anglican cathedral built in Britain and Ireland following the reformation. The first non-Roman Catholic cathedral constructed in Western Europe."

"Yet you said that this side of the river is heavily Catholic," Terence commented.

"It is, but not exclusively. From the pub closer to the river is only about sixty percent Catholic. To the west and north this side of the river becomes overwhelmingly Catholic. Derry is eighty percent Catholic, the most Catholic city in Northern Ireland. In contrast, Catholics represent only a third of Belfast's population, about the same proportion as for all the six counties of Northern Ireland."

Liam led the way to the ancient high walls walking through the Butcher's Gate to the inside streets lined with shops. Pointing to his right, Liam said, "Just down there is the Apprentice Boy's House."

"Isn't that one of those Orangemen loyalist clubs I read about?"

"Yes it is. One of Paisley's most aggressive Protestant arsehole organizations. In early August of 1969, thousands of Catholic residents of the Bogside planned a civil rights march under the banner of the Derry Citizens' Defence Association. The Royal Ulster Constabulary prohibited the Catholic march supposedly fearing violence yet allowing a march by the Protestant loyalist Apprentice Boy's to proceed. I believe the RUC intended the provocation to produce a clash giving reason for the police to come in heavy-handed against the Catholic residents.

"All hell broke out. Three days of rioting between Catholics battling the RUC supported by their Special Constabulary auxiliary forces. Resulted in injuries to 1,000 Catholic civilians and 350 injuries to the police. Half of the RUC's total deployed force. Not a bad showing for residents just throwing rocks and bottles. Kept the fuckers from penetrating deeper into the Catholic neighborhoods. The exhausted RUC eventually withdrew to be replaced by British Army troops."

"The hostilities seem to have gotten worse since then," Terence commented.

"That they have. The situation can never go back to what it was just a few years ago even as bad as it was then for Catholics in Northen Ireland. The violence now can't be turned around."

After wandering about within the Derry walls, Liam said, "Here's a bit of history that explains the significance of the name *Apprentice Boy's*. Goes to the heart of Irish resentment of British rule. In 1688 a group of Protestant trade apprentices hid the keys to the gates of these protective walls of Derry. Thousands of Protestants huddled inside against a threatening regiment of Catholic Jacobite forces of King James II. King James had converted to Catholicism later in adulthood yet had a Protestant daughter named Mary. Mary was married to William II Prince of the Principality of Orange and heir apparent to the throne of the Netherlands.

"Fearing a return to a Catholic dynasty monarchy with the birth of a son, a largely bloodless rebellion deposed Catholic

King James II. Prominent individuals among the British aristocracy then invited William to assume the British throne to preserve Protestant rule, legitimized by Mary's lineage to the British crown. The deposed James II came to Ireland attempting to reclaim the throne. Forces under the new King of England, crowned as William III, defeated former King James' forces consisting mostly of raw recruits at the Battle of the Boyne, a river close to Drogheda in County Louth. That was in 1690. This became the origin of the *Orange Order* and the label *Orangemen.* Protestant loyalists celebrate that Protestant loyalist victory at the Battle of the Boyne as if it was recent history."

Terence knew the general outlines of that old history but was more concerned with the present. "Can we walk the areas where the rioting took place two years ago?" That event had become the catalyst for his obsession to visit Northern Ireland.

"Goin' to do just that, Terry. Started right here from this spot. Let's first climb up on the ramparts of the wall. A one-mile promenade all around provides a grand view of the Bogside from up there. Get an elevated look at the battleground then we'll go down and walk through those terrible days."

Standing on the rampart looking north, Liam said, "That's Waterloo Street below us. Great James Street, where the pub is located, intersects Waterloo about a quarter of a mile away. The pub is located just outside the area that experienced the worst of the violence. "Waterloo, Chamberlain, Abbey, William, Fahan, and Rossville Streets formed the boundaries of the war zone. Catholic civilians erected barricades all over the Bogside further to the west. Defended by throwing rocks and petrol bottle bombs at the RUC. Much to your grandmother's dismay, I went out to get a closer look for myself."

As they walked the streets, Liam narrated the progression of the rioting over the three days. "Helplessness brought actual tears of frustration. Felt the same as I did in 1919, fifty years ago, battling the oppression by British police. The Royal Irish Constabulary back then. Now it's the Royal Ulster Constabulary. A worse bunch. After the Battle of the Bogside, I decided to do something more than sit on the sidelines. This institutionalized oppression of Catholics in the North had gone on all my life. Needed to keep a low profile, so I didn't officially join the Provisional IRA. Safer to use my clandestine skills learned from working undercover for Mick Collins."

Terence let his grandfather talk and just listened.

"I'm too old to take an active part in field operations. Besides, I must think of Agnes. Been married forty-seven years. Should something happen to me there's no family here in Derry to take care of her. So, I turned to what I know best. Operating in the shadows. Counterintelligence working for Mick Collins in Dublin taught me useful skills. Mick used to send me outside Dublin to work with IRA brigades throughout Ireland. Helping get them weapons. Passing on intelligence. Made me skilled in smuggling weapons and learning how to avoid arrest."

"Is that what you and my Da are doing? Smuggling weapons to the IRA?"

Liam nodded. Looking at his grandson for several moments considering how much to tell him, he said, "You are my blood. Son of my only son. It's only right you should know what I'm about. What I 'm about to tell you goes no further to anyone. Not to your mother or even acknowledging to your father that you know details of what we are doing together."

"I understand, Granda. Been hearing about what you did fifty years ago. Now being in the middle of what's going on in Northern Ireland, I couldn't believe you could just stand aside. Had to meet you face to face. Be with you. Experience what I read about in the newspapers and see on television. Makes me angry beyond words."

Liam reached his arm around Terence drawing him close in an embrace. "Can't begin to tell you how much it means seeing you, Terry. Only right you should know what your father and I are up to. The struggle is about supplying arms and explosives to the IRA.

"America with its great numbers of Irish descendants is our best source of money necessary to purchase weapons. However, smuggling weapons into Northern Ireland whether from America or Europe becomes a challenge. Getting them shipped from any country violates the laws of those countries. Getting them into Northern Ireland becomes more difficult. No need to share specific details but bringing contraband into the Republic is still easier than directly into Northern Ireland. While the Guardia in the Republic is vigilant to cross-border smuggling of weapons, it's a long border. Most of that border runs through remote areas affording excellent smuggling opportunities. We also have connections with many in the Republic sympathetic to our cause."

"Doesn't that put you in danger?" Terence asked.

"Can't say there's no danger, but I've gone to lengths to minimize that. Although I'm known to the local IRA, it's largely because of my former background. Just an old timer with an infamous background from working closely with legendary Michael Collins. No one locally knows anything about my smuggling activities."

Terence stopped walking to look at him with a quizzical expression.

Liam said, "My arrangements are with the much larger Belfast Brigade. Even then only two senior officers know what I'm doing. The brigade OC and quartermaster. When I decided to take an active role, I decided how best to remain undetected by the enemy. You see the greatest danger of discovery by the RUC comes from their network of loyalist spies. That and *touts*, those giving up information to save their own hide after being captured. Sometimes after undergoing terrible physical abuse. Same problem the IRA faced in 1919."

Liam Kelly did not add that he had the regrettable task of executing several such individuals fifty years ago. "In addition to keeping those aware of my involvement to the barest minimum, I also chose to avoid any subversive activities in my own environment. Play the retired old rebel that just runs a pub. Besides, the Belfast Brigade is the largest IRA operating unit. They're the ones in most need of weapons and explosives.

"When deciding to lend my services a couple of years ago, I thought immediately of helping by smuggling contraband. Although I didn't participate in the failed IRA *Border Campaign* of the late 1950s, I knew of the principal smuggling connection from America. An enterprising Irish American fellow in New York put together a network that brought over a good deal of weaponry. Your father now living in Boston always wanted to do something for the cause of Irish freedom. I therefore put him in contact with this person in New York.

"On this end, I conspired with the Belfast Brigade quartermaster to complete the smuggling conduit. The lads in Belfast being in the greatest need of arms had the means to supply the smaller Derry Brigade and South Armagh Brigade.

"I'm going to give you the only two names in the IRA that know my part in organizing arms smuggling. Keep that absolutely secret. I only mention their names should something happen to me and God forbidden you find yourself in trouble. The Belfast quartermaster that handles arms is named Brian Keenan. A young lad not that much older than you. Tough and smart. I deal exclusively only with Brian. His superior is Belfast Brigade OC Seamus Twomey who knows my involvement, but I never deal with him. Never even met Twomey."

"How is it you connected with Keenan without involving anyone else?" Terence asked.

"IRA Derry OC Martin McGuinness is your age, Terry. That's how the Provos began. Mostly a bunch of young lads thinkin' about how bad things are. Same feelings I felt back in the old days when I was their age. McGuinness brings Keenan into the *Black Goat* one afternoon. Seems Keenan wanted to meet this old legend from the time of the War of Independence. Keenan impressed me. Same cunning intelligence that drew me to Mick Collins.

"When I decided to do more than just be an ancient figurehead of Irish armed rebellion, I approached Keenan. Excellent move. Brian has already proven exceptionally resourceful."

They walked the streets of the rioting of the *Battle of the Bogside*. Liam ended the tour at Free Derry Corner at the intersection of Rossville Street, Lecky Road, and Fahan Street. On a gable wall at the end of a housing terrace, graffiti read *You are now entering Free Derry*.

Terence said, "Saw that on the television news footage."

Liam said, "A local artist painted that in January of 1969 following an unprovoked midnight incursion by the RUC. That was months before those Protestant loyalist arseholes the Apprentice Boys began their march past the Catholic Bogside that the RUC used to provoke violence against Catholics.

"The RUC drove back the gathering Catholic crowd then pushed forward into the Bogside. Organized groups of loyalists then followed the RUC and began attacking Catholic homes. The fuckers misjudged the outrage of the Bogside residents. Thousands beat back the RUC by hurling stones and petrol bombs. It became a siege. Barricades went up to impede the RUC who responded by firing tear gas. Most of us feared wholesale bloodshed should the Ulster Special Constabulary be sent in. A bunch of undisciplined thugs with no police training.

"The rioting lasted three days. Came to end when the prime minister of Northern Ireland requested the British prime minister send in regular British Army troops. The 1st Battalion, Prince of Wales's Own Regiment of Yorkshire arrived and took over from the exhausted RUC police. Hundreds of civilians suffered injury but gave a good accounting of themselves in battle. Brought the RUC to their knees by inflicting over three hundred injuries on their forces. The RUC was a spent force by the time British troops arrived."

Liam and Terence continued walking a short distance before turning onto Great James Street to return to the pub when Liam stopped. "Remember, everything I told you today about my connection with the IRA is to remain secret. Also don't forget to stick to your story of going back to Boston in the fall. Nothing about you going to Belfast to attend Queen's University. Obviously you'll be chatting with our lovely Maureen. I saw your grin when she smiled at you."

Terence blushed. "She's a pretty one for sure."

"That she is. All the local young men buzz around her like flies to honey. Good for business. Caution is advised, however. Not only from her feminine wiles but because her father is prominent in the Derry IRA. He's a good friend but even he believes that I'm nothing more than a sympathetic old timer with no active role in IRA affairs. Let's keep it that way."

"Okay, Granda. I'll stay as clear of politics as much as possible. Won't deny my sympathies given my heritage but I'll play on that heritage as an Irish Catholic growing up in America. In Northern Ireland for the first time after finishing college and getting my engineering degree. Came here to spend the summer with my grandparents. Worried about them with all the violence. Returning to Boston to find a job. Won't let on that I know anything about the IRA, which I really don't."

Liam slapped Terence on the back. "You're a good lad, Terry. A smart one too. Agnes and I'll be sticking to the story come fall that you returned to Boston. Still concerned about your staying in Belfast with tensions worsening. Pleased that you'll be occupied as a university student. And thanks to your mother, providing you with a name that doesn't link you to an IRA gunman from the past. Living in retirement as a proprietor of a pub, yet this is still the largest Catholic enclave in Northern Ireland, and the RUC believes everyone is somehow connected to the IRA. Keep your wits about you and watch what you're saying to everyone."

CHAPTER 4

Derry, Northern Ireland | Spring 1971

Beginning late afternoon on Friday through Sunday night was the busiest time at the *Black Goat*. That meant days off for Maureen Lynch were Monday and Tuesday. Somewhat crimped her social life but tending bar provided a perfect way of meeting men of interest. Good looking, unattached, educated, and Irish American made Terence Kelly exceptionally interesting.

Having arrived just in Derry before the weekend, she saw him every day at the pub. Unmistakably he was eyeing her with his own interest. Come Sunday she said to him sitting alone in the pub while serving him lunch, "Tomorrow's my day off. Care to take a drive and see something of the countryside?"

Terence grinned, "I'd love that, Maureen."

"Wonderful. Dying to hear what life's like in America. Thought maybe we might drive over the border into the Republic to the town of Letterkenny in County Donegal. Only twenty-five miles from Derry. A scenic drive. Letterkenny's a pretty town. Quiet place without the likes of the RUC attacking Catholics. The police in the Republic, the Garda Síochána, are not even armed."

Maureen returned to serving other patrons, remaining busy until late in the evening when the clientele thinned out leaving just the drinkers at the bar tended by Liam. Terence stayed until closing time, chatting off and on with his grandparents waiting to speak with Maureen.

After clearing the tables, she returned with two pints to sit down with Terence.

Looking to any subject to further conversing with Maureen, Terence asked, "Does County Donegal have a large Catholic population?"

"Oh, yes. But a fair number of Protestants also live there. It's one of the counties of the ancient Province of Ulster that did not become part of the Republic. According to my father, the British felt there were too many Catholics in County Donegal when they drew up the lines for partitioning off Northern Ireland from the southern counties. The British intended Northern Ireland to have a Protestant loyalist population majority. Anyway, things are completely different in Donegal yet it's just a short drive from Derry."

Terence said, "Glad you suggested taking me there. Although I don't live here, all of Ireland is still my heritage. I'm very close to my Granda. Know all the stories of what he did fifty years ago in Dublin. How the IRA achieved something close to Irish independence, but in the end Northern Ireland was partitioned to remain under British rule. How London has supported this oppressive regional loyalist government that has forever denied equal rights for Catholics. No different than Apartheid in South Africa."

"Except in Northern Ireland we have the IRA to fight back with bullets," Maureen said.

"How's that working out? Are they making a difference?" Terence said trying to sound politically uninvolved.

Maureen said, "Too early to tell. The Provisional IRA just came together a couple of years ago. My father says the old IRA had become a bunch of Communists. All talk with no action. Not like the IRA of your grandfather's time."

"Yeah, Granda was somethin' in his day. Must frustrate him to be too old to get into this fight."

In the morning, Maureen walked into the pub where Terence sat drinking coffee. She was dressed in jeans with leather boots and a button-front heavy knit top. Springtime in Northern Ireland was no more than a high of 60 degrees F in May.

"Ready to get going?" she asked.

"Sure enough."

Liam raised an eyebrow after Terence told him he was taking a ride with Maureen for the day. "Have a good time but mind what we discussed," Liam said. Not so worried about Terence watching what he said but more about his hormones and Maureen's flirtatious inclinations encouraged by ample breasts displayed in tight sweaters.

They set out early in Maureen's father's car, a 1965 Ford Cortina 4-door hatchback painted an ugly pale mustard color. Maureen said, "We're goin' to link up with my girlfriend Diana and her boyfriend Fergus. You up for a couple of hours boating on Lough Swilly?"

"Sure. It'll be chilly out there on the water though."

"Fergus has use of a cabin cruiser. We can stay mostly inside staying out of the wind."

"Fair enough. I should be fine. Warm shirt and this fleece lined coat."

Crossing the border into the Republic of Ireland was uneventful. Generally, it was an open border without passport control between divided Ireland. For the Republic, certain border crossings might experience heighten security under circumstances triggered by events in Northern Ireland. Concerns centered on IRA individuals crossing the border to avoid arrest by the Northern Ireland RUC, or smuggled weapons and explosives moving north. In 1971, the situation had not yet deteriorated to a point warranting tightened security along the entire 300-mile common border.

It was only a four-mile drive from Derry to the border. The remainder of the drive to Letterkenny took them through farmland dotted with small farms. Terence commented, "Not much different from many places in New England once outside large cities like Boston. Less trees perhaps but pretty country with everything green."

As they got closer to Letterkenny the grandeur of the Donegal Mountains caused Terence to comment, "This is a spectacular view. Can you stop so I can take some photos? Got this 35mm camera as a graduation present. Just learning how to use it."

Exiting the car, he said, "Stand over there. I want to get you in the picture with the mountains in the background."

Striking a pose, Maureen said, "This afternoon you can get beautiful shots of the mountains from out on the water. Fergus' father owns a couple of hotels. The boat is used for touring Lough Swilly during the summer months. Part of his hotel business where he offers tours for guests wanting to experience the rugged Donegal coast. Fergus captains the boat during his summer break from school. He attends University College in Dublin."

"Really? What's his major?"

"Not sure. Something involving business I think, but I don't know the specifics."

"We should have much in common with our university experience. I also used to sail occasionally in Boston with friends. I like being out on the water. Are we dressed warm enough for the cold sea air?"

Maureen said, "Should be comfortable enough protected inside the boat's cabin. Plenty of room for the four of us."

As Maureen drove into Letterkenny she navigated the streets with familiarity to her friend Diana's house "I come to Letterkenny often. Lively place. Young people in the Republic our age aren't weighed down by politics. Having a good time comes easy here. Sometimes I spend the night at Diana's if I've had too much to drink."

Pulling into a driveway of a neatly kept house, "I'll fetch Diana while you stretch your legs. Then we'll drive over to Fahan on the Inishowen Peninsula. About a half hour drive. There's a small marina there where Fergus is waiting for us at the boat. Diana's packing us food for lunch. I brought along plenty of beer in an ice cooler tucked in the boot."

Exiting the car, Terence said, "Looks like we might be getting some sun today. Clouds seem to be parting. I appreciate you spending your day off to show me around, Maureen."

Maureen grinned. "Spending a day with friends in Letterkenny accompanied by a handsome bloke from America is my idea of an enjoyable day. Hope you enjoy your day too, Terence." Looking into his eyes she touched his face and drew her fingers along his cheek before turning to walk to the front door of Diana's house.

Fergus and Diana were a delightful couple. Terence found Fergus to be an interesting fellow. Studying business with another year remaining before receiving his bachelor's degree, Fergus spoke of joining the family business. As he piloted the cabin cruiser, he said to Terence, "I want to explore opportunities of expanding my family's modest hospitality business. I believe there are unexploited opportunities along the entire rugged western coastline of Ireland. I'm speaking of the counties of Donegal, Sligo, Mayo, and down to Galway. There's more to western Ireland than just the popular Kerry and Dingle Peninsulas in the southwest."

While Fergus was thinking about a professional future, Maureen and Diana seemed more into the moment of just enjoying life. Terence got the sense neither were looking yet to marry and settle down with children. Both had regular jobs, Maureen tending bar at the *Black Goat*, Diana as a secretary in a local law firm office.

A good deal of the conversation turned to everyone asking Terence about America. Seems most Irish families had extended family living in America. Emigration from Irish impoverishment and the lack of economic opportunities all contributed to the great Irish diaspora since the time of the Great Famine in the previous century. For Catholics sealed off in Northern Ireland, institutionalized governmental oppression added further reason to seeking out more favorable English-speaking countries.

All of them including Terence spoke passionately about the *Great Famine*. The fundamental cause coming from a widespread infection by a blight affecting potato crops across all of Europe but inflicting a far worse devastating famine on Ireland.

Terence remarked, "Read a lot about Irish history. Although studying engineering, I took a course in Irish history at Boston College. Lots of Irish emigrated to Boston over the last hundred years. Even though Europe suffered, the loss from starvation and disease was estimated at only about a hundred thousand. In Ireland the estimate ran to one million dead and another million leaving Ireland in less than ten years. The famine caused continued emigration from Ireland. Worst of all was the decade after the famine. Life in Ireland became just too difficult for the poor. The statistic that most stuck with me estimates the population of Ireland at 8.5 million before 1845 then dropping to just half that by 1901. Absentee British landowners lay at the cause of making circumstances far worse for Ireland."

Diana, said, "Enough of sad talk about the plight of the Irish. How 'bout some lunch? Can you idle the boat engine while we have lunch, Fergus?"

Fergus said, "I can do that. Could also use a pint of stout to go with lunch. How 'bout anyone else?"

Maureen replied, "Got everyone covered. Brought along plenty of beer."

Everyone had more than just one pint of beer. After their long lunch, Fergus engaged the engine and continued running north toward the Atlantic. Somewhere along the way Maureen and Diana disappeared below into the cabin. When they came back up, they were both smoking marijuana, each handing a second lit joint to Terence and Fergus.

When they reached the mouth of Lough Swilly where it emptied into the North Sea, Fergus announced, "There's Fanan Head Lighthouse." Diana was standing next to him at the wheel with her arm around his waist under his jacket. Turning around toward Terence, "I'll slow up a bit then come about so you can get some pictures before turning back south, Terence."

Diana laughed, "Looks like Terence has found something else to capture his interest."

Snuggling together on a bench, Terence and Maureen were doing more than keeping warm. When Diana spoke out, Maureen moved her hand discreetly away from Terence's thigh to his chest. Nonetheless, they continued exchanging lengthy kisses, ignored by Diana, who was doing the same with Fergus as he kept the boat on course.

All of them high from the cannabis with lowered inhibitions did what came naturally to young adults attracted to the opposite sex. Terence got his photographs of the mountains on the journey north. Now he could enjoy the boat ride back to the marina at Fahan enjoying Maureen's amorous attentions.

Arriving at the marina, it was early evening with a setting sun. Diana asked Maureen, "Are you and Terence coming back with us to Letterkenny to make a night of it?"

Maureen looked at Terence and smiled, "Sounds smashing, love, but I think Terence and I will leave that for another get-together. He's here for all the summer. Had enough booze and pot for this day. Since we're already halfway back to Derry, best to be on our way back home."

"A smashing day! Spectacular scenery with super people. Hugging Maureen, Terence said, "Couldn't image a more delightful time."

After exchanging kisses all around, Maureen said to Terence, "Want to drive?"

"Sure. I'll see how good I manage driving on the left."

Just a couple of miles after leaving Fergus and Diana, Maureen said, "You said you couldn't image a more delightful time. I think I can manage to add something more to your day."

He looked over at her and noticed she had unfastened the top buttons to her top. Not only had she exposed a deep cleavage of her full breasts, but she placed her right hand on his thigh.

"Take a right turn on a road that's coming up in just a few hundred feet."

Smiling broadly, he watched her as she proceeded to unbutton her top down fully to her waist. After unfastening the front-closure bra exposing her breasts, she moved her left hand to his groin. The sensation of her touch encouraged his already growing erection."

"Pull off the road under that stand of trees. No one lives down this way. The road ends just a short distance down toward the bank of the lough. We'll be alone here shielded from the road."

As he downshifted pulling into a secluded spot, Maureen took matters further by unbuckling his belt then unfastening his jeans then zipping down the fly. Stopping the car, he set the parking brake. Terence looked greedily at her breasts then turned reaching over to cup a breast in his right hand. Simultaneously, she slipped her hand under the waistband of his underwear, causing him to gasp at the pleasurable sensation.

As Maureen extracted his erection she said, "Leave the engine running with the heater on. We 're going to the back seat. Take all your clothes off."

Terence began doing just that while watching Maureen doing the same. Somewhat awkward sitting behind the wheel, the sight of her naked body left him wide-eyed with anticipation. She said, "Told you I could make your day even better. There's a blanket on the back seat. Arrange it so I can lay down. Do it quickly!"

Both stepped out of the car entirely naked while he opened the back door. As he spread the blanket across the seat, Maureen entered from the other side of the car. She positioned herself on her back with her head toward the opposite side. With his erect cock only inches from her face, she pulled him closer to take it fully into her mouth but only for a few moments before saying,

"Get in here and shut the damn door if you want more of that! I'm freezing. Ever do sixty-nine?"

He knew the term cunnilingus for female oral stimulation but never made love that way. He managed to place both feet on the back floor then closed the door behind him. Leaning over her she said, "Throw your left knee over me and put your face between my legs."

Once situated, the heater made them comfortable as they give each other oral stimulation. They kept this up until he reached a point that took concentration to hold off his approaching orgasm. Sensing his state of arousal, Maureen said, "Don't come yet. Turn around and get inside me."

Terence hurried awkwardly to turn around and rearrange himself by changing to his other knee on the seat as Maureen opened her legs. Orgasm for both came quickly after entering her.

Remaining locked together in post-coital relaxation for a time, they soon untangled to sit more comfortably in the backseat. They sat embracing and kissing each other in the warm interior with the windows obscured by their breath condensing on the cold glass.

"Well, did that make your day complete, Love?" Maureen said.

He replied, "That it did. Fantasied about making love with you from the first time I set eyes on you last week. You are one sexy creature, Maureen Lynch. Promises to be a fabulous summer."

Terence Kelly fantasized about the hedonistic pleasures awaiting him during the weeks ahead. Maureen Lynch clearly liked sex. He did not have a particularly wide range of experience with women, but Maureen knew what she liked. He never had a steady girlfriend nor even what he could call a romantic relationship. His few sexual encounters were spontaneous and rarely repeated with the same partner. None of those experiences involved the female taking charge like what just transpired with Maureen.

That first encounter with Maureen Lynch in early May that began euphorically promising a delightful stay in Derry turned sour during their next sexual encounter. This time Maureen lured him to the refrigeration room area in back of the bar to help her hook up a new keg of beer. With the door closed, she kissed him passionately while rubbing his crotch. "I'm feeling horny."

Startled, he said, "You're not suggesting we do it right here are you?"

"Course not. Going to tell Agnes I need to duck out for an hour. Meet me outside but down the street going toward my house. My parents aren't home. We can sneak into my bedroom for a quick one." Anticipation instantly aroused him as he messaged her breasts.

Maureen's house was only a quarter of a mile away. Her father's car was gone. Entering, she made sure her mother was also gone before dragging Terence into her bedroom upstairs. Knowing she looked good, she removed her shirt and bra baring her breasts. To Terence, "Pull off your pants and underwear. I'm going to get your hard."

Grabbing a pillow from the bed, she knelt in front of him. Holding his already erect member, she said, "Looks good, but I can get your harder."

While giving him fellatio both lost track of how close she had brought him to climaxing. Unable to contain himself he pulled out from her mouth, "Can't hold it." His ejaculation sprayed her running down between her breasts."

"Bloody fuck! What about me? You goddamn well better keep hard and get inside me."

She pulled off her skirt and panties dragging him to the bed. Instead of laying down, she rested her hands on the bed. "Do me from the back dog-style."

Terence did his best. Although again reaching climax, Maureen found it lacking. Pulling away she angrily turned on him. "Stupid bloody sod! Just about pleasing yourself. Forgetting about satisfying me. The American bigshot having his way with this poor Irish bitch. Well, that wasn't an acceptable performance!"

Terence made profuse apologies. As her anger dissipated, she eventually accepted his embrace, making temporary peace.

Their next encounter only days later troubled him in a different way. Once again in Maureen's bed she demanded that he perform cunnilingus. "You need to make up for the last time." While she guided him in detail with what she wanted, he felt she was unnecessarily being domineering. Sex should be mutually satisfying not a test of wills.

Unfortunately, the following weeks proved a rollercoaster of sexual experiences. Terence found that Maureen exhibited wide emotional swings that he attributed to increased use of liquor and marijuana. Arguments became commonplace.

By early June, Terence made up his mind to move to Belfast sooner than planned. Classes at the university would not start until September. He would use the time to get acclimated to Belfast. Locate an affordable apartment within walking distance of the university. Begin looking for possible employment opportunities that could fit his class schedule.

Before leaving Derry, Liam told Terence that his relocation to Belfast becomes safer by using his other name. Stewart sounds more Protestant than Kelly. "Disappear into that new identity. The tensions are rising in Derry. Since the Battle of the Bogside in August of 1969 when Catholic civilians clashed with the RUC, things had changed. At that time, the Catholics looked favorably when the British Army interceded by taking over from the RUC. Subsequent circumstances have dramatically changed that view. The British Army can no longer be seen as neutral. The situation in Belfast is equally unstable. Only ten days ago the IRA threw a time bomb into Springfield Road British Army and RUC joint security base in Belfast. A British Army sergeant died. The blast also wounded two other British soldiers, seven RUC officers, and eighteen civilians.

"Just last summer major rioting erupted in Derry and Belfast following the arrest of Bernadette Devlin. More rioting followed in Belfast when the Orangemen marched through Catholic neighborhoods. Running gunbattles between republicans and loyalists killed seven people. London has deployed additional British Army personnel to Northern Ireland. Not to replace the RUC but to provide them with vastly greater numbers for conducting military operations."

"Not to worry, Granda. I plan to absorb myself in my studies."

"Do that and avoid politics. Disappearing into your Protestant background identity offers a degree of safety. Don't try appearing as a loyalist. You're just a bloody foreigner. What about Maureen? Seems you two have become close."

"On again off again. Maureen is a highly temperamental woman. We argue all the time. Can never lead to anything lasting. Becomes a good excuse to break it off. As you say, disappear into my new identity far enough away in Belfast to avoid running into each other. Are you and Grandma okay with furthering the lie that I returned to Boston?"

What he did not relate to his grandfather was his feeling that Maureen was far more than just temperamental. Possessive. Obsessive. Insecure. Unrealistic. Unstable to a scary degree. Accusing him of looking at other women. *Am I not pretty enough? Where are you going? You can't leave me at the end of summer. Why can't I go to Boston and be with you? I always wanted to go to America. You do love me don't you?* The very idea of Maureen accompanying him to Boston became a frightening thought.

Liam nodded. "Yes. Regardless, I suspect Maureen will be hurt. But she'll get over it. Certainly, can't reveal to her that you'll be attending the university in Belfast, especially using another name. When do you plan on leaving?"

"Sooner than I originally planned. Next week I think. Need to find a place to live. Also want to explore the possibility of getting a job that might fit with my university schedule."

"You be watching yourself, Terry. Play the part of the American outsider. Shy away from political discussion. Things are worsening not only in Derry but also in Belfast."

"I know, Granda. The month of May was a bad one in Belfast. June will probably be no better. Shootings by security forces and IRA bombings. An IRA member is shot dead by British soldiers then a British soldier is killed by the IRA. That's becoming a common occurrence throughout Northern Ireland. Back and forth. Is that how this is going to be, going forward?"

Liam replied, "Hard to say. I suspect that will be the case for the immediate future. The newly appointed commanding general of British Army forces in Northern Ireland said that achieving a military solution was not possible. If London takes that to heart maybe the Provisional IRA is making headway. But it's still likely to be a very long fight."

Planning to confront Maureen by telling her of his leaving Derry to return to Boston earlier than planned because of an expected job opportunity, Terence almost lost his resolve. After a strenuous bout of lovemaking, he even considered postponing leaving prematurely for Belfast until August. The next day brought him back to his senses. Maureen was never meant to be more than an exciting summer vacation experience. He wasn't ready to settle into a long-term relationship with someone of Maureen's unstable nature. Her talk of wanting to join him when returning to Boston at the end of summer meant ending things between them would prove difficult. Terminating their relationship without explanation therefore became the easiest solution. Cruel and self-serving, but pragmatically his best course of action.

A forthright announcement of his breaking off and going back to Boston alone would probably incite an unpredictable volatile reaction. He instead deliberately said something intended to precipitate a lesser argument. Something she might see the following morning after learning of his leaving Derry for good as partly her doing.

As agreed, his grandfather told Maureen when she arrived at the pub, "Terence left very upset early this morning. Wanted to tell you that he was returning to Boston sooner than planned. Said your frequent arguments left him feeling that staying longer in Derry would only make matters worse. Told me to tell you he was sorry that things did not work out better and wished you well."

CHAPTER 5

Boston, Massachusetts | January 2025

Terence Kelly sat in Father O'Brien's office at Boston College. While recalling the joyous reunion with his grandparents his first days after arriving in Derry, much of his narrative turned toward his relationship with Maureen Lynch.

"I was young, not experienced with women. Maureen was pretty and overtly sexy. Flirted with the male pub clients. My ego got the better of me when she took a shine to me. In hindsight I think because I was American. Also because of my family connection with Liam and Agnes. Without getting into details our relationship quickly devolved into sex. Often fueled by liquor and marijuana. I believe the word tumultuous best describes our relationship. Frequent arguments. Since I was in Derry only temporarily before relocating to Belfast to attend Queen's University, I decided to leave Derry earlier than planned.

"After an argument I intentionally provoked, I left Derry the following day taking the train to Belfast. Left my grandparents to explain to Maureen my sudden departure using the lie that I was returning to America. Felt guilty but immensely relieved. Except for the sex the relationship with Maureen became intolerable after several weeks."

"You say there were frequent arguments, yet you stayed involved until you decided to break it off. How do you think Maureen felt about the relationship?"

Kelly grunted, "Hard to say. In retrospect, I think it was perhaps nothing more than my being an American. Ties to Ireland but still a foreigner. A novelty maybe. Not because she was in love with me. Nor was I in love with her. I stayed because I hooked up with a pretty woman that liked sex. Youthful stupidity. Living in the moment until her volatility became too much. Emotionally unstable. Perhaps what today is known as bipolar. Maureen reminded me of the female character in that movie *Fatal Attraction* from the eighties. Obsessive like those individuals described as stalkers. I still felt shitty for just upping and leaving her without a word."

O'Brien switched the subject. Maureen Lynch appeared just a footnote in the larger story of Kelly's admission of complicity in widespread carnage. "Tell me how you disappeared into this new identity as Terence Stewart after relocating to Belfast."

"Easier than I thought it might be because it wasn't about religion. I wasn't a practicing Catholic, only sympathetically aligned with Irish nationalism because of my family background. Posing as coming from a Protestant background by my mother's heritage held only the implication that I was tacitly loyalist, or at least not sympathetic to Irish nationalism. No middle ground accepted back then, or even now I should imagine. Adopting a new identity living as if a Protestant was difficult only in being cautious to avoid any pitfalls inconsistent with that label. Didn't usually require professing loyalist views.

"I was Irish American. Raised in Boston from infancy. This conflict in Northern Ireland was no longer about realistically achieving independence from the British. That became the most jarring realization. The Anglo-Irish War of my grandfather's time was rebellion against British rule. Experiencing Northern Ireland, I came to understand the situation in Ulster was never that clear. British rule might be at the heart of the historic problem, but reality was the age-old ethnic divide. Here a Catholic minority had always been denied equal rights by a Protestant majority descended from earlier settlers from Great Britain. As a colonial power, Britain encouraged and supported repression of Catholics in the Northern Ireland regional government.

"More directly to your question, I felt like a clandestine subversive bent on assisting in the overthrow of that unjust government. Being American, it seemed like the civil rights struggle for African Americans in the United States. Don't know that I ever fully realized there was never to be any expectation of Great Britain relinquishing Northern Ireland to join the Republic of Ireland."

"How did this period of your arrival in Belfast fit into your subsequent partisan activist engagement with the IRA?" O'Brien asked.

"From the beginning I became aware of just how sharp the demarcation was between those identified as Catholic or Protestant. This was still rebellion against British rule. British security forces had far more weapons. The Provisional IRA offered the only military response. The difficulty was two-thirds of the civilian population sided with British rule. The IRA could therefore never enjoy widespread support.

"Looking for an apartment meant finding a Protestant neighborhood. Everyone is immediately categorized by that distinction. As a newcomer my interchanges went something like *I'm Irish born in Belfast but raised in America since the age of two.* Where in Belfast did your parents live? *In a neighborhood north of Crumlin Road. Not far from my grandparents' home where I was born. Both my father and Grandfather worked at Harlan & Wolff. Father lost his job at the shipyard following the war due to lack of shipbuilding work. The family then emigrated to America. All my grandparents have now passed.* Any such variations identified you as Catholic or Protestant.

"Becoming my alternate identify as a Protestant became easier than I expected. Growing up in America with no relatives in Northern Ireland made a reasonable excuse for avoiding expressing loyalist views. In that regard, although Irish, I was treated somewhat as a foreigner. Equally easy to avoid expressing hostilities toward Catholics. Said that was not an issue in America therefore I had no strong anti-Catholic feelings. Professing no religious inclinations of any persuasion allowed stepping back from charged discussions. The only remaining issue of conversation to stay clear of concerned the violence. For that I denounced what looked to me like another Irish civil war. I faulted both sides. *Look at each bombing or shooting. Each justified as nothing more than retaliation for acts perpetrated by the other side. Doomed to end badly regardless of the outcome.* Criticized by some for not supporting their side, but not enough to consider that my views supported the opposing side.

"I became identified as Protestant by the same questions faced by everyone when meeting someone for the first time. What's your favorite pub, mate? Football team? Any reference that placed you in either demographic. Never asked directly. Seemed to be no middle ground. None of this was about religion. Catholic or Protestant simply the easiest way of defining your heritage as native Irish or immigrant ancestry that colonized Ireland from Great Britain. I survived by avoiding controversial issues.

"What about at Queen's University? By today's standard it includes a fair percentage of students that might be considered Catholic."

"In 1971 the religious demographic of Belfast was about two-thirds Protestant. There were a fair number of Catholic students at QUB. Probably a lesser percentage than the overall population because of the economic divide. The Catholic population being predominately less affluent. Within the university I found noticeably fewer outward expressions of sectarian antagonism. Among faculty as well as students. Easier for me with my social interactions mostly with others on campus. I worked nights and weekends mostly by myself. What few fellow employees I encountered were undoubtedly Protestant therefore probably loyalists, but I rarely found interactions politically awkward. Being from America seemed always the focus of everyone's conversation with me.

"I knew something of Queen's University from following the Northern Ireland civil rights movement when I was attending college in Boston. The *People's Democracy* political organization was founded at QUB in 1968. Admittedly by politically left-leaning students, but nonetheless, even with a Protestant majority student body, there was less a hostile environment compared to off-campus life. Political activist Bernadette Devlin was a student at the time and frequently featured in American news. Events in Northen Ireland followed closely in Boston with its large, mostly Catholic, ethnic Irish population."

O'Brien asked, "You mentioned finding employment. Doing what type of work?"

"I found part time work at a large television and radio retail store that also offered repair services. Able to work evenings and weekends with flexible hours since it was solitary work. The following year I found work at Belfast 2BE radio station. Today it's BBC Radio Ulster. Worked in the technical department. Rigging gear, trouble-shooting problems, and making repairs. The radio station was in central Belfast just off Crumlin Road about two miles north of QUB. The electronics store was even closer. Both conveniently located since I lived not far from the campus."

O'Brien said, "In our first conversation you said you made radio-controlled detonating devices for IRA bombs. Did your places of employment figure into your covert efforts?"

"Very much so. The retail job particularly afforded access to electronic components. The same type of components used in any radio or television equipment. My detonators were nothing more than modified two-way radio circuitry. I got the idea from working for Comet Electronics. They sold American-made two-way radios, walkie-talkies, to commercial customers. For example, the shipyard or railroads, anywhere requiring outdoor communications. My work and my curriculum at the university also allowed me to openly have electronic components and related equipment at my apartment should I ever come under suspicion. I'll go into greater detail later as I further my story."

"When did you decide to become actively involved on the side of the Provisional IRA?"

"Not my motivation for visiting Northern Ireland. Perhaps the idea occurred after learning that my grandfather was involved with smuggling arms, along with learning of my father's complicity from America. Something like a family calling. The implicit feeling even from an early age that Irish rebellion to free all of Ireland from Britain was in my bloodline. However, by the time I relocated to Belfast I initially became consumed by more immediate things. Finding an affordable apartment. Part time employment to pay my way. Knuckling down with studies. Engineering is a demanding field of study, especially at the graduate level.

"However, over the remaining months of 1971 a sequence of events pushed me closer to contributing in some material way. Didn't immediately know what form that might take. Wasn't about to take up the gun and go underground. What was one more foreign Irishman going to accomplish? Didn't possess that kind of fanatical commitment either. Anyway, couldn't do that to my family. My grandfather's joining the fight in some covert way might be understood, but not an Irish lad having grown up in South Boston. If anything were to happen to me it would devastate everyone in the family, most of all to my grandfather."

"What events are you speaking of that caused you to take this rather bold and dangerous course of involvement?" O'Brien asked.

"Started in Derry. This time it was the British Army not the RUC. Soldiers shot two Catholic civilians in July. New rioting resulted. The Social Democratic Labor Party withdrew from Stormont in protest. London upped the stakes by introducing internment in August. Arrest and imprisonment without trial. *Operation Demetrius* jointly executed by the British Army and the RUC. Sounded to me little different than Nazi-like tactics before World War Two.

"In September Protestant loyalists formed the paramilitary Ulster Defence Association to counter the militant IRA. At the same time the UDA created a parallel organization they called the Ulster Freedom Fighters. The UFF was not a separate organization just an alter ego cover when the UDA chose to engage in violent actions to avoid legal backlash. The Northern Ireland government recognized the UDA as a legal organization during the seventies but by 1973 classified the UFF as a terrorist organization.

"In November, the IRA exploded a bomb inside the *Red Lion Pub* on Shankill Road. Three Protestant civilians were killed and thirty others wounded. A second bomb exploded in an adjacent shop injuring more people. A month later another loyalist paramilitary organization, the Ulster Volunteer Force, detonated a bomb in a Catholic-owned *McGurk's Bar* located at the corner of North Queen Street and Great George's Street. Fifteen killed, including two children, and seventeen wounded.

"The continued violence had by now grown more extreme. The security forces with far greater resources increased attacks directed almost exclusively toward only the IRA, never to the loyalist paramilitary groups. The IRA could respond only by using guerrilla warfare tactics. Attack vulnerable targets then disappear into the general population. In all such conflicts using bombs, civilians always suffered.

"With limited manpower, the IRA's principal means of armed aggression was explosives. Their success at detonating bombs up to this time was mixed at best. Premature detonations killed many inexperienced bombmakers. It became evident to me that the means of detonation was a serious problem. Premature detonations killed those inexperienced. Reliance on improvised timing devices left the bomber exposed. Once set to explode, unintended targets inevitably became casualties.

"The remedy seemed clear to me. Radio control triggering of the bombs. Allowed reliable detonation determined by a bomber from a safe distance transmitting a radio signal of a specific frequency. I possessed the necessary technical knowhow. Simple radio transmission and receiver circuitry. By transmission command, a signal closes contacts in the receiving device connecting a battery source necessary to trigger the bomb's detonating sequence. I not only possessed the knowledge but also had access to all the required electronic components necessary to make the modifications to the commercial two-way radios."

"How did your grandfather play into this?"

"Granda's participation was the only way I could pull this off. If I wanted to remain unknown from the IRA, he became the means. Granda already admitted he was smuggling arms and explosives to the IRA from America. I would build radio-controlled detonator systems that he would provide to the IRA claiming they came from America. He alone would deliver them to the IRA."

"When did you approach your grandfather with this idea and offer your services to design and produce these devices?"

"Not until after *Bloody Sunday* happened in January of the new year 1972. But I started working on making a working prototype well before that."

"Did this require knowledge of bomb making?"

"To some extent. Needed to understand what was necessary for delivering an electrical discharge of the necessary voltage and energy provided by dry cell batteries for initiating the detonation sequence. Mostly needed to understand the ignition demands of blasting caps, the primary ignition source that detonated various types of high explosives. Depending on availability, the IRA used different high explosives for the main destructive charge of their improvised bombs. Dynamite, gelignite, ammonium-nitrate with fuel oil, or so-called military-grade *plastic explosives* like Semtex that contain RDX and PETN.

"I didn't need to understand how much or what type of explosives required detonation or anything about the chemistry. Only the electrical circuit requirements of the ignition source and the required battery supply. The university library provided all the technical information needed."

O'Brien said, "I need to have a better understanding of your motivation for going to Northen Ireland. Of course, it was to see your grandfather who was a legendary figure in your family. Yet enrolling in graduate studies at Queen's University went far beyond just visiting for a summer. Now you say the events of what you experienced in 1971 even before the cataclysmic event of *Bloody Sunday* turned you to participate in a violent form of activism. How do you explain that progression, Mr. Kelly?"

Terence Kelly nodded in understanding. "A very good question, Father. One that I have agonized to answer to myself for fifty years without much success. What I embarked upon demonstrated exceedingly bad judgement no matter my attempts at justification. Completing my undergraduate degree in engineering afforded excellent employment opportunities. I obtained my American naturalization citizenship once I turned eighteen. Everything seemed directed toward securing a well-paying professional career. However, there was a very pronounced obstacle to that picture. The ongoing war in Vietnam. Having finished my undergraduate degree, furthering my education with a graduate degree might not defer me from the military draft. Why not accomplish that in Northern Ireland using my British citizenship?

"While that was foremost on my mind in considering attending Queen's University in Belfast, what transpired became something inexplicable. Perhaps the youthful attraction to adventure. Perhaps my Irishness? A sense of belonging to that great diaspora so much a part of my identity. Part of some larger personal history.

"My father loved the song *Danny Boy*. The first lines of *Danny Boy* I took as a call to action. Listened to it all the time during my youth. From my earliest years the first lines never failed to provoke a feeling of sad lament. *Oh, Danny boy, the pipes, the pipes are calling, from glen to glen, and down the mountain side.* Sung by a great tenor's voice it can bring tears to the blackest of hearts. Often sung at funerals, the words suggest a call to arms as a sad lament of farewell. For me perhaps subconsciously a siren call to return to my origins. You're Irish, Father. You perhaps know something of the feeling we Irish all carry from our historical victimization.

"For me and undoubtedly for countless others, cultural heritage played a significant part in my views. All the more so with my heritage of a living, breathing immediate family reality. I lived the events of my grandfather from fifty years earlier in my mind. Read every book on Irish history, including your books, Father. The centuries of Ireland as a colony under the heel of Great Britain finally giving way in 1922. While I'm Irish, my family originated in Northern Ireland. That was a big deal in 1922 when the British partitioned Ireland in the Anglo-Irish Treaty. The southern twenty-six counties achieving semi-independence from Britain while Northern Ireland remained an integral part of Great Britain. Obviously those circumstances reignited latent hostilities during the tumultuous thirty years of the *Troubles*.

"The conflict in Northen Ireland by 1969 much different than from 1919. Irish rebellion seeking independence from the UK became more immediately one of civil rights for an oppressed Catholic minority. An unfortunate labelling just like calling the opposing side Protestants. Groupings where religion paid no part other than describing one's ancestorial ethnicity. But if you're Irish living in an American city with a large Irish Catholic population, anti-Irish oppression provoked emotions well beyond mere intellectual rebellion.

"I believe that my circumstances combined to instill in me the same ideological fervor of my grandfather and those of earlier generations I read about. Irishness taken to these lengths becomes a way of life. As to your question about what caused me to take up arms at the risk of great personal sacrifice, I never settled that in my own mind. A monumental mistake. What happened those few years in Northern Ireland fifty years ago forever distorted my life. A largely unhappy life.

"Like most occurrences in the world whether successes or disasters, multiple causes combine to determine events. No different for individuals. In my case being Irish, embracing a cause of oppression for that cultural identity, motivated by a legendary grandfather now reengaging in the historical struggle makes for a heady mix. Add to this my youthful immaturity, impressionable, headstrong, immune to identifying risk thinking to live forever.

"All of these factors probably came into play, but perhaps what pushed me over the edge was thinking myself clever enough to pull it off. Using my technical skills to create something useful to attack the enemy while remaining unknown. What better security with only my beloved grandfather knowing what I was doing. Protected by an alternate official identity allowing me to live openly among the opposition while secretly playing as a real spy. The arrogant self-confidence of a talented amateur.

"That I survived to live until taken by cancer rather than wasting fifty years in some depressing prison might validate that self-confidence. However, the reality points more to the fortunes of chance. Those fifty years instead became wasted in self-recrimination rather than accomplishment. Self-loathing is hardly conducive to forging social bonds. A lonely fifty years. Stephen King's line in one of his novels, *life sucks, then you die* accurately sums up my existence. As I recount my story in its many sordid details, I believe you will see the reasons for why I sought you out, Father."

CHAPTER 6

Belfast, Northern Ireland | Summer 1971

Terence Kelly silently left his bedroom before dawn. Sleep eluded him thinking of what lay ahead. Assuming a new identity made him feel like a spy. Before departing Boston in the spring, he received his acceptance letter from QUB. Nothing however illicit by using his official British passport with the name Terence Stewart. Planning enrollment in Queen's University Belfast seemed like a clever idea to remain in Northern Ireland for a sustained period but that was not fully formed. He now sat in the Derry train station sparsely populated with passengers at this early hour feeling uncertain and very alone.

Tuition would make a sizable dent in his modest savings. He did not know rent costs in Belfast or how much he needed for living expenses. Finding employment therefore became essential. Yet he had no idea if that would prove possible. Once he made the tuition payment he would become committed.

After arriving in Belfast, he lugged his bags walking the mile to Queen's University. Waiting until the administration offices opened, he made his way to the bursar's office. Already enrolled, it was just a matter of paying his tuition using a cashier's check made out to Terence Brendan Stewart matching his British passport identity. Student services provided him with a current list of available apartments suited toward students. From there he gained an audience with a counselor in the office of student employment.

Settled into the youth hostel, he would postpone writing to his parents until finding a permanent accommodation. Neither parent knew of his intention to stay on in Northern Ireland by attending graduate school at Queen's University in Belfast. The thought formed in the back of his mind even before graduating from Benjamin Franklin Cummings Institute of Technology in May of 1971. See his beloved grandfather for the first time. The notorious IRA gunman Liam Kelly that fought at the side of Michael Collins in the Anglo-Irish War in the early twenties. A secret IRA assassin like some character in a novel. Yet staying on longer in Northern Ireland made the experience something far more than then just a visit for the summer.

That experience now turned into real adventure living among frequent occurrences of killings and bombings. No matter whether loyalist or Irish nationalist, British controlled Northern Ireland did not feel part of the United Kingdom. More like a rebellious colony. Attending university provided reason to stay on in Northern Ireland in relative safety beyond immediate exposure to the worst of the violence. At least that was his rationalization.

Holding dual citizenship with a British passport allowed reduced tuition and the ability to find part time employment without requiring obtaining a work permit as a foreign national student. The British passport identity also provided him a Protestant heritage should his background be examined. Beneficial in Protestant loyalist dominated Northern Ireland. Leaving the United States also resolved the looming threat of being call up for American military service engaged in the continuing Vietnam War.

After a couple of days of looking over available apartments, he settled on an upstairs unit in a two-story house in the Protestant loyalist neighborhood of the Windsor district only a mile west of the university. The owners were a middle-aged couple. Years earlier they converted two second-floor bedrooms into a self-contained one-bedroom apartment with living area and small kitchen. Access was by an external flight of stairs. After their children moved out, they made the conversion to provide supplemental income. They took a liking to him when he revealed why he came to Belfast. Where his family originally came from before emigrating to America twenty years ago. A modified fiction citing the former careers of his grandfather Brendan Stewart and uncle David Stewart at Harland & Wolff. The landlord currently worked at the shipyard providing a conversational connection.

Before leaving Boston, Terence changed most of the funds in his bank account into British pound notes. Enough to open a Belfast bank account and sustain him for a limited period in Northern Ireland. Having shortened his time in Derry staying with his grandparents now added additional weeks of lodging and food expenses. At least without the distraction of Maureen Lynch, he had uncommitted time to devote to finding work before classes commenced in early September.

Staying consistent with his Protestant identity, he took the list of current businesses advertising for help wanted. Aware of his ethnic classification, he began walking the city armed with a map looking at businesses in what appeared to be predominantly loyalist areas between Crumlin and Shankill Roads. In the course of making inquiries from the university list, he crossed the River Lagan to East Belfast on the Ormeau Bridge. This was an ethnically mixed sector of Belfast roughly populated equally by Catholics and Protestants. Walking south down Ormeau Road, he passed a large retail store. The windows of Comet Electronic displayed televisions and radios. While there was no help wanted sign, he would nonetheless try his luck.

Asking for the manager, Terence made his pitch. "I'm going to be attending graduate school in electrical engineering at Queen's, Sir. Wondering if you might have need for a technician. Your sign says you repair televisions and radios? I could use a job to help pay for living expenses."

"You say you're studying electrical engineering. That covers a lot of different things. You know anything about electronics?"

"Yes, sir. My undergraduate major was electronics. I managed the college amateur radio station in Boston. Installed and repaired equipment. Operated my own amateur radio setup at home."

"Boston? You're American?"

"Irish American. But I was born right here in Belfast. My family emigrated to America when I was an infant. Once I graduated college thought it was about time I returned and saw something of my Irish roots. Made sense to combine that with continuing my education. Being born here I have British citizenship. So, there's be no problem with employment, Sir."

Terence produced his passport and handed it to the store manager.

The manager looked at the passport then said, "Fact is, I just might have need for another technician. We've got more repair work than we can handle. Robert has been with us for a long time. Good man. Taken with the flu so he's not in today. Tell you what. Interested in showing me how skilled you are?"

"Yes, Sir. Be glad to."

"Good, let we show you the repair backlog. Try your hand at fixing a couple of radios. If you've the skills, we could use someone part-time to help Robert. Can you work nights?"

"Yes, Sir. And more hours on weekends if necessary."

A couple of hours later, finishing work on several radios and a television, he got the job. Not having to start classes for many weeks, he began work the next day. A large workload kept him very busy for several full days before the regular technician returned. More than enough to impress the manager. Terence and Robert took an instant liking to each other after discovering their mutual enthusiasm with amateur radio.

As Terence Stewart, he settled into life in Belfast with weeks remaining before orientation at QUB the first week of September. He was able to put in substantial hours at Comet Electronics that greatly improved his financial circumstances. Having brought with him a significant amount of cash converted to British pounds for living expenses, making the tuition payment greatly depleted his U.S. bank account.

Purchasing textbooks for his upcoming classes allowed him to get a head start on the demands of advanced course studies. Between that and work hours, he kept busy. Not knowing anyone, his recreation became solitary walks about Belfast. From the onset, he understood he must remain vigilant to preserve his Protestant identity. While he could never attempt to portray loyalist political views, he also understood he must be careful not to inadvertently slip up by inadvertently revealing his Irish nationalism.

Although sectarian tensions continued unabated, violence did not directly touch most of the population. However, those in the Catholic neighborhoods lived in constant fear. Whether by government security forces, Protestant loyalist paramilitaries, or even acts of outrage perpetrated by the IRA resulting in collective retaliation became ever present concerns. Living in a Protestant neighborhood, Terence avoided much of that. His newly constructed existence took on its own sense of normalcy. Kept busy by sustaining his financial needs, his thoughts turned toward the challenge to expand his technical skills pursuing an advanced engineering degree.

On the morning of Monday 9 August 1971 any complacency became dispelled when he turned on the radio. *For those of you just tuning in, beginning in the predawn hours this morning the British Army began conducting sweeping raids throughout Northern Ireland looking to arrest those suspected of being involved with the Provisional Irish Republican Army. The IRA has for some time mounted an armed campaign directed against the British state of Northern Ireland. A spokesman for Northern Ireland Prime Minister Brian Faulkner announced commencement of Operation Demetrius, a joint military operation involving 3,000 British Army troops and unknown numbers of Royal Ulster Constabulary personnel. Authorized under the Special Powers Act, the objective of the security mobilization is to weaken the IRA thereby reducing their capacity to engage in vio-*

lent attacks. British Army command reports the initial arrest of over 300 individuals associated with the IRA. Those detainees are in the process of being moved to three regional holding centers. Belfast, Ballykinlar in County Down, and Magilligan in County Londonderry. Detainees will undergo thorough investigation including interrogation. This would lead either to release or indefinite internment at long-term internment facilities in Belfast. These include the Crumlin Road Prison in Belfast or confinement onboard HMS Maidstone, a Second World War prison ship anchored in Belfast Harbor.

The crude methods employed by the security forces frequently mimicked Gestapo-like tactics of inflicting severe physical abuse on detainees. Violence erupted immediately with protests, riots, and attacks on the security forces. Within a few days, the death toll numbered 20 civilians, two known IRA members, and two British soldiers.

For Terence, any complacency was shattered. The idea that the British could be so stupid as to again resort to internment only fortified his Irish nationalistic fervor. Terence recalled his grandfather's account of the disastrous effect of the British attempt at introducing military conscription in Ireland in 1918 to replace losses during World War Two. It was the final British affront toward Ireland that sparked the onset of the Anglo-Irish War, or as called by the Irish, the War of Independence. Liam Kelly told his grandson about internment that added final insult to the Irish. Indefinite imprisonment without trial or recourse. Ballykinlar Internment Camp in County Down became the first mass internment camp in 1920. The Internees faced harsh conditions. Maltreatment and even cases of deaths. Once again, the British demonstrated total lack of restraint by applying unjust and brutal methods. Terence knew the history of British atrocities in South Africa at the turn of the 20th century during the Boer War. Nothing had changed in seventy years. Northern Ireland was still nothing more than a British colony. A restive colony to be suppressed by military force.

He began cautiously walking to work at Comet Electronics. At least the route took him through predominantly loyalist areas or past important Belfast institutions. A massive presence of British Army troops patrolled in a high state of readiness against possible threat. Arriving at Comet Electronics, a handwritten sign hung on the door. *Closed until further notice.*

Returning back to his apartment he listened to continued radio news reporting the rest of the day. This latest round of violence provoked by the British signaled a turning point in the escalating conflict. On Thursday he returned to work after the worst of the violence had subsided. On Monday alone, 24 people were killed. 20 of these were civilians. Eleven of these were shot in the West Belfast's Ballymurphy housing estate by the British Army's 1st Battalion, Parachute Regiment in what was already being called the *Ballymurphy Massacre.* In the Northern Belfast district of Ardoyne, soldiers shot another three civilians.

Catholic homes were burned. Both Catholics and Protestants fled from areas of mixed ethnicity. 7,000 people, mostly Catholic were left homeless. Eventually that migration became the basis for establishing the various peace line boundaries in Belfast. An estimated 2,500 Catholics became refugees fleeing south across the border into the Republic of Ireland settling into temporary camps.

The first day of internment netted 342 arrests. All were Catholic. No Protestant loyalists were among those detained. The IRA chief of staff declared only 30 IRA members as being among the detainees. The provocation by London and the Northern Ireland government would undoubtedly increase IRA recruitment. The following months of 1971 would see increased violence. A harbinger of worst to come.

What just happened left no room for returning to anything resembling normalcy. The idea of completing his master's degree no longer would entirely shape his time in Northern Ireland. To be true to his heritage meant he must do something material to side against this naked institutionalized oppression. If his elderly grandfather could rejoin the fight, he must also do the same if he intended to remain in Northern Ireland. Granda would of course argue against it. Yet he could not image abandoning him and Grandma to these butchers when they were taking up the fight even at their advanced age.

It became obvious to Terence that the principal weapon of the IRA must become bombs. They did not have enough manpower or firearms to openly contest militarily against the armed forces arrayed against them. The loyalist paramilitary Ulster Volunteer Force alone was estimated to be larger than IRA membership probably only 1,000 in 1971. The official policing force, the Royal Ulster Constabulary, had an estimated 8,500 officers and 4,500 reservists. By 1972, 22,000 British Army troops were deployed in Northern Ireland, including 27 infantry and two armored battalions with support from 5,300 soldiers from the local British Army Ulster Defence Regiment formed in 1970 for the sole purpose of protecting life and property from sabotage. The size of the security forces for a population of only 1.5 million people for all of Northen Ireland gave indication of the scope of the developing conflict.

It became obvious to Terence that the IRA had no choice but to resort to bombing as their principal weapon. More damage than individual firearms for a limited fighting force engaged in guerrilla warfare tactics. While bomb making was used internationally by all sorts of political groups and could be constructed from comparatively available materials, it still required a level of technical expertise. Accidents abounded for those inexperienced. Bombs were also an imprecise weapon difficult to deploy against a specific target.

Terence possessed no expertise in bomb making. He was not IRA. Nor did he intend to join and thereby expose his identity. He might be Irish, but also an American. Not prepared to give his life even for the cause of Irish Catholic civil rights. Yet drawn to assist the struggle in a material way.

He had no contacts in Northern Ireland except his grandparents. Intended to keep it that way. He may have crossed his own Rubicon, but he still believed he had a conventional future even though not clearly formed. He wanted to actively assist the cause but do so in the most secretive way possible. Martyrdom may have been in his grandfather's makeup but not his.

The solution turned out to be exceptionally simple. Comet Electronics sold walkie-talkies. U.S. manufactured by Motorola and General Electric two-way radios. Two-way radio devices incorporating transmission and receiving functions. A pair could be used to transmit a radio signal to another unit modified to receive the signal and initiate an electrical detonation sequence of a bomb. The range could be significant by using only short antennas affixed to each device. Much of Comet's lucrative repair business centered on two-way radios. The Harlan & Wolff shipyard and personnel of the commercial harbor were both good clients. Lots of units were in service at any time. The radios were necessary for providing communications over a large diverse area requiring mobile communications.

Detonating a bomb consisted of triggering a small primary explosive that in turn initiated the destructive larger main explosive. That is the way a firearm cartridge works. Striking the primer cap at the end of the cartridge causes a spark that ignites the gun powder causing the gas to propel the bullet down the gun barrel. As an alternative to some sort of timer device or fuse, the radio signaling device provided the means to engage an electrical circuit from a battery pack and trigger explosion on command.

Two-way radios could transmit a radio signal at a specific frequency to a receiving unit that could close the circuit to a battery source to detonate a small primary explosive charge to set off the explosion of the larger main explosive charge. Triggering from a considerable distance by choosing the precise instant afforded the ability to place bombs well in advance. Easier to disguise. Far more effective than relying on various improvised timers. Exploding the bomb at the instant to affect the most damage to the intended objective.

He knew nothing about explosives but did not intend to make bombs. Just radio-controlled detonators. Something to detonate blasting caps universally suitable for exploding bombs consisting of different types of high explosives. All he needed to know was the electrical circuit characteristics necessary to trigger a manageable number of blasting caps. Easy enough to research in the university library.

The transmission unit for delivering the radio signal required only minor modification. The other unit serving as the receiver would take some creative work. The transmitting unit would be nothing more than the familiar commercial two-way hand-held radio unit with modifications to the existing function buttons. The receiving unit, however, required removing the unnecessary voice communications components to make space for added components required for creating the detonating circuitry. The design work entailed fitting the modifications within the standard package of the commercial unit. Only the original radio receiver circuity remained. Added items included additional batteries, a high discharge capacitor, and micro-relay to activate the electrical detonating circuit. All these components were readily available commercially.

Would his grandfather buy the idea? Would his grandfather allow him to participate? Would successful radio control detonating devices be important to the IRA? He realized the only way to sell his grandfather would be to build a working prototype. Comet enjoyed a profitable business with continual repairs for two-way radios seeing hard use and replacing units damaged beyond repair. There was a bone yard in the store's repair area used for cannibalizing parts. Plenty of components from which he could experiment. The first step was to study the manufacturer's schematics. From there he would create his specific purpose modifications.

The task became how to fit everything into the existing original manufactured case. If successful it provided a compact package that required the bombmaker to safely attach only two wires to whatever size or type of main high explosive used. No premature explosions. Detonation on command from a safe distance at the precise time rather than reliance on preset timers.

CHAPTER 7

Belfast, Northern Ireland | Winter 1971

Terence began classes at Queen's University in early September. While cordial, he avoided becoming too friendly, still wary about inadvertently saying something deemed inconsistent with his alternative identity. Everyone became politically labeled. Unionist or Nationalist irrespective of your political views or even claiming to harbor no political views was considered impossible. Better to avoid conversations as much as possible. Encountering interactions that could be uncomfortable, he reverted to his Americanism. The tactic afforded an understandable lack of declarative political comment on Northen Ireland issues.

Easy enough to avoid social interaction all together with his full schedule. The first week of classes made him realize the course material was not going to be easy. Integrated circuit technology was evolving at an exponential pace. Published textbooks could not keep pace. Course material at the post graduate level relied heavily on recently published papers and patent applications. Lectures could not be missed.

Classroom hours, study time, working at least twenty-fives hours a week at Comet left little time even for sleep. His full schedule favored retreat into his self-absorbed technical world yet mindful of the climate of pervasive violence. Since implementing internment at the point of a gun by government forces, circumstances worsened across Northern Ireland for Catholics.

From a public telephone Terence spoke to his grandfather for the first time since leaving Derry. They were mindful to be guarded about what they said. Neither knew if conversations might be monitored at the telephone exchange. By prior arrangement, Terence initiated the call since he had no telephone at his apartment. He placed the call to his grandparents' telephone at their residence above the pub. After exchanging pleasantries, both exchanged comments on the perilous situations in both Derry and Belfast, assuring each other of their safety. Terence brought Liam up to date on beginning his classes and gave him the address of his apartment in Belfast. He finally came to the question, "How did Maureen take my leaving without my saying goodbye?"

"Not very well. After showing up for work the following day, she left the pub immediately after I told her you had left to return to Boston. Told her you received a telegram about a possible job opportunity."

"Did she accept that?"

"Couldn't rightly tell, Terry. Tears ran down her cheeks, but she didn't weep. Far too angry. Stormed out of the pub. Didn't return for two days. Then told me she never wanted to talk about you again. Called you some nasty names I don't need to repeat. Anyway, she's bitter but seems to be putting it behind her."

"Hope so, Granda. Didn't want to hurt her but it wasn't ever going to work out between us."

Preferring to change the awkward subject, Liam said, "You must have a full schedule working a job and attending classes? Make sure you find time to relax. You're young with your whole life ahead of you. Any regrets about staying on over here in Northern Ireland rather than returning to Boston?"

"Not at all, Granda. Wonderful seeing you and Grandma. A terrible sadness what's happening though. But necessary for me to experience what it's like for Catholic nationalists living in Northern Ireland."

"That it is, Terry. The Brits have been a curse on the Irish people for hundreds of years. Caught up in their history of misplaced glory of subjugating other people throughout the world. The British Empire now entirely dissolved yet they hold on to Northen Ireland. The only colony left. Expect us Catholics to live under oppression enforced by the British Army and a ruthless colonial police force biased to loyalists."

Terence realized they should not be getting into such conversations on the telephone, "Would like to be seein' you, Granda. Perhaps one day around Christmas. No classes for two weeks for the holidays. Best not to do that in Derry of course. Was thinking about each of us taking the train to Coleraine. What do you think?"

"Grand idea, my boy."

"Of course I'd love to see Grandma too, but I was thinking maybe just you and I. Something I want to discuss something important. Better left between just the two of us."

Understanding that Terence was reluctant to be more specific worried Liam. Might this involve something Liam wanted his grandson to avoid? Regretted having mentioned anything about his active support of the Provisional IRA, or that Terence's father too was secretly involved in smuggling contraband from Boston. "Of course, Terry. That's a grand idea. Nothing I should be worried about is there?"

For Terence, feeling his need to do something material in this fight became an obsession. He believed he may have found a way for an outsider to Northern Ireland. He came to Northern Ireland to experience his heritage. Understand what that meant in terms of this present-day oppression of the Irish. He believed this struggle a remnant of unfulfilled Irish independence ambitions from fifty years ago. Not necessarily just Irish Catholic but decidedly not British loyalists. Committed to remaining here for an indefinite period, he could not stand aside as a mere observer.

"No, Granda. No need to worry. Better though if I explain in person. I'll telephone you again a couple of weeks in advance so we can set a date. You and Grandma stay safe. Derry seems at the greatest threat from British military forces. In Belfast it's more from Protestant loyalist paramilitary thugs."

What Terence wanted to show his grandfather was a prototype of his radio-controlled detonation device. He had not yet constructed a working prototype. He accomplished a functional schematic design by early October after studying the two-way radio manufacturer's schematics and doing reverse engineering on actual radios at Comet he believed he had a functional design. The circuitry was simple. The challenge was physically accommodating the alien components within the commercial radio case to convert the receiver unit to deliver an electrical firing circuit for detonating a bomb. Keeping only components necessary for receiving radio frequency transmission, he eventually devised how to accommodate the added components after removing the unnecessary components used for two-way voice communication. Those additional components included a dry cell battery pack dedicated to providing the firing circuit power and a capacitor fitting better within a Motorola HT220 walkie-talkie case than another commercial product manufactured by General Electric also offered by Comet Electronics.

Terence's first attempts at practical testing on a solderless breadboard on his kitchen table revealed various minor modifications to achieve optimal performance. While the basic circuit design proved functional, the user-related details for status indicator lights required refinement. By November, after making improvements, he was satisfied with the finished product. Given a cursory glance, the two handsets looked like commercial walkie-talkies. The only exception being the receiver module that would become part of the actual bomb had two protruding insulated wires tipped with alligator clips. The bombmaker only had to attach these wires to the imbedded blasting caps to make the bomb operational.

The missing element was the inability of proofing the prototype under actual use. He had no access to explosive blasting caps. All he could do to test for ignition capability consisted of using an electrical multimeter to measure the delivered output voltage and amperage when discharging the capacitor. While far greater than the required electrical parameters, he would feel better by validating functionality in actual practice.

A problem he hoped to resolve before he met with his grandfather. Working on this project with such intensity, he needed to first sell his grandfather on allowing him to participate. Granda would not understand the underlying engineering. Far better to see a live visual demonstration. The thought immediately came to him that he could demonstrate the effect by using a common camera flashbulb providing a visual result. Not explosive like a blasting cap but both devices functioned similarly when activated by a burst of electrical current.

Subsequent bombing events in November convinced Terence that the IRA's principal military weapon was improvised explosive devices. Increasing the utility of IEDs with the advantage of using radio detonator triggers for remote command detonation could greatly expand their effectiveness against more difficult high-value targets.

By the first week of December Terence had refined his design by physical testing. Having experimentally determined the best means of securing the many new components into the receiver-triggering unit, he had a workable prototype. With no further refinements necessary, it was time to scrupulously remove any traces of fingerprints by removing and reinstalling every component. Should this prototype see actual use, he wanted no evidence leading back to him. Producing further units would be done while wearing surgical latex gloves at all times.

On Saturday 11 December, the IRA exploded a bomb outside the Balmoral Furniture Company showroom in the predominantly Protestant loyalist area on Lower Shankill Road in Belfast. A crude bombing of an entirely non-combatant target. Four people killed. Two adults, one Protestant the other Catholic, and two infants. Nineteen others were injured. A senseless attack that set forth reciprocal bombings and shootings by loyalist paramilitaries. Each side justifying their next attack by that executed by the opposing side. Everyone, including Terence, knew this incident of carnage involving ordinary citizens as the victims would have negative long-term consequences for the IRA.

Perhaps naïvely, Terence thought that his radio detonators might allow the IRA to be more judicious by restricting their bombing primarily to military or economic targets. His rationale was based on the ability to secretly set bombs in place well before the time of intended use and control the timing for optimal detonation on command. That became possible by the ability of the individual triggering detonation to stand off at a significant distance while observing the target environment. Even from a considerable distance using binoculars. Moving military targets therefore could come under greater threat. Also provided inducing the similar emotional effect of unknown threat created by snipers.

The next day after completion of his prototype, Terence telephoned his grandfather. They arranged to meet at a specific pub in Coleraine close to the train station on Tuesday, three days after Christmas. Both would arrive by train from opposite directions midway between Belfast and Derry.

Liam Kelly arrived in Coleraine late in the morning and was waiting in the train station for Terence. Stepping down from the train carriage, Liam was standing on the platform. "Terry my boy!"

Embracing each other, "Granda. So good to see you. Everything well with you and Grandma?"

"As good as can be expected in these difficult times. What's with the duffle bag?"

"Something to show you after we talk, Granda."

Liam was impatient to hear what was on his grandson's mind but would let Terence direct the conversation. "Then we'll have a spot of lunch and have that talk. The *Railway Arms* is a fine place serving good food. Close by just outside the train station."

As they entered the *Railway Arms* pub there were few patrons since it was just late morning. Liam and Terence took a table in a corner well away from two elderly men seated at the bar. Making small talk, the bartender approached. "What'll it be gentlemen?"

"How 'bout a couple of pints of stout before taking lunch. Got a couple of hours before catching a train."

"Right you are. Got some good corned beef and cabbage with freshly baked bread just delivered. Where you headed?"

"Jolly good. Headed for Belfast. Taking a trip by airplane with my grandson here," Liam replied. The bartender was probing to identify the strangers' political leanings. As he left their table, Liam said to Terence, "Keep what we have to say just between us, Terry."

Terence nodded. "I want to help you and the IRA."

Liam shook his head vigorously. "Can't allow that, Terry. Your mother would have my head. Your father too. He might be helping me but doing so more safely from America. You can't become involved, Terry. You've already started at the university. What can you possibly contribute?"

"Detonators for bombs, Granda. Radio-controlled detonators. Something that can be used from a great distance. Triggering a bomb to explode using a radio signal whenever you choose. Can be done by someone who remains out of sight. No reliance on timers. No accidental detonations."

Liam's eyes widened then he looked around ensuring no one was within earshot. "Where would you get such a thing?"

"I'll make them. The basic hardware utilizes two-way radios called walkie-talkies. I modify them by adding other electrical components. Everything I need is available commercially. Nothing specifically associated with bombs or anything illegal to obtain."

"What makes you think the IRA needs such devices?"

"Because it's clear that bombs are the IRA's principal weapon. The bombs they've used show a lack of ability to plan a proper attack. That bombing of a furniture store in Belfast a week ago was a stupid thing to do. Blowing up civilians just hurts our cause. The security forces are the enemy, not civilians.

"The IRA must focus on targeting the RUC and British Army not civilian targets. Doing that requires better ways to use bombs. Allows being creative by pre-locating bombs in well-concealed places. But most of all by triggering explosions on command at the right time. When the enemy gathers in a group. As a truck passes for example. My radio detonating devices make the explosives the IRA already possesses far more effective. All the advantages I just mention while easier and safer to use for IRA bombmakers."

"You've designed such a device?" Liam asked. What his grandson described did have merit if it did all he said.

"Yes I have, Granda. Designed and even tested. Better yet, I brought along a working prototype to show you."

Terence patted the small duffle bag. "Not only show you but actually demonstrate how it works."

Liam raised his eyebrows.

"Do you know how high explosives are detonated?" Terence asked.

Liam said, "Can't say I know much about bomb making. Nor much about explosives. I'm more involved with finding sources of the stuff."

"Newspapers report that IRA bombs, or for that matter loyalist paramilitary bombs, use a variety of high explosives. Dynamite, gelignite, sometimes a mixture of ammonium nitrate and fuel oil sometimes called ANFO, and sometimes military-grade explosives called plastique like Semtex. However, the newspapers do not go into the details of how these powerful explosives are detonated. All bombs have in common the need for a detonator powerful enough to explode a small primary high explosive that provides the necessary energy to set off the stable main high explosive charge that does all the damage.

"These detonators are usually blasting caps. What my radio-controlled trigger device does is deliver an electrical circuit burst to ignite the blasting cap that begins the detonation sequence. All the bombmaker needs to do is rig his high explosive charge with my detonator by connecting just two wires from my triggering device that consists of one modified walkie-talkie. A second walkie-talkie serves as the transmitting unit. The operator stands at a safe distance needing only to press a switch to first arm the detonation circuit then activate a second switch to trigger the explosion."

"From what distance?" Liam asked clearly impressed by his grandson's idea.

"Manufacture's specs say one to two miles in urban areas, maybe twice as far in open terrain. My design uses a UHF signal providing a greater range of frequencies than VHF. Also works better in urban areas where the signal may encounter more obstacles. I would suggest keeping the operating range to less than half a mile regardless the environment."

"I'll be gobsmacked!" Liam exclaimed realizing the tactical implications. "How're goin' to demonstrate this? You'll not be igniting one of these exploding blasting caps will you, my boy?"

"Nothing like that, Granda. Never even seen a blasting cap except in a book. Created my design from researching specifications in the university's technical library. High explosives are commonly used in construction and mining so there's a lot of information readily available about how to cause them to explode."

Liam nodded. "Well, let's have lunch and another pint. Then we'll take a walk and find a good spot for you to show me your creation."

After lunch, Liam said, "What kind of place are we looking for to perform your demonstration?"

"Just an open area. Doesn't even have to be secluded but better there are no people about that might become curious. There's just two units that look to be nothing more than walkie-talkies."

"Without exploding a blasting cap, how can you demonstrate?"

"I could just use an electrical multimeter which I used to validate my design. Then the idea struck me that a photography flashbulb functions essentially the same as a blasting cap. The flashbulb works by releasing an electrical charge that burns a magnesium filament inside a bulb filled with oxygen that ignites instantly with a bright flash. In a blasting cap the electrical current does the same thing that ignites a small quantity of explosive material that will then ignite the main high explosive charge of the bomb."

Liam said, "Let's take a walk towards the river and find a suitable spot." After a few blocks a sign pointed to Anderson Park just a short distance further.

"This should be perfect, Granda." Terence led them to a stand of trees. Reaching into the duffle bag, he extracted the two units. Handing the transmitter unit to his grandfather, "This is the transmitter. Nothing more than the transmission circuitry of a two-way radio with the antenna. Powered by a dry cell battery. Note the two switches on the side with plastic flip-up covers. I added these. The green one is the arming circuit, and the red one is the firing circuit. Don't touch anything yet."

Holding the receiver unit in his hand, he said, "This is the receiver unit that will be attached to the bomb. These protruding wires with alligator clips that are now gripping the flashbulb holder terminals will attach to the blasting cap wires or multiple blasting caps connected together. This walkie-talkie unit is where I made most of my modifications. Without going into too much technical detail, I added a battery pack to power the ignition circuit requiring relays to close when triggered by the radio signal. A capacitor then increases the voltage while storing energy from the batteries. That arms the bomb. A second signal discharges the capacitor stored charge igniting the blasting caps.

"Nothing need be done to the receiver unit other than extending the antenna and attaching the wires to the blasting caps. Now back to your control transmitter. After placing the bomb and preparing to trigger an explosion you first arm the bomb using the green switch. When the small green light glows then the bomb is armed. That means the capacitor is charged and ready to fire."

Terence extended the antennas several inches on both walkie-talkie units. "Now switch the green switch to on."

Liam holding the transmitting unit activated the switch and the indicator light came on. "Green light came on."

"Now you can't disarm the detonator other than by disconnecting it from the blasting caps. Now I'll step away a few yards so you can see the flash. Go ahead and detonate the bomb by flipping the red switch when you're ready, Granda."

The flashbulb ignited.

Liam said, "I'll be damned."

Terence said, "Let's try it again with a new flashbulb but from a much further distance. So, we'll first reset both switches on the transmitter back to the off position and connect a new flashbulb. This time I will operate the transmitter. You take the receiving unit that acts as the trigger. Walk a hundred yards away from me. I'll wave when I arm the receiver. Step back, then wave giving me a couple of seconds to ignite the flashbulb."

Even from this distance Terence saw the flash. Liam walked back to Terence at a lively pace clearly excited. "Holy shit! This thing really works. You say it can work from a much further distance?"

"That's right, Granda. The distance is determined by the strength of the radio signal transmission."

"I see how this can be of great use. You made this from commercially available items?"

"Yup. Started out as two-way radios we sell and repair at the electronics store I work at. This is a Motorola product. Made in America. The parts I added are just common items I use in my daily repair work."

"You could make more of these.... what do you call them?"

"Radio-controlled command detonators."

Liam said, "Let's sit over there on that bench and have a talk." Once seated, Liam resumed. "You sure you want to become this involved, Terry?"

"If I'm to stay on in Northern Ireland, can't stand by just observing. Is this any different than what you faced fifty years ago when you were my age, Granda?"

"No. Suppose not. No matter how well you hide what you're doing, there's always the possibility of unknown dangers with becoming involved."

"I understand there is risk no matter my precautions. But I can accept that if you are the only one that knows what I'm doing. The only way I produce these triggers is if you can obtain two-way radios. Too suspicious if purchased in quantity from here in Northern Ireland. Best they come directly from America. From what you've told me, you have ways of secretly getting things into Northern Ireland. Maybe even something my Da can help by locating them."

Liam instantly said, "Terry, even if Eoin gets involved, he must never know that is what these are radios are being used for or that you are involved in any way. Nor is your mother to know."

"Of course, Granda. These radios are not even contraband. Even if discovered, they would appear as nothing more than what they are, communication equipment. The police and military use such radios, why not the IRA? If it is just you providing me the radios without anyone else knowing, then we should both feel more secure."

Liam Kelly absorbed his grandson's comments. "That's possible I guess. I bring you radios I get through my network of contacts. After you convert them into bomb triggers, you return them to me. We simply exchange bags here in Coleraine."

Terence said, "On my end, I will perform my work using latex gloves. You are not to handle the radios without gloves either, Granda. Neither of us must leave any fingerprints. They might be extracted from recovered bomb fragments."

Liam nodded. "Very well, Terry. Let me see about getting some of these two-way radios."

"Just one thing, Granda. When you deliver me the two-way radios, I need a dozen or so blasting caps. Demonstrating with flashbulbs and taking electrical measurements proves the design. But in engineering, nothing replaces proofing by actual test. I don't need explosives like gelignite or dynamite, that's for the bombmaker. My detonators are to explode blasting caps. I'd feel better making at least a couple of live tests. Been thinking about where I might do that."

"Holy Jesus!, How you goin' to do that without attracting attention? I've seen blasting caps explode. They make a bloody awful noise. Where can you conduct such a test?"

"I took a short train ride out of Belfast up the coast. The train stops between Whitehead and Larne. Lot of open area without many houses. Remember, I can set my receiver with the blasting cap far away from me. Nobody will even notice."

"Very well, you're the engineer. I'll include the blasting caps when I deliver you a quantity of walkie-talkies. Remember, blasting caps are contraband so hide them well. Never let your guard down, Terry."

"I'll be careful, Granda."

On a lighter subject, Liam asked, "how goes your studies at the university?"

"Fine. Challenging I'd say. But I'm learning new stuff."

Back at the train station, Liam embraced Terence at the platform as his grandson boarded his train to return to Belfast. Terence turned as he mounted the train carriage steps, "Merry Christmas to you and Grandma, Granda. Stay safe. I love you."

CHAPTER 8

Belfast, Northern Ireland | January 1972

Liam Kelly telephoned his son Eoin in Boston. Led by his father, Eoin Kelly became a key figure in smuggling money and arms from the United States to the newly organized Provisional IRA. Liam's activities transcended procurement for the IRA. He was a close friend of Martin McGuinness, second in command of the Derry Brigade at the time. Through McGuinness, Liam Kelly became an important figure to the IRA Army Council with his smuggling connections in America.

It was Liam Kelly who previously teamed through his son Eoin with Irish-born George Harrison located in New York City to run guns to the IRA in the 1950's for the IRA. With formation of the Provisional IRA in 1969, Kelly became instrumental in resurrecting Harrison's network after discontinuing gun running to the IRA following the failed *Border Campaign* in 1962.

Eoin said, "Good to hear from you, Father. Are things well with you and Mother?"

"Staying safe if that's what you mean. What's goin' on is bad for the pub business though. Terry sends his love."

"Got a letter and Christmas card from him. Came as a surprise to Francis and me his enrolling at Queen's University in Belfast. He never let on to us that he was planning to stay in Northern Ireland indefinitely."

Liam replied "Well, you know how it is when you're his age. But he's doing fine. Busy with his studies while working a fair number of hours at an electronics store. I'm calling about something I need you to purchase and ship over, Eoin. Nothing illegal but better that it still goes by an indirect route. Got something at hand where you can write this down?"

"Sure. Give me a minute."

After Eoin returned to the phone, Liam said, "I need a quantity of two-way radios. Walkie- talkies like the military and police use. Preferably Motorola model HT-220 with standard antennas. If not available, General Electric model 3-5961C will do. Would like twenty pairs to start with. Buy these through different retail sources if possible to obscure the sourcing. Arrange shipment by airfreight addressed to Grafton Electronics to the attention of Jack Quinn at No. 21 Grafton Street, Dublin 2, Republic of Ireland."

"I'll get right on it, Da. Use the regular account to pay for these?"

"Right. Wire me when they're scheduled to ship. Telephone me if you have any problem locating that many pairs. Would like to get them over here within a couple of weeks if possible."

Eoin with his connections in Boston and New York made good on his father's request. Paid from a bank account funded by the IRA with Eoin Kelly using a fake identity. He assumed the walkie-talkies were meant for IRA communications use. Reason enough for keeping them secret from the security forces in Northern Ireland.

From Dublin, Liam had people that would drive the radios across the border. Liam had already established the means of getting them to Terence who would then return them after transformation into radio-command bomb triggers. That preserved the secrecy of Terence as the source. That left only getting the modified radio detonators into the right hands within the IRA.

When Liam Kelly decided to support the newly created Provisional IRA in 1969, he gave considerable thought to his own security. Too old to risk being caught up in a roundup of known IRA members. With his reputation he became an obvious suspect. Not likely as an active member directly engaged in violent acts, but possibly by helping to obtain and smuggle in contraband weaponry. Something where he could limit the number of IRA that would have knowledge of his activities.

Infiltration by loyalist spies working for the government had been an IRA problem since his active days in 1919. He knew of several uncovered *touts* that received a bullet to the head. He would use only his principal IRA contact used for coordinating illicit shipments of arms and explosives. Whereas otherwise using intermediaries as plausibly deniable cutouts, these radio detonators produced by his grandson must be handled directly. Security dictated no involvement with intermediaries.

Brian Keenan was Liam Kelly's principal contact. A dedicated clever young man of about thirty that had already risen to become quartermaster of the IRA Belfast Brigade. It was foremost to get these radio detonating devices into the Belfast IRA, by far the largest and most active IRA organization operating in Northern Ireland.

Liam came to appreciate Keenan's fanatical devotion to the Irish cause of rebellion. Keenan also displayed a range of exceptional skills. He not only dealt with Kelly for the all-important connection with the United States but traveled throughout Europe and even the Middle East looking for sources of weapons. Keenan even possessed some basic knowledge of electrical equipment from his past employment. More importantly, Kelly knew that Keenan was closely associated with IRA bomb making activities and operational strategy.

Most of all, Liam Kelly trusted Brian Keenan. Receiving the detonators from his grandson, he would personally deliver them directly to Keenan. The only other person to know of Liam's involvement was Seamus Twomey, OC of the Belfast Brigade and Keenan's superior. Not even Liam's close Derry IRA friend Martin McGuinness was to know about these bomb detonators. Even Keenan and Twomey were led to believe these were produced in the United States. Everything geared to protecting the secrecy of Terence's involvement.

Liam Kelly received twenty pairs of walkie-talkies from America in the third week of January 1972. He delivered ten pairs of walkie-talkies to Terence along with ten blasting caps after making the exchange at the Coleraine train station. A brief interlude this time over a pint of stout at the *Railway Arms* before Terence boarded his return train to Belfast. Liam Kelly watched him board wondering about the wisdom of allowing his grandson to join this new Irish war.

On Sunday 30 January 1972, both Liam and Terence came to realize that something seismic was happening in Derry as radio and television reports dominated the air waves in the late afternoon. Terence was working at his workbench at Comet Electronics when a television in the showroom could be heard loudly announcing that the broadcasting station was breaking into regular programming with a special news alert. *Forces of the British Army Parachute Regiment have clashed with thousands of civil rights marchers in Derry. A seeming repeat of what happened in 1969 when the Royal Ulster Constabulary attempted a raid in the Bogside district of Londonderry. An anti-internment protest march had been scheduled for today however it is unclear why elite British Army paratroops were called in to provide security backup to the RUC. Regrettably, sporadic gunfire has been reported in this latest incident, but no information is currently available regarding casualties. We will continue uninterrupted broadcast coverage until the violence subsides.* Although there was no live coverage of what was happening in Derry the news anchor continued describing the scene accompanied by audio conversation with a local reporter on the scene in Derry. All the Comet employees and a few customers stood listening in rapt silence.

From a telephone at Comet, Terence called his grandparents' apartment over the pub. His grandmother answered. "Grandma! Are you and Granda alright?"

"We're both fine. We closed the pub when learning of the civil rights march that was to start today in Creggan Heights and ending at the Guildhall close to the river at the northern end of the Derry walls. Yesterday, the police and British soldiers began placing barriers on all streets leading into the march route. Wait just a minute, Terry. Your Granda just walked in."

Liam came on the line, "You've been following what's happening in Derry I trust? Can't begin to tell you how bad this is. The worst of the violence looks to be over though."

"How many injured?"

"Don't know. I was watching with binoculars from well back behind a police barricade on Little James Street where it intersects with Great James Street. People were shot, Terry. Live rounds, not rubber bullets. Must be many deaths among the victims. Knew there was probably goin' to be trouble but nothing as bad as this. Got information early on that locally garrisoned troops of the British 8th Brigade would back up the RUC. Among the 8th Brigade is the feared 1st Battalion of the Parachute Regiment. The 1st Battalion are special forces. A nasty bunch of buggers.

"Weren't those the same soldiers that killed ten suspected IRA here in the Ballymurphy neighborhood of Belfast last summer?"

"The same. Part of *Operation Demetrius* to round up IRA for internment. Just a week ago they became involved in another violent confrontation against protestors outside Magilligan internment center in County Londonderry. The soldiers of *One Para* are a hard-edged bunch of killers meant only for the battlefield. Not the kind of troops you'd put into a sensitive policing situation involving unarmed civilians."

"Unless those in charge wanted this violence to happen," Terence commented.

"Could be that. This had all the beginnings of what happened in '69 when the RUC tried to seal off the Catholic Bogside streets to protect a Protestant loyalist march. Bad as that was, no one at least died. The march today started out around three o'clock. I took up my position beyond a barricade at the end of Little James Street to monitor what happened.

"As this large crowd of marchers came up William Street the situation began turning ugly. Hundreds of marchers spilled into Rossville Street. Bottles and rocks started to be thrown at the police and soldiers behind the barbed wire barricades. The security forces responded first with water cannons. Then firing could be heard. I incorrectly assumed that these were rubber bullets. Then all of Rossville Street became obscured by clouds of tear gas."

"But you think people have been killed?" Terence said.

"Seems likely. Around four o'clock a great many British soldiers located behind the barrier sealing off Little James Street at Sackville Street pushed aside the barrier and began moving down Rossville Street. I could see by their shoulder patches these were parachute troops. Pushing ahead of them where diehard remnants of the marchers trying escape. I'm watching with the binoculars but now there is a pitched battle raging about a quarter mile down Rossville Street from where I was observing. I can hear more weapons firing.

"That was about an hour ago. From my vantage point I saw four or five bodies lying on the street. No one was helping them. British soldiers just stood around with weapons at the ready ignoring the wounded. Maybe knowing the victims were dead.

"I'd seen enough by then. Assumed the military would soon begin making wider sweeps to root out any remaining threats. They came expecting trouble but there was no provocation for this. No one fired on the army or the RUC. I have firsthand knowledge that the Derry IRA was ordered to stand down. Those murderous pigs of *One Para* countered bottles and rocks being thrown at them with live fire!"

Whereas the *Battle of the Bogside* in 1969 looked as if it was the beginning of what would become called the *Troubles,* the events of this winter day in January would carry far more dire implications. Another *Bloody Sunday.* For Terence Kelly growing up listening to his grandfather's stories, he immediately related to his grandfather's account of *Bloody Sunday of 1920* in Dublin. In a reprisal attack for IRA assassinations of British agents, British Royal Irish Constabulary Auxiliaries comprised of former British Army officers, killed 30 civilians and injured another 80 at a Gaelic football match at Croke Park in Dublin. Liam Kelly felt exceptional anguish over the carnage. He was among those ordered by Michael Collins to assassinate British undercover intelligence operatives that resulted in the reprisal attack at Croke Park.

Terence recalled watching television coverage of *Bloody Sunday of 1965* in Selma, Alabama where police inflicted beatings on non-violent African American civil rights protestors. All these *Bloody Sunda*ys had in common incidents of governmental forces killing and brutalizing unarmed civilians.

On this Sunday in late January in Derry, Northern Ireland, British soldiers shot and killed 13 unarmed civilians that day and injured another 14. All the victims were Catholic. A fourteenth person died later of wounds. One victim was shot in the back of the head while waving a white handkerchief. By any definition, an execution. A state declaring war on an oppressed segment of its own citizenry.

The following day, as the reconstruction of events demonstrated, this felt like an inflection point for every Catholic in Northern Ireland. The Republic of Ireland recalled its ambassador from London in protest. For expatriate Irish around the world, this truly now became yet another war of Irish freedom. A war beyond the corrupt racist apartheid-like provincial government of Northen Ireland made the British government the foremost enemy of Irish Catholics worldwide. What existed for the Irish for hundreds of years had not changed.

Even for Protestant loyalists they could now expect proportional retaliation. This was a war where civilians regularly became casualties. First internment without due process of trial, now outright massacre. Especially for Northern Ireland Catholics, this looked like a real war. Shootings, bombings, destruction of property. Essentially martial law enforced by a biased oppressive government fully supported by London. The British and their puppet statelet of Northern Ireland demonstrated there was never to be any hope for collective Catholic civil rights. London would exercise its intent to dominate by force of brutality.

The immediate aftermath of *Bloody Sunday,* reverberated around the world. In Dublin in the Republic of Ireland, a very large crowd protested at the British Embassy located at Merrion Square. Attacked with stones, bottles, and petrol burns the elegant building was burned to the ground three days after *Bloody Sunday.*

Irish Americans experienced widespread condemnation and outrage. With its large Irish ethnic population from 125 years of continual Irish immigration to the United States, support for the beleaguered Irish Catholics in Northern Ireland took on tangible material and financial support. That took the form of both nonviolent assistance as well as covert smuggling of arms and money to the IRA. As for the Provisional IRA of Northern Ireland, they became overwhelmed with new volunteers.

Terence wondered if he was witnessing a repeat of the war of 1919. At least it felt like the beginning of a wider armed struggle. Already more violent than in recent memory such feelings became well-founded. The year 1972 would go on to become the bloodiest year of the decades of the Northern Ireland *Troubles.* Kelly felt ideally positioned to play an active part. Bombs would undoubtedly become the principal IRA weapon. His radio-command bomb triggers would provide greater tactical advantage.

Within a week, he produced two sets of triggers. After making slight modifications to improve the component mountings within the receiver unit, he wanted to confirm everything with live tests. Although he had blasting caps, the thought intrigued him that perhaps he could conduct a full-blown test if he could construct an actual mini bomb. Louder noise, but he intended to perform his tests in a remote area.

Making a miniature bomb using high explosives was not completely necessary, but an actual test would provide absolute validation of his design. However, the challenge was obtaining an experimental quantity of high explosives. He had no access to gelignite, dynamite, much less military grade plastique explosives like Semtex. That left only ANFO. Ammonium nitrate mixed with fuel oil.

ANFO is the acronym for a common bulk high explosive commonly used in mining and construction. It consisted of the commercially available fertilizer ammonium-nitrate in a 94% mixture with 6% fuel oil. The ammonium-nitrate acts as an oxidizer to the fuel oil acting as the fuel. Highly stable, ANFO required a high explosive booster explosive to achieve detonation. Something with greater energy than a blasting cap. The improvised explosive devices assembled by the IRA favored using primer cord or gelignite requiring detonation by blasting caps. The detonation sequence therefore became the small high intensity blasting cap igniting the larger energy produced by primer cord or gelignite necessary for detonating the larger bulk of the ANFO main secondary explosive. The IRA extensively used ANFO for car bombs where large quantities of the explosive could easily be concealed.

ANFO also provided the ability to easily make a suitable small quantity. According to the literature, even farmers used it to remove tree stumps and large boulders. Ammonium nitrate should be readily available given its principal use as fertilizer. However, research indicated ANFO required a greater ignition source than provided by a blasting cap alone. This meant a comparatively significant amount of energy from a precursor detonation of a primary high explosive became necessary to cause ANFO to explode. Detonation therefore required a firing sequence called an explosive train. This began with detonating the blasting cap by delivering an electrical discharge that would detonate a booster charge of a yet more powerful explosive charge sufficient to then detonate the main secondary high explosive of ANFO. Another challenge to resolve if he intended to prove his detonator system with a full live test of a miniature bomb.

At a garden supply outlet, he purchased a ten-pound bag of ammonium nitrate prills, small porous spheres. Prilled ammonium nitrate facilitated absorption of water for use as a fertilizer, or absorption of fuel oil to increase reactivity as an oxidizer when used as a high explosive. Fuel oil used for heating is essentially the same petroleum product as diesel oil available at any filling station.

His grandfather had provided the essential blasting caps but obtaining material to act as the booster charge presented the problem. For non-military uses, booster charges often included a stick of dynamite or gelignite according to published information. The active ingredient in both was nitroglycerin mixed with inert stabilizers making it safer to handle. However, Terence had no way to obtain dynamite nor gelignite. He did not want to go that far by asking his grandfather who would surely have refused.

Nitroglycerin can be produced by acid-catalyzed nitration of glycerol using sulfuric and nitric acid in a simple although exceptionally dangerous process. The synthesis procedure releases a great amount of heat and must be monitored closely to avoid becoming a runaway reaction. The synthesized nitroglycerin in pure form remains extremely unstable. In reference material in the Queen's University library, Kelly found the process for creating nitroglycerin could be accomplished in any kitchen. The process did not require much time nor any special equipment or any expertise in chemistry. The key requirement seemed to be only scrupulously maintaining the temperature throughout the *cooking* of the mixture to prevent premature detonation or releasing toxic gas. Plenty of fearlessness required for a first-time amateur.

Obtaining the basic ingredients for making nitroglycerin proved remarkably easy. A fellow chemistry student at the university provided pint bottles of the necessary ingredients. Terence used the vague excuse that he wanted to use them to experiment cleaning some antique metal items for his landlord. All Terence needed was plenty of nerve making his first attempt at making enough nitroglycerin to fill several small vials. Thereafter, avoid dropping them or exposing them to elevated temperatures until used for his first live tests of his radio detonators.

Striking a couple of drops of nitroglycerin with a hammer on a hard surface was enough to cause a very small explosion according to technical reference. He chose not to go that far with experimentation.

Kelly's miniature bomb design consisted of a 3-inch diameter by 12-inch PVC drainpipe filled with 94% ammonium nitrate and 6% diesel fuel substituting for number 2 fuel oil. The mixture thoroughly mixed then tightly compressed inside the PVC pipe around an imbedded blasting cap that itself was imbedded within a sealed glass vial containing approximately an ounce of nitroglycerin. With the blasting cap wires protruded through a sealed hole in the PVC cap at one end, he had what he thought was a workable high explosive device filled with three pounds of ANFO.

With his radio transmitter, receiver trigger, and miniature bomb in a backpack, Terence took a mid-morning train from Belfast Grand Central station to the small town of Magheramorne on the western side of Larne Lough. The one-hour trip snaked up the coast of the Irish Sea before turning inward toward Magheramorne. The library guidebook was correct about the area being remote with only a few scattered houses.

Walking a quarter of a mile from the small train station to a deserted stretch of land on Larne Lough, he found the ideal spot. No trees but a slight hill allowed him to remain completely unseen from any structure, road, or the railroad tracks. No one should hear even a loud sound from this location.

Getting quickly to the task at hand, he attached the blasting cap wires to the radio receiver unit. He nestled the receiver into the sand then covered it with a towel adding more sand. A precaution to avoid damaging the trigger unit that could be reused. Stepping back thirty yards, he armed the device then fired.

The towel kicked up as the blasting cap exploded with a much louder noise than expected. Proved the design worked as expected. Now for a test of an actual ANFO bomb.

Having prepared the miniature bomb in advance, even the gentle jostling of the train produced anxiety with concerns about the hypersensitivity to shock of the concentrated nitroglycerin imbedded into the ANFO. Hollowing out a depression in the sand with his hands, he carefully placed the bomb then covered it with handfuls of sand.

After again covering the radio receiver with the towel and adding sand for protection of the unit, he now retreated to a much further distance. Looking around to ensure no unexpected visitors, he rearmed the device confirming by the green indicator light. Flipping the firing switch this time produced a tremendous noise throwing sand into the air. Excitement over having successfully tested an actual bomb, he ran to examine the effect. Only a small crater existed.

He recovered the undamaged receiver that could again be used and put it into his backpack. To think of the damage caused by a much greater quantity of ANFO, dynamite, or gelignite placed in the right place was a frightening thought. An indiscriminate horrific weapon when the target became people. That was an uncomfortable thought. Making these detonators crossed him over the line from ideological supporter to active combatant. Once he made them available to the IRA he would have blood on his hands.

CHAPTER 9

Belfast, Northern Ireland | February 1972

Terence completed all ten pairs of radio command triggering devices a week after successfully performing live tests. Once again when he disembarked the train at Coleraine his grandfather was waiting. Both of them carried duffle bags.

Embracing his grandfather after they both put down their duffle bags, Terence said, "What should we do with these?"

"We'll lock them in the station lockers until we both leave."

After locking the bags away, they exchanged locker keys.

Terence said, "Have things settled down in Derry these last few weeks?"

"On the surface, but the wounds of that Sunday will not heal anytime soon. Maybe never. Christ, British soldiers just murdered unarmed civilians!"

"What about those you know in the IRA, Granda. What do they say?"

"My closest local contact in the IRA Derry Brigade is Martin McGuinness. Exceptional young fellow about your age. Second in command of the Derry Brigade. He was out and about that day. Confirmed to me that no one in the Provisional IRA participated that day. No IRA fired on the British troops."

Liam and Terence made the short walk to the *Railway Arms* and found a table. Liam brought back two pints of stout from the bar and sat down. "McGuinness is well connected beyond Derry.

Has a good friend involved in the civil rights movement and Sinn Féin. Another young man named Gerry Adams. Comes from Belfast from a family with a republican background. I knew Adams grandfather of the same name. A fellow member of the Irish Republican Brotherhood back in 1919. Gerry is now on the run since the introduction of internment last year. That's how it is. British security forces can detainee anybody they chose and put 'em away for as long as they want.

"Anyway, McGuinness is well connected. The next day he said he spoke with Adams who has connections with those on the IRA Army Council. New recruits are flocking to join the Provisional IRA. No question that military action will ramp up. British troops will advance to the head of the line as prime targets. Yet, McGuinness says there are indications that what happened in Derry has given London pause before expanding military resources further."

"What's that mean?"

"Don't know. Neither does McGuinness. But it does show just how much stature he has in the IRA."

"Does he know about your arms smuggling?"

"Not directly from me telling him, but likely from his connections with the Belfast Brigade. Yet even then, only the Belfast OC and quartermaster know details of my active involvement. Same goes for those things you brought in your bag. I will personally deliver those to my only direct contact, the Belfast quartermaster. Belfast will believe they came from America. We both shall keep it that way, Terry."

"I understand, Granda." Terence took a sip of his beer. "Tell'm these can improve the use of bombs. Allow them to target police and military rather than targets that harm civilians. Doesn't the IRA leadership realize how counterproductive killing civilians hurts the cause?"

"I agree, Terry. Can't defend these ill-advised bombings. I'm not in a leadership position but have the sense that many of these actions are planned at lower organizational levels."

"You mean ordinary IRA are running amuck? Not much of an army if that's how they operate. Was that the way it was back fifty years ago, Granda."

Liam sighed. "Not at all. Discipline prevailed, especially among the active service units that engaged in military actions."

"Was being part of Michael Collins' *Squad* in Dublin considered an active service unit?"

Liam said, "I suppose so. Everything we did was directed by orders. We didn't act on independent initiative."

Terence nodded. Not the time or place to get into criticism of IRA strategy and tactics with his grandfather. "I performed live tests using my radio command detonators, Granda. They will work as expected. I even made a miniature bomb. Exploded it on a barren stretch of land up the coast just south of Larne."

Stunned by his grandson's pronouncement, Liam said. "Jesus, Terry! Why'd you take the risk?"

"Needed to make completely sure they function as intended. Bad enough to make something to kill the enemy, don't want it to fail some young IRA fighter risking his neck."

"What kind of explosive did you use?"

"ANFO. Ammonium nitrate and diesel fuel substituting for fuel oil. Stuffed into a PVC pipe with a blasting cap detonator and a booster of nitroglycerin. The information about mixing the right proportions and blast effects I found in reference materials in the university library. Afterall, this is just fertilizer and fuel oil. Used for all sorts of blasting applications for decades."

"What about the nitroglycerin. Where did that come from?"

"Made it in my kitchen."

"Good God, are you serious? Could have blown yourself up. Nitroglycerin is what's in dynamite and gelignite but made safer by adding fillers."

"It's delicate work alright. Simple enough process but you have to mind what you're doing. Anyway, won't be making any more nitro. Just needed it to act as the booster to set off the ANFO."

After eating lunch and another pint of stout, they exchanged duffle bags and made their way to Terence's platform. Liam embraced him saying, "You be careful. Stay away from any further bomb making. Ten more pairs of two-way radios are in there. Stick to modifying those. Spend your time on studies and living some sort of normal life."

"Will you know when any of my detonators are used?"

"Probably. I'll at least find out what Belfast thinks of them."

A few days after taking possession of Terence's radio triggers. Liam Kelly drove his old Ford Cortina to a small farm well outside Derry. This was one of many IRA safe locations in County Londonderry. A barn sat a short distance from a small stone house. Following instructions, he opened the two barn doors and drove inside. After closing the doors behind him, a light came on illuminating the barn interior.

"Good seeing you Liam," a young man with a beard dressed in a work coat and flat cap said as he approached Kelly. Peering out a side door was another man holding an Armalite semiautomatic assault rifle, a favorite IRA weapon made in the United States.

"Brian, my lad. Good of you to make time to meet me." Brian Keenan was quartermaster of the IRA Belfast Brigade. By far the largest IRA brigade, Keenan was the most important source for obtaining weapons and explosives for the entire IRA operating throughout Northern Ireland.

"Not a problem, Liam. What is this you're so anxious to show me?"

"What's called a radio-command bomb detonator. I'm not an expert on such things so I'll relate what I've been told by my sources in America. Even had them type out operational instructions. You'll be a better judge of their worth than I am, Brian."

Kelly knew Keenan's background involved working for a time as a television repairman with his brother in Northamptonshire, England. Returning to Belfast, Keenan then worked at an appliance and consumer electronics store. Undoubtedly he possessed a working familiarity with electronics. More importantly, Kelly knew Keenan understood explosives and was intimately involved with planning IRA bombings.

Liam opened the boot of his car. From a box, he extracted a transmitter unit handing it to Keenan, "This is the transmitter control. Modified from a standard commercial walkie-talkie. Note the two covered switches replacing the transmit-receive buttons on the side. Green is to remotely arm the bomb. Red is to detonate explosion. All done by radio signals."

Keenan was immediately intrigued. "Range?"

"I'm told conservatively that it's best to keep to no more than half a mile. The manufacture says the signal range is one to two miles for urban environments, but specific signal obstructions can make a difference."

Liam then removed the companion receiver unit. "This is the receiver-triggering unit. Substantially modified to add a firing circuit to detonate the blasting cap. The protruding wires are to be connected to the blasting cap, or as many as five blasting caps connected in series. I'm not sure what that means exactly."

Keenan said, "Has this been given an actual test?"

"My sources say it's been proven but didn't provide details. Paid a handsome price for these. They're expecting further orders if that's any assurance. I didn't test them myself. Don't know anything about explosives. Even blasting caps are dangerous. Didn't fancy losing my fingers by making a mistake. Here's what they furnished in the way of operational instructions."

Handing Keenan an envelope from his pocket, Liam said, "Best you make your own test, Brian. I brought along a few blasting caps if you want to test. I'm told that you can repeat test firing with blasting caps without damage to the receiver if connected from a couple of feet away. Obviously the receiver goes up in the blast along with the high explosives since it becomes part of a real bomb."

"Sounds interesting. Let's do that test, Liam. Nobody within a mile from here. Blasting caps are not that loud." Looking at the typewritten instructions, he said, "Says here it's only necessary to connect the two leads to the blasting cap, or a string of series connected blasting caps. For safety, discharge the internal capacitor before making any connection to the blasting cap. Holy shit, I'd say so!"

"What's this capacitor do?" Liam said feigning ignorance of the explanation given by his grandson.

Keenan said, "Since the firing circuit is obviously dry cell batteries, the capacitor boosts the voltage while also storing energy. When attached to a load, in this case the blasting caps, the energy is released in a burst of energy. Enough to detonate the blasting cap. The bomb blasting caps are imbedded in a booster charge of a primary high explosive material necessary to detonate the main secondary high explosive that does all the damage. If the capacitor is holding enough of a charge, you might lose more than your fingers."

Keenan took the exposed wires from the receiver trigger and grounded the circuit on an electrical panel inside the barn. He twisted the leads from two blasting caps together in series then connected them to the two receiver leads. Keenan turned toward the man with the assault rifle, "Jimmie, need you over here."

Jimmie Flanagan came over pointing the assault rifle upward with the stock on his hip.

"Take this out back. Walk about a hundred yards across the field then put it on this box so we can see it from here. I'll hold your weapon."

The man looked at the receiver recognizing the blasting caps hanging from the wires with some uneasiness. Keenan said, "No danger, Jimmie. We're not going to touch the transmitter until you walk back here. Even then, there's a built-in safety feature requiring a two-step firing command. The first step just arms the bomb. "Now go ahead. Let's see if thing works."

"Are the benefits of this radio controller that important, Brian?"

"Damn right they are. If it does what it claims to do. Allows triggering the bomb at the precise time of the bomber's choosing. No reliance on fucking timers requiring setting the time delay when placing the bomb. No more accidental detonations. With the range, the bomber can remain concealed or even work with a spotter closer by. The advantage allows the bomber to place the bomb at the best opportunity then explode it at the right time while staying far enough away to disappear after the explosion."

When Jimmie returned, all three men stepped to the back of the barn. Keenan extended the transmitter antenna then said, "Here we go." flipping the green switch, the small indicator light illuminated. "Ready?" He uncovered the red switch and fired. They heard a distant sound, and the cardboard box jumped up from the blasting caps exploding."

"Well, I'll be fucked! Jimmie, retrieve that device. We'll rig it for another test."

At over two hundred yards a second test was repeated successfully.

"Sonofabitch, Liam. You outdid yourself with this. Even after fifty years you're a right dangerous bugger," Brian Keenan affectionately slapping Liam on the back.

Liam smiled weakly. Not sure that he wasn't losing his edge. This fellow Jimmie now knew of him. Should have made sure to stipulate to Keenan about meeting alone. A mistake he should not have made. That's how you died or ended up in prison. Then again he must expect Keenan was important enough to always move about with a bodyguard. However, Liam still admonished himself. Be more careful you old bugger.

Like every Catholic in Northern Ireland, Terence felt the murder of unarmed civilians by the British Army represented a fundamental change in the resurgence of violence. This was state-sponsored oppression at the barrel of a gun. No different than the Soviet Union putting down protests in the Eastern Bloc countries of Hungary in 1956 and Czechoslovakia in 1968. The enemy was Britain and their puppet regional government in Northern Ireland. The inherent antagonisms between ethnic Catholics and Protestants literally made everyone a friend or foe according to that label. Every act of violence justified within that context. Terence succumbed to that same blind anger.

On 4 March at 4:30 in the afternoon, a bomb exploded inside the Abercorn Restaurant on Castle Lane in central Belfast. A senseless stupid act. At 4:28 a call to the emergency services number warned of a bomb set to explode in five minutes but gave no specific location. A bomb exploded underneath a table. Two young women seated close to the bomb died instantly. Another 130 were injured. Many suffered horrific wounds. Limbs blown off. Others maimed with terrible head and facial injuries. Three were blinded by shards of flying glass. Two sisters, one due to be married were mutilated. One lost both legs, the bride-to-be lost not only both her legs but also an eye and her right arm.

No organization either nationalist or loyalist claimed responsibility. A witness that had been inside the restaurant before the bomb exploded identified two teenage girls leaving behind a handbag under their table. Bomb experts determined gelignite as the high explosive used. The extent of the damage suggested just five pounds did enough damage to even bring down the ceiling into the ground-floor restaurant area. Regardless of political leanings, the scope of the carnage provoked revulsion among the citizenry of Belfast.

The RUC and British military intelligence cast the blame on the Provisional IRA, even speculating that it was the work of the 1st Battalion of the IRA Belfast Brigade. A possible motive sighted was that an upstairs bar was often frequented by off duty British Army personnel. Terence Kelly hoped that was not true but could not feel certain. Seemed unconscionable for the IRA to sacrifice so many civilians to go after British soldiers.

Both sides in this war seemed willing to go after soft targets as bombing targets. That meant civilian casualties. A troubling tactic with seemingly counterproductive strategic implications according to Terence's logic. Nonetheless, he had just completed converting the next ten pairs of walkie-talkies into radio-command bomb detonators. The Abercorn bombing occurred on Saturday. The following day he telephoned his grandfather.

They agreed to meet in Coleraine on Tuesday. "I have a package ready for you, Granda." Liam replied, "Very good. Just got a belated Christmas present for you from Boston."

On Monday 20 March, a merchant on Church Street in central Belfast received a telephone call warning of a bomb set to explode during the busy lunch hour. RUC and British Army troops began evacuating people into Lower Donegall Street. A second warning call to the newspaper offices of the *Irish News* also warned of a bombing on Church Street at noon. Then a final call came in at 11:55 am to the newspaper offices of the *News Letter* located at 55-59 Donegall Street. The caller warned the bomb would explode in 15 minutes.

Three minutes later a massive 100-pound gelignite bomb concealed in a green Ford Cortina parked in front of the *News Letter* offices exploded. The newspaper staff had no chance to evacuate. Two RUC constables examining the Ford Cortina were dismembered from being only a few feet from the bomb.

The blast wave rolled down Donegall Street now crowded by the misleading calls identifying Church Street as the location. Four men were killed outright along with the RUC officers. Another man would later die of his injuries. 148 people suffered injuries, 19 of them seriously. Included among those injured were about one hundred school children and many of the *News Letter* staff.

Hearing the news report deeply distressed Terence. This is just wholesale killing where the victims might be anyone, but usually not security forces. The scene of the carnage was only a mile from his apartment. Arriving at Donegall Street, he joined small numbers of people observing the aftermath. The *News Letter* office building was totally destroyed. The remnant of the Ford Cortina that detonated in front of the building had been removed. Shattered windows along the opposite side of the street combined with debris on the sidewalk. Terence looked at the pools of dried blood scattered everywhere with revulsion. Minutes later a street sweeping machine spraying water entered the area to begin removing blood and remnants of human tissue.

Returning home, although upset, he wanted to wall off these disturbing images to continue working on the next batch of radio triggers. He did not know but could not help wondering if this might be the first use of his radio-command detonators. The chronology of events suggested that might be a possibility. Herding the victims into a place of slaughter. The bomber possibly then waiting to the last moment before detonating from a safe distance. Perhaps anticipating the RUC checking the vehicle might be about to discover the bomb hidden in the boot.

Liam Kelly had greater reason to believe this was the first use of his grandson's triggering devices. Brian Keenan called him days later confirming that indeed one of those devices was used in the bombing. "Performed beautifully." Liam Kelly saw nothing beautiful about what happened on Donegall Street. Like Terence, he hoped the IRA would focus on using these radio command detonators to go after more important hard targets involving the security forces. They were the real enemy.

Changing the subject, Keenan said, "Just got distressing news though, Liam. My close friend Gerry Adams, an important figure in Sinn Fein and wanted fugitive was just arrested. Currently being interned on that fucking prison ship *HMS Maidstone* in Belfast Harbor.

Liam replied. "Tough times. You keep your head down, Brian. You're the one keeping the IRA equipped to wage war.

"You do the same, Liam. You're too old a soldier to end your days in some fucking British prison."

On the 30 March 1972, the British government suspended the Northen Ireland Parliament at Stormont. Westminster now adopted responsibility for governing Northern Ireland directly from London. Liam Kelly saw this as nothing more than the equivalent of imposing martial law on a rebellious colony. The imposition of internment without trial was the first move, now taking over the regional government the next move was to attempt crushing this new rebellion. That undoubtedly meant deploying more military resources.

Two weeks later eleven bombs exploded in Belfast. Nine people were killed and a further 130 injured, some of them horrifically mutilated. Of those injured, 77 were women and children. Six of the deaths occurred as a bomb exploded at the Oxford Street bus depot.

As for Terence, he reflected more on the nature of the escalating violence. Both sides professing retaliation for a bombing perpetrated by the other side. Balancing the scale of justice as justification. To those not actively involved in the conflict, much of the violence appeared nothing more than terrorist atrocities. As Terence read accounts of torture against Catholics he steeled himself against too rigorous a self-examination of his contribution of making more effective bombs. Was he engaged in legitimate war or just terrorism?

Resolving to avoid over-intellectualizing, he began working on this latest delivery of ten new pairs of walkie-talkies. Terence would later look back on the unease he felt about the Donegall Street bombing as the beginning of his disillusionment.

CHAPTER 10

Belfast, Northern Ireland | Spring 1972

The *Bloody Sunday* killings in Derry in January caused the Provisional IRA to go on the offensive. Bombings became the principal weapon. For Terence Kelly, it regrettably appeared as nothing more than an undirected spasm of random targeting of loyalist civilians rather than security forces. The massacres of the Abercorn Restaurant and Donegall Street in March were followed in April by as many as two dozen IRA bombings across Northern Ireland. Although there were also incidents of shootouts between the IRA and the security forces, these did not result in significant casualties for either side.

A week after the series of bombings in April, Terence once again joined his grandfather in Coleraine. He exchanged another ten completed radio triggers for ten new sets delivered by his grandfather. The reason for these measured incremental shipments was to create a plausible reason should transport over the border from the republic ever be compromised. Smaller shipments more easily explained as for legitimate communications use not smuggled contraband. Even the exchange of devices between Belfast and Coleraine carried danger only if security forces were to discover modified units during a random checkpoint search. As a safeguard, both Terence and Liam placed their respective deliveries immediately in train station lockers until just before departing Coleraine.

As they sat in the *Railway Arms,* Terence said to Liam, "Why these indiscriminate bombings of civilians by the IRA?"

Liam replied with a long sigh, "I believed the IRA has been knocked back on their heels with this imposition of internment. There're over 800 Catholic men imprisoned under internment. Not all are actually IRA members but enough are that it's affected IRA military operations."

Terence said to his grandfather, "But killing civilians will never help the cause. Makes the world see the IRA as terrorists. Even Catholics in the Republic condemn the killings of civilians. Those Irish in America can't be thinking this is right no matter the violence inflicted by British security forces. You didn't kill civilians like this in the War of Independence, Granda. Everything you told me of your experiences, and everything I read, the IRA fought a guerrilla war against British military forces and the Royal Irish Constabulary, not the population."

"That is true, Terry. The situation was also clearer fifty years ago. The civilian population broadly supported the IRA. But that was only in the Catholic dominated southern counties. Ulster was always different. The situation in Northern Ireland today looks much like 1920. I was fighting the British in Dublin at that time but in the northern counties, Catholics were being murdered."

Terence said, "Yes. The *Belfast Pogroms.* Read about it but you never told me much about it."

Liam said, "Belfast saw the worst of it, but Derry wasn't sparred. During the Anglo-Irish War the northern counties experienced an earlier version of the *Troubles* now being experienced again. Irish history repeats like that. Started with the expulsion of 8,000 Catholics employed at Harlan & Wolff. Your father only found employment as a Catholic many years later because of the need for welders at the shipyard at the beginning of the Second World War when Britain had its back to the wall.

"Rioting and ethnic violence took a terrible toll in Belfast. Something like 500 people died. More Catholics than Protestants. Across Northern Ireland 20,000 were made homeless and 50,000 emigrated. Most of those were Catholics although making up less than a third of the population. Another surge of Irish migration resulted."

Terence said, "What you're saying is this isn't so much about Irish independence to join Northern Ireland with the Republic of Ireland. It's about Catholic civil rights."

"In simplest terms, perhaps yes. But the British lay at the heart of the problem. Their puppet government, a colonial government, enables oppression of Catholics. Now with Stormont dissolved, some see that as evidence of IRA success. Nonsense. Just the British forced to concede the problem rests squarely with London not Belfast. Hard to believe that Catholics can ever live as equal citizens as long as Northern Ireland remains part of the UK.

"Northern Ireland is the last colony of the British Empire. The Irish Free State, India, South Africa, Malaysia, Kenya, Rhodesia, Canada, Australia, and New Zealand all gained independence since the Second World War. Intrenched loyalist support of a majority of the Northern Ireland population makes any prospect of a united Ireland seem unattainable. Without that, equality for Catholics in the northern six counties seems unrealistic. Peace therefore becomes an elusive dream."

Terence did not wish to further debate his grandfather's dire outlook. It did nothing to diminish Terence's angst against IRA killing of civilians as unproductive no matter how one cherished the cause of unified Irish independence. For Catholics, the die was already cast with their position now expressed by the Provisional IRA. Not always in their best interests as evidenced by suffering retaliatory violence. Yet the hatred for the power structure in Northern Ireland did not dissuade him from continuing his newfound active participation. War in whatever form is always ugly in its execution regardless of either side's belief in the rightness of their cause.

As the calendar advanced to May, Terence looked forward to an easier academic schedule. Classes would conclude by month's end. A tough first year with so much demand on his time and absorbing challenging new technical material. At least he felt comfortable with approaching finals. One thing about highly technical fields of study, once you grasp a good understanding of the fundamentals testing becomes less a challenge by comparison with non-technical fields of study. Still a difficult first year made more so with the distractions of his self-made circumstances.

Since leaving Derry and his unfortunate affair with Maureen Lynch, Terence lived the life of a social recluse. Not at all his given nature. The intensity of life in Belfast simply forced that existence by demands on all his time. Getting enough sleep proved difficult enough without devoting discretionary time to relaxation. Most acquaintances at the university remained just acquaintances. Getting close to anyone held all manner of pitfalls. He did not relish playing the role of a Protestant loyalist even to the extent of having to avoid any political comments. Yet labelled as a Protestant in this extremely polarized environment limited his circle of associations. Meant he had to associate with only those identifying as such to avoid drawing unwanted attention. Even playing on his American identity did not insulate him from being expected to appreciate loyalist prospectives.

The summer break from classes afforded some easing of stress. A couple of fellow graduate students with whom he became friendly asked if he was returning to Boston for the summer. Told them that he needed to remain in Belfast and earn next year's tuition by working full-time. They replied that financial needs required them to do the same.

Upon completing final exams, Terence agreed to join them to celebrate at a pub. His relationship with them during the school year had been mostly sharing lunch and walking the campus between classes. They were studying law and political science, and Terence found their comments surprisingly objective. Protestant backgrounds but neither expressed strident loyalist positions. They seemed more focused on their futures. Terence welcomed the social diversion.

Terence gleaned from conversations that both had thoughts about leaving Northern Ireland once completing graduate degrees. Better job opportunities existed in other parts of the UK. America and Canada also of interest. Terence felt guardedly comfortable with their interactions that if political, were more about the climate of ceaseless unrest. Disparaging the uncertain economic climate of Northern Ireland, conversations usually turned to future employment opportunities, girls, or America.

They gathered at a pub frequented largely by university students close to campus. Given the neighborhood, the patrons generally younger, mostly Protestant students. Enjoying pints of Guinness while munching on chips, Duncan said to Terence, "Never thought to ask you, do you have family here in Northen Ireland.?"

"Not anymore. My maternal grandparents passed away years ago. My mother's brother emigrated to Boston before she and my father emigrated a couple of years later with me. Both my uncle and father worked at Harlan & Wolff. Work slowed down after the war. The British economy was in bad shape. Boston offered work for experienced welders in the ship making industry. Lots of Irish in Boston. South Boston where I'm from is heavily Irish."

"Why come to Northern Ireland to attend graduate school."

Terence said, "Made sense after I got my undergraduate degree. Good time to spend my summer visiting where I came from over the summer last year. QUB has a good academic reputation so that made sense. I also became concerned that having just graduated with my undergraduate degree, I might now be facing the United States military draft."

Henry asked, "The draft?"

"Conscription. The Vietnam War is still sucking up young men to go fight in that shithole. Didn't relish goin' to war that's not going well in a stinking jungle. Lots of guys my age coming back in body bags."

"Looks like you got yourself in the middle of a different kind of war. Don't you have to return to America?" Henry asked.

"Not necessarily. Certainly not by any deadline. You see I hold dual citizenship. Naturalized citizen in the United States and in the UK because I was born in Belfast. Coming to Northern Ireland seemed like a good idea all around."

Both Duncan and Henry laughed. "Good thinking mate."

That first social get-together led to regular weekend socializing among all three through the month of June and into early July. A couple of times they were joined by three girls, arranged by Henry the most gregarious of their group.

While Terence experienced brief episodes of relaxation, remaining constantly vigilant to stay in character took away much of the enjoyment. Before coming to Belfast, he was exceptionally sociable. Guarded from repeating a mistake like Maureen, he became decidedly taciturn around women. Most female students possessed little interest in engineering, and he found he had little interest in pop music or movies. Not always good company for the opposite sex. Never far from his thoughts was devoting enough time to work on converting the next group of two-way radios into bomb detonators.

Unknown to either Liam or Terence Kelly, secret talks between the British government and the Provisional IRA began in June. First contact involved a preliminary lower-level meeting between British MI6, the foreign Intelligence service, and the IRA at a private residence in the Ballyarnett district of Derry. That early effort led to the IRA declaring a temporary ceasefire starting on 20 June.

The high-level talks began in London on 26 June 1972. William Whitelaw represented the British government from his ministerial position as First Secretary of State for Northern Ireland. Whitelaw therefore was currently the de facto head of the Northen Ireland government previously administered by the former Stormont regional government in Belfast. Provisional IRA representatives included IRA Chief of Staff Seán Mac-

Stíofáin, Dáithí Ó Conaill, a member of the IRA Army Council, Seamus Twomey, OC of the Belfast Brigade, Martin McGuinness of the Derry Brigade, and Gerry Adams, representing the republican political party Sinn Féin. At the insistence of the IRA, the British released Adams from incarceration under internment to allow his participation in the talks.

The talks broke down two weeks later. The IRA demands included British withdrawal from Northern Ireland by 1975, immediate retreat to barracks of the British Army, and the release of republican prisoners. Far too extreme for the British to agree at least at this stage in the growing conflict. A failed opportunity on both sides. The underlying antagonisms of a polarized Northern Ireland population combined with the interests of a former colonial power made the situation intractable. Decades of continued conflict would eventually result in 3,600 deaths and 30,000-40,000 injured in the violence. Civilians accounted for 50% of the deaths and 70% of the injured largely coming from the estimated 16,000 bombings.

For Terence, the almost daily reporting of not just civilian casualties but incidents describing the vilest barbarity perpetrated by all three warring factions was incomprehensible. This was the twentieth century in a western democracy. Reports of torture, summary executions, and horrific maltreatment of those incarcerated by security forces recalled descriptions of Nazi SS and Gestapo inhumanity.

While conflicted and disillusioned, he rationalized excesses must be expected in war. His radio-command bomb detonators were simply weapons of war. Weapons intended to kill the enemy. Justified only by the cause necessitating those killings. The first week of July, he delivered newly completed radio detonators to his grandfather in Coleraine and returned to Belfast with another batch of two-way radios. Every soldier perhaps experienced disillusionment once thrust into the ugliness of war. Self-examination only became natural. Harboring a lifelong belief in the cause of Irish independence, he was not about to cave into his doubts. He was new to life in Northern Ireland. He admonished himself to toughen up. There was no way to back away from the commitment made to his grandfather. He alone went to great lengths to convince his grandfather to allow his active participation in this struggle. To quit now would become an inexplicable breach of faith to the one person he honored above all others.

CHAPTER 11

Boston, Massachusetts | 2025

Father O'Brien began the next interview session with Terence Kelly. "You say that you first began experiencing reservations about what you got yourself into even before you had constructed your radio detonators. Did the events of *Bloody Sunday* change those feelings?"

"Probably. *Bloody Sunday* undoubtedly reinforced my commitment. Yet my reservations had nothing to do with the cause I signed up for. *Bloody Sunday* made clear the principal enemy was the British. Haven't they always been the true enemy of the Irish?

"My reservations centered on the conduct of the IRA. Fighting a guerrilla war, bombing obviously became the primary weapon. The reason I saw it as a way of materially contributing by providing significant technical improvement. The problem for me was the selection of targets.

"The bombings in November and December were highly disappointing. The *Red Lion Pub* in Belfast and a month later the *Balmoral Furniture* showroom. Soft targets. Civilians killed and injured. Between these IRA bombings the UVF retaliated with the *McGurk's Pub* bombing. More dead civilians. Both sides target civilians depending on religious identification. Thereafter, this became the tone of bombings throughout 1972, the bloodiest year of the entire thirty years of the *Troubles*. Tit-for-tac retaliation between the IRA and the loyalist paramilitaries both targeting opposing civilian non-combatants. I hoped the IRA would change tactics. Their principal enemy was the British military and the RUC police. Theorized that the use of radio-command detonators would provide the means for promoting attacks on the more difficult hard targets of security forces. Unfortunately, it never turned out that way even during the later years of the conflict. Never understood why."

O'Brien said, "Yet you continued making your radio control devices. All of 1972 was more of the same. *Bloody Friday* might be considered somewhat different with some targeting of infrastructure, but the results still led to heavy civilian casualties. What made you continue?"

"Many factors. Once you start something you feel strongly about, it's hard to quit. Like admitting to a mistake. Couldn't see myself just continuing at Queen's University and doing nothing while masquerading as a Protestant of all things. Pragmatically, returning to Boston might also result in being called up in the draft. Better to stay in this war swirling around me than winding up in Vietnam.

"Then there's the matter of family. I came to Northern Ireland without my parents knowing that I was going to stay for an indefinite period. Never told them of my plans to attend Queen's University. Didn't wanted to face up to that being a mistake by leaving prematurely. However, the bigger issue was letting my grandfather down."

"How so? It was your idea to get involved. You said yourself you had to convince your grandfather to allow you to make these radio devices?"

"True enough. By letting him down, I meant appearing afraid to continue when circumstances did not meet my expectations. Quitting without seeing through with my commitment. Young Irish men of all types were willing to risk all by picking up a gun or bomb. Given my family's republican background, I'd be looked upon in a very poor light."

"What about your father Eoin Kelly? You said only that he was working to assist in smuggling weapons from the United States. How active was he really in the conflict?"

"More than I thought. Grandfather was close-lipped about providing details of what my father did. When I returned to Boston, Granda cautioned me only not to allow my father to suck me into any of his illegal activities in America. With my education, I had a life to live. Don't ruin that by getting involved with illegal activity. It wasn't until years later that my father explained just how deeply he was connected into smuggling for the IRA in Northern Ireland. How much that also involved my grandfather."

"Care to explain? You speak of your family's involvement in Irish republicanism. Was this more than just your grandfather? Seems your mother didn't support the IRA. That leaves only your father. It's important that I understand the various influences that shaped your life."

Kelly nodded in understanding. "With the *Good Friday Agreement* in 1998, my father was seventy-two. Thirty years of the *Troubles* had finally ended. Grandfather had long ago passed away. Never thought of my father in the same way as Granda. Anyway, he explained just how deeply he contributed. Not without considerable legal risk for violating U.S. laws.

"Eoin Kelly was twenty-four with a wife and me as a young child when we emigrated to Boston in 1950. Given his father's famous background, he naturally wanted to follow in the continuing struggle for Irish independence. As a scholar of Irish history, you know that the Anglo-Irish Treaty of 1922 did not satisfy Irish aspirations. For Catholics in the partitioned northern six counties it meant nothing changed. The minority Catholic population continued living under terrible sectarian oppression.

"With the establishment of the Irish Free State of the southern counties, the IRA became a depleted organization by the 1950s. Irish independence remained only an issue for Northern Ireland. Father left Ireland well before the last IRA attempt at armed relevance with the failed *Border Campaign*. However, with the resurgence of sectarian violence against Catholics in Northen

Ireland by Protestant loyalists, the IRA found a new life. With the split from the former IRA, the Provisional IRA infused new life in the struggle for Northern Ireland. The legendary rebel Liam Kelly found new meaning to carrying on the fight for Irish justice. It was Liam that gave his son Eoin his first opportunity to take part in smuggling weapons from the United States.

"Grandfather connected with a former IRA member named Michael Flannery who emigrated to New York City after fighting in the War of Irish Independence. For forty years Flannery worked at the Metropolitan Life insurance Company. Drawn back into the republican struggle, Flannery founded NORAID, the North American Aid Committee, in 1969. Disguised as humanitarian aid, its purpose was to raise funds to support Provisional IRA military efforts. Flannery concealed the funds through offshore tax haven subsidiaries coming into use at the time. Liam Kelly orchestrated the recipient end of the conduit in Northern Ireland and Dublin.

"My father became involved in IRA arms smuggling when Liam introduced him to another Irishman in New York named George Harrison. Liam had worked with Harrison in the 1950s supporting the failed IRA *Border Campaign*. With the revived militancy of the Provisional IRA in 1969, Liam resurrected Harrison's smuggling network with my father Eoin playing an intermediary role. Liam never told my father the real purpose of the walkie-talkies until after I left Northern Ireland.

"My father likely assumed it was for IRA communications. Still contraband if found destined to the IRA, he routed them through a Harrison former IRA connection in Dublin whose son owned a commercial electronics distribution business. The radios were then transported across the border into Northern Ireland to Enniskillen in County Fermanagh. From there, Liam had them delivered to a security cutout in Derry that did not know he was the ultimate recipient. My grandfather personally delivered my improvised radio detonators to Brian Keenan. All this secrecy designed to insulate me from involvement."

O'Brien commented, "Yet all this secrecy did not stop your grandfather from abetting you in a dangerous endeavor. If caught, you likely faced imprisonment for life for complicity in multiple murders."

"I understood there were still risks. Yet you can see my grandfather's level of commitment to the Irish republican cause, Father. I worshipped him, therefore, I couldn't let him down."

"How did you then explain your eventual leaving Belfast?"

"That was not until eighteen months later. "I had reason to be concerned about my security. Been at it long enough to have dozens of my radio detonators placed into the hands of the IRA. Eventually my triggering devices would be discovered in some failed bombing or recovered from bomb fragments. If any forensics led to me, I would become a prime suspect. Electronics background. Working with two-way radios at Comet. Especially uncovering my use of alternate identities. Masquerading as a Protestant alone would condemn me."

"How old was your grandfather in 1972?"

"Seventy-five."

O'Brien said, "I know of Flannery and Harrison from researching my book on the *Troubles.* Both older men in 1972 after being inactive in militant IRA activities for decades. Quite an achievement for your grandfather to resurrect what became the all-important connection of America support throughout the early years of the *Troubles.* I can now understand the breadth of your adoration. What explanation did you give your parents for returning to Boston? Were you still attending classes at Queen's University?"

"Finished my course work but hadn't completed my master's thesis. Fact was I was far too distracted therefore I delayed leaving when I should have. Partly from hubris. Mistakenly thinking I had everything under covered. You'll understand the circumstances when I get to that part of my story further on. I gave my parents a fictional explanation. Explained as being dismayed by the continuing violence particularly in Belfast. Came to Northern Ireland to visit my paternal grandparents and experience my Irish heritage. Not this oppressive environment where everyone lived in fear. Using my British citizenship identity as a Protestant became increasing awkward. Father didn't know of that or even the origin of my British identity as Terence Stewart. Created a terrible argument between my parents when he found out. My father was deeply hurt by my mother using her family name on my birth registration."

"Was the breakdown of the talks between the IRA and British government and collapse of the ceasefire a disappointment?" O'Brien asked.

Kelly shrugged. "I suppose so. Granda and I talked about the prospects before fighting resumed. Granda said the IRA demands were unrealistic. He correctly predicted that Secretary of State for Northern Ireland Whitelaw would likely dismiss the IRA demands without countering with an offer of something substantial from London. Whitelaw made no substantive offer, and the talks collapsed. The result became *Bloody Friday* less than two weeks later. The IRA exploded twenty-two bombs in Belfast within an hour. Must have involved complex planning in the works for weeks involving a great many IRA active service members."

"Did you blame the IRA leadership or the British for failing to make any headway in the ceasefire talks?"

Kelly smiled. "Blamed both sides. Even at the time I thought both sides miscalculated. With the benefit of time and books like yours, Father, I saw it as something far more distressing. Typical failure of those in power. Decisions made from emotion, self-interest, but mostly for political calculation to stay in power. No one willing to take a political risk that might lead to an end of bloodletting. No statesmen stood among those on either side. No shortage of fanatics though. Whether freedom fighter or terrorist depends on the perspective of the observer. I saw fanatics contesting with intrenched interests."

"*Bloody Friday* involved mostly car bombs. Seemingly targeting infrastructure. Still killed and injured a lot of people," O'Brien offered. "Caused people to leave Belfast in large numbers."

"A terrible afternoon it was. Set Belfast into a state of chaos. People everywhere panicked expecting more explosions. Some hunkered down, others ran but without knowing where they might be safe. For me that day became another milestone. I felt sure that many of those bombs, maybe most of them, were probably triggered by my radio devices."

"What made you think that?"

"To detonate over twenty bombs in such a short time span required positioning cars containing the bombs at specific locations within a very short time frame. Then someone inside the car would have to set unreliable timing devices if using the IRA's typical improvised means for detonation. Twenty-some individuals meant not everyone could have been experienced. Remaining unseen by people passing on the sidewalks would add pressure to rigging the bomb then getting the hell far enough away. All the while the bloke setting the bomb is terrified as he connects the detonators making sure he does not cause a premature explosion and blow himself to pieces.

"Timing fuses likewise seemed very unlikely for coordinating so many explosions within a compressed time frame. My detonating system allowed the bomber to set the explosive well in advance requiring only driving the car into position and walking away without drawing attention. I believed the only means for triggering that many bombs within a predetermined narrow time schedule meant triggering detonation by every bomber looking at a watch then flipping a switch. All from a safe distance to easily disappear in the confusion."

"With the thought that you were instrumental in the resulting human carnage, how did you feel?"

Kelly paused for a moment. "Held myself emotionally in check. Although not seeing any of the scenes of the bombings until later, *Bloody Friday* made me immediately feel a shared responsibility for the carnage. Easy enough to profess my personal distress like everyone, however the nature of my discomfort came from a different origin. Disoriented by the sheer size of the IRA attack, I still forced myself to carry through with my commitment like any soldier. Still felt motivated by the cause. Emotionally however, I felt physically ill. Civilian non-combatants again accounted for the of majority of casualties. On the darker side, I admonished myself to come to terms with this fight. Non-combatants would always bear the brunt of bombing attacks. More disturbing, I recall feeling a sense of accomplishment. If in fact these bombs were triggered by my radio detonators, I felt a sense of technical accomplishment that conflicted with my gnawing sense of guilt."

CHAPTER 12

Belfast, Northen Ireland | July 1972

It was Friday 21 July 1972. Terence was working that afternoon at Comet Electronics on Ormeau Road. Summer break from his studies. Classes at Queen's University would not resume until September affording the opportunity to work full-time and earn next year's tuition. He planned to meet Duncan and Henry at their usual pub that evening.

In the early afternoon while working in the back-office repair area, he suddenly heard a television news broadcast. Someone had increased the volume of a showroom television to listen to a news announcement. *We are breaking into our regular programming with this special alert. Belfast is currently experiencing multiple bombing attacks across the city.* Terence and his colleague Robert immediately ran into the showroom. Other Comet employees and a few customers stood watching as the news anchor referred to a map of Belfast displayed in split-screen.

For over an hour, they listened mostly in silence as the newscast reported 22 bombs exploding in different locations throughout Belfast. Over a dozen other bombs exploded in other Northern Ireland cities. However, it was Belfast that suffered the casualties. Already reports placed the casualties at nine dead and an estimated 130 injured with some losing limbs and others horribly disfigured. If *Bloody Sunday* in Derry in January demonstrated British brutality, *Bloody Friday* in Belfast six months later demonstrated a proportional response by the IRA. The breakdown of the secret peace talks between the British government and the IRA only twelve days earlier likely becoming the catalyst for the large-scale response by the Provisional IRA Belfast Brigade. The scale of the attack set the tone for 1972 that would eventually claim nearly 500 lives and another 5,000 injured. The worst year of the *Troubles* marking the beginning of twenty-five more years of bloodletting.

The day's events signaled IRA willingness to resort to increased violence while the British would undoubtedly respond by increased use of the weight of the British Army. That response began that same night when 2,000 British Army troops carried out raids in Belfast's Catholic nationalist neighborhoods attempting to seize those suspected as IRA. 58 people were arrested. Small amounts of explosives and weapons were seized. Gun battles broke out sporadically. Over the next three days more than 100 people were arrested.

The Ulster Defense Association took to the streets to protect Protestant areas. In the process of mounting patrols and erecting barricade checkpoints, the UDA killed four Catholic civilians.

The Belfast bombings took place within a span of about 80 minutes. Like all the employees at Comet Electronics, Terence waited until about 5:30 pm before deciding to leave for home following a period of no further explosions. Among the many locations bombed, the news reported that a car bomb exploded on Botanic Avenue only a quarter mile north of Queen's University. His normal route home took him on a parallel street, so he decided to see the damage firsthand.

Largely a semi-residential area, Terence came upon a scene of widespread destruction. Emergency personnel were still working the scene. The epicenter of the bomb was outside the small York Hotel. Heavily damaged along with row houses on one side of the street and commercial businesses on the opposite side, the windows of all the buildings were blown out. However, the most striking damage was 20 heavily damaged cars, including several overturned by the blast. As he walked past, he overheard two RUC officers talking and pointing to a piece of metal with a logo for a bread company, apparently the vehicle containing the bomb.

The impact of seeing this scene first-hand made a jarring impression on Terence. This could have been a bomb detonated by using one of his triggers. Regardless, his contribution to bomb making meant he shared in this. Were there many victims here? The news already reported deaths and large numbers of injuries among the 22 explosions. The worst locations mentioned were Oxford Street in the center of Belfast near the river and Cavehill Road over two miles to the north.

The following morning, he ventured out with his camera to visit the sites of other bombings. A map printed in the newspaper located a cluster of bombing locations in central Belfast. His first stop was the Oxford Street bus station. A telephone warning did not provide sufficient time to evacuate the area. Unlike Botanic Avenue, Oxford Street still held evidence of human remains among the rubble.

Terence could see what appeared as dried pools of blood and what might be human tissue on the sidewalk and in the street. Six died here along with a much larger number of those badly injured. Before a street-cleaning truck approaching from down the street arrived to wash away the gore, he captured close-up photographs. The sight turned his stomach. On the front page of the prior evening edition of the *Belfast Telegraph* a photograph appeared of a firefighter shoveling the remains of a victim into a bag.

Moving on, Terence visited the damaged sites of bombs set on the Queen Elizabeth Bridge, the Liverpool ferry terminal at Donegall Quay, the bus station next to the train station on Great Victoria Street, the Northen Ireland Carriers public transportation depot on Grosvenor Road, and the Star Taxi depot on Crumlin Road. Sick at heart, he returned to his apartment. Comet Electronics closed the store for the weekend.

He brooded over his decision to become involved in supporting IRA bombings. What possessed him to become actively involved? To prove his Irishness to his beloved grandfather? Prove his technical expertise with a more efficient means of killing people? Yesterday's open warfare on the citizenry of Belfast would never lead to achieving IRA objectives. Killing non-combatants certainly would not restore civil rights to Catholics. None of the bombs targeted police barracks or army barracks, or even important infrastructure. Why not? Had he not provided the means for implementing such tactics?

His thoughts suddenly turned to genuine concern. Reports cited several bombs that failed to detonate and were then defused. That meant that his triggers may have been discovered. The number of bombs and the compressed span of time left him concerned that his radio triggering devices probably played a large part. If so, then intact radio receiver devices attached to the high explosives were now in the hands of police and the British Army. Yet there was no way of knowing where lines of investigation by the intelligence services might lead. Where were the devices made? How were they smuggled into Northern Ireland? Who in the IRA took possession of the devices and may know more of their origin? How many people within the IRA knew something about the origin of his devices other than his grandfather and Brian Keenan?

Were the unexploded bombs even rigged with his radio detonators? If so, why might they have failed? Any of many possible reasons he speculated. Nothing is infallible, especially when human participation is involved. A faulty connection to the blasting caps? Failure of the bomber to extend the antenna? Too far out of range? Signal interference? Handling damage? Component failure?

His thoughts turned to chiding himself for useless speculation. Stick to thinking about his precautions. The meticulous use of latex gloves when handling each component. His grandfather's strict adherence to secrecy acting as the sole person knowing the origin of the devices. His mother's fortuitous decision to provide him an alternate identity distancing him from his famous grandfather while giving him a Protestant background. Sooner or later, the use of his radio-command detonators would however be discovered. No such thing as a perfect crime. Too many factors beyond his awareness might eventually lead to some line of inquiry that could envelop him circumstantially.

While dealing with imagined fears of discovery his thoughts turned to the horror stories of physical abuse inflicted on those detained by security forces. In the midst of his dark thoughts, there came a loud knocking on his apartment door, Terence's heart skipped a beat. Nobody ever came to his door. "Who is it?"

"It's Duncan, Terence. Henry's here with me. Come to fetch you. Looking to get to any fucking pub that might be open and get bloody drunk tonight! Open up, mate!"

Relieved, Terence opened the door letting his friends come in.

"Were you at work when this shit went down?" Duncan asked.

"Yeah. Everyone stayed at the store until we felt the bombings stopped. Just got back here an hour ago. What about you guys?"

Henry said, "I was at my father's garage. We all stopped working to listened to the radio for an hour as reports kept coming in. Duncan called me at the garage. Said he'd be right over."

"Got there and Henry's old man was plenty pissed off cursing out the IRA as nothing but fucking terrorist butchers," Duncan said. "All the bombing locations pointed to the IRA as undoubtedly being responsible. Thought we'd come by and see how you were doing."

Henry said. "This fuckin' war is a real shit. Not goin' to end soon unless London sends in more army troops. Not a goddamn thing any of us can do. At least we're not as fucked as the Catholics."

Duncan piped in, "Except there's plenty enough Catholics supporting the IRA. It's the IRA that has gone over to bombing civilians. Terrorism tactics. That's how guerrilla war works. Isn't possible without support from the general population. What do'ya say, Terence?"

Terence said, "Sickens the hell out of me. Came over here to experience my Irish heritage. Didn't expect this. Knew some bad things were happening between the paramilitaries on both sides, but nothing like this. Walked by a couple of the bombing locations after leaving work. Pretty awful."

Duncan asked, "Thinkin' 'bout returning to America leaving all this behind?"

"The thought has crossed my mind. My parents aren't keen about me staying, but I've got another year of school to finish. After that I've got to get a permanent job. Maybe things might eventually settle down in Belfast."

"Not sure about that. Well, at least it's Friday. Got a whole weekend to drown our sorrows so let's get started," Duncan said. "Got a new pub to try out. Solid Protestant loyalist area on the east side of the river on Ravenhill Road. *The Raven Pub.* Heard rumors from my father that UVF blokes have been known to frequent the place."

The mention of a hangout for the Protestant paramilitary Ulster Volunteer Force formed in the late sixties to counter the Catholic IRA caused Terence to respond, "Jesus! We don't want to become targets of the IRA."

Duncan replied, "At least for tonight, the IRA are hunkered down. Radio says there's a massive sweep by British Army troops targeting suspected IRA going on right now. Good idea to spend this evening in East Belfast, Terence."

The evening with Duncan and Henry relaxed Terence's anxiety. Aided substantially by several pints of stout, Duncan and Henry were not bad sorts. Clearly viewing events generally from the Protestant perspective, they however did not hold fanatical political views. Although condemning the IRA as terrorists, both understood that Catholics suffered flagrant civil rights abuses. Duncan was studying law and Henry political science. The exercise of authoritative power by the Northern Ireland government abetted from Westminster in London ran counter to both his friends' intellectual leanings. That was what attracted Terence to their friendship.

As for their views concerning the IRA, the targets of IRA bombings lay at the heart of his own disillusionment. Civilian non-combatant casualties far outnumbered police and army casualties. Increasingly becoming difficult to argue in his own mind that he was nothing more than a terrorist. For outsiders that called violent activists terrorists, it was not about the justification of their cause but the nature of the violence that was denounced.

Terence was unwilling to go as far as admitting to some unprincipled cause, but he was nonetheless deeply disaffected by IRA tactics. He could not accept that bombings causing civilian casualties was the only available weapon to confront government oppression. Why were they not doing more to attack the RUC and British Army? In the War of Independence fifty years ago his grandfather did not kill civilians. His IRA killed British security forces.

Northern Ireland Catholics suffered denial of civil rights. Forcing the British to give up Northern Ireland to unify with the Republic of Ireland was an unrealistic expectation. The civilian population of whichever political leanings were not the enemy. Peace could only come about when that population reconciled to live in equality.

The problem was biased elected officials from both sides concerned more about their party position than collectively governing along with the opposition. The problem seemed inherent to all representative democratic governments. Perhaps the situation was more complicated in Northern Ireland because of latent British colonialism. Terence came to the realization that his fervor for Irish nationalism handed down by his grandfather was overwhelmed by far different circumstances than those faced fifty years ago in the South. The military aspects of this conflict in 1972 Northern Ireland differed fundamentally from his grandfather's war for Irish independence in 1919 in places like Dublin and Cork.

The following morning, Terence called his grandfather. All he said was to call him at a particular number in exactly thirty minutes. Liam Kelly understand by prior arrangement the number was a public telephone. He would then place the call from a nearby public telephone in Derry to circumvent monitoring of communications by security forces.

"Are you okay?" Liam asked at once when Terence answered.

"I'm fine. And you and Grandma?"

"Several bombings. One large bomb in a van did a lot of damage to Waterloo Place. Shook us up some. Several other bombs exploded around the city, but no casualties reported."

Terence replied "Can't say the same for Belfast. Lots of dead. People with horrible injuries. Not like a war between armed soldiers. The casualties almost all civilians."

"Unfortunately, that's the case in all wars," Liam offered.

Terence replied, "Back in 1920, civilians undoubtedly suffered greatly in that war but did not dominate the casualty count."

Liam remained silent for a moment. His grandson's comment was fundamentally correct. All wars are different in character, yet this was not the time to debate with Terence. "Just keep safe and mind your whereabouts. This challenge by the IRA will undoubtedly require a proportional response by security forces and probably by loyalist paramilitaries."

Ten days later, on Monday 31 July, Terence woke up prepared for work. Turning on the radio, he was stunned to hear, *'For those just tuning in this morning, security forces have mobilized in massive strength to dislodge and disrupt military operations by the Provisional IRA. Events in Belfast from Bloody Friday have elevated the conflict to open rebellion according to a spokesperson for Northern Ireland British Army command. That response began at 4:00 am this morning under the banner of Operation Motorman. The most heavily affected areas have been Derry and Belfast. Additional military person-*

nel are also reported deploying to Newry, Armagh, Lugan, and Coalisland.

In the preceding days, 4,000 addition British army troops arrived in Northen Ireland for a major offensive against the IRA. *Operation Motorman* involved 22,000 British regular troops consisting of 27 infantry and two armored battalions. To these forces were added another 5,300 soldiers from the locally based reserve Ulster Defence Regiment. The objective was to reoccupy areas taken over by the IRA and declared by the IRA as *no-go areas* to government security forces. To avoid confrontation the RUC and British Army had refrained from entering these areas for two years. *Operation Motorman* marked a reversal in that failed strategy.

The most formidable no-go area was the Bogside sector of Londonderry west of the River Foyle, known to the predominantly Catholic population simply as Derry. 29 barricades blocked access to what became known as *Free Derry*. All were manned by armed IRA. 16 barricades consisted of reinforced construction making them impassable even to British Army armored vehicles. To breach this armed camp, the British Army delivered to the port of Derry by the naval vessel *HMS Fearless* several Centurion AVRE demolition vehicles, essentially tanks outfitted with bulldozer blades.

During his lunch break, Terence eventually connected with his grandfather by their public telephone routine. "Heard what's going on, Everything okay with you?" Terence said.

"Yes. Lots of soldiers moving about like an invasion. Gunfire has been minimal. Four people have been shot though. Three of those were young cousins. One a fifteen-year-old died and another man also killed. Could have been far worse but the opposing team all left town days ago. Bad weather forecast. Didn't favor playing under these inclement conditions. Other than the senseless murders by British soldiers without provocation, the day so far has been filled by the sound of tanks fitted out as bulldozers clearing nearby streets of barricades. How are things where you are?"

"Staying safe. Getting by. Much distressed though. The news reports about bombings in Claudy are truly a tragedy. The tit-for-tat appears to be what can be expected from here on out. Both sides claim the other is to blame then repeat the same outrages against more unsuspecting civilians. More butchery than warfare I should say."

While the IRA abandoned Derry after intelligence indicated an attack by the British Army, they did not abandon County Londonderry. Shortly before 10:00 am that same morning as British soldiers were invading the Catholic Bogside of Derry, the IRA retaliated by placing three car bombs in the center of the small village of Claudy, nine miles southeast of Derry.

At 10:15 the first bomb concealed in a stolen Ford Cortina exploded outside McElhinney's pub on Main Street. A police officer spotted a Morris Mini Traveler station wagon parked outside the post office on Main Street. Suspicious after hearing of everything going on that morning in Derry the officer had begun directing people away from the area by directing them toward Church Street before the first bomb exploded in front of the pub. At 10:30 a bomb inside a Morris Mini Van exploded outside the Beaufort Hotel on Church Street. This blast killed three people, two of whom had been injured in the first explosion. The bomb in the Morris Mini Traveler parked outside the post office then exploded almost simultaneously. This occurred only moments after clearing the street of people causing extensive damage to buildings and vehicles but without further loss of life.

In total nine people died and another 30 were injured that morning in Claudy. Total population of only about 1,200, Claudy was also 80% Catholic. The UDA and UVF denied responsibility. Provisional IRA chief of staff Seán Mac Stíofáin denied IRA responsibility. That would ultimately be proven false. Terence only learned the truth from his grandfather months later. The unsanctioned rogue IRA bombing was inexplicably the work of

Catholic priest Father James Chesney the operations chief of the IRA South Derry Brigade. Both Liam and Terence were dismayed about what possible motivation accounted for the Claudy atrocity perpetrated on a predominantly Catholic community. For Terence it reinforced his decision to abandon his ill-conceived adventurism in becoming part of this war. Was he any different by enabling deranged IRA fanatics like Chesney to continue indiscriminately killing civilians?

CHAPTER 13

Belfast, Northen Ireland | Fall 1972

Deployment of two dozen bombs in Belfast on *Bloody Friday* was reason enough for Terence to leave Comet Electronics. Fear that unexploded bombs meant the possibility that his modified two-way radios may have been discovered became a concern. His job at Comet regularly working with these same walkie-talkies combined with his technical background made him uncomfortable. Made him no different than the bombmaker that assembled the high-explosive destructive part of the bomb, or the person placing the bomb.

Any brush with the RUC could be dangerous regardless of his identification as someone with a Protestant heritage. He was raised in America from infancy not in Northern Ireland. Protestant parents and grandparents might not mean that much. Not to mention a deeper investigation into his birth registration would name his parents as Francis and David Stewart. David was his mother's brother, used as a convenience to supply the same surnames. If ever discovered by investigators as Terence Kelly, it would add an unexplainable incriminating element when linked with his real father's name leading to his infamous paternal grandfather.

In early August he left Comet Electronics to take a technician position at the Belfast 2BE radio station. His academic background and experience with amateur radio easily landed the nighttime technician position opening. The nighttime work schedule left the daytime available for his classroom schedule and studying. Work at the radio station involved installing equipment, trouble-shooting problems, and making repairs. The radio station located in central Belfast just off Crumlin Road about two miles north of QUB was easily walkable affording some daily exercise.

Perhaps just an emotional feeling, he felt less exposed hidden away in the backrooms of the radio station during the night. Employed at Comet working on the very same two-way radio gear used in the improvised detonation triggers seemed inherently dangerous. Even having past employment at Comet might be of concern if police investigations targeted the use of walkie-talkies as the means of connecting to possible suspects.

It was the middle of September when Terence completed re-configuring the next batch of two-way radios into radio detonators. A longer than normal interval since his last delivery explained by the necessity to source the added electronic components previously scavenged from Comet's repair parts inventory. Somewhat disingenuous but he did not want to explain procrastination due to his lack of enthusiasm for assisting in IRA bomb making.

Terence made the train journey to Coleraine to meet his grandfather on a Saturday just three weeks after another deadly IRA bombing followed by a retaliatory UVF bombing just two days ago.

The IRA bombing occurred in the city of Newry, the principal city closest to the southern border of Northern Ireland with the Republic of Ireland on 22 August. The target was a customs office. While a government economic target that did not prevent the deaths of essentially six civilians, five of which were customs officials and a lorry driver. Not individuals that could be legitimately construed as the enemy. A lorry entered the weighing station next to the main building of the customs clearing house when a 100-pound bomb detonated prematurely. Along with the six civilians, the three IRA perpetrators also died in the blast.

Reported as a timer-detonated bomb, notoriously prone to accidental detonation, Terence wondered why such a large bomb intended for an important target was not rigged with his radio-command detonator? Perhaps all had been expended in Belfast during *Bloody Friday*? This accidental explosion would never have occurred if the bomb had been rigged with his safer radio command detonator. Then again, Newry was outside Belfast and IRA operations fell under a different brigade command. This IRA unit maybe did not have access to such detonators.

The retaliatory bombing by the Ulster Volunteer Force took place in Belfast on 14 September. A car bomb loaded with a massive 200-pound bomb exploded near the Imperial Hotel on Clifton Street. The bomb destroyed the hotel and heavily damaged the nursing home next door. The casualty count was three killed and another 50 injured. This was not a target of suspected IRA. The Protestant loyalist paramilitaries seemingly acting out in kind to the back-and-forth bombings with no regard that it involved only civilians. No different than the IRA.

The Protestant paramilitary organizations however enjoyed a fundamentally different stature from the IRA. The loyalist paramilitaries were allied with the Northen Ireland government and therefore part of the institutionalized oppression of the Catholic minority.

For Terence, escalated loyalist indiscriminate bombings became another consequence of the IRA's failed tactics. The IRA consistently demonstrated an unwillingness to target the harder targets of the RUC or British Army. That was the war his grandfather fought fifty years ago. The IRA operating in Northern Ireland today did not possess the discipline to make this a proper fight between armed combatants. Resorting to terror through bombing killing civilians both Protestant and Catholic even denied the IRA wide support among the minority Catholic population. Worse than tactically unproductive, it alienated those that might otherwise be empathetic. This included those Irish in America who sought to equate this as a struggle of Irish independence to unite Northern Ireland with the Republic of Ireland.

The unrealistic remedy to the contentious partition of the island fifty years ago had no chance of succeeding.

Terence understood guerrilla insurgencies cannot succeed without popular support. Resisting oppression of Irish Catholics is what stimulated him to active participation in the cause he envisioned akin to that which his grandfather fought. This rebellion bore little resemblance to that earlier successful Irish struggle for freedom. That war was fought predominately in the southern twenty-six counties. Northern Ireland was different then as it is now.

Bloody Friday made Terence realize his naivety into thinking that his superior radio-command detonating triggers might alter tactics by directing bombings against the armed enemy. *Bloody Friday* must have employed at least some of his devices. Why wouldn't the IRA have used them against better targets? They possessed enough of them by now. They required no expertise for safely arming bombs while providing optimum timing of detonation from a distance.

Once again in Coleraine, Terence and Liam stowed their respective duffle bags of new walkie-talkies and those modified into bomb detonation triggers into train station lockers when they arrived. This was their usual security precaution while they enjoyed their brief time together.

Sharing a pint of stout at the *Railway Arms* pub, Terence said, "I don't understand the bombings at Claudy. Newspapers say it's a small predominantly Catholic town. Why would Protestant paramilitaries target it?"

Liam sighed, "Because they didn't. They denied responsibility. That happens to be the truth. It was a rogue IRA operation. I know this directly coming from the Derry Brigade OC. Furious over the unsanctioned action, but he can't do much other than remain silent. Let the public assume it must be the UDA or UVF."

"Jesus Christ! Why?"

Liam Kelly was more than just troubled over the Claudy bombings. He knew something more that he chose not to share with Terence."

"Don't know. Don't believe the Derry OC knows either."

Angrily, Terence said, "The IRA are no better than the UDA or UVF. Both sides are becoming nothing more than terrorists. Fucking psychopaths all of them." Terence paused to get control of his anger. "Not sure I should continue contributing to this carnage, Granda. Civilians are being killed in large numbers. Everything the IRA has done since *Bloody Sunday* has accomplished nothing. These bombings have only brought about internment without trial, essentially martial law. Suspended the Stormont regional government then causing Northern Ireland to become occupied with thousands more British Army troops. Ready to shoot to kill anyone suspected of being IRA. Detain and imprison any Catholic suspected of helping the IRA.

Liam said, "I appreciate you being disheartened, Terry. I too feel we are experiencing dark days. Been through this before. War takes different turns. Setbacks are part of that. Each war is unique. Bear in mind the enemy, the British and their Northern Ireland stooges, do not have the upper hand. They are just reacting to IRA attacks. Heavy-handed as the British have always done. No different than how things went during the War of Independence. Executing the leaders of the Easter Rising of 1916 is a prime example.

"Eventually the British will become exhausted. British citizenry will either pressure a change in Westminster, or the sheer cost of waging a war indefinitely becomes untenable. At some point London will be forced to come to the negotiating table when the ruling party in Parliament is threatened with falling out of power."

"Peace talks a few months ago didn't lead to anything," Terence said.

"Premature. We didn't have enough leverage for the demands set forth. The Brits haven't yet reached a point of futility. They haven't figured out how to deal with the likes of those loyalist diehard fanatics like Ian Paisley. Makes for achieving any form of settlement much more difficult.

"Almost every day from 1919 to 1922 was a dark day. Pissing into the wind risking our lives for something that seemed unattainable. Looking to be just another failed rebellion to drive the British out of Ireland. Obviously we prevailed. At least for the southern twenty-six counties. We must stay the present course. I have long ago made that commitment. You must make your own decision, Terry."

Terence nodded. "Tell me this, Granda, are my radio detonating devices being used?"

"Oh yes. Don't know specifics but I believe they were widely used in Belfast on *Bloody Friday*. My contact in the Belfast Brigade has already inquired about getting more."

"By the publicly reported details of those detonated in Claudy and Newry, unreliable timers were used. Does the IRA leadership realize these should be used to go after the RUC or British Army? Maybe even important economic targets. Ships. Port infrastructure. Communications centers. Factories. Warehouses. Bring London to the negotiating table. Quit killing civilians!"

"I've made such comments to the few influential IRA that I interact with. Remember, I'm not an official member of the IRA. Just an old fossil that helps to obtain weapons Too old and out of the mainstream to exert strategic influence."

Terence nodded. Understanding the depth of his grandfather's commitment to the cause of Irish freedom and Catholic civil rights, he must make up his own mind. "I'll consider what you said about war, Granda. Still think the IRA should go after military targets. I designed the radio detonators to make that possible without losing their own people in the process. I'll work on converting this next batch and let you know when they're ready. The last group took longer than expected because I changed jobs. For security reasons."

A look of concern came over Liam's face. "What do'ya mean?"

"Several bombs on *Bloody Friday* did not explode. Reasons unknown. Have to assume the possibility that my radio detonator might have been among those. If so, the security forces will be looking into where they came from. Their experts will recognize the increased utility of these detonators even if the IRA doesn't. These walkie-talkies are commercially available in Northern Ireland. I repaired many of them at Comet. Might be smuggled from America but possibly made right here. That means looking into places and people handling them."

"Even leaving Comet doesn't mean you still might not come under scrutiny," Liam said. "Where do you assemble these things, Terry?"

"At my apartment."

"Jesus! You can't be doin' that!"

"I know, Granda. Right after the massive bombing attack on Belfast, I immediately removed anything incriminating against me from my apartment. Any tools and electronic components remaining are easily explained as a graduate electrical engineering student. I also just started working as a technician at a radio station. Night shift. Haven't yet figured out where I can safely do my secret work but possibly there. Plenty of places to hide things safely out of sight among all the transmitting equipment."

"Will your identity hold up if questioned?"

"It should. Got a British passport as a citizen backed up by a birth registration. Identifies me as having a Protestant background from my mother's side." Terence knew that actually would depend on how deeply into his identity investigators might delve if ever detained. If they discovered that Terence Stewart had no history in the United States, then his subterfuge would quickly unravel.

Terence chose not to fully express his disillusionment to his grandfather. Nor his plans to leave Northern Ireland once he completed his graduate degree at Queen's University. He was beginning his final year of academic course work required for a master's degree in electronics. He had yet to submit a proposal for his dissertation required for obtaining a master of science degree in electronics at QUB. That meant leaving Belfast by the end of the next calendar year.

The graduate degree would enhance his professional credentials if he was able to satisfactorily explain his academic degrees under different surnames. Applying to QUB he accomplished that with a smoke and mirrors explanation of his mother divorcing when he was very young. Subsequent adoption by his step-father accounted for the name Kelly whereas his British birth surname Stewart explained by his legal British citizenship name from birth. That might not work again so easily when seeking employment in the United States even though having different legal names in different countries was not illegal.

Terence departed back to Belfast with his next consignment of two-way radios for conversion to detonators. Hugging his grandfather, he said only, "Love you, Granda. Give my love to Grandma. Both of you stay safe. I'll let you know when I have these radios modified and ready to deliver to you."

The remainder of 1972 continued its record of slaughter. On 31 October, Halloween, members of the violent Ulster Freedom Fighters faction of the Ulster Defence Association detonated a no-warning car bomb outside Catholic-owned *Benny's Bar* near the Belfast docks. Two young girls ages six and four were killed while trick or treating. 12 other people were injured.

Five days before Christmas the UFF struck again. This time in the Waterside district of Derry on the east side of the River Foyle. Five people died by gunfire, four Catholic and one Protestant, along with the wounding of four others. As customers watched a football match on television, two gunmen entered a pub. One armed assailant sprayed rounds from a Sterling submachine gun into the *Top of the Hill Ba*r on the Strabane Old Road. This was a small Catholic neighborhood in the mainly Protestant sector of Derry.

Across Northern Ireland, casualties during 1972 amounted to 479 deaths, 4,876 injured from 10,628 shootings, and almost 1,900 bombs. Over half of the deaths were civilians. Belfast suffered disproportionately and would continue to do so eventually accounting for 1,200 deaths over the course of thirty years of the *Troubles*.

From a Belfast population of 417,000 in 1971, the unrelenting violence eventually resulted in the population falling to 298,000 by 1981 through an exodus to the Republic of Ireland or abroad. The first decade of the *Troubles* would see a devastating economic impact across Northern Ireland. Industrial output declined dramatically with major industries such as shipbuilding and linen textiles particularly vulnerable. The damage to private industry began with the disastrous violence of 1972 causing a decline in Northern Ireland capital investment that further affected employment.

The stress of leading a dangerous clandestine life while conflicted by a crisis of faith in his Irish nationalism, the chaos centered in Belfast further added to Terence's despondency.

CHAPTER 14

Belfast, Northen Ireland | Winter 1972-73

Terence assumed that unexploded bombs recovered from the two dozen bombs planted around Belfast on 21 July 1972, *Bloody Friday,* exposed undamaged radio detonator triggers. His grandfather confirmed that they were used. Yet he still felt that his precautions did not warrant immediately leaving Northern Ireland.

Although not made public for reasons of security, police recovered two such radio signal detonators intact, wired into blasting caps embedded into unexploded gelignite bombs. RUC officers discovered the first bomb on the Albert Bridge spanning the River Lagan south of Queen's Bridge where another large bomb had exploded.

Alerted to the possible danger with so many car bombs detonated across Belfast that afternoon, the abandoned Leyland Mini Van on the busy commercial route immediately aroused suspicion. Looking inside, the officers backed away without opening any doors. They wisely closed the bridge then radioed dispatch to notify the British Army 321 Explosive Ordinance Company, Royal Logistic Corps responsible for bomb disposal.

An army transport soon arrived and an EOC engineer suited up in protective gear approached the Mini Van. Dangerous work since it is almost impossible to check for booby traps connected to doors. The army engineer chose to smash out a window to allow for better examination for a trip device affixed to the inside of the passenger-side door. Not foolproof but the move allowed for opening the door after careful examination inside with a flashlight. Inside the rear of the van, his flashlight illuminated a wooden crate sitting by itself on the floor. On top of the crate rested what appeared to be a walkie-talkie with its antenna extended. From the device, protruding wires disappeared through a hole in the top of the crate.

Climbing into the vehicle, the army engineering bomb disposal sergeant carefully entered the suspect vehicle then made his way to the crate. Examination revealed no concealed booby trap allowing for straightforward defusing by cutting wires. The engineer extracted the radio receiver triggering device and exited the vehicle. Walking back to the armored vehicle where others of the bomb disposal team stood observing from a safe distance, he held up the triggering device signaling he had disarmed the bomb.

"Take a look at this, Sergeant Major," the bomb disposal junior sergeant dressed in his cumbersome protective gear said as he handed the modified walkie-talkie unit to a burly older soldier with a great white mustache.

Sergeant-Major Samuel Dunsford took the device to the rear of the armored vehicle with the tailgate down. Carefully he unscrewed the cover making sure it was not internally booby trapped. Letter bombs could contain enough explosive material to blind or take off fingers therefore this device also could be wired.

Opening the cover Dunsford said, "Well, what do you know. These Fenian fuckers are finally becoming more sophisticated. This is one half of the radio detonator system. Triggers detonation of the bomb by a radio signal from long range. Got a battery pack hooked to a capacitor to increase voltage when discharged. What kind of explosives did you find, Sergeant?"

"Gelignite. Big fucking bomb. Something like 100 pounds I'd estimate. No booby trap. I just cut the leads from this triggering device."

The sergeant-major said, "Could account for how the IRA were able to detonate so many bombs within such a tight time frame. Can't understand why these fuckers haven't done something like this sooner. This radio device isn't even particularly sophisticated. Just safer and allows for precise timing of detonation. Advantages are obvious compared with using electronic timer detonators or some dumbass mashup using a kitchen timer or some such thing. That's how they lose people to premature explosions. What's more interesting is using gelignite rather than ANFO. The IRA must smuggle gelignite into the country. For car bombs, mor economical to make very large bombs from ANFO easily hidden within delivery vans then detonate with blasting caps setting off just a single stick of gelignite to set off the ANFO."

A short time after arriving at Albert Bridge, the British Army Explosive Ordnance Disposal unit was alerted to another undetonated bomb wired with the same type of radio detonator. The discovery of these improved radio detonation triggers launched a new line of investigation involving various elements of British security. This involved British MI5 the UK's counterintelligence service, the Royal Ulster Constabulary, and British Army intelligence. Word went out to begin investigating for the source of these new radio bomb detonating devices.

One of the tentacles of British military intelligence was a secret unit created in the summer of 1971 specifically for the growing problem of Northern Ireland. The *Military Reaction Force* was the brainchild of Brigadier General Frank Kitson, a colorful character in the tradition produced by Britain through history. Brigadier Kitson earned his counterinsurgency experience in the crown colony of Kenya during the Mau Mau rebellion of the 1950s. Kitson now commanded the British Army 39th Infantry Brigade serving in Northern Ireland.

The MRF became a small covert intelligence-gathering and counterinsurgency unit consisting of 40 men handpicked from the British Army. These soldiers operated largely independent of any higher command and control. Their function was to gather intelligence and disrupt the IRA in any way possible. That meant employing any tactics producing results with little concern for oversight.

While based at the Palace Barracks in the Belfast suburb of Holywood, the MRF operated far outside of official British Army control. They did not wear uniforms and instead used covert identities while in Belfast. In practice they became another independent force practicing unrestrained shootings and bombings no different than the IRA or the UDA and UVF Protestant paramilitaries.

The British Army MRF unit organized the *McGurk's Bar* bombing in December 1971 that killed 15. They shot and killed two Catholic brothers in April 1972, then shot five others, killing one in the Andersonstown area in May. They murdered a young woman on Glen Road in June then wounded three men in another shooting on Glen Road the same month. In September, they shot two men, killing one, in the Falls Road district.

However, in September, the IRA discovered that two of their members were double agents working for the MRF. Interrogation yielded information that the MRF was running front companies to aid in their covert activities. The *Four Square Laundry*, a mobile laundry service operating in Catholic nationalist West Belfast, and the *Gemini Message Parlour* on Antrim Road provided opportunities for gathering intelligence and running a network of sources. The IRA Belfast Brigade 2nd Battalion attacked the *Four Square Laundry* and the 3rd Battalion hit the *Gemini Massage Parlour* on 2 October 1972. The IRA inflicted six deaths that day on the MRF. After giving up information on the MRF, each of the two IRA double agents died cleanly by a bullet to the back of the head.

Public exposure caused the clandestine MRF to be disbanded. However, immediately following the demise of the MRF, the British Army replaced the unit with a new undercover intelligence organization called the *Special Reconnaissance Unit,* acronym SRU. Like the MRF, members of the SUR were recruited from across the British Army then trained in an eight-week course on interrogation tactics by the *Special Air Service*, the SAS. As elite special forces, SAS training imbued the reincarnated

Special Reconnaissance Unit with excessively brutal tactical skills developed in British colonial conflicts against rebels. Tactics wholly out of place for policing an urban environment within an integral part of the United Kingdom.

One of those British soldiers recruited for the *Special Reconnaissance Unit* was Sergeant-Major Samuel Dunsford. He was the Royal Engineers' leading expert on bombs being used in Northern Ireland. Following that first discovery on Albert Bridge, Dunsford led the investigation from the technical side. A thirty-year British Army veteran. Enlisting in the Royal Engineers in 1944, he first learned his trade in bomb disposal by diffusing endless unexploded ordinance discovered throughout southern England following the Second World War.

Stationed at SRU headquarters at RAF Aldergrove airbase south of Antrim, Dunsford was placed in charge of a small technical team of royal engineers schooled in explosives and IEDs. Dunsford had joined the SRU at its inception because of his knowledge of bomb making. He therefore bypassed the physical rigors of the SAS training.

On 8 March 1973, the IRA renewed their bombing campaign. This time with a widened geography that included planting four car bombs using ANFO explosives in London. One exploded near the venerable London seat of justice, the Old Bailey Courthouse, killing one civilian and injuring over 200. Simultaneously another explosion occurred at the Ministry of Agriculture in Whitehall. Two other bombs, one outside the post office on Broadway in Westminster and the other at the BBC's armed forces radio studio on Dean Stanley Street failed to explode and were defused. That same day, five bombs also exploded in Belfast, five more in Derry, and one in Lugan, County Armagh. All these bombs exploded within less than an hour.

Reporting to his superior, SRU executive officer Major Robertson, Dunsford briefed Robertson on the status of the investigations of these new radio detonating triggers. "These radio devices were first discovered in the mass bombings in Belfast in July last year. Army intelligence, the RUC, and MI5 have not yet discovered the origins of these devices. Since the bombing in Newry last August, there have been no IRA bombings until just a couple of weeks ago. Two recovered unexploded bombs were discovered in the Belfast bombings. Because of the compressed time frame of the 22 Belfast bombs detonated, we feel most bombs that day were probably triggered by these new radio devices."

"Why does the time frame indicate these devices were used rather than other means of detonation?" Robertson asked.

"The compressed time frame indicates the ability to detonate multiple devices in different locations at roughly the same time by each individual bomber simply looking at a watch, Sir. Difficult to coordinate bombings at multiple locations using imprecise timing detonators with different individuals placing bombs having to actuate individual timers. Remotely triggering command by radio signal allows for selecting the precise moment of detonation. Unfortunately finding small remnants of detonators from exploded ordinance is extremely difficult so we cannot conclusively determine every bomb was triggered by radio command. However, radio signal triggering devices offer a great technical advantage for IRA bombers. Should the IRA exploit those advantages, we could be in for some nasty surprises, Sir."

"What about these London bombs? Two failed to detonate. Why is that?" Robertson asked.

"They did not include these radio triggering devices, Sir. Bomb disposal personnel defused them before ordinary preset timing devices triggered detonation. Typical shortcoming of using timers. Radio triggers can detonate instantly on command from a safe distance for the bomber. Also, the bombs used ANFO instead of gelignite in the July Belfast bombings. May indicate a different group of bombmakers. Maybe even IRA residing in England.

"The eleven bombs exploded that same day in Northern Ireland however all detonated successfully with an hour of each other. They may very well have been fitted with these radio trigger systems. Got lots of soldiers out there looking through debris for any fragments that might confirm these bombings employed the same radio devices. But that's looking for a needle in a haystack."

"Yet two such bombs rigged with these radio devices recovered in Belfast in July failed to explode. What's your best guess why they failed to detonate, Sergeant Major?"

"Could be something as simple as damage to the transmitter. Too far away from the receiver physically connected to the explosives, or something interfering with the radio signal. Perhaps just human failure. With multiple bombs planted in different locations, perhaps mixing up the pairing of the transmitter to the specific receiver tuned to the corresponding radio frequency. Then again, maybe nothing more than a bomber getting cold feet and aborting detonation."

Robinson said, "Very well. Where does the investigation stand regarding the origin of these devices, Sergeant Major?"

"Scotland Yard's Metropolitan Police Forensic Science Laboratory in London analyzed the recovered radio receiver units from Belfast. Reported finding fingerprints recovered but no matches yet to anyone in government files. Interestingly, those fingerprints all came from exposed areas of the devices. Obviously through handling by the bombers. The Metropolitan Police Lab could not find any prints on internal components. The bloke that assembled these probably used surgical latex gloves. The fellow knows what he's doing. Knows something about electrical circuitry. However, the design is not particularly ingenious. Nothing beyond elementary circuitry and a knowledge of radios. But it's an operational leap from relying on improvised mechanical timers or timed fuses. Surprised, the IRA has not gone to something like this long ago. Don't understand why the bombmakers did not use these radio devices after the apparent success in Belfast in July."

The frustrated major responded, "Because they're ignorant Catholics living on the public dole that know nothing beyond drinking, fucking, and brawling. Give 'em a gun or bomb they just become lethal. What about the origin of these devices?"

Unlike Dunsford, Major Robertson knew that an IRA informer mole led to information resulting in the arrest of the ten IRA arrested at Heathrow Airport trying to escape London immediately following the bombings. Nothing having to do with bomb making technology. Contrary to his disparaging remarks about Irish Catholics, he understood these radio devices could well advance IRA bombing effectivity.

Dunsford said "Nothing special about the basic hardware. They're converted from American-made walkie-talkies. Motorola model HT220 two-way radios. Commercially available here and elsewhere around the world. Other manufacturers produce equivalent products. Used by construction firms and law enforcement. Wherever necessary communications are unavailable by fixed telephone lines. Tracking commercial distribution of walkie-talkies will not likely lead to anything without making a connection using other means of intelligence. Unless the modified walkie-talkies are produced in America that probably means someone here in Northern Ireland, or possibly in the Republic, is making the modifications for use in detonating bombs."

Shifting through debris collected from the recent bombings in Belfast and Derry did yield fragments that the Metropolitan Police Forensic Science Laboratory in London confirmed came from Motorola walkie-talkies. If these became universally adopted for IRA bomb making then Northern Ireland and even England itself would become far more vulnerable. Like Terence, Sergeant Major Dunsford understood radio command detonators provided advantages for striking security forces directly.

Unknown to Dunsford, MI5 had already begun collecting information on the commercial distribution of Motorola walkie-talkies and similar products from other manufacturers in the United States like General Electric. The FBI and the Republic of Ireland Guardia all contributed information on legitimate distribution channels as well as those suspected of smuggling contraband into Northern Ireland.

Since walkie-talkies were legitimate commercial products, Eoin Kelly arranged shipments from the United States to Dublin without resorting to the clandestine channels of George Harrison's New York IRA smuggling network. Once in Dublin, a commercial distributor of radio equipment routinely shipped walkie-talkies across the border to Belfast and Derry to commercial businesses or directly to law enforcement. Arrangements by those sympathetic to the IRA easily diverted quantities of walkie-talkies once inside Northern Ireland using double sets of purchase orders. Using cutouts, Liam Kelly acquired the radio sets he delivered to his grandson for conversion into detonation triggering systems without becoming identified.

CHAPTER 15

Boston, Massachusetts | 2025

"Where did we last leave off, Father?" Terence Kelly said as he sat in Father Connor O'Brien's office at Boston College to resume his narrative.

"I believe you were relating your conflicted feelings following the Belfast bombings of *Bloody Friday* in 1972."

"Yes. *Bloody Friday* was undoubtedly a turning point in the early years of the *Troubles*. That included for me personally. My first awareness that my radio detonators may have played a major role. So many bombs exploding within a compressed time frame suggested remote detonation following a prescribed schedule by the IRA. Hearing that two unexploded bombs were diffused meant that my radio devices may have discovered intact. That prompted concern about my employment at Comet Electronics. Routinely repairing the same model walkie-talkies could lead to questioning if ever caught up in an investigation by security forces. That led to leaving Comet and taking a position as a technician working for a radio station."

"How were you feeling about these bombings that left mostly civilian casualties?"

"Profoundly disturbed. My grandfather told me he delivered my devices to the Belfast Brigade. The very unit responsible for the *Bloody Friday* Belfast bombings. Why did they not select more important targets? Belfast provided all sorts of opportunities that could directly affect the real enemy. Security forces, government infrastructure, economic targets. Outside of bombs placed on a couple of bridges over the river, the locations could only result in civilian casualties. Counterproductive to the interests of the IRA. Totally disappointed that my devices had not altered the tactics affecting the choice of targets. Made all the worse by the inexplicable bombings in Claudy."

"The same day as *Operation Motorman* began as I recall," O'Brien said.

"Yes. I spoke with my grandfather the same day as British troops invaded Derry to clear the barricades and retake the *Free Derry* no-go areas. The British murdered a couple of people that day in Derry. *Operation Motorman* was the British reaction to *Bloody Friday*. May have been the intention of the IRA leadership but I don't think they ever thought strategically in those early years. Anyway, what happened in Claudy was truly inexplicable. Claudy was predominately Catholic. Three car bombs killed nine and injured another 30. Turned out to be the work of a demented priest instigating a rogue operation of the IRA Derry Brigade."

"Did you cease making these devices after *Bloody Friday* and the Claudy bombings?"

"Not immediately."

"Why not if you were so disheartened?"

"It's complicated, Father. I wasn't IRA. Just a volunteer who makes hardware. At the time, I may have subconsciously rationalized that somehow mitigated my complicity for the bombing casualties. Like a gunrunner, just an enabler. More importantly, I made a commitment to my grandfather. Someone with whom I had special affection. Remember, I grew up immersed with the ideological lore surrounding Irish nationalism. My own father revered his father as much as I did. We both lived the history of the Irish twentieth-century struggle through recounting Liam Kelly's exploits. Granda's resurrection in the cause of Catholic oppression in his native Derry naturally invoked the implicit motivation for us actively participate.

"Then given my youth with its attraction to adventurism without proper for regard for consequences in an environment I did not understand, it became difficult to extract myself. Quitting would seem like denying my professed ideological commitment to Irish freedom. An admission of youthful foolishness for coming to Northern Ireland then overwhelmed by discovering the reality. More than anything it concerned disappointing my grandfather and difficulty explaining to my parents. Finishing out my master's degree at QUB provided an explainable conclusion to extending my time in Northern Ireland. The ability to relate the difficult experiences of the *Troubles* while concealing what my covert activities."

"How did your mother feel about you going to Northern Ireland?"

"She did not like the idea but thought it was only for the summer of 1971. I hid the fact from my parents that I applied for admission to Queen's University to study for my master's degree. Obviously that meant an extended period to remain in Northern Ireland they would find concerning with the rising tensions.

"Had your mother known, what might have been her reaction?"

"She would have been beside herself with concern with the violence of 1972. She was never fond of Granda Liam. Remember it was her doing to register my birth under her family name. Even stating the father's name on my birth registration as Stewart using her brother's name as the father. Intended for distancing us from the potentially compromising association with the infamous IRA gunman Liam Kelly. She came from a Protestant background. Easier to keep that identification in predominantly Protestant loyalist Northen Ireland."

"When did you discontinue making these radio detonation devices?"

Kelly sighed. "Not until the summer of 1973."

O'Brien raised an eyebrow. "Considering your distaste for how you believed they were being used, what caused you to continue for another year?"

"I have never adequately explained that to myself. Like most everything in life, a combination of factors. In my situation it was easier to continue than making the seemingly logical decision to quit. Inertia. Somehow the death of civilians by IRA bombs did not rise to the level of sufficient disgust. Repeating my culpability in murder rationalized as somehow different by only supplying the means rather than actually exploding the bombs. I was just a gunrunner. Continuing not explainable by a single factor, Father."

Kelly sat back in his chair and remained silent for a protracted time before continuing. When he did continue it was to resume the chronology of events rather than delving deeper into the pathology of his behavior while in Belfast.

"Bombings dominated the remaining months of 1972. A poorly executed IRA bombing in Newry took the lives of six civilians along with the three IRA bombers. A faulty timer detonator caused a premature explosion. Not one of my radio devices.

"The other bombings were the work of UDA or UVF loyalist paramilitaries. All these violent events clearly imprinted in my memory. The *Imperial Hotel* in Belfast. Three killed, 50 injured. *Benny's Bar* in Belfast. Two killed, 12 injured. In December Ulster loyalists took the fight to Dublin. Who's to explain the questionable strategy of expanding the conflict into the Republic? Two car bombs killed two and injured 127. In Belturbet, County Cavan a bomb killed two and injured eight when a bomb exploded in Clones, County Monaghan. Both locations targeted as bordering counties with Northern Ireland known for cross-border incursions by IRA, yet the casualties of course were all civilians.

"Consistent with the tit-for-tat reciprocal exchanges of bombings, the IRA responded in early March of 1973. Two bombs exploded in central London outside the Old Baily Courthouse and another at the Ministry of Agriculture injuring over 200 people. Two other bombs failed to explode. Neither were reported as rigged with my radio detonating triggers. The perpetrators were arrested trying to flee London were from the IRA Belfast Brigade. Why my devices were not used I do not know. Made enough of them. Yet that same day five IRA bombs exploded in

Belfast and another five exploded in Derry. Once again the compressed time frame of the explosions suggested my devices may have been used.

"Same flawed strategy of bombing mostly soft targets. My radio detonating devices did not alter tactics to hard targets or the armed enemy. Had I introduced them a decade later maybe they would have seen wider usage. IRA bombings in the 1980s dramatically shifted to hard targets of the real enemy. However, not the case during those earlier years. I had already made up my mind to leave Northern Ireland by the end of 1973."

"Did these IRA bombings in March make your decision to quit making these radio detonators?"

"No. Something far more immediate. Something that made what I was participating in far more personal. From your research and the long list of bombings do you recall the bombs exploded in Coleraine in June of 1973, Father?"

"Oh yes. A deadly IRA bombing. Caused the UDA to respond by creating the cover name Ulster Freedom Fighters to insulate the UDA from its violent actions. Coleraine was where you periodically met with your grandfather to exchange your reconfigured two-way radios with a new supply from your grandfather."

"Correct. Doing just that on Tuesday the 12th of June, the day of that terrible bombing. A sunny day. Granda and I arrived in Coleraine by train as usual. Over lunch I was pouring out my dissatisfaction over the way the IRA was waging war with bombings. Killing civilians sickened me. Much like what I've been relating to you, Father. Leading up to telling him that my covert activities would soon come to an end. Needed to focus on my studies to complete my degree from QUB. Planning on leaving Belfast by the end of the year. Need to return to Boston to find employment." Kelly then paused for a moment as if gathering his thoughts experiencing that day so long ago.

"You were there the day the bombs exploded?" O'Brien.

Terence nodded. "A bad day for everyone. Mostly for the citizens of Coleraine. That they were mostly of Protestant heritage was irrelevant. As for me, I was scared out of my wits. Not about dying but being caught. Imagine us sitting there at the pub talking about bombings when all hell breaks loose. My grandfather and I have virgin two-way radios along with those modified to radio detonators stashed in train station lockers. Arrest meant life imprisonment if convicted since the UK abolished capital punishment. For Granda, with his IRA history and me as his grandson, we would surely become infamous assuring conviction. For Northern Ireland Catholics convicted of murders committed by acts of terrorism, prison became nothing more than suffering a brutalized protracted death. Let me then tell you about my experiences that summer in Coleraine. The first-hand details will enliven your written account, Father."

CHAPTER 16

Coleraine, Northern Ireland | June 1973

On Tuesday 12 June 1973, Terence boarded the train to Coleraine to meet his grandfather. He was delivering his latest group of radio detonating triggering systems. Expecting his grandfather to give him another quantity of walkie-talkies for conversion, he intended to tell his grandfather those would be the last he would produce. More than that, he would announce his plans to leave Northern Ireland and return to Boston by the end of the year.

Arriving earlier than Terence, Liam Kelly was seated outside near the platform as Terence stepped down from the train carrying a duffle bag. Approaching Terence they embraced, "Doin' well, Terry?"

"Getting by, Granda."

"Let's get your bag into a locker and have a spot of lunch," Liam said.

After placing Terence's bag in a locker, Liam pocketed the key and gave Terence another locker key from a different jacket pocket. That locker held another duffle bag with unmodified walkie-talkies. This was their normal exchange practice. Always the first thing they did upon arrival. Possession of either the unmodified walkie-talkies or the modified detonating was dangerous. They would then spend a precious couple of hours together before taking their respective trains back to Derry and Belfast, retrieving the duffle bags just prior to boarding.

They made their way as usual to the *Railway Arms* pub across the street from the small train station depot. Since they periodically made this trip to meet to Coleraine and frequented the *Railway Arms,* Liam created an appropriate cover. Coleraine was a Protestant town. Better to establish a cover fitting into that cultural demographic.

Liam portrayed himself as a retired pub owner from the predominately Protestant Waterside district of Derry. In conversations with the barman at the *Railway Arms* on the first trip to Coleraine to meet Terence, Liam introduced himself as Brendon Stewart and his grandson Terence Stewart. *"Retired long ago now living outside of Derry on a small farm with my son and his wife. Raising sheep. Terence is my grandson. Studies engineering at Queen's University in Belfast. Trains up here to Coleraine to have lunch and a couple of pints with me when he can spare the time from his studies. Proud of the lad. Smart and hard working. Holds a job to support himself while going to college. Goin' to make a successful professional career for himself."*

As usual they took a table away from the bar where they could talk without being overheard. Once seated with their beers, Terence began by saying, "Got some weighty things to discuss, Granda. To begin with, this new batch of walkie-talkies you brought will the last ones I'll be modifying. Let me explain why.

"Last time we met you could see that I was upset. I began making these detonators because I wanted to help support the Irish cause. Your cause. The IRA cause. Wanted a way to work alongside you. Wasn't about to officially join the IRA. Don't believe you'd have allowed that."

"Right you are there, Terry. You'd stick out like a nun at a brothel. Boston accent pegs you as Irish American. Besides, just being known as IRA by other members would place you at risk. Even I avoided ever officially joining the Provisional IRA. My past made me too well known. The other reason is the constant concern of informers within the IRA. Infiltrated spies or those arrested then coerced by the RUC to give up information."

Terence continued with his difficult announcement by further explaining his decision. "As a military force fighting a guerrilla war, I figured improvised explosives must become the weapon of choice for the IRA. Obviously that's proven to be the case. Problem is they're fixed more on indiscriminate bombing of the wrong targets. They're killing civilians not the real enemy. They should be going after loyalist paramilitaries, the RUC, the Army, especially economic targets. This is not how you waged war against the British in the War of Independence. You attacked Royal Irish Constabulary barracks, ambushed the hated Black & Tans and RIC Auxiliaries, even British Army regular soldiers. You yourself worked with Michael Collins assassinating covert British intelligence agents in Dublin. Civilians died at the hands of the British not the IRA in your war, Granda."

"Can't argue with you there, Terry. Like you, I wish the IRA would take on proper targets. Every war is different though. This one included. Far different than the War of Independence fifty years ago in the South. That was strictly about forcing the British out of Ireland. The civilian population overwhelmingly supported the IRA in that struggle. Not the same situation in Northern Ireland. This is more a civil rights fight for the minority Catholic population under the thumb of a repressive colonial government backed by London. Yet IRA military strategy might be moving in the direction you suggest. The London bombings in March might be a start."

"There you are. The bombs planted there didn't even use my radio detonators. I thought the advantages of being able to detonate bombs remotely from a safe distance at the precisely desired time would logically lead to going after the more difficult targets of armed security forces. Targets minimizing collateral civilian casualties not alienating the Catholic population. The world sees the IRA as nothing more than terrorists. Not because of their cause but because of their methods. I too have begun seeing it that way."

"The IRA has changed nothing about selecting bombing targets. The Belfast bombings in Belfast in July proved that. More disappointing, those bombs may have used my radio detonators. I say that because so many bombs were exploded in such a narrow time frame. Yet elsewhere the IRA still relies on inferior means of detonation. Look what happen in Newry. A premature detonation killed the three IRA bombers while killing six civilians. From this I conclude that my radio detonators have made no difference in changing to more strategic targets.

"But that doesn't matter anymore. I've decided that I can no longer continue making devices used to explode bombs that kill civilians. I've got blood on my hands that I can't feel right about. Tell me how the IRA is any different from other politically violent organizations in the world? The PLO in Palestine, the Red Brigades in Italy, the Basque separatist ETA in Spain. The world labels them terrorist organizations because they primarily kill civilians."

Liam nodded in understanding. "Don't want to debate our struggle by comparing to different struggles in the world. Yet I've been fighting British domination of Ireland all my life. Might disagree with current IRA tactics but I can't influence changes. Today in Northern Ireland there's no middle ground. No standing neutral. Either you are nationalist or loyalist. Given only those two choices, I must stand with the nationalists. That means Irish Catholics. Their civil rights are so severely denied that it alone is the best argument for Irish nationalism.

"Partitioning the northern six counties in 1922 to remain under British rule left those of us from Ulster worse off than before the War of Independence. During that war, the British and their regional government in Belfast violently fell upon the Catholic population in the North. Between 1920 and 1922 Belfast suffered what some call Catholic pogroms. Not unlike the Jewish pogroms of that time in Russia. In Belfast 500 people were killed. Another 500 interned in prison without trail. 23,000 made homeless. 50,000 Catholics fled Ulster. A desired exodus for the racist Protestant loyalist majority population to increase their segregated domination.

"I'm not at all arguing against your feelings, Terry. Just needed you to know my deepest motivations for what I'm involved in."

Liam put his hand on Terence's shoulder and squeezed affectionately.

Terence smiled in return. "There's more, Granda. I'm also concerned about eventually coming under suspicion. My radio devices have undoubtedly been used. That means the probability of British intelligence conducting an intensive investigation. Unlike the IRA, they might recognize the tactical potential should my wireless radio signal detonators become widely adopted. Although having left Comet, I cannot erase having been there working on commercial walkie-talkies. I'm still worried that I might get a knock on my door. Anyway, I'm planning on leaving Northen Ireland by the end of this year. Need just the fall semester to complete my academic work."

Liam nodded with a weak smile. "A wise move, Terry. I suspect things will only worsen in Northern Ireland. As careful as we've been, there is always some risk. If you were to ever get that knock on your door it would be too late. Discovery of your real name, masquerading under a different name as a Protestant, and your relationship to me would condemn you."

"Glad you understand, Granda. Don't want you to feel that I'm letting you down. Here's the schematic and component specifications for the modifications made to both the transmitter and receiver units. Find some Irishman in America with electronics expertise committed to the cause to modify commercial walkie-talkies. Might even be able to make improvements to my design. Something I might have done had I not lost enthusiasm. Anyway, I'll fulfill my commitment at least to modify this batch of radios sitting in the locker. Give me a few weeks and I'll return them to you here in Coleraine."

Liam said, "Hope that won't be the last time I see you before you return to Boston."

"Oh no. Want to say a proper goodbye before I leave. Maybe you and Grandma could come together to Coleraine just before Christmas. This is safe Protestant territory where both of us have created the allusion of being Protestant. The *Railway Arms* feels like a familiar place where you and I have been able to share a few hours occasionally. Grandma will like it. Food's not fancy but good. Speaking of food, shall we have some lunch?"

As they settled into large bowls of the pub's stew, Terence felt relieved. Granda did not appear disappointed. Maybe even relieved. Probably worried more about him than he let on. This was the perfect way out of what had become a regrettable misadventure since coming to Northern Ireland. He could bury what he had done with only his beloved grandfather ever knowing the truth. Grandma likely did not know, but that would not matter. He satisfied his professed reason given to his parents for coming to Northern Ireland. Earned a post graduate degree, useful on a resume if successful in explaining the different names on his academic degrees. Once back in Boston he could begin putting the consequences of what he did in better perspective.

That morning, members of an Active Service Unit of the South Derry Provisional IRA stole two cars from South County Londonderry. ASUs consisted of IRA field operatives that engaged in violent actions. Both vehicles were then packed with ammonium-nitrate fuel oil bombs rigged with timed fuses attached to sticks of gelignite to act as boost detonators for the ANFO. Driving to the north of the county not far from the scenic northern coastline of Northern Ireland, they stopped in the outskirts of the city of Coleraine, population 50,000 in 1973 of which 75% identified as Protestant heritage. At 2:30 pm, the telephone exchange received a call warning about bombs placed on Hanover Place and Society Street. Unfortunately, Society Street turned out not to be the correct location.

Minutes before 3:00 pm a Ford Cortina driven by Sean McGlinchey became confused by the one-way traffic system in Coleraine. Having already primed the bomb for detonation with a short timing fuse he was forced to abandon the car on Railway

Road in front of a wine shop. At 3:00 a bomb consisting of over 100 pounds of high-explosive ammonium-nitrate and fuel oil exploded. Six pensioners, four women and two men, were killed and 33 other people injured, including several schoolchildren. Some of the injured suffered horrific injuries leaving them maimed or disabled for life.

Sitting in the *Railway Arms* enjoying their beer after lunch, Liam and Terence were jolted by the nearby blast. Bottles toppled from behind the bar. Rushing outside everyone looked south further down Railway Road to a scene of terrible devastation. Windows blown out, the wine shop in flames, bodies scattered about. The *Railway Arms* was located at No. 53 Railway Road. The Wine Market where the car bomb exploded was located just south at No. 18 Railway Road only 200 yards away.

Both Liam and Terence hurried toward the scene of the blast. Getting closer a ghastly sight became apparent. Destroyed bodies laid within enlarging pools of blood. Body parts torn from some scattered about.

Five minutes later a second bomb less than a half mile away exploded on Hanover Place near the river. While causing no casualties, it added to the fear and confusion as people waited in terror for further explosions.

On Railway Road, Terence stood transfixed looking at victims. Unlike observing the aftermath of the *Bloody Friday* bombings in Belfast, the carnage in Coleraine was immediate and deeply personal. Bodies and body parts freshly torn apart.

After several minutes, Liam pulled his arm, "Best we get back to the train station. What time does your train leave?" Terence did not immediately respond. "Terry, what time?"

Looking at his watch, Terence replied, "Three-thirty."

"Good. We get back to the station and you get on the train before this place becomes overrun with police."

"What about you, Granda?"

"I'll be fine. Going to wander off to distance myself further away from Railway Road. Maybe spend the night with someone I know that lives here. Tomorrow morning I'll place a call to Derry and arrange for someone to drive up and take me back home. Only an hour's drive from here. Best that I retrieve the devices you brought when things settle down after a couple of days."

Hours after the explosions, police and emergency personnel were still conducting investigations while efforts at clearing the debris on Railway Road began. Within the train station there appeared no unusual police activity. As his train arrived, Terence retrieved his duffle bag with a new supply of walkie-talkies just before stepping up into the train carriage. He placed the duffle bag in the baggage area. It carried no identification. Should police discover it in a search, it would not identify him as the owner. Although just commercial walkie-talkies, why so many being transported in an unmarked piece of luggage might still provoke questioning of every passenger in the carriage by security personnel. Tense minutes passed before the train departed on schedule.

Within days, loyalist UDA paramilitaries set in motion retaliatory attacks against Northern Ireland Catholics. Using their alternative cover identification as the Ulster Freedom Fighters, gunmen set out to avenge the murder of the six pensioners in Coleraine and the maiming of many schoolchildren.

UFF members kidnapped a 17-year-old in Catholic Andersonstown Belfast and killed him with a shot to the back of the head. The following day the body of a 25-year-old Catholic was found at Corr's Corner near the Belfast-Larne Road. The UFF claimed responsibility for throwing a bomb into a North Belfast Catholic pub. Two weeks after the Coleraine bombing the UFF stabbed to death a prominent Catholic politician and his Protestant woman friend. The viciously mutilated bodies were discovered in a quarry off Hightown Road in North Belfast.

CHAPTER 17

Belfast, Northern Ireland | July 1973

Witnessing the gore of mangled human bodies and dismembered bodies parts closeup in Coleraine made an overpowering impression on Terence. Regardless of how graphic, no photographs could ever convey the sense of revulsion standing within feet of mangled victims. Far worse those of children. This was no accidental disaster. Civilians senselessly murdered for no reason other than being of a different social category. Nothing distinguished the Northern Ireland population except by an arbitrary classification based on centuries-old cultural-religious heritage.

A regional government originating from legacy colonial rule by Great Britain corrupted with institutionalized oppression of Catholics in Northern Ireland since the 17th century. So deeply entrenched nothing in the current century pointed to possible change. Quite the contrary, it was only through violent revolt that the counties comprising the Republic of Ireland eventually shook off British rule fifty years earlier. Catholics in this last British colonial-governed territory of ancient Ulster could never hope for change through parliamentary process.

The origin of Catholic oppression went back four hundred to what became known as the *Ulster Planation.* A colonization effort by King James I to establish British Protestant domination of the region. The objective was to displace native Irish Gaelic landowners by giving English and Scottish colonials half a million acres of the best appropriated arable land. The result was a legacy of ethnic division exacerbated by strident religious differences of that earlier time. This was only a hundred years after Henry VIII broke with the Roman Catholic Church during the Protestant Reformation that diminished Roman Catholic hegemony across Europe. That legacy of sharp social division never dissipated over time in Ireland ruled by Great Britian.

Events of the 20th century only sharpened hostilities. Given the minority status of Catholics with partition of Ireland in 1922, the northern six counties that became Northern Ireland remaining part of Great Britain. Protestants held a two-thirds population majority. That led to Protestant domination at every level of government by subverting every fundamental precept of the representative democratic process to ensure Protestant loyalist control over an oppressed minority.

For Terence, all that he experienced since coming to Northern Ireland did not diminish the righteousness of the reason for rebellion, nor the resorting to violence by the IRA. His problem lay in the blind barbarity that only led to the same response from security forces and their allied loyalist paramilitaries. Both sides killing civilians along religious demographic lines. For Terence, who harbored no religious feelings, this seemed logically absurd. A western supposedly democratic country dividing into opposing sides, differing only by historical circumstances spanning centuries. Nothing about Irish sectarian violence related to differences over religious observance. *Catholic* or *Protestant* was only a socio-economic-political label of convenience. Everyone racially looked the same and spoke a common language.

Sickened by the experiences of civilian casualties from IRA bombings in 1972 and personal confrontation with the mass bloodshed in Coleraine left Terence with no choice but to plan leaving Northern Ireland. There was no life for him to be had here. However, he would fulfill his promise to his grandfather to reconfigure this last batch of walkie-talkies. Upholding his relationship with his beloved grandfather overrode his own conscience demanding he immediately cease assisting in bomb making. Maybe the IRA would eventually come around to going after proper enemy targets, the true enemies with guns backed by a racist provincial government. However, he had no interest in living his life in Northern Ireland.

By the end of the semester in May he completed all the course work required for his master's degree. This now allowed him to devote all his efforts toward working on his thesis. Even during his new night job at the radio station, he often had uninterrupted free time to devote to the thesis. It involved designing a new technical approach for advancing radio communications. Advances in integrated circuitry made a theoretical approach possible. Possibly original enough to have commercial significance. Enough for his academic advisory committee to have given advance approval for the thesis subject. The theoretical concept protocol therefore was deemed to have merit if he could devise a workable circuit design capable of achieving expected results.

Among the challenges he faced was devising the necessary microprocessor program to accomplish the complex switching involved. Even then, how could he deliver acceptable proof of the theory as a practical concept rather than just theoretical? Constructing a functional prototype might be necessary to accomplish that. That might prove a daunting undertaking involving the emerging technology of digital computing.

Even though the utility of the post graduate degree might be compromised because of the name Stewart instead of Kelly, it represented a worthy personal achievement. Enough to cause him to remain in Belfast a while longer. Freed from the burden of engaging in dangerous covert activities, four months should be sufficient time to complete the work unless his fundamental ideas proved flawed. In that case, he would still leave Northern Ireland.

Putting Northern Ireland behind him and returning to familiar normality consumed his thoughts. Maybe in time the dark side of what he did would fade into buried memory. Begin a professional life in Boston. Everything put in order explained by his two-and-a-half-year adventure as just that, an adventure.

Part of growing into maturity. Not a youthful mistake of hubris. Seemingly to his family, a successful outcome given he funded advancing his education through earning money with a second job in a foreign country. Only his grandfather knew of his active involvement in the violence of those early years of the *Troubles*. With the eventual passing of his grandfather, his secret should be forever buried.

These thoughts consumed Terence for the less than two-hour train ride from Coleraine to Belfast Grand Central. His thoughts focused more on concerns that his grandfather left Coleraine and returned to Derry without incident. The following morning Liam answered his telephone call at the apartment. Relieved, Terence asked, "Made it home safely?"

Liam replied, "No problems. You doin' okay?"

Terence as usual was calling from a public telephone. "Good as can be expected. Seeing such things can change you."

"Focus on what you can control, my boy. Can't be changing the unpleasantness in this world."

Terence replied in a tone of profound sadness, "Don't need to be adding any further unpleasantness either. Hard to see that things aren't headed for a very long conflict. Read in the newspaper that Gerry Adams was just rearrested. Reinterned in Maze Prison."

"Yes, I read that too. Adams is the foremost political spokesman for Sinn Féin and therefore the IRA. Putting him back in lockup doesn't bode well for any possible resumption of peace talks.

Terence followed their security protocol to avoid saying anything that might compromise him by revealing his relationship to Liam should security forces be monitoring Liam's telephone. Liam Kelly had a notorious past. Terence Stewart did not exist. He ended the call unable to make any expression of endearment. "Be seeing you soon. Will call you in advance. Take good care."

Coleraine pushed Terence into a period of depression. Having started his new job, it was all he could do to get through several weeks of familiarization with his responsibilities sufficiently to work by himself as the only technician during the nighttime hours. Busying himself by immersion into commercial radio transmitting equipment at least provided diversion. Once on his own starting at 9:00 pm until relieved at 6:00 am, his work consisted of completing work orders for repairs and equipment installation. He welcomed the solitude.

During the daytime hours he became reclusive, devoting his few non- sleeping hours to working on his thesis project. Declining invitations from his friends Duncan and Henry by his conflicting work hours with their normal daytime jobs during the summer break of classes was easier than trying to be sociable. He liked both Duncan and Henry, but the friendship would soon end when he left Belfast. Known to them as Terence Stewart, carrying on a long-distance correspondence when returning to Boston was ill-advised. To bury the circumstances of his time in Northern Ireland required making a complete break. Duncan and Henry must be abandoned no different than Maureen Lynch.

Granda and Grandma would not likely live beyond the next decade. Once they passed, then what personally transpired in Northern Ireland became relegated only in his memory. Time might heal those emotional scars as the cliché said.

Duncan and Henry refused to continue taking no for an answer with his excuses about his nighttime job or working days on his master's thesis. However, locking himself away did not completely allow concentrating on work to dispel a latent anxiety. A gnawing sense of dread that at any time there could come a knock on his door continually intruded into his thoughts. Or the door smashed open then being hauled away. Graphic depictions of the physical maltreatment inflicted on suspects by the RUC or Army made his skin crawl. While knowing that at some point his radio detonators would be discovered, he imagined how he might be possibly discovered regardless of his precautions.

Terence finally relented to his friends. He had weekends off from Belfast 2BE radio station. Late on a Saturday afternoon he was to meet Duncan and Henry at a new pub in East Belfast just across the river. The *Raven Pub* was located on Ravenhill Road deep in loyalist territory. Not far from Ormeau Road where he previously worked at Comet Electronics. The pub was located just a short distance south of Albert Bridge.

Terence arrived at five o'clock. The pub was crowded but Duncan and Henry were already seated at a small table. Immediately he was glad he agreed to join them. The atmosphere felt like his grandfather's pub. Typically Irish. Lots of wood. Smells of food mixed with beer and spirits. The place where the Irish found social comfort even during the worst of times. Made no difference whether the patrons were Catholic or Protestant. The only distinction came when conversation turned political.

Spotting Terence, Duncan waved him over and they all shook hands. "Glad you could break away to join us, mate. About time you relaxed. You've become a fucking recluse since you took that night job at the radio station."

Henry said, "It's summer. No more classes for any of us. Time for livin' a little, Terence."

As Terence raised a hand to get the attention of a particularly attractive young waitress, he said, "Fine for you fellows. I completed all my course work for my master's this last semester, but I've still got my thesis project to worry about. Want to complete it by Christmas."

"Then what, Terence? Get a real job? What sort of position would suit you?" Henry asked.

The waitress interrupted. Terence looked up and locked eyes with her. Long dark hair, exceptionally dark eyes. A face of classical beauty. Trim shapely body. "What'll you be havin', Sir?"

"You don't have to address him as Sir, Adele. He's just a student like all of us," Henry said. "This beautiful young woman is Adele Thompson. And this bloke, Adele, is Terence Stewart."

Adele smiled, "Pleased to meet you, Terence. What'll you be having?"

"A pint of Guiness, if you please."

Henry said, "Adele here is also a student at Queen's. Her father owns the pub. What is it again you're studying Adele?"

"English literature. Humanities department. One more year to complete my undergraduate degree."

"Ah yes. Adele can quote all manner of appropriate lines from Shakespeare. Give us an example will you, Adele?" Henry said.

Adele gave Henry a friendly sigh of resignation. *"O, speak to me no more. These words like daggers enter in mine ears."* Hamlet, act 3, scene 4. For those of you that are unread in classical literature, a more sophisticated way of saying *keep your gob shut."* With a smile, she added, "I can quote further if you like?"

The three men laughed. "Ever hear a waitress quote Shakespeare in a pub, Terence?" Henry asked.

Terence replied, "Most impressive. I apologize for my unsophisticated friends here, Adele."

"No need. I've learned to ignore them. Now, your accent says you're Irish yet from somewhere other than Belfast."

"You're correct. Grew up in America. Boston. Born here in Belfast though. My family emigrated when I was very young. Came back to the old country for the first time. Using the opportunity to stay longer by studying for my master's degree in engineering."

"Oh, my. That's grand. Glad Duncan and Henry brought you here this evening." Looking at Duncan and Henry, "Do you two want another round?"

"That we do," Henry replied. As Adele turned and walked toward the bar, he sighed watching her shapely behind in tight jeans then said to Terence, "Adele's a real looker for someone so smart."

Terence was clearly taken by Adele Thompson. He liked women and women liked him. He recalled his past relationships fondly. Maureen Lynch being the glaring exception. Looking at Adele Thompson made him realize how out of character his seclusion and enforced celibacy was since coming to Belfast. With his misadventure of making bomb detonators soon to end perhaps his last months in Northern Ireland might be different.

Adele appeared self-assured and intellectual. A far cry from obsessive Maureen. The sex with Maureen might have been initially exciting but dealing with her controlling nature and manic mood swings was too much. No choice other than to cut short the relationship. Looking at Adele brought a feeling of wellbeing not experienced for a very long time.

Terence's relaxed mood carried through the entire evening. Interrupting their drinking, they ordered dinner enjoying the pleasant atmosphere of the many other patrons. The congeniality of Irish pubs as a social place for even families made everyone feel welcome. His grandfather's pub in Derry felt the same. Irish bars in South Boston did not always exhibit the same atmosphere found in the old country.

As the evening wore on, Terence and his two friends decidedly showed signs of too much alcohol. Adele then surprised them by coming over with a cup of coffee in hand and sitting down at the table. "I'm done for the night. Looks like the three of you should also be calling it a night.

Terence said, "Got that right, Adele. I'll get myself a cup of coffee. How 'bout you guys?"

Duncan said, "No thanks. Time to settle our tab and call it a night."

Terence said, "I'll take care of the bill. My thanks for encouraging me to come along with you. It's been a wonderful evening," turning to smile at Adele.

Duncan and Henry took their cues to leave Terence alone with Adele. Obviously the two of them had become very friendly.

Sharing coffee with Adele was a perfect ending to the evening.

She asked, "What brought you to Belfast to enroll at Queen's University?"

Terence recited his well-rehearsed narrative used for employers, his landlord, Duncan, and Henry. "South Boston is an Irish town. Everyone speaks of relatives still living in Ireland. My mum's family came from Belfast, my father's family came from Coleraine." Terence chose Coleraine instead of Derry because it was predominantly Protestant, yet he avoided delving more deeply into family background.

"I had elderly grandparents on my father's side still living in Coleraine when I decided to make my first visit to the old country. I had just graduated with my bachelor's degree in engineering. That was two years ago. Planned to spend the summer but the thought stuck me, why not stay longer? Since I held dual American and British citizenship having been born here, I was accepted at QUB to pursue a post-graduate degree. Less costly for tuition and preferential enrollment compared with universities in the United States. Completed my course studies for my master's degree just last semester. The degree requires a thesis. Working now on that. If that is successful, should complete everything for the degree by the end of the year."

"Do you have many close relatives in Northern Ireland?"

"Not really. My mum's parents died years ago. My paternal grandfather in Coleraine died a year ago. Unfortunately, my grandmother resides in a nursing home in Coleraine. Suffers from declining memory difficulties. Haven't had any contact with my few scattered cousins."

"What field of engineering are you studying?"

"Electrical engineering. More specifically, electronics. Things involving control circuitry. Communications, radio, and television. That's how I landed a technician position at BBC radio station 2BE."

Adele said, "Maybe you'll stay on in Belfast in spite of all the terrible goings on. That's wonderful to combine furthering your education while taking the opportunity to experience your heritage. Regrettably, this growing political violence must be distressing."

"Certainly distressing. But hasn't that always been the fate of Ireland? I do my best to focus on my studies. I'm now consumed with the challenge of completing something original for my thesis. Working nights at the radio station leaves little time for agonizing over this recurring violence."

Adele added, "Unfortunately, Ulster has seen nothing but violence throughout the twentieth century. Those in the south now live in peace. Northern Ireland has always been more complicated. Finding a different path forward to peace seems so very far off."

Terence was not certain what Adele's last comment revealed about her political views, but he wanted to avoid any political discussion. His long-nurtured feelings about Irish republicanism although compromised by the IRA resorting to terrorist tactics had not been completely abandoned. He must remain vigilant to avoid that deep-seated ideology to resurface.

His attraction to Adele Thompson overrode any ethnic background differences. A Protestant background did not necessarily mean fervent loyalist. Now stuck in this contrived alternative identity, he just wanted to find internal peace and get on with his life.

"Couldn't agree more, Adele. Although Irish, I'm also American. Don't have the background to hold strong political views since I did not grow up in Belfast. However, bombings and shootings can never lead to an equitable settlement for the entire population. That's the only way that Northern Ireland can ever experience peace."

"Well expressed, Terence. Now I must also be calling it a night. Will I be seeing you again?"

"Absolutely. When do you work at the pub?"

"During the summer with no classes, Thursday through Monday from three in the afternoon until we close. When classes resume in September, usually I work only the busy Saturday and Sunday evenings."

"Wonderful. I work nights during the weekdays from nine at night to early the following morning, but I have Saturdays and Sundays off. How about I stop by here at the pub next Saturday around nine o'clock in the morning? We can rent bicycles and spend the day at the nearby park by the river. We'll get some sandwiches and have a picnic then get you back to the pub by three o'clock to go to work."

She smiled warmly. "Sounds lovely. If it's a rainy day then perhaps we can instead spend a couple of hours at the Ulster Museum near the university. I'll see you next Saturday, Terence."

The following day after the evening at the *Raven Pub,* Terence reluctantly resumed working on conversion of the remaining walkie-talkies into bomb detonating triggers. Although his heart was no longer in the task he would fulfill the commitment made to his grandfather.

Soon after *Bloody Friday* the previous year, he took to hiding the two-way radios from sight. The only place possible was the attic. Access was in what had been the second-floor hallway before the owners converted one of the two bedrooms into a small kitchen and living area. The hinged door to the attic was now located in the kitchen ceiling.

Converted to an apartment, the owners no longer used the attic for storage. After moving in, Terence had opened the access door while standing on a chair and peered inside with a flashlight. Nothing was visible except for a wooden ladder laying on the floor. Plywood covered the ceiling joists affording flooring covering half the attic. Fiberglass insulation between the ceiling joists was visible in those areas not covered by plywood.

The unmounted ladder was apparently available for infrequent use requiring some other means of reaching it by hand to pull into position to ascend into the attic. It was by pulling away insulation from the exposed areas between the ceiling joists that he hid both unmodified and modified sets of walkie-talkies along with components required for conversion to radio detonators. Placing the contraband under the plywood flooring then replacing the insulation left the area appearing untouched. Awkward accessibility and not secure should police ever conduct a thorough search, it nonetheless provided adequate visual concealment from simply opening the ceiling access door.

As for the small assortment of electronic tools and measuring instruments, these easily fit within a toolbox left in plain sight in the apartment. Explainable as an electronics engineer working on his graduate degree thesis. Arguably necessary for conducting empirical testing of circuitry. Proof of that existed with pages of annotated schematics and solderless breadboards populated with components in support of his thesis abstract defining the project in technical detail.

CHAPTER 18

Belfast, Northern Ireland | July 1973

July became a turning point for Terence. He felt a sense of mixed emotions about the events of the last twelve months. Fervor for his sense of Irish nationalism fostered by his relationship with his grandfather became far more complicated. A maturity acquired with examining how that ideal was being expressed in the much different socio-political environment of Northern Ireland. Nothing at all comparable to how he thought of events from the time of the Anglo-Irish War that eventually led to Irish independence from Great Britian for the southern twenty-six counties.

He still harbored resentment toward the British. The British created a monster in the evolution of retaining Northern Ireland. Its colonialization gave rise to the regional government that either feared or simply chose to oppress a third of the population. However, for Terence, he could no longer actively support IRA tactics by directly contributing to the wholesale killing of noncombatant civilians. Now putting that put behind him still left his thoughts unsettled about his Irish heritage.

Yet for those same feelings, he could not deny the seemingly incompatible feeling of accomplishment of having contributed to his Irish identity in a material way. Honored the exploits of his grandfather by volunteering for this fight. Granda's understanding of his reluctance to not continue further. In effect, bestowing his blessing for his grandson's comradery.

Terence reflected that his grandfather's understanding may have come from his own experience. Liam Kelly did not agree with the terms of the 1922 Treaty that partitioned Northern Ireland from the Irish Free State. However, he chose not to continue the conflict that became the Irish Civil War fought between opposing IRA veterans. Liam chose not to make war against former comrades in a useless fight. Terence chose not to continue involvement in killing any more civilians.

He also felt a rewarding accomplishment to have somehow forged ahead amidst difficult distractions to earn a post graduate degree. Returning to Boston in a few months with the prospect of getting on with a normal life a much-welcomed expectation. Better off for having experienced and survived a life-changing experience.

However, he selfishly chose to ignore the ramifications of his developing feelings for Adele Thompson. When would tell her of his plans to leave Belfast at the end of the year? Should the relationship become something more, would he stay in Belfast? That seemed unwise. His radio detonators were still out there. Danger of being discovered remained a possibility. Adele following him to Boston was out of the question. How could he explain concealing living under two different identities? A long-term relationship with Adele seemed impossible. Morally, he should not pursue the relationship further.

Yet he did not possess the moral strength to do the right thing. Dwelling on the problem he unrealistically believed he might find a solution. Therefore, he again took the easy way out. Let things play out. Their attraction had yet to transform into a serious relationship. Quit agonizing over circumstances that could not be changed. Fatalistically, just gave in to living in the moment with disregard for the consequences.

On the last Saturday in July, Terence and Adele celebrated a sunny summer day by renting bicycles and roaming through the vast Ormeau Park that stretched between Ravenhill Road and the east bank of the River Lagan. Adele had brought along sandwiches and sodas for a picnic lunch. They had until three o'clock in the afternoon when Adele must get to the pub for the busy Saturday night crowd.

The park was peaceful, full of trees with a large enough expanse to not feel crowded. Children played and dogs ran about enjoying the perfect summer day. An atmosphere of normality. The park seemed like an oasis. However, life in Belfast was anything but normal. The expectation of violence never far from anyone's thoughts.

Sitting on a blanket eating lunch, Adele asked, "What's the subject of your master's thesis?"

"It's actually a design project. Titled, *Advanced Channel Queuing Protocol for Packet Switching.* Technical paper titles usually sound incomprehensible for those outside the field. Packet switching is a newly created method of transferring electronic data more efficiently. Wireless communications like radio or hardwired communications. I already received approval for pursuing my project protocol theory that suggests it has technical merit provided I can devise a practical solution."

"Sounds deeply technical. Why the name *packet switching*?"

"The concept involves moving electronic data in packets, groupings of data, rather than a single transmission that occupies the entire channel bandwidth until completion. Data packets allow for maximizing the bandwidth load carrying capability by allowing multiple transmission traffic to simultaneously use a communications channel. The protocol differs from circuit switching that uses a fixed path between two points for the duration of a single transmission. Packet switching routs data packets through independent paths. These packets then travel over a shared network using variable bandwidths with different routings with the data packets arriving at different intervals. The challenge becomes reassembling the data fragments into the original intelligible message."

"Good grief. I have no idea what that all means."

"Forgive me for rambling on. Engineers can do that."

"Quite alright. I can see your enthusiasm. "How does your idea contribute to this technology?"

"Well, it involves what I believe might be a new protocol for improving dynamic bandwidth allocation efficiency. Hard to explain without getting even deeper into technical mathematics, but it could be commercially important if my theoretical concept proves practical."

"Sounds impressive. How'd you get into this area of electronics?"

"Started out when in high school. I became involved with amateur radio. Had my own amateur radio license. An impressive setup in my bedroom in Boston. Able to communicate all over the world with other radio enthusiasts. That led to studying electrical engineering in college. When I came to Belfast to pursue my master's degree in electronics, the engineering school at QUB had a newly acquired PDP-11 computer made by Digital Equipment just outside of Boston. Had some experience with the same computer at my undergraduate university in Boston. I took a couple of advanced courses that got me interested with how computer technology could be used in radio. That eventually led to hitting upon the subject for my required master's thesis."

"Impressive. Working now at a radio station does that suggest where you're your professional career might be headed?"

Terence did not want to venture into talking about the future. "Maybe. But computer technology opens up all sorts of possibilities. But enough about me. Tell me about your field of study. Can't say that I'm very well read. Tend to read mystery novels mostly. Dashiell Hammett's Sam Spade books. Raymond Chandler's Philip Marlowe character. That sort of stuff. I also enjoy film noir movies like Humphrey Bogart in *The Maltese Falcon* and *The Big Sleep*."

"Nothing wrong with that. I enjoy a wide range of writing. My love for classical literature is an acquired taste. Takes a bit of effort to delve deeply enough to discover why such writing has endured for hundreds of years. For me it's what I call the texture of the writing. Some indefinable combination of word choice, syntax, and structure of sentence and paragraph. Easier to explain by the result when it works for the reader. Speaking more about fiction, it's about the conveying of emotion, the painting of a mental image of characters against a background of time and place. Simply the ability of the author to draw the reader into his or her creation."

Terence said, "Wow! That's some explanation. Sounds as technical as my field of study. I remember required reading of Shakespeare from high school. Like everyone, I struggled with grasping the old English. Made for slow reading. Often difficult to understand. How's that different for you?"

"Not sure I can explain. Partly practice I guess. When you get into Shakespeare his language takes on the expressive quality of poetry. At least for me it does. It partly breaks down to learning new words, or familiar words used in a different context. Gets easier as you read more Shakespeare. I also took two years of French. Reading the old English used by Shakespeare and his contemporaries like Christopher Marlowe and Ben Jonson is somewhat like reading a foreign language in which you are familiar but not entirely fluent. With practice you become accustomed to the unique qualities of the language.

"But for me, it's far more than the beauty of how Shakespeare expresses his stories. His characters are well drawn and fit perfectly into the storyline of his plays. Like any great writer, some of Shakespeare's plays are better than others. He wrote plays to make money through theatrical performances. Sometimes economic demands overshadowed his literary genius."

Adele's intellectual faculties were impressive. He had never met a woman like Adele Thompson. Physically as attractive as Maureen Lynch but otherwise a completely opposite personality to the emotionally erratic Maureen. "Now it is me who is beyond understanding of your obvious expertise. I can see your admiration for the written word."

"I do love words. Writing opens the world to me. Places, people, all manner of differing philosophies. Couldn't see my life unless populated with books."

Their conversation continued with both absorbed by listening to the other. Neither of them wanted to cut short their time together on this glorious day but Adele needed to get to the pub by three o'clock. After returning their bicycles, they walked to the pub.

Standing outside the *Raven Pub,* Terence said, "A marvelous afternoon, Adele. Didn't want it to end. How about I come back tonight? I'll have a good dinner and maybe a whiskey or two. Then walk you home when you get off work."

Adele held his upper arm with a hand and pulled him closer. "I'd like that, Terry." She leaned in closer and gave him a lingering kiss on the lips before saying, "I'll see you this evening then."

Terence felt the emotional surge conveyed by her kiss. Pushed concerns of difficult decisions down the road. Enjoy the moment by reveling in their developing emotional connection.

Returning to the apartment, he set to work on the remaining walkie-talkie conversions. The last batch. To be delivered to his grandfather as soon as possible. By six o'clock he finished the last of the devices. A milestone now ridding himself of what became an unfortunate diversion be believed honored the legacy of his grandfather. Fulfilling an obligation to the person closest to his heart. Someone with whom he shared what he called a dark secret that nonetheless expressed their special relationship. Regardless of the regret over making bomb-related devices for the IRA, there existed a feeling of accomplishment. However, something better put behind him. Experience the remaining months in Northern Ireland as a bridge to the rest of his life. His youthful idealism and attraction to adventure replaced by the sobering realities acquired from experience.

Terence arrived back at the *Raven Pub* at seven o'clock that evening. The place was again full. He acknowledged Alfred

Thompson behind the bar with a nod of his head. Adele's father knew that his daughter was fond of the good looking Irish American Terence Stewart. Alfred liked him. Also approved of the smart young man dating his daughter as having excellent professional prospects. Liked the idea that being American he did not seem to possess strong political feelings about the situation in Northern Ireland. At least he did not come from a Catholic background. Adele was strong willed and cautious with men. He thought she could do worse than Terence Stewart.

As Terence entered the pub making his way to an empty seat at the bar, Adele gave him a warm smile. Alfred extended his hand across the bar, "Good evening, Terence. Good to see you. What'll it be?"

"Good evening to you, Sir. A pint of Guinness if you please. Thought I'd also treat myself to a good dinner this evening. Some of your excellent stew and bread sounds just right. Adele and I shared this fine summer day bicycling in the park. Dinner at the *Raven* rounds out a perfect day."

Around nine o'clock everything changed.

Crowded with patrons, the blast from a large explosion from outside the *Raven Pub* blew in the front door and damaged heavy shutters covering the large front windows. The shutters reduced some of the blast energy, but the window glass still shattered spreading shards throughout the interior. Bottles and the mirror behind the bar shattered.

Facing away from the blast with his back turned sitting at the bar, Terence was knocked from his bar stool onto the floor. Disoriented, he rose to his knees. With the power knocked out, the interior of the pub went dark. Women were crying. Those injured could be heard pleading for help or groaning in agony. Terence's thoughts turned to Adele. Yelling her name, he was joined by her father also calling out for her as he rose from the floor behind the bar.

Alfred Thompson flicked on a flashlight and began surveying the scene. Dust from the damaged interior filtered through the beam of the flashlight. A couple of men stood up. Everyone else lay about on the floor. The distance wail of sirens joined the distressed sounds of the injured against an otherwise eerie stillness.

From the back kitchen, Alfred's flashlight beam caught the face of his daughter emerging. Terence immediately saw her walking dazed and unsteady but appearing uninjured. Running to her they embraced to be joined by her father moments later.

Alfred said to Terence and Adele, "Start helping those that are uninjured outside. Don't move those badly injured. Grab some towels. Try to stop the bleeding of anyone seriously at risk of bleeding out."

Within thirty minutes fire and rescue personnel arrived and took charge of treating the casualties. Terence, Adele, and Alfred Thompson surveyed the scene from outside. A car bomb. Large enough to cut the vehicle in half with the intact front half laying on its side. The rear section consisted only of large pieces of scattered sheet metal. The bomb obviously located in the boot.

Alfred Thompson knew something like this could happen. This was solidly loyalist territory. If Terence's friend Duncan was correct, possibly even frequented by UVF paramilitaries. Alfred Thompson had taken precautions. Sandbags reinforced the lower three feet of the exterior walls below the windows. The windows had been covered by heavy wooden shutters. Now blown away with only one of the four hanging by a single hinge, it appeared they mitigated some of the blast force. The modifications intended as a blast barrier served that purpose. As a result, they prevented wholesale structural damage although the front portion of the roof suffered damage. Undoubtedly the precautions saved lives.

Three hours after the blast Terence watched as a tow truck lifted the remains of the engine half of the bomb vehicle onto a flatbread truck. Firefighters and police gathered debris from the destroyed car while searching for any forensic evidence of the bomb. Terence heard one officer call out, "Look for any small fragments of debris that could be from the car or even the pieces of the bomb." Terence immediately speculated of the possible irony if the bomb might have been triggered by one of his radio devices. Undoubtedly this was an IRA bombing.

A RUC constable came up to Alfred Thompson after all the injured were removed. "Glad to see you and your daughter are uninjured, Mr. Thompson."

Thompson just nodded. "How many casualties, Constable?"

"Fortunately, only one death. Older gentleman. Malcolm Greene. Took a piece of glass in the throat. Surprisingly only sixteen injured. Four look to have suffered severe injuries, however. Looks like your modifications helped limit the carnage."

"When I repair the damage I'll be more thorough," Thompson said. Turning to Terence, "Terence would you mind taking my car and driving Adele home? I've already called my wife telling her Adele and I are both okay, but I need to look after securing things here."

"Yes, Sir. Be glad to."

Thompson kissed Adele's cheek. "Tell your Mum I may be a few hours. Not to worry. Someone will bring me home."

Inside the car, Terence asked Adele, "Doin' okay?"

She began to cry uncontrollably. He said nothing only putting his arm around her and pulling her to his shoulder. After several minutes she regained her composure. "Sorry about falling apart like that."

"No need. You're just coming down from the effects of shock. I'm feeling it too. Terrible thing to see people injured like that. You did remarkably well. Helped a lot of those victims."

"Most of the victims are people I know. Some will carry scars for life. Malcolm Greene was a wonderful man. Retired Royal Navy officer. Imagine surviving the Second World War to end his days like this," she said.

Handing Adele off to her mother, Terence said he would call her tomorrow. As for him, a troubling walk back to his apartment. A perfect day instantly turned into tragedy. What did he expect from living in a war zone?

He recognized his dilemma not so much as denial as being unwilling to cut and run. Seeing this through on his own terms became his preoccupation. Remaining to the end of the year felt necessary for demonstrating his reasons expressed to his family for coming to Northern Ireland. By ending his misadventure of choosing to actively participate in the armed rebellion, he felt he should now be relatively safe. The truth about his covert activities known only by his grandfather seemed to ensure that remained secret. No reason he should become a suspect.

Finishing his thesis now became the reason to stay in Belfast. Not entirely true if being totally honest with himself. There was still Adele Thompson. Unrealistic perhaps, but he rationalized there might be a way to continue their relationship. Unlikely, but his entire time since coming to Northern Ireland had been an unrelenting improbable sequence of experiences. Only the alignment of unrelated circumstances made his secretive existence possible. Except for his disillusionment over IRA tactics in prosecuting the Irish Catholic side of the conflict, and the unfortunate misadventure with Maureen Lynch, the last couple of years had been an enlightening experience. Exciting and at times even frightening. Isn't that the nature of adventurism?

Even though a sustaining relationship with Adele Thompson seemed improbable why deny the possibility? She was intelligent. She might forgive his subterfuge if explained as an innocent act not intended as misrepresentation. Accepting of someone with a Catholic background by her family would probably be more of an issue. However, his parents came from different ethnic backgrounds. Maybe give Adele that choice when the time came to announcing his leaving. Should their relationship go that far, possibly spinning his background to account for having different surnames might be enough. His mother's second marriage and adoption at an early age by his stepfather? Admittedly a longshot but nothing to lose. Remaining indefinitely in Northern Ireland was not an option.

CHAPTER 19

Coleraine, Northern Ireland | August 1973

The aftermath of the *Raven Pub* bombing brought Terence closer to the Thompson family. For over two weeks, he helped Alfred make repairs and reopen for business. Rumors that the pub was frequented by UVF proved correct. Several of those helping out with the recovery clearly appeared to be loyalist paramilitaries. Terence not only observed handguns sticking out of waist bands, but noticeable respectful regard paid to Alfred Thompson. Snatches of overheard comments led him to speculate about Thompson having far more than just a connection to those dangerous looking individuals appearing almost as bodyguards.

None of that came as a surprise but still unsettling to be in such close proximity to the enemy given Terence's subversive activities with the IRA. Spies discovered by either side in this conflict suffered execution often following horrific physical abuse. Continuing a relationship with Adele Thompson carried grave danger should he make any mistake. This new knowledge caused him to abandon any thought of ever being able to reveal his real identity to Adele. Foolish to have considered such a possibility. Then the thought struck him that he could not even do the right thing and severe their relationship. That also might prove to be a fatal error.

The bombing of the *Raven Pub* brought him to his senses, introducing reason for depressive thoughts replacing his unrealistic sense of euphoria. Nothing would change until he left Northern Ireland. He needed to focus on that truth and follow his plan. That included delivering the last of the converted walkie-talkies to his grandfather. Fulfill that obligation. His participating in covert IRA efforts forever cementing a special bond of shared Irish nationalism with his grandfather. Remaining in Northern Ireland to complete his thesis became necessary to fulfill his purported reason for attending post-graduate studies at QUB. Aborting that by leaving without completing the required thesis invited speculation. After accomplishing the academic work, acquiring the degree also took on importance for his professional future.

Terence boarded a train for Coleraine in early August. This trip was to deliver the last group of radio detonators to his grandfather. Perhaps his last trip before a final rendezvous with both grandparents around the holidays before leaving Northern Ireland for good.

The train arrived in Coleraine as usual at 11:40 am. Liam Kelly walked toward the train as it came to a stop. He stood looking across the platform for Terence. Carrying the duffle bag, Terence waved when spotting his grandfather. Following their usual routine, Terence deposited his duffle bags in a station locker. This time there was to be no exchange of bags, Terence handed the locker key to his grandfather as they made their way to the *Railway Arms* pub.

Seated with their pints of stout, Liam said, "As much as I appreciate your contribution to the cause, I'm relieved you're getting out of this, Terry. I'm too old to turn back, however, you're too young to risk the rest of your life. This struggle may continue until well after I'm gone."

"You've got lots of years left, Granda. Fifty years ago, you helped defeat the British and gain independence for the twenty-six counties of the South. The situation today in Northern Ireland is something quite different."

"That it is." Liam changed the subject to avoid further discussion of Terence's reasons for dissatisfaction with the IRA. "How are things with your new job at the radio station?"

"Fine. Not especially fond of working in the middle of the night but getting used to it. Gives me enough free time to devote to developing my thesis project. It's a design concept for a more efficient method of transmitting electronic data."

"An academic project or something with commercial value?"

Terence smiled, "That's a very perceptive question, Granda. If it has merit, could be useful in various ways. Have you ever heard of digital computers, Granda?"

"No. Something that might use what you're working on?"

"Not exactly. Digital computers are essential to managing modern communications networks. Their capabilities are necessary for my concept to function. The commercial possibilities are in the field of communications."

"Sounds as if your studies at Queen's University have paid off. Still expect to complete this project by the end of the year?"

"That's the plan. By Christmas. Believe it best I then return to Boston. Time to get a job. Much better prospects in the United States. For my professional field, Massachusetts is an ideal high-tech location."

Liam nodded. "Wish your time here could have been under better circumstances. Yet even with your disappointments, it's been grand to have you, Terry. For your grandmother too. We're very proud of you. I'm also proud of how you volunteered to do something useful for the cause. Continuing on even after becoming disillusioned. Is that the right word to use about how you feel?"

"I'd say that's accurate, Granda. I know you also share my feelings about the IRA making a better fight by avoiding the killing of so many civilians. But neither of us can change that."

"True enough. I see the fight from the point of view of an old warrior in the large cause of Irish freedom. You still have a long life ahead of you after all this unpleasantness passes no matter what the outcome. It would hurt me something awful to see your life ruined by having come to Northern Ireland."

Terence said, "Been thinking about spending Christmas with you and Grandma. What about getting away for a couple of days and we all train down to Dublin? Spend a couple of nights at a hotel. My Christmas present. You can show me something of Dublin. The places where you and Michael Collins waged war against the British. We'll have Christmas dinner together before I take a flight from Dublin to Boston."

Liam smiled and a tear rolled down his cheek. He reached out putting his hand on Terence's forearm giving it a firm squeeze. "That would be grand, Terry. Your grandmother will be delighted. Let's plan on doing just that."

Although saddened by how things turned out, Liam Kelly knew he bore responsibility for allowing his grandson's participation. A terrible mistake. Knew full well his culpability. Kept what Terence was doing a secret from Agnes. Once Terence became active in his illicit covert IRA activities, Liam did not dare share with his wife the dangerous reason. Told her only that he periodically met Terence in Coleraine to share a few hours. Agnes understood the secrecy having to do from the unfortunate failed relationship between Terence and Maureen. Necessary to preserve the fact that Terence had not returned to Boston. Living in Belfast under a different name attending Queen's University would ignite the volatile Maureen. Agnus liked Maureen since she was a child but understood she had a wild side.

A couple of pints later Terence and Liam began eating lunch. Suddenly from outside came the loud sound of multiple lorries down-shifting to decelerate. The unusual noise brought the bartender and the few patrons to investigate the commotion. Liam and Terence joined those now standing on the sidewalk outside the pub.

The lorries were British Army Bedford RL all-wheel drive lorries painted in Northern British Army camouflage green and dark grey, capable of transporting an infantry platoon of troops. *8th Infantry Brigade, British Army* displayed on the door panels. It was a large convoy proceeding along Railway Road and the adjoining street running between the front entrance of the train station and the pub. Two of the lorries came to an abrupt stop as others continued traveling south. From behind the *Railway Arms* on the intervening street, additional lorries braked to a stop in front of the train station entrance.

Liam Kelly immediately recognized this as a security sweep. Predominantly Protestant Coleraine, having been previously bombed by the IRA in June, left him no doubt the British Army was looking for IRA. That likely meant British Intelligence had uncovered information likely from an infiltrator or maybe a captured IRA member succumbing to harsh interrogation.

Liam took Terence by the arm and guided him back inside the pub. "Stay calm. I'll settle our bill then we'll just leave quietly."

"What's going on outside?"

"A security sweep. Just keep your head about you. You are doing nothing incriminating. The detonators are secure in the station locker. Listen to me carefully. Here's your story should you be questioned. You've trained up from Belfast to meet your great uncle who drove up from Londonderry. Remember, it's Londonderry not Derry. Uncle's name is William Campbell. We spent the day seeing the scenic north coastline. There's a real William Campbell with a bar in the Waterside district. The *Waterside Public House*. Campbell is Catholic but has nothing to do with the IRA. That the pub is located in predominantly loyalist Waterside will make you sound non-threatening. Show your student ID from the university. If asked for more information say you were born in Belfast but grew up in Boston. First time visiting Northern Ireland. Ask what's going on. Don't become talkative with the military or any RUC. Just answer their questions. Don't volunteer information."

"What about you?" Terence asked.

"Best if we separate. Don't fancy being questioned by the British Army. By the unit insignia on the army trucks these soldiers are likely stationed in Ebrington Barracks in the Waterside district. Even though I'm not known as active in the IRA, my name is undoubtedly known and probably on a British Army Intelligence watch list. Don't relish having to explain why I'm in Coleraine.

"IRA set off a bomb at the perimeter of Ebrington Barracks in March. Didn't injure any soldiers but they're motivated to go after the IRA since the bombing here in Coleraine in June. You make your way into the train station. Take your scheduled train back to Belfast. If delayed, stay in the station. Relax but go back to Belfast. If you should be questioned, you had lunch with your uncle at the *Railway Arms*. The bartender may remember our faces there. We've had lunch at the *Railway Arms* every time you've come to Coleraine. But they don't know my name. So, I'm your Uncle William that returned back to Londonderry by car."

Terence asked, "But what are you going to do?"

"There're people here in Coleraine that can help me avoid any problems. I'll be fine. Back home by tomorrow. Call me tomorrow night. If your grandmother answers, say nothing to her about what happened today in Coleraine. Say only that I saw you off on the train and you wanted to ask him something about plans for Christmas. As for me, I will spend tonight in a safe house and make my way back to Derry tomorrow when everything blows over. Your grandmother may worry but she's all too familiar with my clandestine activities and won't ask for details."

With that, Liam and Terence stepped outside. Both smiled at each other but did not embrace to avoid drawing attention to soldiers moving along the street. Liam walked north on Railway Road. Terence turned the corner around the pub then walked across Railway Place to enter the train station.

Liam proceeded along Railway Road then turned onto a connecting street. Once out of sight of security personnel, he made turns onto various streets working his way into a residential area. He knew Coleraine enough to navigate his way to a small Catholic neighborhood in otherwise Protestant Coleraine. A fellow aging IRA veteran from the time of the Anglo-Irish War lived here. Like Liam Kelly, Jack Doyle was sympathetic to the new Provisional IRA but at his age no longer active in military operations.

Liam Kelly returned to Derry after the signing of the Anglo-Irish Treaty of 1922, rather than participating in the civil war. He effectively retired from active rebellion until the current start of the *Troubles* and the creation of the Provisional IRA. However, Jack Doyle continued the fight as an anti-treaty IRA dissident in the subsequent Irish Civil War. Once again drawn to driving the British from Northern Ireland, Doyle later participated in the last futile efforts of by then a greatly diminished IRA. Participating in the *Northern Campaign* in the early years of the Second World War then again in the *Border Campaign* of the late fifties ensured Doyle being labelled a potentially dangerous subversive. Pleading innocence to aggressive interrogators would only invite terrible abuse with no regard for his advanced age.

All the more condemning for an IRA fanatic residing in predominantly loyalist Coleraine, Doyle topped the list of people of interest suspected of complicity in the Coleraine bombing in June. Knowing Doyle's background, Liam Kelly approached Doyle's cottage cautiously. From a distance he watched as an RUC armored car backed up by a lorry full of British soldiers came to a halt in front of the house.

RUC constables armed with a battering ram broke down the front door while British soldiers surrounded the house. Minutes later the RUC dragged Jack Doyle by his arms stumbling along the walkway in his stocking feet. A constable tapped Doyle sharply across his back with a baton. "Get up you old Fenian arsehole!" Doyle struggled to his knees. Another constable pushed him off balance with his foot on Doyle's butt. "Not too old to kill other old pensioners you Fenian bastard. You've got a lot to answer for Doyle. We'll make sure you have a rough time but in the end you'll tell us everything."

Partly concealed behind a parked car, Liam Kelly watched from close enough to hear the RUC. Christ, Doyle was damn near his age. His heart might not endure the kind of physical abuse that he was probably going to experience.

Getting out of Coleraine with police and army in such large strength was too risky. His plan was to find some place out of sight until nightfall. At least this was the end of summer and tonight would not be uncomfortably cold. With nightfall and hopefully the withdrawal of security forces, he could settle himself somewhere secure for the night. Early the next morning, telephone someone in Derry to make the thirty-mile drive and retrieve him.

Not only with darkness a low overcast also restricted illumination from the weak moonlight of a quarter-moon. The gloom allowed him to enter unseen into what he believed to be as safe a place as any other location in Coleraine. Jack Doyle's cottage. The police were likely done here. Inside, he felt his way about the ransacked darkened interior. In the kitchen he cautiously opened the refrigerator causing the internal light to come on. Closing it quickly he determined he had access to food and drink should the need arise. He would leave before sunrise to survey the situation. Doyle's phone was probably being monitored requiring him to find a public telephone to first call Agnes then make another call for someone to extract him from Coleraine. Liam was more concerned about Terence's situation. Was he now safely on back in Belfast? Since Terence had no telephone, he must wait until Terence called tomorrow night as instructed.

As Terence stepped inside the train station, British soldiers began corralling people into groups. An officer announced loudly, "This is a security sweep. Nothing to worry about unless you've got mischief in mind. In that case be advised that we have live ammunition in our weapons. Not about to have another day in Coleraine like in June. Everyone is to present identification. Keep calm. Answer any questions directed to you, otherwise keep your mouth shut and you'll soon be on your way. Get too it, Sergeant Winkler."

Terence settled down concentrating on controlling his breathing. Follow Granda's instructions. Looking a little scared was okay just don't look guilty. Answer any questions but don't ramble. He reflected on his grandfather's wisdom to immediately stow their respective duffle bags in lockers. Fortunately, on this trip he had nothing to retrieve before boarding his train back to Belfast.

Told by a soldier for his group to form a single file line, Terence waited his turn behind two other men. As his turn came, a soldier ordered, "Identification." Terence extracted his passport. The soldier looked at the passport for several moments. "Driver's license."

"Don't have a Northern Ireland license."

"Why's that?" the soldier asked.

"Been living in America since I was a child. Born in Belfast. Been going to college at Queen's University. Don't have money for a car."

"What brings you to Coleraine?"

"Met my uncle here this morning. He drove up from Londonderry. Took me for a drive along the scenic north coast. I'm heading back to Belfast on the 3:19 train." He extracted his train ticket and handed it to the soldier. "Name?" the soldier said.

"Excuse me?" Terence replied, not understanding since he gave the soldier his passport.

"What's your uncle's name?"

"Ah, sorry. His name's William Campbell. Owns a pub in the Waterside district of Londonderry."

Satisfied. The soldier said, "Very well. Move along. Be sure to catch that train. Don't be hanging around here. This sort of shit goes on all the time. Not like in America I expect."

Terence just nodded then went outside near the platform to wait for his train. Another unsettling experience following witnessing the bloody aftermath of the bombings here only two months earlier. Too keyed up to sit and wait for the train, he paced the platform. Relieved by having escaped further scrutiny did not diminish worrying about the fate of his grandfather.

The excitement in Coleraine that day died away quickly. Unbeknownst to Liam Kelly, the raid came about after the arrest of a known IRA member in Derry suspected of being connected with the June bombings in Coleraine. Faced with accessory charges to murder, the suspect gave up information in exchange for dubious promises of leniency. Five Catholics in total were arrested that day in Coleraine. None were IRA except seventy-two-year-old Jack Doyle named by the informant. While having nothing to do with the Coleraine bombings, Doyle's long history with the IRA foretold harsh treatment regardless of his advanced age.

CHAPTER 20

Coleraine, Northern Ireland | August 1973

Maureen Lynch also traveled to Coleraine arriving on the same train as Liam Kelly. Liam disembarked and disappeared inside the station building. She found a bench at the farthest end of the boarding platform of the Coleraine train station. From her vantage point she could observe the arriving or departing trains on the single-track platform. She was on a mission. The phrase *heaven has no rage like love to hatred turned, nor hell a fury like a woman scorned,* aptly described Maureen's frame of mind. That morning, she followed Liam and watched him board the train in Derry. Remaining unseen, she boarded a different carriage of the same train.

During the short trip to Coleraine, she walked forward to the train carriage that she observed Liam Kelly boarding. Peering into that carriage from between carriages, she saw Liam sitting there. When the train stopped, she allowed Liam to disembark before her then waited for him to walk away before she stepped down to the platform.

Maureen Lynch had reason to believe Liam might be travelling to Belfast to meet Terence. That meant changing trains in Coleraine. Although it was possible that Terence might be coming to Coleraine to see his grandfather. Either way, she intended to follow either Liam or Terence to Belfast. If Terence Kelly relocated to Belfast instead of returning to Boston two years ago as

Liam told her, then there would be hell to pay. After many weeks engaged in an intense relationship, he abandoned her without explanation. She could not let his deceiving her stand. What was Terence doing in Belfast since leaving Derry? Confront him and demand an explanation for his treating her with such disregard.

The previous night Liam tasked Maureen with closing the bar. Before the last customer left, she was having problems with the pressure on one of the faucets of the draft beer system. Carbon dioxide and nitrogen was introduced into the kegs of beer kept in the cooler behind the bar to push the beer from keg to faucet. The system required regulators at the compressed gas tanks and at each keg to control the pressure. She was not mechanically inclined and after fiddling with the secondary regulator on the suspect keg in the cooler, she was unable to resolve the problem. Tomorrow was Monday with the bar normally closed. Liam would want to fix the problem before reopening on Wednesday.

Locking the pub doors, she made her way up the stairs to Liam's and Agnes' apartment to tell him of the problem with the drafting system. Before knocking she heard Agnes speaking loudly. Not arguing but both she and Liam were hard of hearing and therefore naturally spoke loudly.

Although Maureen could not hear every word clearly she did hear *Terence*. Then something about *Belfast*. Putting her ear to the door she picked up *classes at Queen's University*, then something about *Christmas together with Terence*. What the hell were they saying! Terence returned to Boston two years ago! Or did he? Could it be possible he stayed in Northern Ireland? Why Belfast? Could it be to attend the university? Why the secrecy? She immediately realized the answer. To avoid her. Their last nasty quarrel before Terence suddenly left her two years ago. Not so much as even saying goodbye. The ungrateful sod. With all the sex she offered him, how could he just walk out on her to sneak off to Belfast?

She stood at the apartment door for several minutes. What more she overheard distinctly appeared to support the fact that Terence was living in Belfast. What she further gleaned sounded like Liam saying, *taking the train again tomorrow to Coleraine*. Sonofabitch she thought silently. Did Liam regularly visit Terence in Coleraine? Why Coleraine? Because it was not far from Derry and connected directly to Belfast by train. Easy for Liam to take a train to meet Terence in Belfast, or maybe just part of the way in Coleraine.

Fuck the problem with the beer dispensing. Without knocking, she left and returned home. Tomorrow was her day off with the pub closed. What she just learned called for new plans. Pack a few things. Might be gone for a couple of days she told her parents without explanation.

As the train pulled into Coleraine station, having boarded the last carriage meant Liam was in a carriage further up the platform. Stepping down from the train, she remained in place to watch for Liam. When seeing him disembark, she turned her head away for a moment to hide her face. Turning back, she watched Liam walking into the station building. Coleraine train station was small offering few places of concealment either inside the station building or outside along the platform. The platform area seemed best, yet no obvious place existed from which to observe passengers disembarking while remaining unobserved. Not easy to hide from someone that knows her so well. Before leaving Derry she attempted to modify her appearance as much as possible and stay at a distance.

Planning in advance she radically altered her appearance from her usual provocative attire. A headscarf hid her hair. Her face absent its usual makeup and particularly bright lipstick. Accompanied by dark glasses, the effect even surprised her when looking in her makeup mirror. Flannel shirt instead of her preferred tight knit tops. Corduroy slacks. Sneakers instead of heels or boots. Combined with an old denim jacket of her mother's and carrying a backpack, made for an effective transformation into practical outdoor clothing. A young woman making her way across Northern Ireland on a summer holiday.

Yet Liam and Terence would recognize her if close enough. Not only here in Coleraine but certainly when following Terence on his return to Belfast. Having no idea where he lived meant following close enough without being seen.

She had no intention of confronting Terence in Coleraine. That would come later after learning more about what he had been doing in Belfast since he left her. Not sure what she had in mind. Definitely not to plead her undying love. Although closer to rage than feeling hurt, she still wanted him back. Must have him back. Maybe an obsession but Terence might be her opportunity for leaving Derry. Belfast was better. Boston in America was far better.

As an American, Terence could be her ticket to get to America. Even marrying him if necessary. He was good looking and a satisfactory sex partner. More importantly, educated with good employment prospects. She could seduce him back. He was incapable of resisting her sexuality. Determined to seize the opportunity, she would find the means of getting Terence back under her control.

Liam entered the train station allowing Maureen to find a place of concealment for observing the platform. Liam was either waiting for a change of trains to take him to Belfast or waiting for Terence to join him here in Coleraine. Either way, she needed to observe from near the platform. Terence had not yet arrived otherwise he would have been waiting on the platform for the arrival of Liam. A stressful afternoon would follow.

Waiting in anticipation for Terence to arrive or Liam to appear on the platform elevated her anxiety. Would Terence really show up? Did he look the same? If they were meeting here in Coleraine then she must wait until Terence boarded a train returning to Belfast. That presented her greatest uncertainty. Which train would he take? Then how could she board without either Liam or Terence seeing her? Too many uncertainties to plan for in advance.

She took a bench outside on the platform located where the last carriage stopped on her arriving train. Coleraine is on a single-track line. A train arriving from Belfast would be heading in the opposite direction. Using that point of reference she would situate herself on a bench furthest to the end of the platform where she assumed the engine would stop. This would give a view of all disembarking passengers the length of the train arriving from Belfast. Keep watch for Liam who would likely be waiting on the platform to greet Terence.

Maureen's wait was less than thirty minutes when the public address system announced the arrival of the 11:30 train from Belfast. Liam reappeared from inside the station and took up a position midway along the track platform. Minutes later Terence disembarked. From even a distance she clearly recognized him. Smiling and carrying a duffle bag, he spotted his grandfather. After embracing, the two of them walked into the station.

Maureen followed well behind several other arriving passengers. Inside the station she watched as Liam opened a locker and placed Terence's duffle bag inside then pocketed the key. Both then exited out of the front entrance of the station. Following carefully, Maureen watched them walk a short distance to enter the *Railway Arms* pub.

Returning inside the train station Maureen went to the ticket counter. Looking at the schedule for trains departing that afternoon to Belfast, she decided to buy multiple tickets not knowing how long Terence planned on staying in Coleraine. After purchasing tickets leaving Coleraine at 3:19 pm, and 4:19 pm, and 5:19 pm, she asked the clerk, "Where can I get a sandwich?"

Maybe Terence was not immediately returning to Belfast. Maybe the bag stowed in the locker was for an overnight stay. Couldn't afford to miss him though if he was returning to Belfast that afternoon or evening. Best to remain at the station positioned at the end of the platform. The uncertainty served to increase her anger.

A deli located on Railway Road just a few buildings south of the pub where Liam and Terence went proved convenient. No way of telling when she might get another chance to eat. After purchasing a sandwich and soda Maureen returned to her bench on the far end of the train platform. Returning through the station she bought a newspaper that could prove handy for concealing her face. The newsstand kiosk also offered a city map of Belfast.

Knowing the direction of travel for the southbound train to Belfast, she selected the bench outside on the platform that should be at the end of the train. A position from which to observe Terence boarding hopefully onto a train carriage closer to the engine while she boarded the last carriage with a better chance of avoiding detection. Anticipating a long wait, determination fortified her resolve to stick with her surveillance.

An hour later something startled everyone within the train station. The sound of heavy lorries accelerating then coming to a noisy stop was followed by the sound of banging metal. What she heard were tailgates from British Army troop lorries banging open to discharge soldiers. Moments later, soldiers in full battle gear flooded onto the train platform.

An officer yelled, "Everyone stand. Women proceed to the north end of the platform, men to the south end. Have identification ready for inspection."

Already in the position allocated for women, Maureen stood up. Scared but prepared to explain her reason for being in Coleraine. Any Catholic from Derry knew enough always to be prepared should they ever be stopped for questioning by security forces. Easier for women yet that did not always ensure protection from brutal physical treatment. Protestant Coleraine was a hot spot on edge since the recent bombings.

"Identification," a soldier holding an assault rifle across his chest demanded as her turn in line came. Handing over her driver's license," the soldier remarked, "Londonderry. Bogside from the address. What's a Catholic woman doing here in Coleraine?"

"Taking a short holiday. Goin' to hitchhike my way up along the scenic north coast before starting classes at Magee College back in Derry. Coleraine's a logical place to venture north."

Seemingly dressed for her explained purpose, the soldier returned her driver's license and moved to the next woman in line. Minutes later having checked the few women on the platform, the soldier said, "You're all free to go about your business." A little shaken, Maureen resumed her position on the bench. Her thoughts immediately turned to Liam.

Liam was like an elderly uncle. He didn't smack down young people. Nor anybody for that matter. Strange for someone with such a rumored fearsome reputation as an IRA assassin from fifty years ago in Dublin. Her own father, active in the Derry Provisional IRA, told her stories about his good friend Liam Kelly. Could Liam have returned to the ways of those earlier IRA of the war in the twenties? Maureen hoped Liam was not caught up in whatever was going on with all these soldiers running about.

With those thoughts on her mind, she saw Terence emerge from the station. Liam was not with him. As Terence emerged from the station, a soldier blocked his path. "Get into that line for identification check."

Terence nodded then took his place at the end of the line. Maureen wondered why he had not retrieved his bag from the locker. Raising her newspaper to shield her face, she took furtive glances keeping track of his location.

Twenty minutes later the public address system announced the arrival of the next train to Belfast. Maureen had planned correctly. Terence boarded a carriage midway along the train allowing her to board the last carriage unseen.

The train pulled into Belfast Grand Central station about 5:00 pm. Looking down the platform, Terence should disembark ahead of her. Therefore, it became important to exit immediately after he passed to keep him in sight.

Putting her arms through the backpack straps, she stepped down onto the platform. Terence was walking briskly ahead of her. Now began the most difficult part of her plan, following Terence without being seen. Being daylight helped but also meant he might recognize her should he turn around. Had no idea how far that might be. Carrying nothing meant Terence walked at a brisk pace. Keeping up while avoiding being noticed proved difficult.

It turned out to be only thirty minutes south from Belfast Grand Central train station to the Windsor district just north of the national football stadium. Few twists and turns allowed Maureen to keep at a manageable distance to avoid being noticed. That proved a non-issue with Terence unincumbered carrying no bag walking purposefully without taking notice of the surroundings.

Arriving at his destination, Terence went through a gate in a white fence surrounding the corner house on a quiet street. From the adjacent street and the cover of another perpendicular corner of row housing, Maureen watched him climb an external stairway to a second-floor door. Entering with a key suggested it must be his flat.

Waiting a few minutes, she wanted to confirm that by checking the line of post boxes near the fence gate. Two boxes were labeled with the corresponding house number 21. Looking inside the box marked 21, she found mail addressed to John Graham. Guessing the post box designated 21B to be the upstairs flat, she looked inside quickly. Two pieces of mail, both addressed to Terence Stewart. Stewart? Too much of a coincidence. Was Terence using an assumed name? Why?

Now what was she to do? Following Terence to Belfast with no further plan, she now must decide on her next move. Couldn't very well linger about this residential street corner. If a constable should come by that could prove dangerous. Her identification stated she resided in Derry. The street located in the

Bogside essentially labelled her as Catholic. What was a Catholic woman from Derry doing in a Protestant Belfast neighborhood?

Coming from the train station she passed a bus stop not far from Terence's flat. She decided to wait for a while from the bus stop bench. Pretend reading the newspaper while waiting for a bus. Her line of sight allowed watching the door to number 21B.

An hour later Terence emerged and began walking back up the street in her direction. Immediately seeing him appear on the sidewalk, she stood and disappeared across the street walking a short distance down an intersecting street. Picking him again as he walked past her it seemed he was heading back the same route they had just followed from the train station. After a few blocks he turned onto an unfamiliar street. She wanted to consult the map but didn't dare stop for risk of losing him. After about a mile he ducked into a restaurant. They were in the center of Belfast according to her map.

Passing outside the restaurant window she saw him sitting alone. The smell of food made her hungry. Across the street there was a delicatessen. Didn't relish another sandwich but there was little choice. Needed to see what Terence might be up to after the unexpected experience in Coleraine.

After eating her sandwich, she occupied the time waiting for Terence by walking up and down the sidewalk while keeping watch on the restaurant. It was after 8:00 pm and dark when Terence emerged from the restaurant. Another short walk brought them to a large building on the corner of Ormeau Avenue and Bradford Street. After Terence entered a side entrance marked *employees only,* she went to the front entrance. A brass plate read *Broadcast House*, underneath *BBC Radio Station 2BE.*

Assuming Terence worked at the radio station since entering the employee entrance at this late hour, he probably worked a night shift here. Suited her schedule. Find a hotel for the night. A hot shower and good night's rest with a decent breakfast in the morning before resuming her surveillance of Terence Kelly, or *Terence Stewart*. Consulting the street map from the train station, hotel advertisements populated the reverse side. Among those listed was the *Belfast International Youth Hostel*. According to the map less than a half mile directly south of where she stood on Donegall Road. Perfect. Although unknown to her, this was the same hostel Terence used when he first came to Belfast after leaving Derry two years ago.

The following morning Maureen returned about 8:30 to take up position at the nearby bus stop from which to observe Terence's flat. Perhaps risky since she might stand out by remaining seated on the bus stop bench then repeatedly getting up to walk away rather than boarding passing buses. At least this was a workday with many residents already at work by this hour. However, should a police officer notice her she might look suspicious.

While waiting she concocted a story if that should become necessary. Looking up a young man she recently met on the train but apparently getting the address wrong. Just looking at the map to get myself back to the train station. We were to take the train north to do a backpacking walk together along the Giant's Causeway on the northern coast. Not very convincing but she wasn't doing anything wrong.

Not sure what she was expecting by watching Terence's flat other than learning as much as possible about this new life he chose. If he worked nights, what did he do during the day? Beyond that she had no plan. Too many conflicting emotions left her one moment fantasizing about reconciling then reverting to latent rage that wished for getting her revenge for his having abandoned her. Not sure which obsession might win out when she finally confronted him. Needed time to think things through by returning first to Derry.

Returning to Belfast was easy enough. Next time, knowing the location of Terence's flat and place of employment gave her a sense of power she would exploit. Most assuredly, she intended there to be a next time. She was not through with Terence Kelly.

Trains left every hour from Belfast Grand Central for Derry with a train-change in Coleraine. Her plan was to leave Belfast around midday. Before leaving Belfast, she wanted a last look at Terence. She left the hostel early in the morning stopping to eat a quick breakfast along the way to Terence's flat. Once again she took up her surveillance location at the bus stop. After waiting over an hour, she decided to leave for the train station. Hanging about at the bus stop too long risked becoming suspicious to a watchful local resident. She only guessed that if Terence worked nights, he might sleep when arriving back home in the early morning. Then again, he may not even be home.

As a bus approached, Maureen moved away to avoid appearing as a waiting rider. When the bus stopped, outstepped a tall young woman. Well-dressed. Short skirt with calf-length boots with heels giving her a decided sexy look. A pretty face framed by long dark hair as she turned toward Maureen and smiled.

Maureen watched as the woman walked briskly to climb the outside stairs to 21B then knocked on the door. It took a full minute before the door opened. Maureen recognized Terence standing there dressed only in an open shirt and underwear. The woman immediately embraced him. After several moments of passionate kissing, the woman stepped inside, and the door closed.

Maureen Lynch was dumbfounded. Obviously, having not seen Terence for two years, it was entirely probable that he had found a new girlfriend. That logic did not mitigate the jealous anger of seeing him displaying intimacy with another woman.

Maureen returned to continue her surveillance from the bus stop bench. Two hours passed. Moving away from the bus stop whenever a bus approached, she was determined to wait until the woman emerged from Terence's flat. By now she imagined what Terence and this woman must be doing. No matter how long she needed to wait, she must learn more about this woman.

Having rediscovered Terence Kelly living in Belfast, she was no means done with him. He would resume his position as her lover or suffer the consequences. Given where he was living, was he posing as a Protestant loyalist by using another name? Would the threat of exposing whatever he was doing in Belfast be enough to force him to reunite with her? Maybe enough to even force him to take her to America? Was Terence into something political with his grandfather? Her own father was an important figure in the IRA Derry Brigade. Also, a good friend of Liam Kelly. Never let on about Liam being currently involved but who's to say given Liam's legendary reputation with the old IRA.

CHAPTER 21

Boston, Massachusetts | 2025

The last time we spoke you made reference to being in Coleraine with your grandfather in June 1973, the day of the bombings," Father O'Brien began with their next interview session in O'Brien's office at Boston College.

Terence Kelly nodded. "A day of absolute horror. The images are impossible to erase even to this day. I was already disgusted by IRA failed tactics in their bombing campaign. Taking the conflict to London to bomb targets in March expecting to bring the violence directly to those living in England made strategic sense but their tactics again tactics fell far short. While targeting symbolic government buildings symbols, the bombs only injured civilians. Two bombs even failed to explode. Then the perpetrators were soon arrested. Hard to imagine such incompetence ever achieving any meaningful result.

"However, the Coleraine outrage stood apart from the London bombings as an act intended solely to inflict terror against another ethnic group. No hard targets of security forces. A stupid rogue operation committed by fanatics I learned years later from my grandfather. Completely counterproductive. The carnage physically turned my stomach. Made vivid the basis for my disillusionment. The incident dispelled whatever hesitation remained about terminating my covert contribution to IRA bomb making.

"Granda and I were having a pint over lunch at the *Railway Arms* pub next to the Coleraine train station. I had delivered my latest batch of modified walkie-talkies bomb detonators, secured in a locker in the station along with a new supply of walkie-talkies my grandfather smuggled in from American.

"I directed the conversation by telling Granda that this newest batch of walkie-talkies he delivered would be the last I intended to convert to detonators. Couldn't do this anymore. Told him I did not agree with the IRA targeting civilians with bombs. Those that ordered these bombings might say targets were selected for other reasons. That's all just bullshit. The end result became the same. Civilians are killed and injured. Since my devices became part of these acts, I bore shared responsibility.

"Added that I was also concerned that unexploded bombs could have included intact radio signal receiver units directly connected to the high explosives. I recently left my position at Comet Electronics because of that. Working to repair these same walkie-talkies was what I largely did at Comet. Should the security forces look deeply enough, I might become a person of interest. My using an alternate identity would come unraveled. Identified as the grandson of Liam Kelly would become my undoing.

"I been spilling out my troubled thoughts to Granda. He did not attempt to argue away my feelings. May have even been relieved that I was ending my involvement. Even my pronouncement that I was planning to return to Boston by the end of the year after I completed my post graduate degree may have been a relief. Perhaps feeling his own sense of responsibility for enabling me in this dangerous enterprise. I feared though that with his iconic involvement in Irish independence, he might find me wanting in my otherwise professed commitment. That was not the case.

"My grandfather's deeply ingrained devotion to Irish freedom had not diminished by the passage of time. I believed he shared my dissatisfaction with IRA bombing tactics being counterproductive. However, I felt he placed the loss of civilians in this current struggle as an unfortunate necessity. Unlike the war waged by the IRA fifty years earlier, this current conflict was fundamentally different. In Northern Ireland, the Catholic population was overshadowed by a larger Protestant loyalist citizenry. In 1918, the Irish Catholic population dominated the southern Irish counties and overwhelmingly backed rebellion. An Irish Catholic rebellion. That was never the same situation experienced in Northern Ireland. Not in 1918, not in 1972.

"Having aired my declaration to cease active involvement and announced my intention to return to Boston at year end, and Granda's expressing his understanding, both of us relaxed. Back to being just grandfather and grandson, Granda replied, '*We must get together before Christmas. Your Grandmother already misses seeing you when I periodically come here to Coleraine. Never revealed to her what you are actually doing, though she still worries. Bad enough violence in Derry, but Belfast is worse. Worries about you using what she calls a false name. Agnes is a smart woman. That I never invite her to come along with me to Coleraine, she knows there's likely something more than you just avoiding Maureen. Reads about student protests among QUB students. Thinks you might have become involved with that.*'

"After eating lunch, we ordered another pint. Enjoying our remaining time together, that's when all hell broke loose. A massive explosion just down the same street rocked the pub building. Granda and I along with everyone inside rushed outside. Looking south a dust cloud of debris cloaked the area only a few blocks away. I could see overturned cars in the street. Along with many others, Granda and I ran toward the scene of the explosion. A bomb exploded creating a large crater in front of a wine shop now engulfed in flames. Masonry, roof tiles, and glass lay about a wide area. Most disturbing was witnessing firsthand the destroyed bodies of victims. Blood and gore. Human tissue. Dismembered body parts. That's what struck me. Innocent civilians. Not just statistics. Not something over which to debate as unintended collateral damage.

"Granda and I just stood there. Nothing anyone could do. Rescue personnel began arriving within minutes. Coleraine was predominately Protestant loyalist. Granda knew better than to remain here when security forces descended onto the area given his past association with the IRA. My train was scheduled to leave in less than a half hour. Granda told me to get on it. As for him, he said he knew someone in Coleraine. He'd lay low until tomorrow before returning to Derry. The radio detonators remained concealed in the train station locker for later retrieval."

O'Brien shook his head. "I can image how you felt witnessing the aftermath of an actual bombing. Did you suspect it was the IRA?"

"Oh yes. That was why Granda was careful to portray himself as Protestant. Told the bartender at the *Railway Arms* that he owned a pub in Waterside, Londonderry. Londonderry, not Derry he cautioned me. Gave the name of an actual pub and owner he knew of. Told the bartender since the *Railway Arms* was located conveniently next to the train station, he occasionally met his grandson there. If ever remembered, we would not stick out as Catholics."

"Coming a year after *Bloody Friday* in Belfast, the Coleraine bombing must have made quite an impression," O'Brien commented.

"That it did. Nothing again ever came close to the trauma of looking at the dead and injured of Coleraine. Yet that was by no means the end of my proximity to violence where people died."

O'Brien raised his eyebrows.

Kelly said, "As the saying goes, *you ain't heard nothing yet.* By the time I finish my story, I believe you'll agree that my tragic experiences will make for riveting reading.

"Being in Coleraine experiencing the bombings firsthand confirmed my decision to cease involvement with subversive activities. Felt I had honored my commitment to my grandfather. Believe he also understood that I did not share the same passion that shaped his lifelong struggle for Irish freedom from the British. As things would turn out, I should have left immediately to return to Boston."

"Yet you remained in Belfast? Had you completed classes at QUB?"

"Yes. However, QUB required a thesis for a master's degree. Already had an approved project but still faced months of work for completion. In my case complicated by it requiring a creative technical solution to an immerging problem related to electronic data transmittal. Meant that my thesis abstract required measurable scientific validation to be deemed worthy of awarding my master's degree."

"Why did you not just leave after the Coleraine experience and present your thesis after returning to Boston?"

"Never have ceased thinking about that. A couple of reasons. It would raise questions among my family why I left prematurely without staying in Belfast until finishing my degree work. Other than my grandfather, no one knew of my subversive covert activities materially aiding the IRA. I had a good job working nights allowing ample time to work on my thesis that consisted of a design project related to data transmission. Being highly technical, my thesis would undoubtedly require incremental review by the committee to validate its merit. That's better accomplished face to face. Unlike subjective judgement evaluation of a thesis in many other fields, my technical concept either had merit or didn't. No middle ground.

"However, my real reason was something more emotional. Another woman unexpectedly entered my life. Adele Thompson."

"Yet you still planned to leave Belfast by the end of 1973. Where was that developing romantic relationship headed if you intended leaving Belfast in a few months?"

Kelly had already beat himself up over the pain he must have caused for Adele. His sense of loss and her undoubtedly deep hurt made recounting those memories as difficult as anything else.

"Uncertain as to what Adele meant to me. Chose to deny that I was probably in love. Instead, I procrastinated making a decision that I knew would only become more difficult. Couldn't however bring myself to do the right thing by severing the relationship.

"Adele Thompson was an extraordinary woman. Intelligent, attractive, loving. Our differing ethnic backgrounds nevertheless made for an impossibly tragic Shakespearian romance. I was not just Catholic, but IRA. Adele was not just Protestant, but her father was a Belfast commander in the UVF loyalist paramilitary. Of course I didn't know that at the time. Couldn't get much further apart socially or politically. She knew me as Terence Stewart. Could never hope to explain the reason of my real surname being different."

O'Brien exhibited a slight scowl. "So, what was your plan when the time came to leave Belfast? Did you perhaps find some way of preserving the relationship?"

"Not until too late. At the time, it seemed impossible. Making no excuses, though, Father. I stand guilty of whatever sin that might be called. Told myself I might be able to eventually concoct something explainable. Started as nothing more than chatting up a pretty girl at a pub that a couple of fellow QUB students took me to. I had become a social recluse for almost a year. Emotionally susceptible and starved of female companionship, I easily succumbed to the many charms of Adele Thompson."

"Did you engage in intimate relations with her?"

"Not immediately, but eventually we enjoyed fulfilling intimacy. Adele was nothing like Maureen Lynch. Very attractive which made me notice her, but it was our intellectual connection that made her more than just a pretty face.

"Dated several times before another traumatic experience brought us closer. Another bombing. This time the target was her father's pub. Car bomb outside. Adele and I were inside the pub at the time. After a pleasant Sunday spent riding bicycles in a park she had to go to work at the pub that afternoon. I showed up at the pub later to have dinner with her. Around nine that evening an explosion rocked the pub doing considerable damage. You can look up an account of the bombing, Father. Saturday 28 July 1973. The *Raven Pub* on Ravenhill Road.

"Alfred Thompson anticipated this could happen. Had taken some precautions to the front of the building facing the street.

Sandbags and heavy shutters covering the windows reduced the damage, but the inside of the pub sustained considerable damage. Adele and I were knocked to the floor but uninjured. We both tried to help the injured. One fatality with 16 injured. This time became a unique experience by becoming a victim. My efforts were inadequate when trying to help the injured until medical personnel arrived.

"The next couple of weeks were difficult. Adele was still traumatized. Both of us became preoccupied with helping to put the pub back in operation. She had classes to attend. I had the challenges of completing my thesis.

"What happened to your grandfather the day of the Coleraine bombing?" O'Brien asked.

"Granda obviously got away. In a secure public telephone conversation, the following evening he explained his harrowing night spent in the home of a local IRA contact. This was after observing an old IRA colleague still actively involved being dragged away by soldiers who then ransacked the house. Granda guessed the raid stemmed from insider information obtained by British intelligence. Anyway, you can image how rattled I became with these successive incidents and the narrow escape by my grandfather."

"Did you continue to see things through according to your plan to complete your thesis by year-end?"

"Yes. To my endless regret. You will see what I mean as I continue my story."

"What made you not just cut and run? Was it Adele Thompson?"

"She undoubtedly had a bearing on my staying, but I blame it on my stubbornness to carry through with my plans having felt I had covered my tracks. Never wanted to admit to myself this had been a monumental mistake coming to Northern Ireland, made far worse by volunteering to make weapons for the IRA. Thinking I was doing something to impress my grandfather. Perhaps someday even telling my own father what I did. Other than smuggling arms, my father missed his chance to participate in the IRA operations because of emigrating to Boston. I therefore had a family reputation to uphold. At least the paternal family side. My mother wouldn't have seen it that way. Thankfully, she never knew otherwise. Nor did my father. So, I just procrastinated. Spent several marvelous weeks together with Adele. Didn't want to throw all that away. Still deluded myself by expecting to find a solution to have literally gotten away with murder and thereafter returning to a normal future life in the United States.

CHAPTER 22

Belfast, Northern Ireland | August 1973

Terence arrived back in Belfast after the scare of the security sweep in Coleraine. Just when thinking that his plans had fallen into place to extricate himself from this misadventure, realization of the remaining threat persisted. Most worrisome was wondering what happened to his grandfather. Did Granda find refuge with someone in Coleraine? Did he make it safely back to Derry? He would not know until telephoning tomorrow evening. Obviously, being careful with what he said should his grandmother answer. She undoubtedly knew that Liam was in some way connected with the IRA if for no other reason than his friendship with IRA Derry Brigade OC Martin McGuinness and Maureen's father Sean Lynch.

Arriving at his flat, Terence's anxieties ran high. Having no walkie-talkies either modified or unmodified in his possession in Coleraine saved him. Even so many pairs of unmodified devices would have been difficult to explain. The obvious conclusion by security forces would be illicit communications intended for the IRA or paramilitary loyalists. That could easily have led to disaster. At least he must go to work at 9:00 pm. Better to remain occupied rather than facing a sleepless night. Collecting his thesis project notes he stuffed them into his briefcase, then left his flat setting off walking to the radio station. Although not particularly hungry, if he was going to eat anything it must be before clocking in for work. In a few hours restaurants will close for the night. Dinner at his favorite Italian eatery not far from the radio station might improve his spirits.

By 6:30 am the following morning, he was back in his flat. A long night. Emotionally exhausted, he fell asleep. A couple of hours later persistent knocking on his front door aroused him from a sound sleep. Fear invaded the grogginess of just waking up. The police? Slipping on a shirt as the subtle knocking continued, concern began fading. Police would not be timid with their knocking.

Opening the door enough to stick his head around to see who it was, Adele Thompson said, "Did I wake you?"

Still slightly groggy, this was a pleasant surprise. "No problem as long as it's you waking me." Opening the door wide he stepped closer to give her a kiss. She threw her arms around him in a tight embrace engaging his lips with her own passionate response. After several moments, he pulled her inside and closed the door.

Once inside, Adele renewed kissing him. Tears ran down her cheeks, "I'm so sorry about the other night. I shouldn't have put you off from making love. Just uncertain about committing. Came here this morning to remedy that."

Bewildered, but aroused by her attention, his growing erection became prominent within his underwear briefs. Without hesitation, Adele's hand ran down to his groin. Rubbing him not enough, she quickly slipped her hand inside the waistband to grasp him. Stepping back, she then seized his briefs with both hands yanking them down below his knees.

From that point there began a flurry as she disrobed shedding her skirt followed by panties then moving against him allowing him to unfasten her bra and shed her remaining clothing.

For the next hour they enjoyed exploring each other. The tenderness toward pleasing each other only intensified their state of arousal. Finally entering her, neither could prolong their orgasms for very long.

They laid spent in each other's arms. Terence reflected on the extraordinary feeling. Something never experienced before with a woman. Thinking this defined the difference between lovemaking and fornicating. Or just fucking as better typifying Maureen Lynch's style of sexual intercourse. Raw, selfish, competitive, even combative. Lovemaking with Adele proved entirely different. Both concentrated on offering mutual pleasure to the other. Discovering their own satisfaction thereby intensified creating a profound bonding inexplicable by words.

Adele got out of bed and put on Terence's shirt. Brazenly displaying her nakedness, she neither buttoned the shirt nor pulled on her panties. "How about I make us some coffee?"

Terence smiled. "I'd like that. Need my morning coffee although making love with you is a much better way to start the day."

As she stood preparing a pot of coffee, he came up behind her and wrapped his arms around her. Rubbing her breasts, one hand soon wandered downward to her pubic area.

Not resisting, she continued concentrating on making coffee. After setting the burner alight, she turned facing him. Kissing him she stroked his beginning erection. After several moments, she said, "Save that for later once you're fully restored. I can stay only a couple of hours. Need to stop by the pub then get to my one-o'clock class."

Terence made an expression of a contrived sense of disappointment then set out two coffee mugs then returned to the bedroom to put on jeans.

Sitting at the small dining table drinking coffee. Adele asked, "How are your studies progressing."

"Completed all the required course work with good grades. Only need to complete the master's thesis. My design concept seems to work on paper. Can't find any flaws. Only question is the ability to create a microprocessor circuit design to reintegrate data packets, chopped up groups of data, into an intelligible message.

"I have an idea about how to augment my thesis with something more than schematics and technical explanation. If I can construct physical hardware possessing circuitry to visually demonstrate my concept, that would dramatically validate my work. People inherently understand something about mechanical engineering or the laws of physics. Electrical engineering deals in abstracts understood best by observable physical results.

"Have a thought that I might be able to make functional circuitry to demonstrate my theoretical concept visually on a CRT display. This is new technology. My concept isn't necessarily original, but if successful it validates my grasp of the underlying cutting-edge work in the field of data communications."

"How long will that take to create such demonstration?"

"A few months I hope. That assumes I'm at least sufficiently successful for the academic advisory committee to declare my concept having merit. That's a black and white question. Either it works as I theorized, or it doesn't. Not sure I'm good enough to make microprocessing hardware to demonstrate the principal which itself is developing technology."

"If your idea proves out, then what?"

"Get a job. Had originally planned to return to Boston. The climate of violence in Belfast has only become worse since I came to Northern Ireland. However, I'm not so sure I want to leave."

"Why is that?"

"Because of you. This morning made me realize just how deeply my feelings for you ran."

Adele smiled broadly and nodded. "I came here this morning because I realized I also have strong feelings for you. How about we spend the afternoon together tomorrow? I have two back-to-back classes early in the morning. I can be here by eleven o'clock in the morning. You can get some sleep. We'll have the rest of the day together until you must get to work tomorrow night. You can devote the rest of today to working on your thesis."

"Sounds wonderful, Adele."

"Since I don't understand electronics, if you could make something like that to show me visible results that would be fantastic. Even for your professors, a visual demonstration would show unusual effort."

"My thoughts exactly. Still, it's a challenging task to assemble functional hardware circuitry to demonstrate my technical principal. Requires a microprocessor with CRT displays to serve as a means of visually showing what is happening. Something like assembling my own minicomputer."

Adele said, "Well, if you can construct such a device, it sounds like an impressive way to validate your theory visually. Somewhat like the result of your evident growing erection providing visualization of what's on your mind."

Laughing, he replied, "Exactly. The natural result of the well understood process of looking at a remarkably sexy half-naked woman."

She reached over to kiss him while rubbing his groin, while his hands cupped her breasts. Disengaging, she stood up. "Both of us need to wash up if we're going to take this further. I'm glad I changed my mind and came here this morning."

"I feel the same, Adele. I believe we're falling in love."

"That we are my love."

Just before noon, Adele Thompson emerged from Terence's flat. She was smartly dressed, with Terence just in jeans, barefoot, and without a shirt as he embraced the woman to engage in a prolonged kiss.

Maureen had been observing from behind a parked automobile on the street for a couple of hours since the woman entered Terence's flat. Hopefully remaining unnoticed, she assumed the woman would eventually leave by bus the same as arriving. As the bus approached, Maureen crossed the street to board following the woman.

After a change to another bus, the woman disembarked on Ravenhill Road then entered the *Raven Pub.* Maureen felt decidedly uncomfortable in yet another obviously Protestant loyalist neighborhood. The British Union Jack flew from a tall masthead outside the pub. Thankfully the woman remained inside the pub for only fifteen minutes before emerging to again board another bus, this time carrying a backpack.

Tying her hair in a scarf to slightly alter her appearance, Maureen boarded the same bus just before the door closed. Maureen walked past the woman seated in the forward section of the bus. Another good look at the woman's attractive face further inflamed Maureen's jealousy.

The woman disembarked at Queen's University with Maureen following. After the woman stopped to chat with two other young women she entered the university grounds, Maureen Lynch had seen enough. She knew where Terence lived. Obviously sleeping with a loyalist. Someone appearing connected with the *Raven Pub.* Armed with that information she could be back in Derry by late afternoon. She would show up at Liam Kelly's *Black Goat Pub* the next morning without ever being missed.

Furious and bent on revenge, she cautioned herself to calm down. If it was revenge she wanted, then why not obtain much more? She could blackmail Terence into doing her bidding. Threaten him with revealing his secret identity. Threaten to reveal him as a spy. For which side did not matter. Exposure meant a very bad way to die. In exchange for her silence, he must take her to America. Once there he must continue to do as she demanded, or she will make up lies about his involvement with the Provisional IRA. She could also threaten to expose his grandfather to British authorities by making up lies. Maybe spin lies to her father that Liam Kelly had been compromised by his grandson working for the loyalists.

Boston was full of mostly Irish Catholics sympathetic to Irish nationalism. Wouldn't take kindly to someone posing as a Protestant loyalist. Terence would realize escaping to America might still have unpleasant consequences if she turned on him. Adding to this was Terence's inability to resist the kind of sex she offered. Susceptible to her carrot and stick manipulation.

On the return train trip back to Derry, Maureen Lynch's anger over Terence's betrayal turned to more pragmatic thoughts. How best to blackmail Terence into getting what she wanted? Could Terence perhaps be involved in something dangerous? Could her threats backfire and put her at risk? Terence didn't seem the type. Devoted to his grandfather but still an American. Unused to what it meant living as an Irish Catholic in Northern Ireland. Unlikely to have gotten involved in Northern Ireland politics. Yet why was he using another name? Did her knowledge of his secret of using different identities represent enough of a threat for him to bend to her demands?

Maureen was far more than an Irish bumpkin from remote Derry. She was street smart. Clever. Strong willed. Obsessive. Willing to take risks to escape her circumstances. What sort of life could she ever expect by remaining in Derry? She was a barmaid with no prospects. Marriage and family in this rural Irish backwater conjured dreadful images. Her good looks would fade with age. Whoever Terence Kelly was he offered an opportunity that she must pursue. The prospect of embarking on an adventure that could change her dreary prospects served to concentrate her thoughts on a plan. As the train pulled into Derry, she had formed her next moves.

After his first intimacy with Adele Thompson, Terence spent the rest of that day forming a plausible narrative of how he might explain occupying different identities. That was a given. He had no intention of becoming Terence Stewart. That would mean remaining in Northen Ireland. Harboring concerns about discovery of his contributing to IRA bomb making therefore making him complicit in untold numbers of deaths and injuries, made that impossible. He was not foolish enough to believe that he covered every eventuality. No perpetrator could ever be sure of having committed the perfect crime.

Revealing his true identity to Adele as Terence Kelly at some point became imperative. Explaining the origin stemming from his mother's concerns over her husband's background made sense. Revealing he came from a mixed ethnic union of his Protestant mother to his Catholic father might go down okay with Adele. Yet why that prompted his mother to create different surnames on his birth-related documents meant revealing to Adele the danger stemming from connection to his notorious IRA paternal grandfather. That became an issue because Liam Kelly was from Derry therefore residing in the United Kingdom. Liam's IRA exploits in the 1920s made him an Irish legend only in the Republic of Ireland. The mere mention of the name Liam Kelly held all manner of pitfalls in the charged political environment of Northern Ireland.

Using the manufactured explanation of allowing preferential entrance and tuition to QUB as a British national lacked credibility. Adding his reason for pursuing a post-graduate degree from QUB to avoid the United States draft was only somewhat better for explaining masquerading under another name. Why not just stay in Northern Ireland as a legal resident until circumstances in the U.S. with respect to the Vietnam War changed? He could think of no answer to that obvious question.

If nothing else, Adele's father's active involvement in the loyalist UVF, represented too serious a threat to ignore. Any explanation of using different identities because of mixed ethnic backgrounds became irrelevant. What was happening in Northern Ireland was equivalent to a civil war with the weight of the British government siding with loyalist paramilitaries. The IRA was condemned as a terrorist organization. Arrest by the RUC would lead to murder charges for participating in bomb making. Loyalist paramilitaries would deem him an IRA spy. Spies suffered a bad death with British security forces turning a blind eye.

Leaving Northern Ireland was the only way to escape the consequences of his participation with IRA violence and to live a normal life in Boston. Yet abandoning Adele Thompson made that imperative gut-wrenching. Not likely that Adele would leave her family to run away with him to America. The situation seemed hopeless. Too premature to consider confiding his circumstances to Adele unless he could construct a better narrative.

Whatever the remaining months in Belfast held, he would make the most of his time with Adele. His dilemma seemed beyond solution. Fatalistically, he would take things as they came while staying focused on leaving Belfast by December.

Their earlier lovemaking did have another unexpected positive effect. The rest of the day put him in a frame of mind for devoting himself to working on his technical project. Armed with a fresh positive perspective, a new approach came into focus. An easily manageable workorder schedule allowed him time for exploring his newly conceived approach to overcome the technological challenge he had wrestled with for weeks. Pieces began falling into place. After a couple of hours, the solution revealed itself. Testing his hypothesis, he could find no flaws. Every proof attempt returned positive confirmation. Not only did this satisfy the thesis abstract, but it also appeared to be a technically elegant solution to a thorny problem. Not merely an academic exercise but a true innovation with immediate practical application. All that remained was to draft descriptive diagrams and graphs accompanied by suitably explanatory content.

The following day, he could not contain his enthusiasm when Adele arrived at his flat. Although the subject matter and the mathematics were beyond Adele's comprehension, he went to great lengths to show his solution with scribbled drawings.

Adele said, "I don't understand anything you are describing, Terry. How does this technology become so important?"

"It will be essential with ever increasing electronic information demands."

Adele said, "Are you still going to attempt constructing something to visually demonstrate how this works?"

"Oh yes. That will take some work, but I've completed a design. All I need now is to obtain the necessary hardware components and see if I can successfully construct a processing circuit to demonstrate the validity of my theory. I think I can obtain the necessary integrated circuits through the university.

"Looks possible on paper. It requires designing what are called interface message processors. Very new technology developed only in the last couple of years in the United States. Published technical work is understandably very thin. It therefore becomes a real challenge. Even without demonstrating my theory in practice, my thesis paper may be sufficient for awarding my master's degree.

"Sounds to be an impressive accomplishment of what you've already achieved, Terry. Do you believe your advisory committee will more enthusiastic if you able to demonstrate your theory in practice by constructing actual circuit hardware?"

"No question. It will show I have a thorough understanding of the underlying hardware elements necessary to accomplish data packet switching for practical applications. I'm very satisfied that I've produced some good work. I have you to thank for my breakthrough."

She raised her eyebrows. "How could I have possibly contributed?"

He came over bending down to kiss her. "Because you turned my attentions to us. Freed my mind from obsessing over technical challenges. The solution was always somewhere in my mind. But I was trying too hard to solve the problem by hammering away without considering alternative approaches."

Adele returned his kiss with passion amplified by tenderly touching his cheeks with both her hands. "We have the entire day. We could start celebrating early."

CHAPTER 23

Derry, Northern Ireland | September 1973

Mixed with her latent jealous anger over Terence's betrayal, Maureen felt the excitement of adventure. Tinged with perhaps danger and the prospects of leaving her confined existence in remote Derry with its violence and institutionalized ethnic oppression. Her first course of action was to learn as much as possible about what Terence was doing. She suspected that Liam had been meeting him occasionally in Coleraine ever since Terence abruptly left Derry. Was the secrecy simply to keep her from learning he was in Belfast? That didn't explain using a different name. How was that even possible? He was an American. Holding a job meant possessing some official identification under the name Terence Stewart. How did that come about?

After Terence left her, she wrote several letters to the address of his parents in Boston that Liam said was the best way to reach him. The sonofabitch never replied. Of course not, he was living these last two years in Belfast just 75 miles away. Liam lied to her about his return to college in Boston. His Belfast girlfriend was either a student or worked at Queen's University in Belfast. Maybe Terence was also attending Queen's as a graduate student? Yet why was he using the name Stewart? Everything came back to that question.

Considering that Liam Kelly was an IRA veteran from the past and her own father's veneration of him along with Derry

Brigade OC Martin McGuinness, she always suspected Liam must be involved in some way with the Provisional IRA. Hiding in plain sight as an aging pub owner in his seventies. That alone cast suspicion on Terence using an assumed name. A false identification having something to do with the IRA? The key might be the girlfriend. Maureen would start with learning more about the *Raven Pub*.

Knowing nothing about how to go about researching, she started at the Londonderry Public Library. A helpful librarian directed her to a Northern Ireland business directory. That led to a public listing with the address for the *Raven Pub*, its establishment fifteen years earlier, the proprietor named Alfred Thompson. From there the librarian suggested other directories to research Alfred Thompson. From there she discovered other significant information. Alfred Thompson, born 1927, married, wife named Luise, two adult children, Fred born 1948, Adele born 1952. Thompson was politically active in the Ulster Unionist Party. Unconfirmed reports identified him as a prominent figure in the Ulster Volunteer Force in Belfast.

The information shocked Maureen. Thompson was not only a loyalist but possibly associated with the Ulster Volunteer Force, the most actively violent of the loyalist paramilitary organizations. The UVF was a familiar group to Maureen as table talk at home by her IRA-connected father, Sean Lynch. This opened up all sorts of speculations. If Adele Thompson was Terence's girlfriend, then Terence could be involved with something very dangerous. IRA spy or IRA traitor?

Before leaving the library, the librarian asked her if she found what she was looking for. Maureen answered, "Maybe. Are there any other references that might be helpful? I'm actually looking for someone that might be associated with a certain business in Belfast."

Everything rested on confirming Adele Thompson as Terence's girlfriend. That would mean Terence had infiltrated a loyalist paramilitary organization either as an IRA spy or IRA traitor.

"Might this business be mentioned in the newspapers for some reason?" the librarian asked.

"I don't know. Is there a way to search that?"

"Oh yes. We could try the archive of the largest Belfast newspaper the *Belfast Telegraph*. We have back issues going back a decade on microfiche?"

"What's that?"

"Microfiche is a way of storing newspaper content on miniaturized images that allows storage of large volumes of material in compact form. It can be read on a viewer that allows enlarging to read on a screen. Let me show you."

Leading Maureen to a desk with a viewing screen, the librarian pulled up a cross-reference index that showed an alphabetized index of names with dates where that name appeared on in the *Belfast Telegraph*. "What is the name you are researching?"

"The *Raven Pub* in Belfast."

"Let's take a look," the librarian said. "You're in luck. Several references, all very recent. Let's start with the earliest date."

The display showed the front page of the Saturday July 28, 1973, edition. A photograph of the destroyed front of the *Raven Pub* featured prominently. The headline read LOYALIST PUB BOMBED IN CENTRAL BELFAST.

"Oh my," the librarian exclaimed. "This was just weeks ago. Is this the business you were looking for?"

Maureen nodded as she began reading the reported details of the incident.

"You can scroll to internal pages of this newspaper edition by clicking on this arrow. You can go back to the cross-reference index and view other editions by clicking here. If you need assistance, I'll be at my desk."

Maureen read the entire coverage of the *Raven Pub* bombing. Moving to the next edition for the following day, the coverage included statements from Alfred Thompson accompanied by his photograph and that of his daughter Adele sighted both as having escaped injury during the explosion that killed one person and injured sixteen.

Maureen enlarged the image of Adele Thompson. Staring at it for several minutes, even with the grainy image, left no doubt this was the woman that entered Terence's flat. Absorbing that, further reading quoted a statement by the RUC identified the *Raven Pub* as a known watering hole for suspected members of the loyalist paramilitary organization the Ulster Volunteer Force.

While that truly scared Maureen with the risk of becoming involved in something with extremely dangerous implications, it also meant Terence would have no choice but to agree to her demands. Regardless of what he was really doing, her knowledge of his using different identities exposed him to either IRA or loyalist retaliation. With her IRA affiliation, she knew full well the fate of spies if discovered by either side. Torture to give up information before execution. Even she could be at risk.

Why would Terence do such a thing? If true, Terence must be acting on something Liam Kelly cooked up. Her father recounted to her the stories of Liam's exploits in Dublin during the War of Independence. Liam Kelly was a clever and dangerous gunman never to be underestimated. Nonetheless, Maureen felt she had the upper hand. Enough to coerce Terence of no choice but to take her to America.

Maureen concocted a simple deceit. She announced her intention of going on a month-long holiday to Paris with two girlfriends from Letterkenny. Both her parents and employer Liam Kelly said they were happy to see her expand her interests beyond Derry.

Instead, she would go to Belfast and confront Terence. Forgive him for abandoning her but declare she wanted him back. Tell him she knew of his living under another name. Assumed the secrecy of meeting his grandfather in Coleraine meant involvement in something dangerous. Didn't want to know any details but threaten to expose his subterfuge if he didn't take her to America. Both could be safe and together there. Confident in her ability to sexually coerce his cooperation, he would see the benefits of the proposal, reinforced with the implicit danger of refusing.

Emptying her bank account, she packed her best clothes and abandoned her unnecessary meager possessions. She would not be returning to Derry.

Terence sat with Adele Thompson on his second-hand well-worn sofa. Both relaxed sipping wine while enjoying the post-coital warmth following their afternoon lovemaking. Life felt good for Terence. Confident of the acceptance of his master's thesis was not only professionally important but it validated his professed reasons to his family for remaining so long in Northen Ireland. He believed he could explain his academic degrees awarded in different surnames to an employer. Nothing more than parental divorce with the subsequent adoption by a stepfather at an early age. Seemed entirely explainable.

Escaping his ill-conceived IRA misadventure without consequences while sharing a profound bond with his grandfather balanced the scale. Looking back with mixed feelings about his traumatic experiences since coming to Northern Ireland would undoubtedly have an unknown impact on the rest of his life. At least there would be a life ahead. Yet the gnawing uncertainty about holding on to Adele disturbed his otherwise sense of well-being.

"What are your plans after completing your undergraduate degree next spring?" Terence asked her.

"Been thinking about pursuing my master's like you. I have aspirations for teaching at the university level. Post graduate degrees therefore become a requirement."

"Teaching literature?"

"Yes. Also been thinking about trying my hand at writing. Fiction. Novels actually."

"That's a bold leap. Aren't short stories easier to write? You are enamored with Shakespeare. Shakespeare's plays are just short stories. Why not do something like that?"

"Because I'm drawn to novels. A bigger canvas. Exploring subplots and mixing together diverse characters. And no, short stories and plays are not easier to write. Just different challenges for the writer. No different than the challenge of writing poetry.

"I'm enamored as you say by Shakespeare because of his use of language. No writer in the English language has even come close to his genius of using words to express emotion with such eloquence and power. However, Shakespeare's storytelling themes are sometimes lacking. His power comes from the shaping of his characters. Without his exceptional use of language, he would never have achieved his place in literary history for over four hundred years. Every fiction writer hopes their work not only tells a compelling story but does so by using those well-drawn crafting elements famously exemplified by Shakespeare's works."

Terence remarked, "I love listening to you recite lines from Shakespeare. Can't always understand the meaning with his use of old English words, but I can hear the beauty of his phrasing you describe."

This conversation provided the opportunity to segue into an idea that began developing since their first intimacy. Terence said, "What if you were to consider pursuing your master's degree in America? New England has some of the most prestigious universities in the world."

Adele's eyes widened. She wasn't expecting this, but the idea immediately sounded intriguing. Admittedly, she wondered what would happen once Terence completed his master's degree at QUB. Finding employment meant a decision to return to America or remain in Belfast. As an American, for professional reasons that was no real choice. If he stayed in Belfast it would only be because of her.

Terence continued, "Assuming acceptance of my thesis, you could join me over the holiday break from QUB. I haven't been back to Boston for two years. Returning no longer holds my attention. That's because of you, Adele. You can explore possible university choices for pursuing your master's, maybe even followed with a PhD. You can return to Belfast for your final semester at QUB.

"Do you know what you're suggesting, Terry?"

He laid his hand over hers. "I think I do. We love each other. Means staying together. Educated, we have the options of exploring the best opportunity of how to enjoy life. I believe the political violence will only get worse in Northern Ireland. Living in Irish populated Boston could be a welcome relief for both of us. You can fly directly from Boston to Dublin in less than seven hours. Not like being on the other side of the world."

Should Adele agree with at least spending a few weeks in America over Christmas, his plan included flying first to New York to spend a few days. This will allow him to spin his fabricated sanitized story before training to Boston and facing the family. That assumes if explaining his mixed ethnic political family background does not kill the prospects of pursuing a future together.

He will confess that he felt he must conceal his background fearing her parents' reaction as well as his father and his notorious grandfather on opposite side Northern Ireland's political divide. The troubled Irish British history should not preclude two people in love rising above that unfortunate history. No one would believe his being raised as a Catholic from South Boston falling in love with a Protestant loyalist, much less the daughter of a loyalist paramilitary leader. He is neither a practicing Catholic nor Protestant. His parents came from opposite backgrounds that accounted for his possessing different legal surnames under each of his dual nationalities. He did not feel it safe enough to reveal his mixed background while still in Northern Ireland. Could not trust Adele's father's reaction learning of his relationship to Liam nor the RUC nor British security forces. Avoiding the U.S. draft and the Vietnam War and pursuing a post-graduate degree in Belfast made sense, especially with the ability to take advantage of his dual British citizenship. Acceptance into QUB and the ability to pay his way with a good technical job fitting his studies' schedule made experiencing his birthplace a memorable experience.

The narrative seemed logical and believable. Everything consistent with factual circumstances when altered by omissions to suit his purpose. His willing participation in IRA bomb making concealed by only his grandfather knowing that regrettable dark secret. Granda would keep that secret to his grave. Granda would also understand his falling in love with a Protestant. Terence's Derry-born Catholic father did just that by marrying his Protestant Belfast mother. Granda wanted both his son and grandson to have a life removed from the political violence that shaped his entire life. Explained under these circumstances, Adele might understand. She never expressed strong political views other than lamenting the unrelenting violence of the *Troubles.* It was worth the try. All the better to present to Adele from the neutral environment of America.

CHAPTER 24

Belfast, Northern Ireland | October 1973

Maureen Lynch took an early train to Belfast driven to the Derry train station by her father. She told her parents it was to be a two-week holiday to Paris with two girlfriends from Letterkenny across the border in County Donegal. They would train to Belfast then train south to Dublin to take a flight to Paris. Liam Kelly her employer gladly gave her the time off from work at the *Black Goat Pub*. Liam and Agnes Kelly were longtime friends of Sean and Mary Lynch and treated their daughter Maureen like a niece from her early age.

Assuming Terence to be home early in the morning with his apparent nighttime job at the radio station, she would surprise him at the same time she previously observed his girlfriend entering. The irony brought a smile.

Setting down her suitcase and backpack, she knocked gently on Terence's front door. Getting no response, repeated louder knocking eventually brought him to open the door. With a shocked expression, she threw her arms around him. Smothering him with kisses she pressed her breasts against him by pulling him tighter. Backing him inside the flat, she kicked the door closed, "I've thought about you for so long. Make love to me right now, Terry!".

"No! What the hell are you doing here? How'd you find me?"

She grabbed both his wrists placing his hands on her breasts. Wearing a low-cut tight-fitting top wearing no bra, she simultaneously began unfastening his belt then unzipping his fly. He could not help himself from responding when she ran her hand inside his underwear.

Giving into the pleasure of the moment, he fondled her breasts as she did the same to his erection. Pushing him back onto the bed after a few moments, she began removing her clothes. He could not help but watch. Maureen possessed an outstanding body. Easy to convince himself to go with the flow rather rebuff her. Her discovery about him living in Belfast put him on dangerous ground given her volatility. That instability combined with obsessive behavior is what made him abruptly leave Derry without saying goodbye. Her showing up in Belfast now represented an existential threat. Better to manage the circumstances after gathering his thoughts undistracted by arousal.

He therefore did not resist as she pulled off his jeans followed by his underwear. With his erection springing forth she knelt on the floor to take him fully in her mouth. Laying back on the bed he gave in to her sexual impulses.

After twenty minutes of furious lovemaking, Maureen disengaged from their entanglement. Lying next to him propped on one elbow, she said, "I should be angry with you for dumping me without even so much as a goodbye. When I discovered you in Coleraine, all I could think about was getting you back. What have you been up to for two years living here in Belfast?"

Unprepared and overwhelmed, he tried to conjure an explanation that would not worsen his circumstances, he replied, "When were you in Coleraine? And why?"

"I was in Coleraine the day you met your grandfather. That chaotic day weeks ago when British security forces swept through the town. Followed your grandfather on the train to Coleraine. Wondered for some time where he went off every once in a while when the pub was closed for business. Watched you board the train in Coleraine to Belfast then followed you all the way here to your flat. Watched from outside that night until you left the flat. Apparently to your job at the radio station."

She omitted for the time being having renewed her surveillance the following morning and observed his girlfriend entering his flat then staying a couple of hours.

"This is clearly a Protestant loyalist neighborhood. I looked in your postbox. Mail addressed to this flat is in the name of Terence Stewart. What's that all about?"

"Nothing sinister. Just my surname that appears on my British passport. Had to do with my mother registering my birth using her family name. She was concerned when we emigrated to America when I was two years old that there might be a problem because of my grandfather Liam's notorious involvement with the IRA. I grew up becoming a naturalized United States citizen using my baptismal registry as Terence Stewart Kelly. My mother naturally used her married name Kelly when we arrived in America. I only used my British identity as Stewart to gain preferential entry into Queen's University and find employment in the UK.

"That sounds like bullshit. You didn't go to all that secrecy just to get away from Derry and attend the university."

"Wasn't about secrecy. After our last argument, didn't want to keep going through further painful arguments. I have affection for you, Maureen, but we weren't getting along very well. Just thought it better to part ways. Had already submitted an application for acceptance at Queen's University."

"Really? You never mentioned that. When were you going to tell me?"

Kelly sighed. "Had our relationship turned out better, I would have told you. Studying in Belfast didn't mean we could not have been together. It's only two hours by train. Took to meeting my grandfather in Coleraine occasionally because it's not far from Derry and easily reached by train."

"To avoid seeing me you mean," Maureen said sharply.

"I suppose that was part of it. Couldn't very well show up at the *Black Goat* and confront you. Once classes started at the end of that summer, just easier not to resurrect old hurts."

Unconvinced that there wasn't something more to Terence's secrecy, Maureen pretended to accept his explanation. Using different names living in a Protestant loyalist neighborhood screwing the daughter of a possible loyalist paramilitary figure provided sufficient reason for him to fear exposure. More important for her to use that as leverage to coerce him to take her to Boston. Also gives her time to make him pliable to the implicit blackmail threat by his willingness to enjoy sex with her.

For Terence, the day passed in a blur. Fear mixed with uncertainty of how to extricate himself from this catastrophe. His dilemma complicated by wanting to prevent further sacrifices having come so close to leaving his secret life behind unscathed while accomplishing so much. Enduring this crazy bitch while losing the love of his life Adele seemed a terrible irony.

Terence telephoned Adele from his radio station the night Maureen showed up. Needed to stall for time to figure out how to deal with Maureen. He concocted a story for Adele that he must leave Belfast for an undetermined number of days. "The nursing home contacted my parents in Boston that my grandmother has been hospitalized in Coleraine. Apparently suffering from pneumonia. She hasn't been physically well for some time. Also suffers from severe memory decline. Will keep in touch but unsure how long I might be away."

The following morning, he woke Maureen when entering the flat from returning from his nightshift at the radio station. It was 6:30 am. Maureen's bipolar mood instantly turned ugly. Mornings not being her best time of day even coffee did not improve her behavior. Her latent raging anger of Terence's betrayal came forth. "Now I know why you never answered my letters I mailed to your parents' address. When are you planning to really return to Boston?"

"Probably by the end of the year. Need to complete a thesis for my degree at Queen's University. What I always planned to do."

"What about your girlfriend, Adele Thompson? She going with you?"

Another shock adding another level of concern. How did Maureen learn about Adele? "Have you been spying on me, Maureen?"

"Enough to learn you're up to something. Something probably dangerous. I know that Adele' Thompson's father is a loyalist paramilitary bloke. Does that have something to do with you using the name Stewart?"

Terence shook his head vigorously. "Let's leave Adele out of this Maureen. I came to Belfast to attend the university. I'm not involved in Northern Ireland politics. Neither my grandfather's nor Adele's father."

"That's all bullshit! You're hiding something. That's why you're using a different name. Something to do with your grandfather, I'm thinking. You know my father's IRA and they're good friends. I think you're into some kind of dangerous shit involving the IRA. You're trying to figure out how to dump me again and get on with whatever that is and continue fucking your Protestant loyalist tart."

Now worked up, Maureen continued, "You want to know how I discovered about Adele Thompson? I watched her that morning after you arrived back in Belfast the previous afternoon. She showed up here. You came to the door in your underwear. Spent a couple of hours fucking before she left.

"When she left I followed her to this pub called the *Raven*. Found out it's a loyalist hangout. Adele is the owner's daughter. Alfred Thompson is suspected of being a loyalist leader of one of those paramilitary organizations."

"How did you come to that conclusion?"

Turning angrier, Maureen responded, "You think I'm just stupid rural Irish. You with your university education. I researched all this from what I found in the newspapers and other references in the Derry Public Library. Know what else I found out? The *Raven Pub* was bombed just weeks ago. Now that began me to wondering if Terence Kelly masquerading as Terence Stewart might have a hand in this."

"Now wait a minute, Maureen. Why would you even speculate about something that crazy?"

"Because you and your grandfather have been meeting in secret. Probably for a very long time. Liam leaves town every few weeks on days when the pub is closed. Agnes always gave some vague excuse for his being away. He was meeting you in Coleraine.

"My father won't confirm it, but I know Liam Kelly is still involved with the IRA. The old leopard didn't change his spots. Perhaps Father didn't know that Liam might be working with the IRA Belfast Brigade. Living in hostile Catholic Derry would make sense for Liam to maintain his cover as long ago retired from IRA activities. Christ, he's in his seventies, but still a clever old fox."

Terence responded shaking his head. "It was a car bomb that damaged the *Raven Pub*. I know nothing about bomb making. Have no reason to become involved with helping the IRA try to kill loyalists. I'm from Boston. This isn't my fight. Look what happened with all the bombs the IRA detonated across Belfast on *Bloody Friday*. They did not need an American to set a car bomb off in front of the *Raven Pub*."

Maureen was not placated. "Too many coincidences. Using different names. Setting yourself up as a university student in Belfast. Living as a Protestant loyalist yet coming from a background as an Irish nationalist with our grandfather's IRA history. Both of you sneaking about meeting secretly in Coleraine. Seducing the daughter of a loyalist paramilitary leader. The bombing of the loyalist pub.

"Don't know what kind of game you're really playing, Terry. I'm convinced though that Liam must somehow be involved with the IRA. Might appear to be nothing more than an elderly proprietor of a Bogside pub. Hard to believe he's not secretly involved in IRA activities with all that's been happening these last few years in Derry. Father told me the stories of what Liam Kelly did fifty years ago. Of all things, he was an assassin for Michael Collins. A right bloody dangerous fellow in his day. Can't believe he put that behind him."

Switching the subject back to the girlfriend, Maureen said, "Get the Protestant bitch out of your mind. Telephone her and make up some reason for not seeing her."

"I already have, Maureen. Called her last night. Told her my grandmother was in the hospital in Coleraine."

Maureen smiled menacingly. "That was smart. Wouldn't do having Adele showing up at the door. You and I'll be leaving Belfast very soon."

"What do you mean?"

"I mean you're going to take me to America. Remember Diana from that day we spent in Letterkenny? She has a cousin that married an American. Her cousin now lives there. Diana explained that if you marry an American citizen you can get what's called a green card. Allows you live and work in the United States as a foreigner. That's what I want."

The mention of marriage became yet another shock with horrifying implications.

Maureen continued. "Call it a marriage of convenience. Not a forever arrangement, Terry. Yet why not? We have great sex together so that's not such an unpleasant thought."

"What if I refuse?"

Maureen's tone turned offensive. "You don't want to do that, Terry. Leave me again and you'll regret it. Don't know what you're into by using another name, but it certainly isn't something you want to become known. That could prove fatal. My father's IRA and your girlfriend's father is Protestant loyalist paramilitary. You're up to something against one side or the other. Either way, you'd be in very deep shit if you were found out."

With that exchange, Terence understood just how dangerous his situation became with someone as unstable as Maureen fixed on blackmailing him to help her get to America. Even once in America, what would happen? Couldn't possibly tolerate her demands while enduring participation in her brand of sex. At risk was the implicit threat of her revealing to her father his closely held secret of using different identities. Sean Lynch undoubtedly was now the OC of the IRA Derry Brigade. Terence guessed that to be the case with the public reporting of Martin McGuinness' recent arrest in the Irish Republic for involvement with a seized large quantity of explosives and ammunition. That placed Maureen with immediate access to exercise her blackmail threat. Sean Lynch wouldn't buy his reason for using a different identity any more than his daughter did not. That might even lead to endangering his grandfather.

"I just need a few more of days to complete my thesis project and submit it. We will leave for Boston immediately after that. It would look odd to my family leaving without first finishing my degree."

"How long?" Maureen asked.

"No more than a week."

"Make it less than a week. I want to leave by this coming Friday," Maureen declared.

Punctuated by Maureen's aggressive sexual appetite, the toxic environment created by her threats became unbearable. Within days, his disgust forced a desperate decision of how to resolve the problem presented by Maureen Lynch with finality. A daring move requiring him to immediately leave Belfast and return to the United States. Submitting his thesis was all that remained. He devoted much of his nightly work schedule for the next couple of shifts to compiling the thesis in finalized textual form. With the design already completed, that left only composing the abstract and descriptive content.

Bringing components to work, he assembled the first iteration of his functional breadboard experimental processing circuitry. To demonstrate his theory visually, he used CRT displays to connect with his processing circuit to display data transfer rates. His solitary environment working nights at the radio station provided the ability to access the latest electronic instrumentation. Initial results encouraged him by producing surprising results. The empirical work also pointed to required modifications in the circuit design.

Completing the thesis abstract and descriptive content, he made an appointment with his thesis advisor at QUB. On the Wednesday before Maureen's imposed Friday deadline, he announced to Maureen that he must meet with his advisory professor at the university.

Maureen replied, "Okay. Until we are on a plane to Boston, I can't be sure you won't run out on me again. Hand over your two passports so I know you'll be returning."

Infuriated, he held his anger in check. What he had in mind would be fitting retribution.

The meeting with his advisor went remarkably well. The professor's review of the design validated Terence's confidence in the technical merits of his innovation. The textual composition became just an essential formality. The degree was dependent on the technical merits not on the writing quality of his textual explanation. Surprising his advisor, Terence added that he also designed a processor circuit board to demonstrate his theory in practice to the advisory committee.

On the walk back to the flat, Kelly's thoughts turned to reaffirming his decision to resolve the problem of Maureen. He repeatedly reviewed the details of his plan looking for any flaws. The means for accomplishing what he had in mind already existed. Important to keep his thoughts focused on executing the plan rather than dwelling on the emotional aspects. Survival left him no other choice.

CHAPTER 25

Boston, Massachusetts | 2025

"When we left off your narrative from our last session, you had just escaped discovery of a British security sweep in Coleraine," Father O'Brien said. "That was not long after the witnessing of the carnage in the aftermath of the Coleraine bombings that killed so many civilians in June. You mentioned your regrets for not having ended your Northern Ireland misadventure of making bomb detonators following that scare of potential arrest. Did your grandfather successfully avoid discovery in Coleraine?"

"Oh yes. Even at his advanced age, Liam Kelly was practiced in survival. He was clever at such things as evidenced by his operating in secrecy during his years fighting in Dublin during the War of Independence. Knew how to remain under the radar for decades after until circumstances came undone in Derry in 1969. Caused him to recognize the remnants of the original IRA had gone soft. Turned political rather than militaristic in pursuit of Irish nationalism. Worse yet, the Original IRA moved far to the left politically. Granda was old school. Therefore, he joined the Provisional IRA, the militarized resurrection of the IRA from fifty years earlier. When I say joined, he did so semi-unofficially. Wanted to stay in the shadows. That's what he knew best when working for Michael Collins.

"Too old to take up the gun, Granda therefore turned to smuggling. My own father helped him reestablish a link with a New York-based Irish smuggling ring. The radio detonator devices I produced found their way to the IRA Belfast Brigade rather than the local Derry Brigade. Even that smuggling channel was known only to the Belfast Brigade quartermaster and OC. In that way Granda maintained his cover as an elderly pub proprietor. At his advanced age, not likely to be suspected as having reverted to an IRA gunman."

"How then did he escape Coleraine that day? You were fortunate having delivered your improvised walkie-talkie devices secured in a station locker when British soldiers descended on Coleraine. Nothing incriminating. With your grandfather's history if caught, he would certainly be detained and questioned."

"Granda snuck away to look up an IRA contact in Coleraine. As Granda told me later, he saw the man arrested and dragged from his house. Coleraine was too hot to attempt an immediate escape, so he spent the night in the man's already ransacked house. Someone arrived by car the following morning to drive him back to Derry. The British Army gone, he retrieved the duffle bag from the train station locker containing my last delivery of modified walkie-talkies."

O'Brian said, "You also spoke about Adele Thompson. Did that relationship contribute to keeping you in Belfast?"

"Adele was very much a major reason for staying in Belfast when I should have left. Women became my downfall as you shall see as I relate subsequent events. I convinced myself I was staying to finish my master's thesis. That would validate my entire cover story to my family for staying so long in Northern Ireland. Having found the love of my life in Adele, I denied what should have been the compelling logic of leaving after discontinuing involvement with the IRA. Finishing up the master's thesis from Boston would have been a prudent move for reasons of safety. Foolish enough to think I had enough time to attempt to find a way of continuing the relationship with Adele.

"Seemingly having buried my secret activities involving the IRA, I believed I may have devised a narrative that might salvage our relationship now having progressed to intimacy. At the same time, my thesis project came into focus. Finally resolving a thorny technical problem, I was able to validate my innovation approach for improving electronic data transmission. I actually designed and assembled processing circuitry to demonstrate my theory. An impressive accomplishment that I wanted to show off. It would ensure being awarded my master's degree.

"Everything was now in place to leave Belfast. My sanitized cover story serving to explain my two years in Northen Ireland to family and to Adele seemed viable. Revisiting my Irishness while furthering my professional credentials, living through the unusual violence, giving testimony to my maturity.

"Waited too long. Maybe by only a matter of days. Maureen Lynch showed up at my flat. Difficult to describe the depth of my shock. She immediately revealed discovering my using another name that turned my shock to genuine fear. Using different names in this charged politically violent climate posed a real threat. Living in a Protestant loyalist neighborhood involved with the daughter of a loyalist paramilitary with my paternal grandfather a former notorious IRA gunman exposed physical danger from every faction engaged in the *Troubles.* Could never be explained satisfactorily."

O'Brien said, "I can well-imagine your concerns. How did Maureen Lynch find you?"

"Told me she followed my grandfather to Coleraine. Wondered where he periodically disappeared every few weeks. Observed me greeting him at the Coleraine train station. Realized I had never returned to Boston after leaving her two years earlier. After the security sweep, she followed me back to Belfast on the same train. A couple of weeks later she returned to Belfast.

"Maureen might be psychologically unstable, obsessive, and given to using sex to get her way, but she was not stupid. Told me how she discovered my alternative name in mail in my post box. Followed me to the radio station. Sat outside my flat the following morning and observed Adele arriving. Waiting a few hours, she then followed Adele to her father's pub then to QUB. Maureen returned to Derry describing how she researched the

Raven Pub at the public library using microfiche archives of the *Belfast Telegraph*. Discovered the car bombing weeks earlier, accompanied by newspaper photographs of Alfred Thompson and his daughter Adele as surviving the bombing. The newspaper article alluded to the alleged association of Alfred Thompson with loyalist paramilitaries.

"Can certainly understand Maureen Lynch showing up as frightening development," O'Brien commented.

"Indeed, it was. Becoming far worse after announcing her demand that I take her to the United States. Even suggested a marriage of convenience allowing her to remain in the U.S. Her way of escaping limited prospects as a young Catholic woman stuck in the Bogside quarter of remote Derry.

"A horrifying thought of Maureen accompanying me to Boston made dangerous when she backed up her demands by blackmailing me with threats of exposure. It was no stretch that exposure of my suspect circumstances using another name in Belfast during that time could turn fatal."

"How did you manage the suddenly altered circumstances imposed by Maureen? What about Adele?"

"Called Adele that night from the radio station. Gave her the excuse for needing to leave for an unknown number of days. My parents in Boston wiring me of my grandmother's hospitalization in Coleraine. Having no telephone at my flat avoided inconvenient calls from Adele. That bought me time. Regarding your question, I did not manage well. No way to manage someone like Maureen. Imprisoned by her for several days was pure hell.

"Her instability during the month or so I spent in Derry convinced me to end the relationship. Entrapped now by her in Belfast, things quickly became intolerable. Maureen did not believe my explanation of using another name for reasons of getting into QUB and finding employment using my British citizenship. Admittedly it was a weak argument. Her father was IRA. She worked for my grandfather and knew his history in the IRA. Natural for her to believe I was working with him covertly in some way. Maybe spying on the loyalist enemy. Whatever it was, she understood just how dangerous that became if exposed.

Having the upper hand only added to giving free reign of her mental instability. I am now convinced Maureen Lynch suffered from bipolar disorder. Unchecked when mixed by holding leverage over me only magnified her instability."

O'Brien nodded while making notes as Kelly paused for a moment to gather his thoughts. "The idea of being indefinitely saddled with this crazy woman was beyond imagining. I decided on what I must do to remove Maureen as a threat. Survival can provoke resorting to extreme measures. Even finding a way of escaping Northen Ireland leaving her behind might not ensure my past deeds would not eventually come back to haunt me. Should she decide to spread rumors about my involvement as either a spy for the IRA or a traitor to Irish nationalism, might that still be a threat even after returning to the United States? Then the more immediate threat to my grandfather's safety could not be ignored.

"I was undoubtedly complicit in the deaths and injuries to unknown numbers of those victims killed by IRA bombs. The United States and the United Kingdom held close ties in matters of criminal legality. Extradition to the UK on terrorism charges could not be ruled out. I might also become a pariah among the Irish population of South Boston. My family unfairly affected. My grandfather quite possibly interned. Taken altogether, I decided on an extreme solution."

O'Brien looked at him immediately realizing what Kelly seemed to be suggesting. "What happened to Maureen, Terence?"

"She died."

"You mean you killed her?"

"Yes."

O'Brien was taken back by Kelly's matter-of-fact response. Killing Maureen Lynch must have been exceedingly personal. Nothing to compare to his more remote guilt over civilians killed by IRA bombings using his improvised radio detonators. "Care to explain how you accomplished killing her then getting away without being caught?"

"Of course, Father. I'm here to relate every detail of my long list of sins. Killing Maureen Lynch may be the lesser of my victims of bloodshed but unquestionably the most troubling. However, I do not offer that as an excuse for murdering her. Nothing I relate to you is intended for any sympathetic treatment. Murdering Maureen has no justification except self-preservation. I could have simply left Northen Ireland. Instead, I reacted in desperation. Instead of cutting bait and just leaving Northern Ireland I wanted to conceal my mistakes. Hardly justifies murder even of a blackmailer. However, I did not appreciate the depth of the emotional scaring until years later. Far greater guilt than my part in the killings from IRA bombings. Probably because that was less remote. The horror of killing Maureen has forever haunted me above all else."

CHAPTER 26

Belfast, Northern Ireland | October 1973

With unstable Maureen Lynch possessing his secret she became a real threat of others discovering his covert identity. Up to now he has remained anonymous with an unknown legitimate identity backed by a British passport. No one knows that alternate identity other than his grandfather. His detonation devices contain no fingerprints. Any electronic components found are commonplace radio, television, and other communications components commercially available in Northern Ireland and Great Britain. Any forensic debris cannot directly lead to him. Only his employment at Comet Electronics working with the same model walkie-talkies could conceivably become an issue. Living in Belfast under the legal name Stewart should also insulate him from being connected with his notorious IRA grandfather.

Self-interest, hubris, and disgust that this obsessive unstable woman could jeopardize everything became too much. Her blackmail left him no alternative. Removing Maureen through an act of violence would never have occurred to him had he not already possessed the means. That means existed, concealed in his attic from long ago.

When first creating his improvised radio detonating triggering devices, he conducted live tests in a remote stretch along the coast of the Irish Sea near Larne Harbour. One small intact test bomb remained hidden in the attic. Along with the bomb was a fully functional radio detonator transmitter and receiver. Assembled just eighteen months ago, it could be made operational after replacing the ignition batteries.

The destructive main secondary explosive was ANFO, ammonium nitrate and fuel oil. His construction used a three-pound high explosive mixture of 94% ammonium nitrate thoroughly combined with 6% diesel fuel substituting for fuel oil, both being chemically identical. He compressed the mixture inside a 3-inch diameter by12-inch length of PVC drainpipe capped on both ends. Imbedded within the ANFO were two blasting caps, inside a vial of nitroglycerin sealed tightly with glue. Insulated wires protruded through a drilled hole in one end of the cap on the pipe. ANFO could be degraded if allowed to absorb moisture, however, he meticulously sealed the cap to the pipe with PVC cement. As for the nitroglycerin, the relatively mild summer climate would not elevate the attic temperature to a dangerous level having set the device next to the attic ventilation opening as a precaution.

Easy enough to quickly install four new 9V batteries that supplied the electrical power source for igniting detonation and testing system functionality with a multimeter. The small bomb was more than enough to kill a person holding it within inches from their body.

All that remained was devising a method for disguising the bomb that would allow Maureen to be holding it. That also meant a way of keeping it out of range from him and ideally from others.

As the deadline imposed by Maureen approached, Terence said to her, "We're leaving Northern Ireland in a couple of days. Obviously I won't have the opportunity to see my grandparents. At their age, I may never see them again. I'll make up an excuse for leaving abruptly. Probably something to do with a job when I telephone them after arriving in America. Thought I might get them an early Christmas present and send it in the mail before leaving Belfast."

Maureen said, "That's a nice thought. We'll go out together today to find something suitable. What do you have in mind?"

"Don't know. Something for the both of them." Mindful of something that would duplicate the size and weight of the small bomb, he suggested, "What about a Waterford crystal piece? That's Irish and makes an elegant gift."

Maureen replied, "Sure. Sounds appropriate. Got a store in mind?"

"For a fine gift, I'm thinking Robinson & Cleaver. Never been there but I've heard it spoken of as very upscale. Should carry Waterford crystal. We can take the bus. The store's downtown across from city hall."

The store indeed had a large selection of Waterford pieces. He selected a flower vase that provided similar size and weight of the small bomb. The store wrapped it in colorful paper in a gift box. "Do you have a sturdy box I could use for shipping the wrapped gift?" The helpful clerk found a suitable box and even gave him masking tape to seal the package for shipment.

Once they returned to the flat, he said to Maureen, "How about you run down to the grocery and get us something for dinner. Could also use something to drink. Bottle of decent whiskey. I'll wrap my grandparents' gift for shipping. Tomorrow we'll go out and drop it off at a post office for shipment to Derry. Then we'll have dinner at a good restaurant. Our last night in Belfast. The following day is Friday. I'll place a call to the radio station and claim a family emergency has unexpectedly called me away. We then train down to Dublin and book a flight to Boston."

Maureen grinned. Overjoyed that her plan was coming together she came over and gave him a kiss. "That sounds wonderful. I'll get dinner, whiskey, and maybe a bottle of wine. Where can we celebrate with a nice dinner at a restaurant tomorrow night in Belfast? Any suggestions?"

"Can't say that I do. We'll ask about for a recommendation when we go out to the post office tomorrow."

He gave Maureen money, returning her kiss. "I won't be long," she said.

Waiting a few minutes making sure she hadn't forgotten something and unexpectedly returning before he accessed the attic. The switching of the Waterford vase for the bomb retrieved from the attic set his nerves on edge as seconds ticked by. Reflecting that Maureen had completely abandoned any reference to Adele suggested she must feel in firm control. The thought strengthened his resolve. Her blackmail threat had brought about this drastic solution. How could he have been so stupid as to succumb to her seduction in Derry? Should have realized then that there was something wrong with her.

Pushing aside those thoughts, he concentrated on making the switch of the vase with the bomb quickly. It took only a couple of minutes to place the wrapped Waterford vase in the attic and return the ladder reclosing the access door. He then set to work on rigging the bomb.

The previous night he brought home fresh 9V batteries necessary for supplying power to detonate the blasting caps. He had no new batteries to power the walkie-talkies but used a meter to verify they were still good having never been previously used.

With the 9V batteries snapped into place, the bomb became operational. He tested all power outputs with a meter as his last act. It must not fail to explode. He stuffed it into the heavy shipping box securing it from moving about with crumpled newspaper. He quickly secured the box with excessive amounts of tape to preclude any chance of opening. The transmitting unit that looked to be a standard walkie talkie he placed in the pocket of his jacket. Should Maureen discover it and ask what it was, he would say it was necessary to communicate when working on the radio station broadcasting equipment located in a separate building.

Looking at his watch, the time transpired since Maureen left was twenty-five minutes. Less than the thirty minutes he allocated for accomplishing the preparations. The grocery market was at least a ten-minute walk each way. Terence sat down to compose his shattered nerves and calm his racing heart rate.

Maureen was no cook. She returned with fresh bread, cheese, and sausages for a cold dinner. She had not forgotten the whiskey, adding both beer and wine. Both having drank too much, Terence was spared having to participate in another night of unwelcomed sex.

In the morning, Terence felt physically terrible. Too much whiskey and spicy sausage combined with interrupted fitful sleep. Probably the same for Maureen who remained sound asleep as he made his way to the kitchen to make coffee.

Keeping as quiet as possible, he was able to get down a cup of coffee before she came out of the bedroom. Sitting down, she yawned, "I feel like shit. Drank too much of your bloody whiskey. What time are we leaving for the post office?"

"Later this morning. After we shower and recover from last night. We'll ask around for a recommendation for a good restaurant. Maybe something different like Italian. Must be an Italian restaurant somewhere in Belfast. In Boston we have a lot of great Italian eateries."

Terence looked at her disheveled hair, blurry eyes wearing no makeup. Wearing his shirt unbuttoned with her exposed breasts caused no sexual arousal. Constraining his disgust, he cautioned himself to remain in control. Only a couple more hours and Maureen Lynch would cease to be a concern. He forced his thoughts to move to practical matters once completing what he just set in motion. Get that horror behind him as if her death was already a fait accompli. Return then to the flat and begin removing any remaining traces of Maureen Lynch.

Terence and Maureen set off by bus to the Botanic Gardens Post Office near Queen's University at ten o'clock. Terence held the box on his lap. He concentrated on holding his concerns in check that something might go wrong. What if the bomb failed to detonate? Did he miss something in rushing to prepare what he assembled months ago? Could he go through with triggering detonation? The thought of it not exploding and the package being shipped to his grandparents caused him a moment of immediate panic. The reaction calmed only by intently looking out the bus window rather than glancing toward Maureen.

He knew the bus stop from having used it often. The Student Guidance Centre was next to Elmwood Hall situated on the same block as the building housing the post office. It occupied corner of the ground floor next to an Ulster branch bank. In front of the post office was a one-way drive for cars to exit off University Road for cars to deposit mail in conveniently situated post boxes. Nearby stood a newsstand kiosk. That was necessary for his plan.

As they disembarked the bus, he said to Maureen, "I'm going to get a couple of American magazines to take along on the trip. Spotting *Newsweek* and *Time Magazine* on the newsstand, he remarked, "Look at that." The cover of *Time Magazine* read *War in the Middle East.* "At least Northern Ireland hasn't become as bad as living in Israel."

Paying for the magazines, he handed Maureen some money then handed her the box. "You take this to the counter for shipment. Address the label to the *Black Goat Pub*. I want to read about what's happening in the Middle East." The ruse was necessary as an excuse for transferring the box to Maureen and appearing distracted by the *Time Magazine* cover.

Entering the post office, Maureen walked toward the counter while Terence hung back just inside the front entrance. Only a few people populated the post office interior. One woman standing at the counter was speaking with the postal clerk. As Maureen drew closer she stopped behind the woman to wait her turn next for service. Terence then stepped back outside the entrance door. Moving to the side of the glass door he was now no more than forty feet away from Maureen.

Extracting the transmitter unit, he stepped clear of the glass entrance door and turned his back to shielding what he was doing from view by anyone entering the post office. The green light appeared after toggling the arming switch. Before losing his nerve, he flipped the firing switch. The force of the blast shattered the glass door from behind him.

Turning around, he immediately reentered the destroyed interior taking in the scene. Debris scattered everywhere. Part of the drop ceiling gave way causing a cloud of dust. Lighting fixtures and wiring hung down. Maureen lay face down on the floor. Terence could see a rapidly expanding pool of blood spreading on the tiled floor next to her. Her right arm outstretched revealed a bloody stump at the wrist missing her hand. The only other obvious victim appeared to be the woman that had been standing at the counter perhaps a few feet in front of Maureen. She was crumpled on the floor leaning awkwardly at an angle against the service counter.

Pocketing the walkie-talkie transmitter, Terence turned away and left the building. Outside a gathering group of people stood stunned. As a dust cloud drawn out the shattered windows by a gentle breeze immerged from the destroyed front of the building, several men entered inside to render assistance to victims. In the distance came the wailing of police sirens.

Terence calmly began walking away shaking his head to appear dazed but also to dispel the vision of the mangled remains of Maureen Lynch. A block away he turned at the first cross street. Proceeding a couple of blocks he came to a trash disposal bid. Removing the transmitter from his jacket pocket, he wiped it thoroughly with a handkerchief to remove fingerprints then placed it under a discarded shopping bag in the trash bin. The horror of what he just did caused a physical reaction. Leaning forward he bent down clutching his knees then began repeatedly vomiting covering the shopping bag in the trash. Within a couple of minutes, the nausea passed enough to steady himself by holding onto the trash bin.

To clear his head, he walked back to the flat rather than take a bus. His thoughts now turned to rewinding the event. Would anyone recall him? What about the newsstand vendor? Nothing should connect him as a bomber.

Reaching his flat, he immediately began gathering Maureen's clothing and toiletry articles. Stuffing them into her suitcase and backpack, he would decide later the safest place to discard them. That night, he would type a letter of resignation at the radio station stating a family emergency in America required him to return there immediately.

Allowing himself no more than two weeks before actually leaving for Boston would allow time to reunite with Adele. Time also to schedule a demonstration of his thesis theory to the university advisory committee. Recovering his composure and put his flat in order, he would wait until the following night at the radio station to call Adele. Tell her of his return from Coleraine after his grandmother's condition improved dramatically. Make arrangements for seeing Adele the following day. Rehearse his story about the need for returning to Boston sooner than planned. This time because of a possible employment opportunity. Tell her he still wants her to join him in New York and Boston over the university's holiday break.

He would remove the Waterford vase from the attic and ship it to his grandparents just before departing Belfast. Once in Boston then telephoning them. That allowed time for him to construct his story of shock after reading of Maureen's death. She never contacted him, but still that was too much of a coincidence. Had she been stalking him? To his grandfather, having completed his degree requirements, thought it best to depart Northern Ireland as soon as possible without elaborating further.

The next morning, the *Belfast Telegraph* published the story. The column title on the front page read, *YOUNG WOMAN KILLED IN BOMBBLAST*. The first paragraph of the article read, *A young woman in her twenties died when a bomb believed she was holding exploded inside the Botanic Gardens Post Office near Queen's University in Belfast. According to a RUC spokesman, the victim's identity is being withheld pending notification of family and a continuing investigation. The spokesman did offer that the circumstances suggested that the comparatively small bomb may have exploded accidentally when the woman was about to ship the package to an intended*

victim that the RUC would not further comment on pending the ongoing investigation. In addition to the deceased woman, two others were injured in the blast. An unidentified woman suffered serious injury, and a male postal clerk sustained lacerations in the blast. Both victims are expected to recover.

Terence heard the news of the blast on the radio hours after the bombing then read the newspaper account in the next day's edition. The RUC undoubtedly knew Maureen's identity from the contents of her handbag. No reason the incident should connect to him. Maureen was not known in Belfast. No photograph was yet posted on television. Living in Belfast under a different name severed any connection with Derry other than with his grandparents. Perhaps the accidental explosion might cast suspicion on Maureen's father who must be suspected of IRA activity in the Derry Brigade. Might the RUC suspicion Sean Lynch of using his daughter to post a bomb to a loyalist politician or paramilitary leader?

Terence must not assume too much. Before Maureen appeared at his door, he felt safe remaining for a few more months in Northern Ireland. Time enough to finish his degree providing a logical explanation to his parents for remaining in Northern Ireland to gain his master's degree. Allowing an orderly exit from making bomb detonators for the IRA fulfilled the commitment made to his grandfather.

Maureen's death now meant leaving Northern Ireland sooner than planned. Yet he should still have time enough to further his plans with Adele. Everything prepared. Nothing incriminating left in the flat. Letters drafted and ready for posting to his employer and landlord. Terence Stewart would then simply vanish.

"Adele, it's Terry. I've returned to Belfast just this evening. I'm at work at the radio station."

"Wonderful! How's your grandmother?"

"Much improved. Her pneumonia seems to be responding to treatment. What's your class schedule tomorrow? I want to see you."

"Just a single class at eleven o'clock."

"How about lunch around one o'clock?"

"How about at the pub? Told Father I'd tend bar tomorrow night giving him a break."

Terence waited outside the *Raven Pub* for Adele to arrive the following day. Thought it better to avoid displaying overt affection in the presence of her father and the pub regulars.

Over lunch, he announced, "I know I just returned, but something else unexpected has come up. When speaking with my parents in Boston, my mother said there was a letter addressed to me from one of my former professors in Boston. The letter says he has a friend with an employment opportunity in the private sector that might be ideal for me. Unfortunately, I need to fly to Boston in a few days. Told my mother to call him and arrange an interview for this coming Monday."

With a disappointed tone in her voice, Adele replied, "Oh my! That's good news, I guess. How long will you be gone? Are you then returning to Belfast?"

Terence let out a sigh, "Probably not. If the interview goes well, I will likely have to start work within weeks. But remember my suggestion about you flying over to spend the holidays with me over the university's holiday break. You can experience New York and Boston. I'll pay for your airfare and hotels." Taking her hand, "We can talk about what comes next with us."

CHAPTER 27

Boston, Massachusetts | 2025

Terence Kelly resumed his narrative after going into the details of how he killed Maureen Lynch. O'Brien listened silently, transfixed, but aghast by Kelly's detailed explanation of the murder. Obviously an event recalled from fifty years ago, yet Kelly's unemotional recounting of how he conceived and executed such a horrific act still came as a surprise. Kelly transformed from repentant activist Irish nationalist to unrepentant confessed murderer. A sharp contrast when measured against his professed greater distress of losing Adele Thompson.

From an envelope Kelly extracted a couple of photocopies he printed from digitized archives. "This is a copy of the *Belfast Telegraph* front page of the 17 October 1973 edition reporting the death of a young woman by a small bomb at the Botanic Garden Post Office in Belfast the prior day. This other group of printouts is the follow-up article appearing in the 18 October edition identifying the victim as Maureen Lynch. The reporting states facts about the victim from a RUC spokesman."

After reading both newspaper articles, O'Brien said, "Explain again how you determined murdering Maureen Lynch to be a better solution than just leaving Northern Ireland immediately after she showed up in Belfast? Was it because you already possessed the means by having a functional bomb at your disposal?"

"That certainly was a major factor. No reason for her death to point to Terence Kelly or even Terence Stewart. Other than to my grandfather, her death should have no connection to me. The newspaper coverage even reported a possible scenario suggested by the RUC. *The victim was the daughter of Sean Lynch believed to be closely associated with the Provisional IRA's Derry Brigade. The RUC believes Maureen Lynch may have been in the process of posting the bomb when the bomb accidentally exploded. Such unintended explosions killing IRA bombers are not uncommon. The intended recipient of the package is not known since no shipping label was recovered from among the bomb debris. The whereabouts of Sean Lynch the victim's father is currently unknown. Maureen Lynch also worked as a barmaid at a Bogside Derry establishment called the Black Goat Pub. Curiously, the Black Goat Pub is owned by Liam Kelly, age 76. Kelly fought during the Anglo-Irish War as an IRA assassin for Michael Collins in Dublin. Kelly became a notorious member of Collin's Squad, also known as the Twelve Apostles. Liam Kelly has been questioned by the RUC but dismissed as a person of interest in the death of Maureen Lynch. Kelly's advanced age with no known involvement in nationalist activities since the early 1920s makes his involvement in the Belfast post office bombing unlikely.*

"Committing murder is a highly personal act. Did the ability to do this from a distance so to speak make the act easier?" O'Brien asked.

"Ah, never thought about that, Father. Perhaps that made a difference. I certainly wasn't about to strangle her. However, the sight of her mutilated body lying on the floor was a ghastly sight. By no means an impersonal way to kill someone. Cannot imagine what her face or the rest of her body must have looked like. Even in recurring nightmares, I fortunately conjure only the image of her handless bloody that is bad enough."

O'Brien remarked, "Did the thought of being known as Terence Stewart with no connection to your notorious grandfather make staying on in Belfast for a few more days seemed safer?"

"Precisely. Only my grandfather could make a connection to me."

"Did you ever explain what happened to Maureen to him?"

"Not really. He never asked me directly and I didn't offer a confession. Didn't like lying to Granda but couldn't bring myself to tell him the truth. Maureen was like his niece. Her father was his friend. I believe he knew, her death was my doing. I'll explain in more detail later on in my narrative.

O'Brien changed back to exploring the motivation for killing Maureen Lynch. "Still unclear how you decided such an extreme solution to rid yourself of Maureen was necessary. You had already planned on leaving Northern Ireland within a couple of months. Why not simply leave Belfast the following day after she showed up at your door? Does that mean you stayed in Belfast for other reasons enough to cause you to kill Maureen?"

Kelly nodded. "That is the heart of the matter is it not, Father? First I lost my idealism as an Irish freedom fighter then becoming a common murderer for misplaced reasons hardly justifying such an act. Irrational from a perspective of logic. Her blackmail could only affect me indirectly. Once in the United States, not likely anything would ever come of my participation with the IRA. Yet Maureen was obsessive enough to follow me to Boston. Not sure what kind of stink she could cause. Could damage me in the eyes of my family but not likely to expose my IRA activities. That seemed secure.

O'Brien said, "That doesn't seem to explain taking such extreme action? That action itself carrying such great risk."

"Never have come to terms with doing what I did, Father. Best I can do is recite reasons that do nothing other than inadequately explaining my blind hatred for Maureen. At the very center of that hatred was her having control over me. Ruining my newfound relationship with Adele Thompson that I believed had long-term possibilities. Leaving Belfast abruptly before waiting to officially accept my master's degree making premature departure difficult to explain. Attending QUB became my professed reason to the family for staying on in Northern Ireland for two years. Whether Maureen made a stink in Northern Ireland or in Boston would make me appear immature for going off on a youthful misadventure. A foolish escapade getting involved with a disturbed woman. Appearing diminished in my grandfather's eyes. My lacking the ideological resolve of aiding the IRA after it was I that convinced him to allow me to make improved bomb detonating triggers. All told, nothing sufficient to justify committing murder with all the risks that entailed. But at the time, sufficient to distort my perception of reality."

O'Brien, "Ideology attempts to justify all manner of violence as the means to accomplishing some greater purpose. Yet it is self-interest that often produces horrific acts of violence that cannot be morally justified. Is that what happened to you?"

"Something along those lines. Difficult to parse out my many moral transgressions by cause and effect. My disillusionment began with questioning the ideology that I embraced since old enough to understand the Irish struggle like so many Irish immigrants in South Boston. My experience from living the brief time in Northern Ireland profoundly disillusioned that ideology. My idealism derived from circumstances of a bygone era. Fifty years ago, when my grandfather fought for Irish independence from British rule. Not the situation in Northern Ireland during the *Troubles*. The IRA was no longer fighting just the British. Sectarian repression dictated a different kind of enemy. That's where I went wrong. The glorious exploits of my grandfather's IRA days as an Irish freedom fighter now looked to be nothing more than terrorism practiced by the Provisional IRA. By the time Maureen reappeared, I was already conflicted by competing emotions with which I was emotionally unable to cope."

Returning to Kelly's narrative chronology, O'Brien asked, "What happened next.? Did you immediately leave Belfast soon after killing Maureen?"

"I intended to. Felt I had little choice. My best laid plans contained a flaw. What else did I miss? Maureen may have told someone after discovering my living under a different name in Belfast. She remained with me for a week in Belfast. Someone may have seen her coming and going. Yet after killing her, I disposed of everything incriminating in my apartment and prepared for leaving Belfast within days. The RUC apparently believed Maureen to be an IRA bomber killed accidentally by a premature explosion. But I deluded myself into thinking that I had some time remaining before leaving Northen Ireland.

"A few days more to make my pitch to Adele seemed to present no risk. Telephoned Adele of having returned to Belfast. My grandmother's medical condition has improved significantly. Announced another fabrication that in speaking to my parents I learned they received a letter from a former professor addressed to me concerning an employment opportunity. Told Adele that it required my return to Boston in days to appear for interviews. Asked if she would spend her holiday break from the university with me in New York and Boston. She could then return to Belfast to finish her last semester for her undergraduate degree. She said she would think about it. That was late October 1973."

"Thought I had matters under control, at least for a short time. Time to try to make an attempt to salvage my relationship with Adele even with leaving Northern Ireland. Unbelievable hubris. Felt I had covered on my bases with enough interlocking secrecy to quite literally get away with murder.

"Interestingly, the damage I've done to Adele Thompson continues to weigh heaviest on my mind. I have two competing nightmares. Both recurring frequently over all these decades since returning to the United States. The visual horror of reliving the grotesque bloody vision of Maureen's bloody handless arm and replaying scenarios that make no sense as often happens with dreams.

"Different variations of another recurring dream where Adele continually rejects me has tormented me for years. Even hours after waking I find myself often replaying this dream. With my many far more terrible crimes, odd that abandoning Adele should be what mostly stands apart in my subconscious."

For O'Brien that was not in any way odd. Pointed more to Terence Kelly's sense of loss rather than guilt.

Kelly resumed. "I successfully buried those crimes committed in Northern Ireland. My manufactured narrative of fictionalized circumstances fit well with the chronology. However, hurting Adele who I believe loved me stands apart in my thoughts even to this day. Illogical, nothing compared to taking lives, but there it is. No question that subconsciously Adele was probably my strongest reason for killing Maureen. Above all else Maureen's implicit threats would clearly result in my losing Adele. Adele became the overriding reason I stayed in Belfast longer than I should have. Little did I know how much worse my predicament would become because of killing Maureen."

CHAPTER 28

Belfast, Northern Ireland | October 1973

The bombing that killed Maureen Lynch occurred on Tuesday 16 October. Terence waited until the following night to telephone Adele from the radio station telling her of his return from Coleraine. After making arrangements to see each other the next day, that same night he set in motion plans for leaving Northen Ireland.

Although the newspapers would report the bombing and announce the name of the victim, he still believed he had time to make an orderly departure. Time to try to convince Adele of following him to United States to spend her holiday break from university classes with him. That was the best he could do to salvage their relationship. Remaining in Northen Ireland no longer was an option. Never his intention anyway. Maureen discovering him made leaving imperative. Her death made it more so.

He gave himself no more than a week to settle things with Adele. That night he typed a letter of resignation to the radio station and to his landlord about leaving his flat. The following day he called his thesis advisor. Describing his construction of circuitry hardware to demonstrate his theory in practice, the professor was impressed by his exceptional initiative. Two days later he conducted a successful demonstration to three engineering professors comprising the faculty advisory committee. The resounding success garnered as much praise for his creation of the possessing hardware as his theoretical work. He left assured of being awarded his master's degree.

The correspondence he mailed cited an unexpected family emergency requiring his immediate return to the United States. Walking home after leaving the radio station he deposited the letters in a post box. He would spend a few days with Adele then depart Belfast that coming Sunday morning. Train to Dublin then board a flight to Boston. Resume life as Terence Kelly.

Unknown to Terence, Maureen had telephoned her mother when she left Terence's flat for the grocery market the day before she died in the bomb blast. In a brief conversation with Maureen said, "Mum, I'm calling from Belfast. Change of plans. I'm not going to Paris as I told you. I just made that up. Going instead to America. You remember Liam's grandson, Terence. Discovered him going to school at Queen's University. Going to spend a few weeks with him in Boston."

Her shocked mother replied, "You can't just run off like that to America. What about your job?"

"I'll let you explain to Liam Kelly. None too happy that Liam and Agnes lied to me about Terence having returned to America after he left Derry. Anyway, I posted a letter to you and dad that will explain everything. Got to go now, Mum. There's no telephone where I'm staying, but don't be worrying. Tell Father I love him." She rang off without further conversation with her mother.

On Thursday 18 October, the article appearing in the *Belfast Telegram* shocked those in Derry. Sean Lynch learned of his daughter's death in this way. Identifying him as prominent in the Derry IRA also meant he must immediately go into hiding or risk being detained. More pressing on his mind was finding out who killed his only child. After consoling his wife as much as possible, he placed a call to Belfast to his principal contact with the IRA Belfast Brigade, intelligence officer Robert Gallagher. In a guarded telephone call from a public telephone booth, Gallagher said, "No word on the street about responsibility for the bombing. If it was the doing of loyalists, nobody is saying anything. What was your daughter doing in Belfast?"

Lynch chose not to mention his daughter's telephone conversation. "Have no idea. Told us she was on holiday in Paris with some girlfriends. Newspaper mentioned me as possibly connected to the Derry IRA. Not waiting for the RUC to come knocking. Need to find out who did this to my daughter. Can you fix me up with a safe house in Belfast, Robert?"

"Right you are, Sean. Very sorry for your loss. Here's an address. Tell the woman answering the door that *my wife's cousin Robert sent me*. She'll be expecting you tonight. Don't share your real name."

Before setting out to make the drive to Belfast, Sean Lynch took keys to an old truck registered to someone diseased along with a forged driver's license in the same name.

Liam Kelly on the other hand could not go underground. Too old, too well known, nowhere to hide, and he must take care of Agnes. He had also been scrupulously careful to distance himself from association with anyone in the IRA Derry. Employing Maureen Lynch being a regrettable exception. Completely unlikely though that she could be acting in something involving her father's IRA activities, especially not in Belfast. A loyalist bomb perhaps, but that made no sense either. Immediately his thoughts turned to his grandson. Had Maureen somehow reconnected with Terence in Belfast? That left ominous speculation about what might have happened.

Liam Kelly's active association with the Provisional IRA was known only to three senior members of the provisional IRA, Seamus Twomey, OC of the Belfast Brigade as well as overall chief of staff of the Provisional IRA, Brian Keenan, Belfast Brigade quartermaster, and Gerry Adams. Furthermore, he restricted his activities to smuggling arms. Far too old to become involved in IRA active service unit attacks. When the RUC came calling, he convincingly toughed out their interrogation that his IRA association ended fifty years ago.

A distraught Sean Lynch spent the next day huddled with Robert Gallagher in the safehouse located in a Catholic Belfast neighborhood. A non-descript residence looking identical to others in a long block of brick row houses, it had the advantage of having an escape route should security forces descend upon the area. A middle-aged woman lived there. A widow of a fallen IRA member supporting herself by maintaining the residence for its occasional use. The escape route was a hidden exit behind a storage closet. The hidden door could be slid into a false wall allowing access to the residence next door occupied by another covert IRA supporter. That residence held a concealed cellar that also served as an IRA armory.

Gallagher told Lynch, "No reliable information floating about the post office bombing yet, Sean. My sources inside the RUC say the police still believe your daughter was most likely in the post office to post the bomb to some target when the bomb exploded prematurely. No evidence among the bomb fragments revealed any address. Premature explosions happen with inexperienced bombmakers."

"Fuck all that shit! Maureen wasn't a bombmaker. Knew nothing about bombs or weapons. Wasn't involved in any IRA activity. Christ, I should know. Been OC ever since Martin McGuinness' arrest in the Republic. There's some bastard out there that tricked her into delivering this bomb to the post office. A stupid bombmaker who botched the rigging of the detonating circuit. The sonofabitch knows he fucked up. Keeping quiet. Knows there's hell to play for doin' something like this without orders. Know any of your lads that could be involved, Robert?"

Gallagher replied, "Definitely not. Can't argue with that logic though. Until some talk on the street produces something, not much we can do. Things like this don't remain secrets forever though. Dumbasses eventually slip up somewhere."

Lynch said, "Need to call my wife. Bad enough suffering the death of our daughter, I'm now forced to leave Mary alone to grieve while I go into hiding."

"Can't call from here, Sean. Telephone exchange might be monitored. I'll come back after dark. Take you a few blocks away to a public telephone booth poorly lit by streetlamps."

Lynch said, "Of course. Don't intend to wind up in some internment lockup. Rather meet my end by taking a few coppers with me."

Placing his call later, Sean Lynch received yet another shock. When his wife answered she was crying. "Mary, you must get hold of yourself, or you'll make yourself sick. Have you eaten anything all day, Dear?"

"Sean, a letter arrived this afternoon in the post. From Maureen." Mary Lynch burst out into another bout of uncontrolled sobbing."

Letting a minute pass to allow his wife to calm down, Sean asked in a calm voice, "What does the letter say, Mary?"

"It's about that young man, Liam Kelly's grandson from America. Seems Terence Kelly never returned to Boston two years ago after he and Maureen broke up. He's been living in Belfast attending Queen's University."

The revelation stunned Sean Lynch. Before he could say anything, his wife said, "Seems Liam and Agnes also knew Terence was in Belfast. Maureen says she learned about that when she followed Liam on a train trip to Coleraine a month or so ago."

"What the hell is that all about? When did Maureen write this letter?"

"Less than a week ago. There's something else that I don't understand, Sean. Maureen says that Terence is going by another name. Calling himself Terence Stewart. She says Terence told her it had something to do with his birth records involving his British citizenship, and his getting into the university. Don't understand what that means."

Sean Lynch did not understand either, "What else does the letter say?"

"Said that Terence has a flat in a decidedly loyalist neighborhood. Even gives the address. Says Terence has been seeing a loyalist woman, a student at the university. Her father owns a pub. The *Raven Pub*. Says she and Terence are flying to America in a few days. Terence has promised to help her immigrate to America. Says she can't abide living the rest of her life in Derry. Says she will telephone us when she gets settled with him in Boston."

Lynch was more than suspicious learning of Terence Kelly using a different name and involved with a loyalist woman. His mind went at once to wondering if Liam Kelly was up to something that involved his grandson. Something that quite possibly led to Maureen's death.

Concluding the telephone call with his wife, Lynch turned to Gallagher standing guard next to the telephone booth. "Know an establishment called the *Raven Pub?*

Gallagher registered surprise as he discarded his cigarette. "I know it. How is it you know the name?"

Lynch related the contents of the letter that arrived today in Derry. "Seems Terence Kelly is going by the name Terence Stewart, Robert."

"Something strange going on, Sean. The *Raven Pub* is owned by Alfred Thompson. Commands an active service unit or whatever the Ulster Volunteer Force calls their violent members. You say Liam Kelly's grandson is mixed up with Alfred Thompson's daughter?"

"My daughter also said that Liam Kelly knew Terence was living in Belfast and kept it a secret from her. Maureen worked in Liam Kelly's pub in Derry."

"Jesus Christ! Smells like somthin' rotten going on, Sean. Got to pass this intelligence to our acting OC."

"Who's that now that Seamus Twomey got himself arrested and jailed in Mountjoy Prison?"

"Acting OC is Éamonn O'Doherty. I'll also be telling Brian Keenan our quartermaster. Keenan grew up in County Londonderry. Heard him speak respectfully of Liam Kelly. Maybe he can shed some light on this information. Terence Stewart you say is the name Liam Kelly's grandson is using?"

"That's what the letter said. Maureen and Terence had a romantic affair two years ago when Terence first came to Derry to spend the summer with his grandparents, Liam and Agnes

Kelly. Lasted a month or so. Maureen always was a bit wild. Not surprising that she might have been more than Terence Kelly could handle. On day she finds he just left without saying goodbye. Liam said Terence returned to the United States. Liam knowing all the time Terence was in Belfast attending Queen's University. That's what bothers me."

"Maybe more worrying is Terence Kelly living under a different name in a loyalist area while talking up with the daughter of a loyalist paramilitary figure."

"Armed with an address, I intend to confront Terence Kelly. Will you help me, Robert?"

"Need to check first with O'Doherty, or maybe Keenan. Don't want to be entering a loyalist area without first reconnoitering the situation. Terence Kelly could be spying for his grandfather. Liam Kelly might be old, but I'm told stories about what he did in Dublin fifty years ago. Twomey and Keenan speak of him as a deadly piece of work in his day. Maybe Liam Kelly may still be doing something secret."

Lynch said, "Could also be that his grandson turned spy or even informer. Maybe working both sides. What's called a double agent. If that's the case, makes him a prime suspect in killing Maureen."

Robert said, "Can't argue against that possibility. Sure it is that all of us need to be gettin' to the bottom of this."

Liam Kelly regularly read the *Belfast Telegraph* as the most authoritative newspaper in Northern Ireland. Reading of Maureen Lynch's death in a Belfast bombing came as a bewildering shock. Immediately he began ticking off questions? Why was she in Belfast instead of on holiday in Paris? Something involving Terence? Had she discovered him living all this time in Belfast after leaving Derry two years ago? Reading further newspaper details presented more questions.

The RUC said she was the only fatality. Holding a small bomb that injured only two other people inside a post office. The conclusion that she appeared in the process of mailing the bomb stunned him further. Intended or unintended victim became the question. Impossible to believe that Maureen, who he knew for so many years, could have been involved in knowingly mailing a bomb. Liam couldn't ignore the implication that somehow his grandson might be involved. He knew Terence had actually produced a small workable ANFO bomb he used for testing his radio detonating triggers. That realization sent a cold shudder of fear through Liam Kelly.

Liam Kelly telephoned Sean Lynch. Mary Lynch answered. In a weak voice she answered, "Hello?"

"Mary, this is Liam."

Immediately she broke down into a fit of uncontrolled sobbing. Liam understood she knew. "Is Sean there? Let me talk with him, Mary."

Softly, she said, "He's not here, Liam."

"Where is he, Mary?"

She hesitated before replying, "I don't know exactly, Liam. You read in the newspaper what happened to Maureen I assume?"

"Yes. I'm so very sorry, Mary. But where's Sean?"

"Staying somewhere safe. We suspect the police might be coming around." With that, Mary Lynch hung up. Maureen's letter said that Liam and Agnes Kelly had lied to her. Why? Unclear about what was going on, but Terence Kelly somehow played a part.

Liam shared the newspaper account with Agnes. She was unaware of Terence's cover activities with Liam. She believed keeping his secret about attending the university in Belfast was because of Maureen's obsessiveness. Terence used the reason for remaining in Northern Ireland to obtain an advanced degree while avoiding military conscription in the United States still fighting the Vietnam War.

With no way to telephone Terence, Liam was at a loss about what to do. The only way to determine if Terence possessed knowledge of Maureen's death was to speak with him. His impulse was to leave immediately for Belfast. He knew Terence's address. A dangerously ill-advised idea after thinking through the possibilities. Firstly, he had no idea if Terence was involved, or if he even knew Maureen was in Belfast. His concern was based only on coincidences. Terence's past affair with Maureen and Terence's secret association with bomb making.

Liam chose instead to reach out to his connection with the Belfast Brigade, Brian Keenan. For years, he and Keenan worked together to smuggle arms and money into Northern Ireland from the United States. Keenan's influence reached well beyond his official position as quartermaster. Brian Keenan was a fanatical proponent of IRA bombing strategy. The Belfast Brigade was the largest Provisional IRA brigade. From Belfast smuggled ordinance then dispersed to the other brigades. OC of the IRA Belfast Brigade Seamus Twomey was recently arrested, therefore Liam turned to Brian Keenan.

After returning to the safehouse, Gallagher said to Lynch, "I'll be discussing this matter with O'Doherty straightaway tonight. I trust you'll be staying put, Sean. Can't be having you wandering over to Terence Kelly's flat this time of night. I'll return tomorrow morning with my orders."

Except for brief interludes of dozing off, sleep alluded Sean Lynch all night. The woman made him a good breakfast with plenty of coffee in the early morning. Thanking her he said, "Need to get some air. Won't wander very far. I'll be back in thirty minutes."

Finding the same public telephone, Lynch placed a call to Derry. The number was always answered any time of day. For security the caller just gave a number then disconnected. Someone designated as a duty officer then returned the call from a public telephone. Ten minutes passed before the public telephone in Belfast rang.

"This is Sean. Who's this?

"Michael Coleman."

"Take a pencil and write this down Michael. I need the Donovan brothers to assemble a bomb. Gelignite. Five or six pounds. Something that can fit easily inside a briefcase. Timed detonator. Maybe a kitchen timer. Something where the person placing the bomb adjusts the desired time delay for detonation. Here's the wrinkle. The detonating circuit is to be booby-trapped. When the dial is turned to the desired setting it is to immediately trigger explosion."

"Can you repeat that, Sir?"

Lynch repeated the instructions and had the man repeat it back to him. "They are to bring the bomb to Belfast tomorrow night. They're to lay up somewhere safe in a hotel where they can be reached. I will call you again tomorrow night with instructions for where they are to deliver the bomb."

Lynch intended to confront Terence Kelly. Not likely Kelly would break down and confess to any knowledge of what happened to Maureen, but he needed to get a read on Kelly's reactions. Regardless, Lynch planned to exact his own brand of justice. Even without specifics, Terence must be dirty. Using different names and living among loyalists was too suspicion. Lynch felt betrayed by his old friend Liam Kelly. This secrecy involved more than Terence hiding from Maureen in Belfast. Why didn't Terence simply return to Boston?

Solving the mystery was beyond Sean Lynch. Instead, he reacted by conceiving a plan that would deliver a blow against the loyalist enemy and take out Terence Kelly in the process. In his mind, circumstantial evidence condemned Terence Kelly. Dealing with him on that basis became a necessary expedient at the very least. Guerrilla warfare made niceties of due process unrealistic.

CHAPTER 29

Belfast, Northern Ireland | October 1973

Liam Kelly was desperate to understand what happened in Belfast. Brian Keenan was his best source. He received dozens of Terence's radio detonating triggers. Watched as Liam demonstrated the functionality with a live test demonstration.

"What can you tell me about that bomb that killed that Derry woman in Belfast, Brian?" Liam asked.

Keenan replied a bit sharply, "Liam old friend, I should be asking you that question.

"What do you mean>"

"Did you know Sean Lynch came to Belfast immediately after reading of his daughter's death in the newspaper? The same article that named you as her employer at your pub in Derry. Lynch contacted our brigade intelligence officer who is our liaison with the Derry Brigade. We put Lynch up in a safehouse. Like you, Lynch came looking for answers. But he also brought us information. Telephoned his wife. Seems she received a letter posted by his daughter before her death. Some troubling information about your grandson Terence.

"Seems he's been leading a double life. Goes by the name of Terence Stewart. Has a flat in a loyalist neighborhood. He may also have a loyalist girlfriend. Worse yet, the girlfriend's father is UVF. Know anything about that, Liam?"

"It's not about the girlfriend. I know that Terry's been attending Queen's University. Working on a master's degree. Didn't want Maureen Lynch to know because he broke off a relationship a couple of years ago. That's why I keep his secret."

Keenan replied, "Liam, it's about why your grandson is using another name. Why he's connected with a UVF loyalist like Alfred Thompson. Your grandson's girlfriend is Thompson's daughter."

"What are you getting at, Brian?"

Liam knew of Alfred Thompson. The UVF was the most violent of loyalist paramilitary organization. Thompson's unit was well known.

"Could very well mean that Terence is connected with Maureen Lynch's death, Liam. From all reports she was holding the bomb when it went off. If this is about protecting his daughter, Alfred Thompson would have instead removed Terence blaming it on the IRA. And he would have done that using a gun not a bomb. It's about Terence consorting with the enemy, Liam. Did you know about him using another name?"

"Yes, but it's complicated. Nothing involving the UVF. Let me explain."

For the next thirty minutes Liam confessed everything to Brian Keenan. The reason for Terence using a different name. The relationship with Maureen Lynch. Finally thinking it better not to withhold anything, Liam told Keenan that Terence had been the one that designed and produced the dozens of radio detonators Liam provided to the Belfast IRA. Hoping to convince Keenan of Terence's loyalty to the Provisional IRA with that admission, Liam still withheld telling Keenan that Terence stopped making any more radio detonators months ago. Nor that Terence wanted out because he disagreed with IRA bombs killing civilians. That would only worsen Terence's situation.

"Jesus Christ, Liam! Why the hell didn't you tell me that before?"

"For reasons of security, Brian. Didn't matter to you whether those radio detonators were made here or America."

"Sure as hell matters now. Makes Terence the prime suspect for involvement in Maureen Lynch's death. Maybe nothing more than removing an unwelcomed personal problem of an old girlfriend. However, that becomes suspect if he's taken up with this loyalist new girlfriend that just happens to be the daughter of a prominent UVF figure."

"Knowing what you just told me, Terence seems the only logical suspect for killing Maureen Lynch. He had a lot to fear with just her knowing he was using another name. We both know Terence probably had the means of constructing a small bomb. The why of it doesn't matter. Only what comes next. Sean Lynch wants to confront Terence. Can't deny him that right. Our brigade intelligence officer will supervise Terence's interrogation. Should we discover Terence's been working with the UVF, don't need to tell you what that means."

"I'm coming to Belfast, Brian. Got to look after my grandson."

"No, Liam. You'll not be coming to Belfast. It's out of your hands. Don't make the situation worse. You'll let us handle this. Best I can do is promise that Terence will get a chance to explain himself. This is now a Belfast problem."

Brian Keenan was certain that Terence Kelly killed Maureen Lynch. Having designed these radio denominators, he knew a great deal about bomb making. Getting explosive material was obviously a problem, but that only might make for stronger suspicion that it could be a UVF bomb. Using one of Terence's radio detonators would have been an ideal way to trigger the explosion remotely from a distance selecting the best opportunity. Not too much a stretch to believe this former girlfriend became a dangerous threat after discovering his subterfuge living in Belfast as a Protestant loyalist under a different name.

Keenan held Liam Kelly in exceptionally high regard as an IRA legend. He would keep his promise to keep their arrangement related to radio detonators and his grandson totally secret. Liam's American smuggling connections continued to provide an important source of arms and money for the IRA. That secret meant withholding knowledge about Terence Kelly's covert activities. Whatever transpired between Kelly and Maureen Lynch in Derry might have become a dangerous threat if she somehow discovered his living a secret life in Belfast under another name. Current circumstances nonetheless took on wider significance.

Regardless of Terence Kelly's IRA activities, his mistakes alone created this current situation. Taking up with a loyalist woman and daughter of prominent UVF commander for someone hiding his IRA affiliation went beyond stupidity. Then reacting by killing Maureen Lynch with the very instrument that could point to him compounded that stupidity. Unlike his grandfather, Terence Kelly was an inexperienced amateur dabbling in high stakes covert activities that got people killed.

That inexperience might now bring Terence Kelly to a bad end. Keenan would not divulge knowledge of Terence Kelly's secret bomb making capabilities, but neither would he shield him from retribution from a vengeful father. This was a situation of Terence Kelly's making. War bred unpleasant circumstances of expediency. Keenan would follow an objective course. Honor his pledge to Liam Kelly for ensuring a fair hearing. Yet he must keep faith with a fellow IRA commander having legitimate reasons for extracting justice.

Acting Belfast Brigade OC O'Doherty had larger problems requiring his attention. "Brian, you handle this mess involving Sean Lynch's daughter. You know Liam Kelly personally but there are larger questions about what happened. Settle the matter in the best interest of the IRA."

Keenan therefore issued orders to intelligence officer Robert Gallagher. "Take Sean Lynch to confront Terence Kelly at his flat. Just the two of you. Careful mind you, this is a loyalist neighborhood. Make sure Lynch is not armed. Both of you interrogate Kelly. See if you can get to the bottom of this or at least learn more. The issue is Kelly's use of a different name and associating with the UVF."

Gallagher asked, "Terence Kelly undoubtedly will deny any involvement with killing Lynch's daughter. We'll still have to decide what to do next if Lynch remains convinced that Kelly was involved."

"That's why I'm sending you to accompany Lynch, Robert. You know Lynch. You're also Belfast intelligence officer for good reasons. I'm looking to hear your best advice about how to resolve the situation in a way that benefits the IRA. This is war. Casualties must be expected. That includes Maureen Lynch and Terence Kelly."

Gallagher returned to the safehouse in the afternoon after consulting with Brian Keenan. To Lynch, he said, "We'll be paying Terence Kelly, also known as Stewart, a visit this evening after dark. You'll have your chance to interrogate him. I'm to do the same. It's now my business to learn what Kelly's been up to associating with the likes of Alfred Thompson. Got two of my people keeping an eye on Kelly's flat. They have orders not to allow Kelly to leave.

This was a delicate assignment for the two Belfast IRA maintaining a surveillance on Terence Kelly's flat in a Protestant neighborhood. Every sector of Belfast that identified strongly with religious ethnicity remained vigilant. Sectarian violence was always a threat. Anyone unknown to the neighborhood fell under suspicion. The IRA watchers therefore positioned themselves in a utility van disguised as *Northern Ireland Electricity Service* used for just this purpose. They wore matching uniform coveralls. The van was outfitted with appropriate utility servicing equipment and two-way radios to facilitate communications.

Friday evening at eight o'clock Terence set off from his flat for his last work shift at the radio station. The previous night he posted his letter of resignation along with a letter to his landlord. Everything set in motion to leave Belfast. The only reason for delaying departure being the opportunity to explain to Adele his reason for leaving for Boston unexpectedly. The delay proved a costly error.

The IRA watchers observed Kelly leaving his flat. Their orders were specific. Should Kelly attempt to leave, detain him and sit on him inside his flat until relieved. Told to use whatever force required meant their suspect was foe not friend.

Terence descended the stairs then began walking. Although dark, the streetlights provided spotty illumination. The IRA watchers must exercise caution not to create a disturbance drawing attention.

Both watchers left the service vehicle and began following Terence. One kept from behind at a good distance while the other proceeded along the opposite side of the street preparing to cut him off.

Terence sensed the man approaching from behind and stopped to turn. Seeing the uniform of the electrical utility and a smile on the man's face, Kelly returned the smile offering, "Good evening."

Terence's smile vanished as the man extracted a revolver fitted with a noise suppressor. "Let's return to your flat. No harm will come to you if you follow instructions. Make no mistake, if you try to run I'll shoot you. I'll try for a leg, but I don't recommend you test me."

Terence stood unmoving, transfixed in terror. A second uniformed man came up behind him. Terence uttered, "Who are you?"

"Just do as we say. Now move!"

Terence led the way as the two men walked behind him, the one with the weapon having shielded it from view by holding it inside his jacket under his opposite armpit.

Inside the flat, the gunman ordered, "Make yourself comfortable. Some people want to talk to you. Might be a long night. Got any coffee?"

Terence nodded to the small kitchen area. The other man found a tin of ground coffee. Next to that a bottle of whiskey. He said, "I'll make us coffee. You might prefer some of this whiskey though. Looks like you're in need of somethin' to settle your nerves."

Sean Lynch and Robert Gallagher arrived an hour later.

Terence recognized Sean Lynch from his time in Derry. Not only Maureen's father but a known leader in the Derry IRA and friend of Liam Kelly. Terence knew Lynch being here meant he was in deeper trouble than he thought possible. Meant Lynch knew of his using another name. Meant Maureen revealed information to him.

Lynch immediately began before even sitting down, "Hello, Terence. Been a long time since you left Derry. You know why I'm here. You're goin' to tell me what happened to Maureen."

"Have no Idea, Mr. Lynch. Just read about it yesterday. Didn't know she was even in Belfast."

"The fuck you didn't! You damn well knew she was here! She discovered you sneaking around with your grandfather then followed you here. Living a new life in Belfast under a different name. Maureen said you were taking her to Boston with you. Instead, you killed her."

Terence vehemently shook his head. "That's nonsense! I haven't seen Maureen for almost two years."

"You're lying. She wrote a letter before she died. Mailed it to Derry."

Terence shook his head again. "Listen, Mr. Lynch. I didn't reunite with Maureen. Hadn't seen her since I came to Belfast to take up my studies at Queen's University. If she had located me here, I would never have offered to take her to Boston. We parted in Derry on bad terms. That's why I left without saying goodbye. You know how Maureen was. It didn't work between us after spending weeks together. Certainly would never again become involved with her. Don't want to speak badly of her, but Maureen was what I call emotionally unstable. All that stuff she wrote in the letter about us going together to Boston was just her fantasy."

"Fuck you say! I don't believe a word of what you're saying. Why are you using the name Terence Stewart? What's the game you're playing?"

"No game. I have dual American and British citizenship. Born in Belfast, my Protestant mother feared my Catholic father being the son of the notorious old IRA gunman Liam Kelly might become a problem. Feared it might become an obstacle for their planned emigration to the United States. Born to a midwife in 1948, my mother registered my surname as Stewart, her family name. When I decided to visit my grandparents in Derry for the first time, I applied for a British passport. Thought that I might try getting into Queen's University to pursue a master's degree and stay on in Northern Ireland longer. UK citizenship gave me admission preference and the ability to find part-time work while going to school. My two names are both officially legal. Nothing suspicious about how that came about."

Terence reached into his pocket and handed over both his passports that he now always carried on his person.

"Don't believe a word of that bullshit. Did your grandfather know about all this?"

"Of course. You can ask him. He kept my secret only because Maureen worked at the *Black Goat*, Granda's pub. Didn't want her to know I was still in Northern Ireland living in Belfast."

"What a bullshit tale. Don't believe a word of it."

Terence said, "What do you think I'm up to?"

"Don't know. But whatever it is has something to do with using different names. As you explain it, your mother's Protestant, your father's Catholic. No question about your grandfather's politics. Maybe you're spying for Liam. Then again, maybe you've fallen in with the loyalists. You see Maureen spoke about your new Belfast girlfriend, Adele Thompson. You know of course who her father is?"

"Of course. Alfred Thompson owns a pub. The *Raven Pub*," Terence said.

Lynch added, "He's also an important figure in the Ulster Volunteer Force. A nasty bunch of loyalist paramilitaries. Bitter enemies of the IRA. So maybe you've gone over to the other side. Maybe you've become what's called a double agent."

Terence rolled his eyes and sighed, "That's simply not true. Why would I be doing such a thing?"

Ignoring Terence's comment, Lynch said, "The newspapers say Maureen was holding the bomb when it exploded." Pausing for a few moments taking a couple of deep breaths before resuming, "I believe it was you who must have given her the bomb. Maybe your girlfriend's father discovered Maureen. Wanted to protect his daughter. Maybe wanted to protect you as a spy with credentials because of your connection to your grandfather."

"That's ridiculous. Just speculation based on nothing. I have no idea how Maureen came into possession of a bomb, but it wasn't my doing. I have not seen her since I came to Belfast! And I know nothing about making bombs."

"Your UVF friends know all about making bombs and you're hiding something. Maureen may have threatened exposing you."

"Mr. Lynch, you're just imagining such things. I know you're grieving, but I had nothing to do with Maureen's death."

This exchange went on for close to two hours. Gallagher finally had enough. To Lynch, he said, "You and Kelly here have argued back and forth. The fact is there's no direct evidence that Kelly is responsible. Only the allegations of Maureen. However, Kelly is still saddled with explaining his use of a different name. His explanation isn't very credible. That and masquerading as a loyalist associating with the daughter of a UVF leader. The circumstances make Kelly look bad but doesn't convincingly prove his involvement with Maureen's death. So, Sean, what is it you want to do?"

"I'm convinced he knows more than he's letting on. Want to take him back to Derry. Do a proper interrogation. Putting him up for trial by IRA court martial."

Gallagher said, "He's not IRA, Sean. You are understandably biased. The verdict would be guilty. The sentence undoubtedly death. Can't allow that to happen, Sean. This is Liam Kelly's grandson for Christ sakes. You need convincing evidence not just accusations. Besides, Maureen was killed in Belfast. That makes this a Belfast matter. Maybe even a matter for the Army Council."

Sean Lynch sat silently, breathing heavily after his emotional expenditure. "Maybe there's another way. Giving me my justice while achieving something of military importance."

Gallagher replied, "Explain, Sean."

"Going to be honest with you, Robert. I already planned to come here and extract revenge. Don't need the legal nicety of certainty beyond a reasonable doubt. I planned on killing Alfred Thompson by forcing Terence to deliver a bomb to the *Raven Pub*. Then I planned on dealing with Terence Kelly after that. I've got some lads already on their way to Belfast bringing a bomb.

"My suspicion since reading Maureen's letter has been her death was the doing of the UVF. Alfred Thompson likely responsible. Something involving his daughter. That means Terence is connected. Why else target Maureen? Where else could the bomb have come from except the UVF? I plan on killing Alfred Thompson. Only fitting that Terence Kelly be the one to do that."

Terence shouted, "What the fuck! I'm not killing anyone for you!"

Gallagher said, "Calm down." Turning to Lynch, he said, "You've no authority bringing your people to Belfast, Sean.

"Listen, Robert. Here's my plan. Can't bring back Maureen but I can strike back at the enemy I know who must have caused her death. Couple of my lads from Derry are bringing me a suitable bomb. Terence Kelly has the ability to get close enough to Alfred Thompson to kill him. Terence simply delivers the bomb inside the *Raven Pub*. Place the bomb where it will kill Thompson and maybe a lot of his UVF thugs. Terence sets the timer then walks away to take a leak but instead sneaks out the back. All he needs is a couple of minutes on the bomb timer to get clear."

Gallagher replied, "Really? When were you going to tell me about this plan of yours, Sean? Mucking about outside of channels where you don't belong could end up putting you in a box." Gallagher meant the threat as a stinging rebuke.

Lynch sat in silence gathering his thoughts. "For the breach of protocol coming into your territory, I truly apologize, Robert.

But think of it. Take the opportunity to get rid of Thompson. I have no doubt that Terence Kelly's mixed up with Maureen 's death. Maybe he was threatened by Thompson. Tricked by Thompson into shipping the bomb. Maybe Thompson meant both Kelly and Maureen to be killed. Maybe the bomb was booby trapped, and Kelly knew that. Any way you look at the circumstances, Terence is somehow connected. For that he must pay. Don't need the legal nicety of certainty beyond a reasonable doubt. If Terence Kelly delivers a bomb that kills Alfred Thompson, I'll consider the debt paid. All I ask then is for you to get Terence Kelly out of Northern Ireland."

Listening to Lynch and Kelly argue back and forth convinced Gallagher only that Kelly was hiding something. Nothing specific but Maureen being killed by a bomb pointed at Terence Kelly being connected. Something more than just his romancing of Alfred Thompson's daughter. Had that been the issue, Thompson would just scare the shit out of Kelly and run him out of Belfast. On the other hand, where did the bomb come from? Kelly didn't have the means or knowhow to produce a bomb. Not likely Liam Kelly was up to anything like using his grandson from America to spy on the UVF. Gallagher also did not find Terence Kelly's reason for using another name convincing.

However, Robert Gallagher was a pragmatist. Devoted to Irish nationalism as fanatical as Brian Keenan, Seamus Twomey, or Éamonn O'Doherty. They all would see the possibility of using Kelly to kill UVF leader Alfred Thompson as an attractive opportunity. Kelly's connection to his famous grandfather did not factor into this situation. Letting Lynch proceed with his plan had merit. Good morale boost for the Belfast IRA. "Tell you what Sean, this is not my call. Need to take the decision higher up. My lads are still hanging about outside. They'll come inside to keep you and Kelly from coming to blows while I'm gone. I'll return here as soon as possible to tell you what comes next. Both you and Kelly just sit tight."

CHAPTER 30

Belfast, Northern Ireland | October 1973

Robert Gallagher met Brian Keenan in a West Belfast pub frequented by IRA. Armed lookouts stationed around the perimeter secured the pub from any surprise incursion from loyalist paramilitaries or the RUC entering the vicinity.

After summarizing the lengthy confrontation between Sean Lynch and Terence Kelly, Gallagher said to Keenan as they sat in a darkened back corner of the pub, "Terence Kelly talks a good story, but it sounds too convenient. His explanation for using different names is not convincing. Don't believe his denial that Maureen Lynch never made contact with him in Belfast. He's the person most likely to have given Lynch's daughter the bomb to post. They had a falling out in Derry soon after Kelly came over from the States. Kelly claims Maureen never reunited with him in Belfast. If that were true it doesn't make sense that she would carry a package from someone unknown. According to Lynch, she never mentioned knowing anyone in Belfast. Her letter that Lynch's wife received explained this was all about Terence Kelly. Kelly claims that the letter was Maureen's fantasy.

"I think Kelly's lying. Makes Terence Kelly clearly the most likely person setting up Maureen Lynch. About what exactly I can't tell. Yet I'm not convinced he's fallen in with the UVF. Kelly may be screwing Thompson's daughter, but I don't believe he's involved politically. Perhaps nothing more than a stupid

Irish American caught in shit over his head. But the bomb exploding prematurely in Maureen Lynch's hands is too coincidental to be believable. Don't frankly know what's goin' on, Brian."

Keenan of course was intimately aware of the extent of Terence Kelly's knowledge of bomb making. Witnessed live tests of his radio detonating triggers. Produced dozens of these improved detonating triggers that Liam Kelly secretly delivered to the Belfast Brigade. However, Keenan would keep the vow he made to Liam Kelly to keep his grandson's involvement secret.

Keenan's knowledge of Kelly's secret bomb making work made him more than the prime suspect in the killing of Maureen Lynch. He possessed the means and the motive. If what Gallagher related about Kelly's comments of Maureen Lynch's emotional instability, it presented Kelly with a strong incentive for eliminating her. If this former girlfriend discovered Kelly living in Belfast under a different name she possessed ample blackmail material. Maybe she demanded Kelly take up with her again. Kelly could not imagine being saddled with her indefinitely. Felt the only way to safely escape was by silencing her.

Gallagher continued. "I listened to Lynch and Kelly going back and until it became repetitious. Kelly stuck to his story. Here's the interesting part, Brian. I asked Sean Lynch what he proposed we do. His solution came as a real surprise but might be of interest to us. Wants to use Terence Kelly to plant a bomb in Alfred Thompson's *Raven Pub*. Kelly is known there because of his relationship with Thompson's daughter. Kelly could easily place the bomb close enough to take out Thompson and maybe some other UVF among the patrons. Lynch threatens Kelly to do this, or he'll be discovering Kelly's part in Maureen's death by using some very unpleasant means."

"I'll hand it to Lynch, that's a clever solution," Keenan said. "The idea might have merit. What do you think, Robert?"

"Let it proceed, Brian. If successful the trail should lead back to Sean Lynch and Derry rather than our brigade. Besides, whatever is going on, I believe Terence Kelly knows far more than letting on. He's not one of us just because his elderly grandfather's a fuckin' legend. If Kelly becomes a casualty, it's of his own making."

"I tend to agree, Robert. Where's Lynch and Kelly now?"

"Sitting in Kelly's flat, "Gerald and Colin are keeping them company. They detained Kelly quietly as he left his flat for his nightshift job at a radio station. Don't expect Adele Thompson showing up announced at least not right away."

"What's Sean Lynch want to do about Kelly even if he's willing to place the bomb?"

"Well, he tells Kelly if he kills Thompson that squares it. Kelly must immediately leave Belfast. I don't believe Lynch's will be satisfied with letting Kelly just leave Northen Ireland. He'll still want to personally deal with Kelly and make him talk before putting a bullet in his head.

"Lynch thinks Kelly's a tout. Gone over to the other side. Evidenced by his masquerading as a loyalist. Romancing Alfred Thompson's daughter, no less. Believes that to be the reason for his own daughter's death. Kelly's involved somehow, but Lynch firmly believes that Alfred Thompson was behind the murder of his daughter. Kelly is somehow involved, but Lynch knows he's not a bombmaker.

"Then Lynch springs yet another surprise. Tells me right in front of Kelly that he has already arranged for a couple of his Derry lads to bring a bomb to Belfast."

Keenan set down his beer. "Is he fuckin' crazy? He can't be engaging in operations in Belfast. Christ, he's acting OC of the Derry Brigade. He's on a RUC list for arrest after his name appeared in the newspapers with the death of his daughter. He's now a liability for us here in Belfast. This whole affair could turn into a great fuckin' bollocks."

Gallagher nodded in agreement, "Lynch is bent on revenge. Not acting rationally. Would prefer snatching Kelly and taking him back to Derry. Forcing Kelly to plant the bomb inside the *Raven Pub* just becomes an acceptable way for us to agree with his plan for taking his revenge. Probably hopes that Kelly will die in the blast or be caught then executed by UVF."

"What do we do about Kelly if he goes through with this?" Keenan asked Gallagher.

"We get Kelly out of Northern Ireland immediately. Send Lynch back to Derry. This is not a personal matter."

However, for Brian Keenan it did have a personal aspect. He wanted to honor his commitment to Liam Kelly. Terence Kelly had also rendered service to the IRA cause. Regardless of making stupid decisions, Terence Kelly was not a *tout*.

"How did you leave it with Lynch?" Keenan asked.

"Told him this was now a Belfast matter. I'd take his proposal for using Terence Kelly to get at Alfred Thompson to someone higher up."

"Okay. Stay put here. I'll be back in an hour," Keenan said. Nodding to someone in the pub, he then slipped out the back door followed by an IRA bodyguard Gallagher recognized.

Keenan placed a call from a public telephone booth watched over by his bodyguard. "Liam, it's Brian. Call me back at this number." He disconnected before Liam Kelly said anything further."

Liam Kelly understood the security protocol. He used a public telephone a block from his residence above the *Black Goat*.

"Seems we have a situation here in Belfast, Liam. Concerns your grandson and the death of Maureen Lynch."

Liam replied, "How are you involved, Brian?"

"Because Sean Lynch showed up in Belfast. Seems Sean Lynch received a letter from his daughter posted before her death. Provides all sorts of information concerning your grandson Terence. Sean Lynch's contact in Belfast is our intelligence officer, Robert Gallagher. A sharp officer. Sean wisely informed Gallagher he was in Belfast after learning from his wife the contents of his daughter's letter. Among other things, Maureen Lynch discovered Terence living in Belfast under the name Terence Stewart. You knew about that, I believe. Maureen's letter said she followed you meeting with Terence in Coleraine. Why's Terence using another name, Liam?"

Liam Kelly said, "Started out perfectly innocently. Terry was romantically involved with Maureen Lynch. Turned out to be badly paired. Terence decided to stay on in Northern Ireland by attending Queen's University. Terence has dual U.S. and UK citizenship under different names. It's a little complicated how that came about but it obviously became useful for security with what my grandson was doing. How 'bout I come to Belfast and help you sort this out?"

"No, Liam. You stay put in Derry. This is now a Belfast problem. Let me tell you how things stand. My intelligence officer has both Sean Lynch and Terence under guard at Terence's flat. Lynch believes Terence was involved with in his daughter's death. Terence is involved with the daughter of Alfred Thompson. You know of Thompson don't you?"

After a pause, Liam replied, "Oh God no! Yes I know Thompson is a prominent UVF figure. Didn't know about a relationship between Terence and his daughter."

"Well, that's the problem. Lynch believes Terence may have gone over to other side. You know what that means?"

"Terence is not a *tout*. You know that, Brian."

"Of course I do. I also know that it would not have been Thompson's doing in killing Maureen Lynch. If he had connected Terence with Maureen the daughter of a Derry IRA officer, he'd have killed Terence. Maureen died with a bomb in her hand. We both know who rigged the bomb and killed her don't we, Liam?"

"Terence wouldn't do such a thing."

"Really? He made dozens of radio detonator triggers. You even told me he made and detonated a demonstration bomb. Maureen's letter supposedly claimed Terence was taking her to Boston. Doesn't sound like Terence would agree to such a thing unless under duress. If Maureen threatened exposing his using another name, Terence would know that could be dangerous because of his involvement with Thompson's daughter.

"Gallagher doesn't believe Terence's version that Maureen never made contact with him in Belfast, claiming her letter was nothing more than fantasy. I don't believe Terence's story either. Why else would Maureen Lynch come to Belfast other than to reconnect with Terence?. It's clear to me that Terence constructed the bomb then used it to kill Maureen Lynch."

"No!" was all Liam could say.

Keenan replied, "He had the means to construct a bomb. Had motive and opportunity."

"What's going to happen to Terence, Brian?"

"Something of interest but something you will find disturbing, Liam. Sean Lynch believes his daughter's death is Thompson's doing with Terence somehow involved. He doesn't know about Terence's knowledge of bomb making. Neither does our intelligence officer. Kept my promise to keep his and your IRA activities a tightly held secret. Lynch's solution is to use Terence's access to kill Alfred Thompson by placing a bomb inside Thompson's pub."

"Jesus, no!"

"Once that's accomplished, we then spirit Terence out of Northern Ireland."

"Are you agreeing to this, Brian?"

"Yes. The alternative is let Sean Lynch take Terence back to Derry and stand before an IRA court martial. You know where that would lead, Liam. Terence made a stupid mistake killing Maureen Lynch. He could then have simply left Northern Ireland immediately after killing her. But no, he decides to stick around for some reason. May have been because of Adele Thompson.

"I don't know your grandson, Liam, but he acts like this is some adventure. Perhaps that comes from living in Boston all his life. Making bomb detonators, playing like a secret agent in the movies using different names. Believing he can kill someone getting in his way and not have it come back on him. He's a dangerous amateur. At least if he removes Alfred Thompson he does the IRA a service."

"Is there no way to just to let me get him out of Northern Ireland now, Brian?"

"Afraid not, Liam. Circumstances have gone too far. I'll keep you informed."

"Very well. A last favor, Brian. Should Terence do as required, promise me to make sure he gets safely out of Northern Ireland."

"You have my word, Liam."

Robert Gallagher returned to Terence's flat after leaving Keenan. To Sean Lynch, he said, "Your idea to take out Alfred Thompson with a bomb is approved. I'm to observe but this'll be your bomb, your operation. If it goes wrong that will become known." Turning to Terence Kelly, he asked, "You willing to do this?"

"Fuck no!"

"Understand the alternative is for us to let Mr. Lynch take you back to Derry for interrogation. I can assure you that will be very unpleasant. Then you'll stand trial before an IRA court martial. I can tell you that under the circumstances you are in some very deep shit. I strongly suggest you take the offer to place a bomb in the *Raven Pub*. Do that successfully then you'll be safely delivered across the border into the Republic. Return to Boston. You don't belong in Ireland. What's your decision?"

Terence remained silent for several moments before nodding his head. "I'll do as you ask.".

Turning to Lynch, Gallagher said, "Come with me Sean." To Gerald and Colin, "Keep watch over Kelly until you hear from me."

An hour later Gallagher called Gerald on the two-way radio, "You're to sit on Kelly tonight. Take turns with Colin standing watch. Lynch and I will return before sunrise in the morning with the bomb. Have Kelly get some rest. Make sure he's not hiding any weapons in the flat. Tomorrow is game on."

Gerald asked, "Should Kelly try to make an escape, what are we to do?"

Gallagher replied, "You have a silenced weapon. Kill him, then leave quietly."

Lynch and Gallagher returned to Kelly's flat early the next morning before sunrise. Callagher arrived first to survey the neighborhood since this was loyalist territory. Minutes later Gallagher signaled Lynch sitting on the bus stop bench to come in. Sean Lynch arrived carrying a briefcase.

The two IRA men had already made coffee. Terence Kelly was still in the bedroom. After using the toilet, he appeared blurry-eyed having spent a sleepless night.

Lynch said pointing, "The bomb is in that briefcase, Terence. You'll be placing it inside the *Raven Pub* this afternoon. Since you're a university student I trust you can explain the briefcase as related to your studies?"

Terence's mind raced searching for a way to escape the situation. "Where am I to place the bomb and how do I get away?"

Lynch replied, "That's your problem. The objective is to kill Thompson because he's a UVF commander. Lots of blood on his hands. Anyone else in the pub is a loyalist and becomes a bonus. Fail to kill Thompson and we'll assume that was intentional making you a tout.

"I assume you've been inside the *Raven*?"

Terence nodded.

"Does Alfred Thompson work behind the bar?" Lynch asked.

"If he's there, he usually tends the bar."

"Then sit at the bar with the briefcase at your feet. I'll show you how to arm the bomb. Nothing more than moving the dial on a kitchen timer. Give yourself just a couple of minutes. Make as if going to the toilet. Is there a back door that you can leave by without being seen?"

"Yes."

"Then that's all there is to it. Don't get cold feet and think you can just walk out without setting the timer. If you're caught placing a bomb that doesn't explode, you're a dead man. After some very rough treatment by the UVF you'll end up with a bullet to the head. Fail to go through with this, then the IRA will do the same.

"I'll show you how to set the timer later just before you set off for the *Raven*."

Gallagher interjected, "After the explosion leave the *Raven* calmly and just walk away. The same service van that will drop you off a short distance from the *Raven* will pick you up at the same location. From there we'll accompany you by train south and drop you off in Newry close to the border with the Republic. You'll take the train on to Dublin then take a flight to Boston."

Terence asked, "When is this to take place?"

Gallagher answered, "Five o'clock this afternoon. Will Thompson's daughter be there at the that time?"

Terence shook his head. "She's not working at the pub today. Has a late class at the university. I made arrangements yesterday to meet her at the pub about seven this evening for dinner."

Gallagher replied, "Good. Then you have no excuse but to go through with this. With that, I'll be leaving. You won't be seeing me again. This is Sean Lynch's operation. Get this done and leave Northern Ireland. Don't come back."

Following the post office bombing, he removed anything incriminating about his covert activities or Maureen's presence from the flat. Terence showered and packed a suitcase to occupy the time before leaving.

An hour before leaving, Lynch said, "Time I explained how to arm the bomb and set the timer. Placing the briefcase on the small kitchen table Lynch opened the lid exposing the bomb.

Terence immediately said, "This briefcase is all wrong. Something a businessman might use. How am I to arm and set the timer inside the pub without being seen?"

It was a Samsonite hard-shell briefcase opening in half when placed on its side. Inside sat the bomb. Twelve sticks of gelignite each with a diameter of 1.25 inches and length of 8 inches bound together with tape. Multiple insulated wires ran to the terminals of a capacitor. The detonator system components lay next to the high explosive gelignite. A kitchen timer with a dial for adjusting minutes. Six 9V dry cell batteries, and a makeshift circuit board with toggle switch and micro relays. Upon casual examination, it appeared conceptually the same circuit design of his radio devices improvised from walkie-talkies with a mechanical timer replacing the radio receiver for arming and detonation.

Terence stood up. "Let me show you my briefcase. Returning from the bedroom he set his top-opening briefcase on the floor. "See what I mean? I can set this at my feet and reach inside from the top. Can possibly reach inside and arm the device by feel alone."

Lynch emptied Terence's briefcase full of papers to determine if the bomb would fit. Terence said, "Let me show you."

"Careful. That toggle switch with a cover is the arming circuit. Do not for any reason touch that until just before setting the timer."

Terence answered, "Okay. You see here these wires coming from the sticks of explosives are long enough to place the explosives on the bottom with these detonating components resisting on top instead of to the side. My briefcase expands sufficiently to accommodate the high explosives at the bottom. I can position the arming switch and timer for easy access from the top."

Lynch nodded. The suitability of Terence's briefcase became immediately obvious.

Feigning ignorance, Kelly allowed Lynch to explain the arming and detonation procedure while he asked appropriate questions.

Lynch said, "Open this protective cover then flip this toggle switch to arm the bomb. Next, wind the timer spring then turn the timer dial to the desired number of minutes before detonation. I suggest two minutes, three at most. Time enough for you to get clear of the building. Any longer than that risks discovery. That's it. Any questions?"

"No. Simple enough," Terence said.

While understandably uncomfortable with what he must do, Terence also felt uneasy about handling a lethal device assembled by someone unknown. IRA bombmakers frequently suffered premature explosions due to inexperience. In bomb making, your first mistake became your last. He wanted badly the chance to examine this device in detail. Didn't come this far to die from someone else's mistake. Suddenly the thought occurred to him or *die by the bombmaker rigging a booby trap.* Essentially that was what he did to Maureen. Might this bomb be rigged to deliver the same outcome for him?

Yet how could he be sure? No opportunity existed for a thorough examination. He had no access to tools or an electrical multimeter. His pocketknife, scissors, and sharp kitchen knives had all been confiscated by the IRA minders as possible weapons. With such troubling thoughts he began searching the kitchen for anything that might prove useful. In a kitchen drawer with miscellaneous items, he found a small screwdriver overlooked by the IRA.

Time dragged on in silence. Lynch and Terence did not resume their argument. No reason for either of them to argue further. Belfast IRA quartermaster Brian Keenan resolved the standoff. Believing Terence had murdered Maureen Lynch, after consulting with Belfast OC Éamonn O'Doherty, Keenan agreed with Sean Lynch's plan to settle the matter by having Terence deliver a bomb killing prominent UVF figure Alfred Thompson.

Keenan believed Terence Kelly killed Maureen Lynch. However, Sean Lynch was a fellow IRA leader. His daughter's killing had nothing to do with the sectarian conflict. Lynch's compromise solution seemed appropriate justice and offered an unexpected opportunity to deliver a blow to the enemy. At 4:30 pm, Robert Gallagher said, "It's showtime, Mr. Kelly. You ready?"

Terence nodded.

Gallagher turned to Lynch, "Anything else?"

Lynch shook his head, then said, "What happens after the bombing?"

Gallagher replied, "We'll transport Kelly out of Northern Ireland."

"What if he doesn't go through with the bombing?" Lynch asked.

"Then we'll deal with that problem in Belfast. We understand your feelings, Sean, but this is now a military matter. A Belfast IRA matter. No reason for you to remain in Belfast. You've got your own troubles to deal with back in Derry. Take care of your wife and go into hiding to avoid the RUC. You and your lads that brought the bomb need to leave Belfast immediately."

With that, Gallagher, the two Belfast IRA, and Terence Kelly left the flat. Robert Gallagher climbed into the passenger seat of the service van while Gerald got behind the wheel. Terence and Colin entered the van through the rear doors.

Terence exited the utility service van a block from the *Raven Pub.* As he walked the short distance his heart raced with the same dread experienced when he walked Maureen to her fate. What he was about to do also brought the realization that he would never again see Adele Thompson.

Entering the pub, he immediately made his way to the toilet down a hallway not far from the bar. Before entering the toilet, he looked at the back door marked exit. He gauged less than thirty seconds was needed to make his escape from the bar. Right now, he needed privacy to examine the device. He was not about to trust his life to an unknown bombmaker. The only possibility was to carry the briefcase into a toilet stall immediately upon first arriving at the *Raven*. If a booby trap existed it would be evident in the circuitry involving either by the arming switch or timer. Entering a stall, he latched the stall door and placed the briefcase on the toilet stool lid.

Reading circuit schematics as an experienced electronics engineer became second nature. He worked out problems by visualizing mental images much like some people visualize maps. Interpretation became like reading a language.

It became obvious that like his detonator circuit design, a capacitor was used to store an electrical charge from a source of 9V batteries and store sufficient energy for detonating a blasting cap inserted into the gelignite high explosives. The covered toggle switch described as the arming circuit allowed the batteries to charge the capacitor. The mechanical timer would close the capacitor output circuit to deliver the stored electrical charge detonating the blasting cap that then detonated the high explosive.

Two leads protruded from the back of what appeared to be mechanical kitchen timer. Using the small screwdriver, he pried off the back cover of the plastic timer. It took several moments to take in how the timer functioned. As Sean Lynch instructed, turning the dial to the maximum time wound the spring. Then turning the dial counterclockwise to the desired run time set in motion the timing function. The kinetic energy of the spring rotated a toothed wheel that engaged with a simple clockwork escapement mechanism moving the wheel at a constant rate.

The firing sequence therefore began by winding the timer spring then actuating the arming circuit by flipping the toggle switch to charge the capacitor. Setting the dial to the desired time began the firing sequence. Reaching the desired set time would discharge the capacitor stored energy detonating the firing sequence.

Nothing immediately looked out of place to Terence. No obvious booby trap. However, a deadly explosive device made by someone else was only inches away. In electrical engineering dealing in abstracts, you learned to take nothing for granted with live circuitry. This prompted the question to Terence, if he wanted to booby trap this bomb, how would he go about that?

Looking at the front dial to the timer set at zero, he turned to the back with the exposed internal workings of the simple device. An indicator arm on the escape wheel held graduations correlating to the front dial. Looking from front to back, something seemed wrong. Repeating the comparison multiple times confirmed what was out of place. With the front dial set at zero, the corresponding position on the escape wheel inside was advanced to a position well beyond zero. He instantly understood the implications. After winding the spring, turning the dial to set the duration would immediately close the firing circuit discharging the capacitor detonating the bomb. The instantaneous explosion would kill both him and Alfred Thompson. Sean Lynch satisfying his revenge.

Terence immediately wondered if the Belfast IRA guy in charge knew about this. Even if he disabled the booby trap modification and carrying through with the bombing, would he then just get a bullet to the back of the head?

With no alternatives, Terence could only deal with resolving the immediate problem. Rectifying the bombmaker's subtle modification proved simple. The axis of the escape mechanism was held in place by a cap screw. He unscrewed the cap screw with his screwdriver allowing for recalibration of the escape mechanism to conform with the front dial. He could now safely activate detonation after setting a delay duration allowing time to escape the blast.

Leaving the toilet, he settled onto a stool at the bar. "Good afternoon, Mr. Thompson."

"Terence, my lad. How you doing this fine afternoon?" Alfred Thompson said.

"Fine, Sir. Celebrating. Just came from the university. Presented my thesis for my master's degree to my academic advisor. A technical project actually. Demonstrated my results with a functional processing circuit I assembled. A way of transmitting electronic data more efficiently. Got it right here in my briefcase."

"How was your presentation received?"

"Couldn't have been better. The visual demonstration made all the difference."

"Good for you. You meeting up with Adele?"

"Yes, Sir. Told her I'd see her about seven o'clock for dinner. Felt like coming here straight from the university. A pint or two sounded a perfect way to celebrate."

"I agree. Coming right up, my lad," Thompson said.

Terence bided his time until downing half his glass of Guinness before reaching into his briefcase. Winding the timer spring, he then opened the safety cover then flipped the arming switch. Waiting a couple of seconds while holding his breath for a moment, he set the timing dial for two minutes and closed the briefcase latch.

"Mr. Thompson, going to the toilet. Don't let anyone touch my briefcase here."

"Right you are, Terence."

Terence exited the back door just beyond the toilets. He turned and began walking toward his rendezvous point. Seeing the fake utility service van only a hundred yards away, he stopped to wait for the sound from the explosion.

As seconds ticked by, the expected blast still caused him to jump. Turning back in that direction, a dust-filled cloud of debris came from the front of the *Raven Pub.* He surmised that unlike the car-bomb detonated when he and Adele were inside, this internal blast was likely far more destructive.

As he began briskly walking back to his pickup location, he reflected on what he had just done. Murdering Alfred Thompson and likely others for no reason other than his own survival. In that respect, no different from murdering Maureen Lynch. Except perhaps even worse. He bore no animosity toward Alfred Thompson.

As Colin opened the rear doors of the fake electrical utility van, Terence climbed inside. Behind the wheel, Gerald accelerated the vehicle leaving the area without attracting attention. Sitting in the passenger seat, Robert Gallagher turned to Kelly, "Where did you place the bomb?"

"At my feet against the bar. Alfred Thompson was on the other side of the bar. I spoke to him before saying I must go to the toilet. Armed the bomb and set it for two minutes. Walked straight away out the back door."

Gallagher said, "Then you lived up to your side of Sean Lynch's bargain. We're driving to the train station. Gerald and Colin will accompany you close to border with the Republic where they will get off the train when it stops in Newry. You stay on the train that will take you to Dublin's Connolly station."

Gallagher turned and handed Terence his U.S. and British passports. "Get yourself to Dublin Airport. Leave Ireland without delay and never return, Mr. Kelly."

CHAPTER 31

Belfast, Northern Ireland | October 1973

Ignoring Brian Keenan's warning not to come to Belfast, the day before the *Raven Pub* bombing, Liam Kelly trained to Belfast. Nothing he could do to intercede with Sean Lynch's plan to force Terence to deliver a bomb to kill Alfred Thompson. However, he could not bear remaining in Derry. Checking into a small hotel under a false name he must sweat out waiting. No telling when this was supposed to happen. If there was no explosion, that could mean Terence's circumstances might be even worse. All he could rely on was Brian Keenan's assurance that Terence would not be harmed if he went through with killing Alfred Thompson.

In the hotel bar late in the afternoon after arriving, a television over the bar broadcast the evening news. The scene showed the destroyed front windows and the intact sign of the *Raven Pub. An hour ago, a bomb detonated inside the Raven Pub. The proprietor Alfred Thompson and three others were killed and several others injured in the blast. The same establishment in this predominantly loyalist area of East Belfast previously suffered a car-bomb attack in July of this year. The RUC declined to comment on rumors that Thompson was associated with the Ulster Volunteer Force loyalist paramilitary organization.*

Liam Kelly telephoned Brian Keenan from a public telephone in the hotel. "I just heard about the bombing of the *Raven Pub* on the television news."

"That's right. It's done, Liam. Your grandson did his part."

"Where is Terry now?"

"He's fine. On his way by train to Dublin. Being escorted by two of our people. Sean Lynch is no longer involved. Your grandson is unharmed. Warned to leave Ireland immediately."

"I'm in Belfast, Brian. How can I link up with Terence?"

"I told you not to come to Belfast, Liam."

"That you did. Too old though to obey orders where it concerns the welfare of my grandson."

"You should have thought about that when you allowed him to participate in the struggle."

"True enough, Brian. Can't undo that mistake. Just trying now to get him safely back to America."

"If you want to make contact you might catch up with him at Dublin's Connolly station. Don't know if perhaps he has already boarded a train or not. Might try Dublin Airport in that case. Make sure he's on his way to America, Liam. Don't want to find out he's returned back to Belfast. He's not welcome here. If Lynch were to find out he's in Northern Ireland, I won't be able to prevent Terence coming to a bad end."

"I understand, Brian. Thank you for keeping our secret and all you've done."

Liam Kelly arrived at Connolly station in Dublin and disembarked immediately to survey the platform should Terence be among those getting off the same train. A quick check of the train schedules indicated trains arriving from Belfast in the late afternoon through evening ran every hour. Considering the time reported for the *Raven* bombing, Terence most likely arrived before his train. Best to get to Dublin Airport. Terence should be taking a direct flight to Boston or perhaps New York. If lucky,

Liam might make it in time to locate Terence before boarding a flight. Possibly the last time he might ever see him.

The taxi to Dublin Airport took thirty minutes. Liam would start first with Aer Lingus after looking at the departure display then other airlines that might have direct flights.

Liam might be in luck. Finding no direct flights to Boston or New York that evening meant that Terence might be booked on an Aer Lingus flight leaving Dublin for Boston the following day at 12:40 pm, or an 11:05 am flight to JFK. That meant Terence might have found a hotel for the night or simply decided to spend the night inside the airport. Liam spent the next hour walking the terminal including bars and eating establishments. With no success he turned to a bank of telephones for nearby hotels. On his third try, he got, "Yes, we have your grandson staying with us tonight. Do you wish me to ring his room?"

"No that won't be necessary. I will come to the hotel. I just arrived on a different flight."

At the hotel, he knocked on Terence's room. Receiving no reply, Liam said, "Terry, it's your grandfather."

Terence opened the door and embraced his grandfather. Tears streamed down his face. Stepping inside, Liam closed the door and said, "Been a long day. I'm a little tired." Liam then sat down in the only chair in the room. "Agnes was thrilled with the Waterford vase you sent. The note inside said you were unexpectedly returning to Boston sooner than planned. Seems even that plan suffered unexpected difficulties."

Terence sat on the bed making no reply.

Liam wanted to ask why Terence did not leave Belfast after the death of Maureen but knew the answer. Like Brian Keenan, Liam believed killing Maureen Lynch was obviously Terence's doing. Liam chose not to put him on the spot. Liam also assumed Terence had remained in Belfast only because of his relationship with Alfred Thompson's daughter. Liam could not imagine how Terence might feel about that twist of fate.

"I regret allowing you to participate in this conflict, Terry. This is not the same as the war against the British that I fought fifty years ago. That was the Irish struggle for independence you grew up hearing about. Different set of circumstances in Northern Ireland."

"It was my doing, Granda. Guess I was not made of strong enough stuff."

Frustrated with the course of events bringing them to this point, Liam could not resist asking, "It was not about you using a different identity. That could be understandably explained, but taking up with the daughter of a loyalist paramilitary made that impossible landing you in this predicament." Liam withheld adding, *that was what led to your killing Maureen fearing her exposing you to your new girlfriend's UVF father.*

Instead, Liam said, "However, the death of Alfred Thompson was a military success for the IRA. Do not regret the part you played, Terry. Put all that happened to you while in Northern Ireland behind you. Time will eventually place everything in perspective. Get on with your life. With all the difficulties you experienced since coming to Northern Ireland, you still advanced your academic credentials. That's worth a great deal. Bury the bad memories. Part of going through life. Someone once wrote, what doesn't kill you makes you stronger. Seems particularly appropriate under the circumstances."

Neither wished to continue the strained conversation by discussing the deaths of Maureen Lynch and Alfred Thompson. Nothing could be undone. Each understood their own responsibility in the sequence of unintended consequences of their actions. Both exhausted they laid down on the bed together propping their heads up with pillows. Before falling asleep they promised to have breakfast together in the morning before parting. Terence to take a flight to Boston and Liam returning by train to Derry.

Using his U.S. passport under the name Terence Kelly, he took the flight to Boston. Therefore, he possessed entry and exit documentation indicating that he left Boston for Dublin in 1971 and returned by the same route in 1973. No entry documentation into Northern Ireland existed on his U.S. passport nor for that matter on his British passport under the name Terence Stewart. An obstacle for British law enforcement to pursue his trail should he ever become connected to criminal activities within the Northern Ireland.

The unexpected pleasure of seeing his grandfather transformed to profound sadness as he took his seat on the Boeing 707. The last time he might ever see his grandfather given his advanced age. Adele Thompson forever lost. While relieved by narrowly escaping Belfast with his life, Terence could not shake the horrors of the last couple of weeks.

Arriving in Boston, he chose to check into a hotel rather than show up unannounced at his parents. He needed time to reconstruct his experiences to fit the circumstances of two years in Northern Ireland. Before leaving Dublin that morning at breakfast with his grandfather, he strategized how to portray those experiences. His grandfather would preserve the subterfuge and forever keep his illicit activities secret.

Central to the reshaped narrative would include the wonderful experience of meeting his paternal grandparents. The achievement of obtaining his master's degree. Achieving valuable work experience. Experiencing Northern Ireland as the place of his birth, notwithstanding the *Troubles*. The violence left no expectations for career opportunities in Northern Ireland. The sectarian divide seemed intractable. The only alternative was to return to the normality of Boston and get on with life in America. Tamp down any return to dwelling on Irish nationalism. Adopt instead any expression of politics involving the *Troubles* as being foremost a Catholic civil rights issue. Unrealistic to believe this violent conflict could conceivably ever lead to the United Kingdom relinquishing Northern Ireland to become part of the Republic of Ireland.

CHAPTER 32

Boston, Massachusetts | 2025

Terence Kelly resumed his narrative in Father O'Brien's office at Boston College. It had been three weeks since their last conversation due to Kelly's deteriorating medical condition. The increased reliance on morphine to control the pain dulled the mind and made him sleepy. The recent experience made evident that his time was limited. Best to move his story toward conclusion while still physically able.

Kelly picked up the narrative from their last session where he discussed killing Maureen Lynch. After spending over an hour relating the disastrous events that followed, O'Brien said, "A remarkable chain of events. What led you to suspicion the possibility of the bomb you were forced to place in Thompson's pub might be booby trapped?

"Sean Lynch's eyes. I could sense his degree of hatred. He believed this was Alfred Thompson's doing but all because of me. Whether I had turned traitor or just became involved with Thompson's daughter made no difference. The fact of my using another name made me complicit in her death. His Derry IRA lads brought a bomb to Belfast to kill Alfred Thompson. As for me, likely a terrible fate awaited me if the Derry IRA were allowed to take me to Derry. You know the sordid history of the many credible accounts of torturing suspected traitors. The compromise of forcing me to place the bomb in the *Raven Pub* was an inspiration to satisfy the Belfast IRA because of my access. I suspicioned that might not be sufficient to satisfy Sean Lynch."

"In a conceptual way, a similar subterfuge that you used to kill Maureen Lynch," O'Brien offered.

Kelly took no offense. He was here to confess everything. "I would agree with the comparison, Father. Therefore, logical to be done with exacting retribution by a single act. From a technical perspective, the bombmaker knew his craft. The booby trap was elegant in its simplicity. I would likely have overlooked it had I not already been suspicious enough to make a thorough examination by removing the back of the kitchen timer.

"A year after my return to Boston, my grandfather told me of Sean Lynch's arrest and internment in the Long Kesh Detention Centre. Learned later that Lynch died from kidney disease while in prison. Granda commented that he never saw or spoke again to Sean Lynch after what happened in Belfast. Other than that, Granda never raised the question about Maureen's death with me. I believe Granda always knew it was my doing."

O'Brien asked, "I did some new research. The record shows Liam Kelly died in 1978. Declassified British intelligence records state he died by his own hand exploding a bomb inside his car when approached by a British Army SAS search and destroy team. Did you know that?"

"Guessed it could have been something like that. My father maintained regular contact with Granda. Told me only that the Brits finally got to him. Said the official report that Liam Kelly blew himself up was British propaganda. I knew differently.

"Two days before my grandfather's death, I spoke with him for the last time. Since leaving Belfast in 1973, we spoke only sporadically. Always felt our relationship had been damaged by my killing of Maureen. Granda would never have been able to understand my motivation. He liked Maureen. Treated her like family. Knew she was flirty with a wild reputation. She related to Granda as if he was her own grandfather. Reliable, Maureen became important to running the pub.

As the Northern Ireland *Troubles* continued after Terence returned to Boston, Liam Kelly could not resist playing a part. Irish nationalism was in his very nature. The nature of government repression of Catholics only worsened throughout the 1970s. Britain ruled Northern Ireland essentially by martial law. He could not stay out of the fight. Supplying his grandson's radio detonators to the Belfast Brigade through Brian Keenan kept him in the game. Liam missed the intrigue that made him a part of the IRA.

Terence had supplied him with the design details when he ceased making the devices. Liam hen enlisted his son Eoin to find someone in the United States to replicate Terence's design. These improvised devices now became contraband, no longer commercial walkie-talkies shipped through a distributor in Dublin. Therefore, Liam created a different smuggling conduit. This involved IRA sympathetic individuals in nearby Letterkenny in County Donegal across the border in the Republic of Ireland. Through this channel starting in New York, Eoin Kelly arranged shipment to Shannon Airport near Limerick in western Ireland, imported as commercial walkie-talkies in their original packaging. From there, they were trucked two hundred miles north to Letterkenny, still within the Irish Republic. Smuggling them across the porous border into Derry became easy. By 1974, the IRA began again receiving radio bomb detonating triggers.

The following year an undercover covert unit of British Army Intelligence known as the *Special Reconnaissance Uni*t discovered the origin of these radio bomb-detonating devices in Letterkenny. Trained by British SAS special forces, SRU personnel became indoctrinated in using excessively brutal interrogation techniques. A captured IRA operative based in Letterkenny succumbed to torture after being kidnapped by a covert SAS team operating over the border. Assisted by the U.S. FBI, the information he divulged eventually led back to the George Harrison smuggling ring in New York. The name Eoin Kelly surfaced in connection with Harrison. British SRU agents connected Eoin Kelly to his father, legendary IRA gunman Liam Kelly from the 1920s. After uncovering the name Liam Kelly as the name of a pub owner in Derry, someone in the SRU asked if this person might be related. A colleague replied, "Not just related, he is the legendary Liam Kelly. Must be in his eighties. Could he once again be active in the IRA?"

In a rare conversation between Terence and his grandfather in 1978, Liam Kelly sounded uncharacteristically fatalistic. Agnus his wife of over fifty years had died the prior year. Following her death, Liam Kelly increased his participation in smuggling efforts to supply the IRA with explosives and weapons.

"I have resumed my old ways, Terry. Found a new source to produce your devices. My colleagues in Belfast will put them to effective use. Ulster will one day become united with a true Republic of Ireland. Not likely I shall see that day, but it's inevitable."

Terence did not share that view but made no comment. His beloved grandfather would choose how to spend his remaining years. Terence only hoped he would not be arrested and die in prison like Sean Lynch.

Two days after that conversation, Liam Kelly sat in his car outside the pub when he spotted a soldier in face-paint camouflage peering around the corner of the building. On the floor of his car in front of the passenger seat rested a small gelignite bomb rigged with a radio-command detonation receiver. The transmitting unit sat next to his left hand on the passenger seat. Something always within reach whenever in his car for exactly this sort of eventuality. Liam Kelly had no intention of ever being taken by British security forces.

Several soldiers suddenly surround his car from a safe distance pointing automatic weapons. With no possibility of escape Liam Kelly immediately armed the bomb followed in seconds by the bomb exploding.

Terence learned of his grandfather's death from his father. Northen Ireland newspapers reported only the death in a car bomb explosion taking the life of legendary IRA gunman Liam

Kelly. *British security forces believe loyalist paramilitaries were responsible for the car-bombing that killed legendary IRA gunman Liam Kelly outside his pub in Derry. Kelly aged 81 was formerly part of Michael Collin's infamous assassination unit known as the Squad during the Anglo-Irish War of 1919-1921.*

O'Brien said, "Since our last session I've been conducting new research related to some of the material you revealed. I can therefore perhaps add information you may not know.

Starting with your immediate family. I unearthed an obscure British intelligence communication from 1978. Background reports about an interrogation of a Belfast IRA operative by the name of James Flanagan. The report connects Flanagan with Belfast Brigade quartermaster Brian Keenan, an unusually important IRA operative. Keenan was responsible for procuring much of the IRA's weapons and explosives in the early years of the *Troubles.* From the United States, Eastern Europe, and even the Middle East. Flanagan got caught. An SRU report dated 1978 indicated Flanagan was turned over to the SAS for questioning. Questioning is of course a euphonism for torture. The report documents that Flannigan provided information that a famous former IRA gunman named Liam Kelly, now an elderly owner of pub in Derry had been an important smuggling conduit of arms and explosives from the United States for many years. The SAS also had other information implicating Liam Kelly with a smuggling channel into Derry from nearby Letterkenny.

"Additionally, I uncovered another remarkably candid exchange between the British SAS commanding officer of Ebrington Barracks in the Waterside sector of Derry. After SRU operatives led them to Liam Kelly, SAS command issued an order to eliminate him. However, the order was more specific. I quote from this order that undoubtedly was mistakenly declassified. *This order is designed to deny any propaganda value to the IRA of the British Army executing an 81-year legendary Irish hero from the 1920s by instead transferring blame to unknown loyalist paramilitaries.*

"You believe your grandfather took his own life when faced with imminent capture by the SAS? That appears possible by this classified order."

Kelly nodded. "Yes. That would have been Granda's style."

"Your grandfather must have understood the increased risk of smuggling fully prepared operational radio bomb detonators. Prior to that, your improvised devices involved only commercially available two-way radios. Your conversion into detonators kept that far more self-contained. Flanagan must have learned of your grandfather through his connection with Brian Keenan in Belfast."

Kelly said, "For years Granda undoubtedly prepared for possible discovery. He understood that few secrets are ever absolute. He was eighty-one with his wife gone. Nothing left to live for. Wasn't about to allow being arrested."

O'Brien said, "Something else I uncovered poking around declassified British Army Intelligence records. Your radio command detonators rather than timer detonators were very much a concern for the security forces. From the time of their first appearance in 1972, I discovered several official reports commenting on the tactical failure of the IRA to deploy them to greater effect against police or army personnel. The same thing that troubled you with the casualties heavily weighted to civilians.

"Also discovered they recognized a period where these radio devices fell from IRA use for a period. They reappeared again around 1976. These devices were probably those sourced by your grandfather from America. These second-generation detonators were discovered to have an insidious modification. After the death of your grandfather an undetonated bomb was discovered intact. This device concealed an embedded blasting cap with a small quantity of high explosive PETN. Apparently concealed in such a way undetected by a bomb disposal technician who attempted inspection of the device without wearing protective equipment resulting in serious injury. British Army Intelligence concluded that the radio detonator triggering systems first discovered in 1972 came from the United States likely through smuggling efforts involving Liam Kelly. Thus, the historical record believes Liam Kelly was behind these radio devices produced by some unknown American bombmaker from the beginning."

"Interesting, but only adding to my legacy of misdeeds," Kelly remarked.

"Now, for your father. You know of course about his legal difficulties in 1980?"

"Yes. Unlike others in New York charged with smuggling weapons and explosives to the IRA in Northen Ireland, my father was never charged."

O'Brien said, "That is correct. Here's some information I uncovered. Those involved with IRA smuggling were arrested by the FBI Joint Terrorism Task Force. Interestingly, they were all acquitted. Excuse the pun, by a hail-Mary unusual defense. Seems the Harrison network used an Italian American arms dealer named to secure and move contraband. That individual had connections to organized crime, but more importantly, his gun running connections also involved the CIA. The defense convincingly asserted the defendants believed they were assisting the CIA and won acquittal.

"While digging into those old FBI files, there were minor references made about you. A search among passport records revealed Terence Kelly departed Boston in 1971 for Dublin. He reentered the United States in October 1973. Employed by Bell Laboratories in 1974. Employment records cited your academic background included a bachelor's degree in electrical engineering from Benjamin Franklin Cummings Institute of Technology Boston in 1970. Additionally, a master's degree from Queen's University in Belfast, Northern Ireland in 1973, awarded under your legal British name of Terence Stewart. Unusual but not illegal. Employed in Belfast by a retail electronics store and later as a technician at a radio station. This accounted for your two years studying in Northern Ireland with no political footnotes.

"A legitimate reason for being in Northern Ireland irrespective of your paternal grandfather's IRA past fifty years earlier. His death attributed by the RUC as a victim of a loyalist paramilitary bombing. In the absence of any incriminating evidence from the British, the FBI found no reason to pursue looking more deeply into your past."

"Amazing the possibilities for searching records in this day and age," Kelly remarked.

"Here's a thumbnail brief of other individuals you mentioned in your narrative. Sean Lynch acting OC of the IRA Derry Brigade was interned for IRA activities in December 1973. The incident resulted from a failed ambush on a British Army patrol in the Creggan District of Derry on 3 December. The British shot dead one IRA volunteer and wounded another. The wounded volunteer implicated Lynch in the planning of the ambush resulted in Lynch's arrest. He would spend several years in internment where he fell ill with kidney disease and died in 1977.

"Brian Keenan was arrested, convicted, and given an 18-year sentence in a London court in 1980 for murders related to IRA bombings in Great Britain. Keenan served his sentence until his release in 1993. By 1996 he had become one of seven members of the IRA's Army Council. Keenan remained a committed militant advocating for continuing the armed struggle until his death by cancer in 2008.

"Newspapers reported Alfred Thompson, age 46 at the time, was killed along with other victims in a second bombing of the Raven *Pub* in East Belfast in October 1973. This bomb was detonated inside the pub with the IRA again believed to be responsible. After his death the UVF acknowledged Thompson commanded a UVF battalion. Your story stands up with corroboration by the public records.

"Care to know what happened to Adele Thompson?"

Kelly nodded with a look of surprise mixed with some apprehension. "Of course. Hopefully not another tragedy?"

"Not at all. Took some doing since she never became a figure related to events during the *Troubles*. Spent a career as a professor of literature at Queen's University. Married a fellow QUB academic in 1981 but kept her family name for professional reasons I assume. One daughter. Widowed in 2015. Retired from QUB in 2019. Lives now in Holywood just a few miles outside Belfast."

Kelly smiled with genuine happiness "That is truly comforting to learn that Adele made a life for herself doing what she wanted. At least I avoided ruining another life."

"How did your parents respond when you returned?" O'Brien asked.

"Both relieved by my being safely back home. The recurring violence in the international news must have been a constant source of worry. Especially for my mother who never trusted her IRA father-in-law. Evident by her giving me an alternate surname on my recorded birth record. They never challenged my fabrications about my time in Northern Ireland.

"As for my father, hard to say. He had secrets of his own he kept from me. I knew my grandfather must have involved my father in finding someone over here to produce my radio detonator design. We rarely discussed what was happening in Northern Ireland following my return. Once I began working at Bell Labs, I saw my parents only occasionally. Mostly during the holidays. Mother always fawned over me. Wondering if I had a girlfriend. What did I do for fun? She developed the idea that I had profoundly changed after my return but did not understand why, nor did she directly confront me with questions.

"Of course, I had changed. Became semi-reclusive. Worked long hours as a means of occupying my time. Avoided making friends. No social orbit, only acquittances. Eventually they even fell away."

"Never another romantic interest all these years?" O'Brien asked.

"Never. Too much emotional baggage. Self-loathing an impossible obstacle to a relationship of any kind."

O'Brien said, "How are you feeling physically?"

"Like I'm dying," Kelly said laughing at his glib response that brought on a coughing spell.

After several minutes to recover, Kelly resumed, "Forgive my poor attempt at dark humor. I admire your forbearance, Father O'Brien. Couldn't have been easy for you all these weeks listening to my horror story. Not exactly a confession even a Catholic priest could absorb without experiencing distress.

Nothing more of relevance to add. My life since the 1970s adds nothing of interest to the story. Nothing in the way of adding to understanding. Certainly nothing that would evoke empathy in anyone reading your chronicle of my misadventures.

"My life of the years of 1971 to 1973 becomes the entire story. I believe all that remains is a concluding interview session. Filling in gaps that I may have overlooked in my narrative. A final discussion concerning what I believe to be my final days. What happens should I lapse into a comma? Any legal considerations of concern requiring something like a dying declaration giving you full rights without reservation to my story.

"How's your schedule over the next couple of days, Father? Feel I don't have all that much time left. Screwed up my life. Want to at least put some order to my death."

CHAPTER 33

Boston, Massachusetts | 2025

Terence Kelly's final session with Father O'Brien scheduled for three days later needed to be postponed to the following week. Kelly appeared at O'Brien's office apologizing for any inconvenience.

O'Brien asked no questions. It was evident by Terence Kelly's appearance that he had taken a turn for the worse. Medical diagnosis of longevity involving terminal disease is never precise because of the interaction of many factors. Yet for O'Brien seeing him regularly over a couple of months it became obvious Kelly's decline had noticeably accelerated.

"Been a difficult week. Caused me to get my affairs in order. I drafted these documents. Perhaps useful, if nothing else at least providing you with documented evidence that your book is not fiction."

Kelly handed O'Brien a folder. Opening it, O'Brien found a signed confession detailing his killing of Maureen Lynch, Alfred Thompson, and the three other victims of the *Raven Pub* bombing. A lengthy confession to having produced dozens of radio command bomb detonators for the Provisional IRA in 1972 and 1973. Included was a schematic design.

"I just realized how presumptuous I have been. I don't believe you ever committed to writing a book. However, that remains entirely your decision. Perhaps you will use my material differently. Maybe reshape it into a novel. Maybe reshape my character into a more empathetic protagonist. That of course has never been my intention. Couldn't very well serve as atonement unless the narrative is completely truthful."

O'Brien replied, "I appreciate your consideration, Terence, however, I assure you that I intend to write a book. The material is compelling on many levels. Haven't completely thought how I will treat your extraordinary experiences during the *Troubles.* Your life is not as simple as good or bad. The darkest circumstances are still shaded more gray than black. Not something I will fictionalize, however. I believe your story as is will read like a novel."

"Thank you, Father. My only stipulation is waiting until my death before publishing. Considering my state of decline that should not become an issue."

"Do you have extended family?"

"Not really. Only a few cousins and maybe their children from my mother's brother David Stewart. Lost contact with them when I went off to college."

"What about your financial estate? Do you have a will?"

"Yes I do. Glad you asked." Kelly handed O'Brien a two-page typed document.

"Prepared by an attorney. My estate consists of entirely financial assets. They are to go Adele Thompson, resident of Holywood, Northern Ireland, UK. I trust you will provide the attorney who will be the executor with her address at the proper time. My only other asset will be any publishing proceeds derived from your book. All such proceeds belong to you, Father O'Brien. Didn't mention that in my will. Would raise questions from my attorney that I wished to avoid. Therefore, I have drafted this separate notarized document granting you all rights to any and all financial proceeds of the book. Shouldn't be necessary under copyright laws and I doubt anyone has stature to contest that, but I prefer no loose ends."

O'Brien said, "Seems then we may have reached the end of our interview sessions, Terence. From our first meeting I sensed the story you wished to make public concerned only those few years in Northern Ireland. That was over fifty years ago. How would you wish me to describe your life after you returned to Boston."

"Describe it as fifty years of penance. Fifty years living in an emotional desert. Just relate facts that might otherwise appear in an ordinary obituary. There's no story there anyway. Nothing of interest to any reader. I have read your work, Father O'Brien. Neither your non-fiction historical books nor your novels are layered with attempts at psychological explanations of the principal figures. That's why I thought you to be particularly suited to writing not a biography, but an examination of that short window in time of my experiences during the early years of the *Troubles.* Better that my story contributes to understanding what it meant living those difficult circumstances rather than attempting to examine underlying reasons for my behavior.

"However, as to your question about the rest of my life, let me just generalize by saying I turned inward. Bell Labs offered a continual environment of technological challenges allowing immersion for what became obsessive behavior with my professional work.

"To fill my discretionary personal time, I turned to reading. Never was much of a reader except for technical material when I was young. Never appreciated the required reading of high school and undergraduate literature courses. Returning to Boston that changed. If for no other reason than I needed to immerse myself in something other than professional work.

"Although my thoughts of Adele Thompson were ones of loss, perhaps it was her enthusiasm for literature that led me to become an avid reader. Perhaps nothing more than the compulsion to escape from within myself. Northen Ireland wrought all manner of changes in me. At least my fifty years after Northern Ireland I did no harm to people.

"I began serious reading beginning with Adele's passion, Shakespeare. A tough slog with the old English and syntax, but I stuck with it. Being somewhat obsessive, I eventually discovered what Adele saw as the magnificent power and beauty of Shakespeare use of language. From there I became a bibliophile with unlimited time to devote to my emotional refuge.

"From Shakespeare I ventured into an eclectic range of literature and historical non-fiction. Of course, Irish history continued to be a particular interest. I may have lost my idealism, but the struggle of the Irish still resonated. Liam Kelly shall always remain a true hero to me. Anyway, that's how I discovered your work, Father. Surprised when discovering that Connor O'Brien was also a Jesuit priest and professor at Boston College. Diagnosed with terminal cancer, turning to you to chronicle by experiences during the *Troubles* seemed providential for what I had in mind."

"How do you intend to spend your remaining time. Terence?"

"Haven't given that much thought. Not sure I have any options. According to my oncologist, I might experience abrupt severe symptoms at any time as the cancer begins impacting other organs. Other than pain, my symptoms currently are a persistent cough, shortness of breath, and fatigue. End-stage lung cancer is an insidious way to die, Father."

"Do you have plans when your symptoms worsen to a point where you need palliative care?"

"No specific plans but someone at my medial provider's office has counselled me on alternatives. Having no family makes such decisions straightforward but no less difficult."

"I can well image. Although I realize you profess having no religious beliefs, I would be glad to offer designating me as your emergency contact in the absence of having any family. Trust me, I won't deliver you the last rites sacrament unless specifically requested."

Kelly smiled and nodded, "Thank you, Father. That is most generous of you."

O'Brien felt the lifelong damage done to Terence Kelly's psyche. Difficult to imagine living in perpetual guilt as a willing penitent but with no means for seeking peace through a meaningful form of atonement.

O'Brien asked, "Did you ever consider suicide to end your emotional distress?"

"Yes, often. Can't tell you why I never did anything about it. Perhaps a long-forgotten subliminal prohibition instilled at an early age by my Catholic upbringing. Perhaps just self-inflicted punishment to live a life barren of joy or even life's ordinary pleasures."

O'Brien said, "Might that be for lacking to find an appropriate means of atonement?"

Kelly smiled saying, "As a writer, historian, and priest you may be better equipped to answer that philosophical question. Becomes rather academic now under my present circumstances don't you think, Father?"

CHAPTER 34

Belfast, Northern Ireland | Chapter

Before boarding his British Airways flight to London Heathrow then making connections to fly on to Belfast, Terence Kelly placed a call to Father O'Brien's Boston College office.

"Good afternoon, Father. It's Terence Kelly."

"Good to hear from you. Everything okay?'

"All circumstances considering, yes. Just calling to say I'm about ready to board a flight to London then connect to a flight to Belfast. Thought I should see Belfast my place of birth for the last time while still physically able. Should something physical happen prematurely, there is no need to make any special arrangements on my behalf. Let things run their course.

"Just wanted to thank you for hearing what I call my last confession even though it certainly did not follow prescribed Roman Catholic protocol. I deposited a letter to you in the mail. I believe you to be the only person capable of understanding. Go with God, Father O'Brien. Goodbye." Kelly disconnected before O'Brien could respond."

Traveling first class and suitably drugged with morphine, Kelly felt rested when the Boeng 747 touched down at London's

Heathrow Airport. He only recently began using a cane. A reliance for support should a sudden episode of acute pain disorient him. The progression of his cancer had aged his appearance beyond his 77 years prompting solicitous assistance from airline staff.

"I see you are connecting to a flight to Belfast. Mr. Kelly, the lead flight attendant said to him." He was traveling on his U.S. passport in the name of Terence Kelly. Terence Stewart ceased to exist in 1973. That now expired passport resided in the hands of Father Connor O'Brien. "That's a three-hour layover. Would you care to relax in our first-class lounge?"

"That's a splendid idea. Which direction when I disembark?"

"It's a long walk. I'll arrange for a wheelchair and someone to take you there?"

Until today, Kelly had not felt the need for such assistance. Evidence of the state of his decline. "Perhaps that would be a good idea. Thank you."

At the British Airways lounge he past the time reading the *Belfast Telegraph* while enjoying coffee and a late breakfast. No front-page headlines of violence since the *Troubles* had long ago passed into history. Yet reading the editorial section, the power sharing between Irish nationalists and British loyalists indicated political ideologies had never fully reconciled. Possible that Northern Ireland might someday become part of the Republic of Ireland, but Kelly doubted that ever happening.

Kelly arrived at Belfast International Airport around noon the day following departing Boston owing to the differences in time zones. He took a taxi to the *Regency House Hotel.* Online he booked a spacious one-bedroom apartment for four nights in the historic building. He chose the *Regency* because of its location within a walkable quarter of a mile from Queen's University. A familiar place with its grand 19th century architecture that had not changed. The Regency's interior reflected an old world British influenced elegance. Before settling into the hotel, he planned to take a stroll to revisit the campus of Queen's University that afternoon. Although advertised as serving an exceptional breakfast, the hotel did not have a restaurant. Yet a cozy bar promised Kelly a perfect place to quietly enjoy a drink later.

Before leaving Boston he made arrangements for a hired driver to chauffeur him about Belfast the day following his arrival. On the agenda was to pass by locations recalled from his time in Belfast fifty years earlier. Using *Google Earth* street view on his mobile phone gave him a sense of what those places looked like today. Although most were drastically altered after fifty years, visiting in person for a last time satisfied an emotional need given the purpose of this trip.

The day after that he would devote himself to relaxing, enjoying the amenities and ambience of this fine hotel. Perhaps venturing out for dinner or maybe deciding to bring back a modest cold dinner of bread, cheese, and charcuterie. Accompanied by an excellent vintage bottle of wine. Since the apartment offered a small kitchen area, a perfect place to relax for someone comfortable with solitude.

Getting ever closer to the end, he cherished each hour of even small pleasures. At some point not that far off, his cancer would overwhelm everything. Death might be swift but more likely protracted. Bedridden with brief periods of consciousness distorted by the effects of heavy pain medication.

Leaving the hotel soon after arriving, he spent over an hour walking around Queen's University. It was a beautiful compact campus. Venturing inside he was amazed that he could recall much of the interior layout.

Before returning to the hotel, he forced himself to pass by the building housing the Botanic Gardens Post Office located close to the university. An act of penance. Not exceptionally different from what he remembered, the location where he murdered Maureen Lynch proved suitably disturbing.

Not hungry, he decided to walk to his former apartment that proved further than he recalled although he was able to navigate the route from memory. From the outside, his upstairs flat looked much as he remembered. Suddenly feeling tired and a bit more emotional than expected, he decided to take the bus back to the hotel. Walking slowly, he sat down at the same familiar bus stop bench looking at the sign posting the bus numbers and schedules. His smart phone displayed the bus routes on *Google Maps* that would put him close to the Regency. Eating could wait until breakfast the next morning. Another less noticeable symptom of end-stage lung cancer was loss of appetite.

Stepping back inside the *Regency* after his strenuous outing what he wanted now was a Scotch at the *Regency's* bar. Perhaps more than just one drink. Instructions were very specific about avoiding alcohol while talking morphine. Considering why he returned to Belfast that was hardly of concern. Yet he kept to a single drink before retiring to room. Needed a clear head to put certain personal items in order.

In his room he began unpacking. Emptying his single suitcase, he organized his clothing in a chest of drawers and armoire. In the bottom was a toiletry bag and package of 9V batteries. Unzipping the bag, he extracted what looked like a travel electric toothbrush and a can of shaving cream. From the end of the cylindrical toothbrush, he extracted the false endcap of what should have been a toothbrush. Instead, he dumped a cardboard cylinder with two protruding insulated wires into the palm of his hand.

Placing these pieces on the round kitchen table, he removed the top of the aerosol can of shaving cream. Again, dumping the contents into his other hand, revealed a cylindrical item with two terminals on top. A capacitor. What lay on the table were components for a bomb detonator system.

Going to his messenger shoulder bag, he extracted what appeared to be another small travel bag. His prescription bottle of morphine, mouthwash, travel size toothbrush, and travel-size atomizer bottle of cologne in its original packaging box. Kelly handled the cologne with utmost care. The bottle contained homemade nitroglycerin. Exceptionally unstable, sensitive to high temperature and impact. The reason for transporting it on the plane inside his carry-on bag allowed for preventing rough jostling. Inside the cologne packaging box, he sprayed actual cologne to help mask any explosive detection during airport security screening. However, the cap was hermetically sealed with glue to prevent any escaping molecules detectable as explosive-related compounds. Two wires also carefully sealed protruded from the cap.

Inside the vial of nitroglycerin was a makeshift exploding bridge-wire detonator. Commercially produced EBWs held a very small charge of a high explosive. A fine wire filament is instantly vaporized when applied with an appropriate electrical charge. This then detonates a very small amount of high explosive material in commercially manufactured EBWs consisting of a nitrate compound pentaerythritol tetranitrate. This detonation then detonates a larger high explosive called a booster sufficient to detonate the larger ANFO main secondary high explosive charge that produces the damage. Having no access to pentaerythritol tetranitrate, Kelly simply incorporated enough of his homemade nitroglycerin to explode when detonated by the bridge-wire filament. The quantity of concentrated nitroglycerin was sufficient to allow foregoing a booster detonation by directly detonating the ANFO main explosive.

All that remained was purchasing the ANFO explosive materials and the means of containment that could only be done after arriving in Belfast. That would be accomplished tomorrow during his chauffeured drive around Belfast. Even in checked luggage, a recognized explosive agent like ammonium nitrate might be detected by screening hardware.

After eating the advertised spectacular breakfast at the hotel the next morning, his driver arrived at 9:00. In the lobby, "Glad to meet you, Mr. Kelly. My name's Albert Blair. At your service for the day. Understand you wished to see Belfast."

"In a way, Mr. Blair. Not necessarily the tourist sites. You see I spent a couple of years here while attending QUB. That was over fifty years ago. During the worst early years of the *Troubles*. Have both fond memories and some less than fond remembrances."

Albert Blair appeared to be in his forties. He replied, "Oh my. This your first time back to Belfast since then?"

"Yes it is. Life sometimes has a way of getting away from you. Born in Belfast but grew up in Boston in America from a young age. Came over only the one time in the early seventies to attend QUB for two years. See the place of my birth. Experience my Irish heritage. So, I want to pass by some of those locations I remember from that time."

"Let's drive around QUB to begin our morning, Mr. Blair," Kelly said. "Although I walked around the grounds yesterday afternoon, the magnificent buildings are worth another last look. The place holds many fond memories amid all the violence afflicting Belfast at the time."

"Understand completely, Mr. Kelly. Other than the university, much of Belfast will be much different than how you remembered it though."

"I expect as such. Still, it's more about the feeling of once again setting foot in Belfast. Don't believe it will take all day, so I have some errands I need to run this afternoon. I'm planning to visit a cousin I never met. An old fellow like me. Lives on a small farm outside Newry. I believe I can train down there?"

"That you can, Sir."

"Fine. When we spoke on the telephone he asked if I could pick up a few items at a hardware store to help him make some small repairs. Image a couple of old men like us doing handy work, but it seems like a good way to bond having never seen each other."

"That sounds grand. Connecting with family in the old country will make your trip memorable."

They spent the morning driving somewhat randomly as Kelly's thoughts turned back in time. The former Comet Electronics' building replaced by an office structure. Belfast 2BE radio station, now BBC Radio Ulster, looked much the same. Driving within sight of the Harlan Wolff shipyard, Kelly remarked, "Only one of the giant gantry cranes was here in 1972. The second one must have been erected after I returned to America."

Blair remarked, "That unique building sitting out there is the Titanic Museum erected in 2012 in time to commemorate the hundred-year anniversary of the famous ship."

Directed to the train station by Kelly, Blair said, "What you knew as Belfast Central Train Station, was renamed Lanyon Place Railway Station several years ago."

Terence Kelly had seen enough after only a couple of hours. This trip was only partly to experience nostalgia. Its purpose was to punctuate his end in a manner of his choosing.

"Tell you what, Albert, I'm feeling a bit tired. Best I get on with my errands so I can get in a nap this afternoon before dinner. Tomorrow I want to feel rested for my visit to Newry."

"Right you are, Sir. Shall we then visit a hardware store next?"

"That'll be just fine.

The hardware store resembled a Home Depot store back in Boston. Kelly said, "Why don't you just drop me off and pick me up in one hour. Have yourself a spot of lunch. I'm not hungry and no reason for you to follow me around. Old age has slowed me down."

"Very good, Sir. I'll meet you right out in front here in one hour."

Inside, Kelly took a cart and began collecting items from a list. Materials included a twelve-inch length of three-inch diameter PVC pipe, two PVC end caps, PVC glue, an extension cord, superglue, two inline cord electrical switches, a roll of duct tape, and bag of ammonium nitrate porous prilled fertilizer from the garden supply department.

Tools purchased included a hacksaw, hand drill, utility knife, diagonal cutting pliers, wire stripping tool, and a gallon-size yellow safety can for filling later with diesel fuel. Checking out he asked the clerk if they might have a couple of empty boxes they could place his purchases in. "I will need someone's help in carrying these items for me. Boxes are easier to handle than bags."

Before leaving the hardware store, he sealed the four boxes with duct tape to conceal what his driver might find to be an unusual collection of items.

Pulling up with the car, Blair commented, "Quite a load of items you have there. Guess you and your cousin have some work ahead of you."

"Perhaps. I'm an engineer, my cousin owns a farm of which I know nothing about. Just want to come prepared. Most of these items are tools. Perhaps overkill, but I'd rather have them if needed. A farmer can never have too many tools.

"A bit tired out now though, Albert. I believe I've had enough for today. What say we head back to the hotel? Help me carry these boxes to my room and you can call it a day."

"Very well, Sir. Sure you don't want to see some of the popular visitor sights. Maybe the peace wall located between Falls Road and Shankill Road in West Belfast? A legacy carryover from those terrible old days you experienced?"

"No, I think not, Albert, but thank you anyway. Don't need reminders about the terrible violence during that time."

After Albert Blair and a bellman carried up the boxes to his room. Only one more task remained. He needed to obtain a quart of diesel fuel. When returning to the hotel, he noticed a filling station only a couple of blocks from the hotel. Feeling a little tired, he had no choice but to make the trek. He could not very well be observed carrying a yellow safety can for flammable liquids to and from the hotel. Selecting the smallest of the cardboard boxes allowed concealing the shallow can. Cutting handholds made for easier carrying when filled with diesel fuel with his cane hooked over his forearm.

Having returned to the hotel from the filling station, Kelly sat down to rest for a while. He planned to assemble his improvised bomb following his original design before venturing out to enjoy an excellent dinner. Then return to the comfortable bar at the Regency. A perfect atmosphere to enjoy a couple of drinks before attempting to get a good night's rest.

With concluding everything planned for tomorrow there remained only one uncertainty that lay beyond his control. The most important aspect of making this brief return to Belfast.

Assembling the bomb took less than an hour. The design clearly established within his memory as if decades of time had never passed. Everything fit inside his messenger shoulder bag. On top of the bomb's explosive material contained in the PVC tube rested the detonation components. Two loops of the extension cord were cannibalized to provide insulated wiring connections to the inline switches. White wires for arming the bomb by connecting the batteries to charge the capacitor. Black wires for connecting the capacitor output to detonate the nitroglycerin that would then detonate the ANFO. Placing the shoulder bag against his chest, he should not experience the near instantaneous death caused by the explosion.

Could he go through with it? Death was death but the vision of a horribly violent death like that he delivered on Maureen was still disturbing. Should he lose his nerve, resting next to the bomb switches was a full bottle of horded morphine tablets of sufficient quantity to cause a fatal overdose. Not sure how painless that might be, but once ingested, it became final.

The evening passed with an excellent dinner and pleasant solitary enjoyment of a couple of Scotches in the Regency bar. Situated in a comfortable corner chair, the solitude in the softly lit bar area displaying the elegant wood décor concluded his final evening.

Although not well rested, Terence Kelly was nonetheless prepared to execute his plan. His mind emptied as much as possible of old memories, he focused on the plan for that morning. In his sport coat pocket, he extracted a piece of paper. It was the current address of Adele Thompson provided by Father O'Brien. When he made plans for returning a last time to Belfast, seeing Adele was not initially included. A reunion could only inflict new pain long ago having receded into the distant past. Unfair to her and quite likely to derail him from carrying out his theatrical demise.

Instead, he wished only to stand close to her for a few minutes. Look into her eyes. She would not recognize him after fifty years, even more so since the cancer had greatly altered his appearance. Looking in the mirror that morning he saw only a dying old man. He would take a taxi and tell the driver only

Church Road in Holywood. Tell the driver he didn't know the exact address but would recognize it when he spotted it. Once passing Adele's address he would have the taxi deposit him a block away.

Holywood was only a short ride. As the taxi passed beyond Adele's address, Kelly said, "Ah, that's it. You can drop me here, driver."

His only fear was Adele not being home. He had no backup plan. This was only a singular opportunity. Ringing the doorbell, he waited an agonizing minute, but the door finally opened. "Yes? Can I help you?" Adele said. Although she had aged fifty years, no question this was Adele.

"My name is John Sullivan. I was looking for Evelen Hughes. A distant relation I have never met. Might that be you?"

"No. "I'm afraid not." She had now opened the door widely to speak to this elderly man.

Kelly gazed into her face and said, "So sorry to have bothered you. My sister-in-law in New York asked if I would look up her cousin Evelyn since I was attending a funeral of one of my cousins in Belfast. The address I was given is 72 Church Avenue. Turns out there's no such number. Wondered if maybe it might be Church Road. Since you are not Evelen, guess the house number might also be incorrect."

"Do you live in the United States?" Adele asked.

"Yes. New York. My parents emigrated to America when I was a child long before the terrible years of the *Troubles.* Still have a few extended family members in Northern Ireland though. Since retiring, I've made the trip a couple of times. Again, I apologize for bothering you, madam. Have a nice day."

"Good luck to you, Sir."

Kelly began walking away turning to wave at Adele. She returned his wave before closing her front door.

On his mobile phone he found directions to the Holywood train station. A manageable walk of only a half mile. Checking train schedules previously he knew trains ran every twenty minutes between Holywood and central Belfast. Back in Belfast he took a 15-minute taxi ride to Stormont, the seat of the regional government of Northern Ireland.

Ending his life on the picturesque grounds of Stormont held no meaning for him. Just a suitable place but with no implied significance.

Finding his end in Belfast held only personal reasons. Visiting the location of his misadventures that cost him so much in life. The opportunity to look into the eyes of Adele Thompson for just a couple of minutes made the effort worthwhile. The imagery of his death by a bomb might become more poignant to her once O'Brien published his story and she discovers the Terence Stewart she once knew was Terence Kelly.

Dropped off by a taxi, he walked to the Reconciliation Sculpture that featured a man and woman kneeling while embracing. It was located only a short distance in front of the Northern Ireland Parliament Building.

For Terence Kelly, the expression of loss suggested by the artist spoke to the larger tragedy of the *Troubles* of Northern Ireland. The scene and silence on this overcast day created an appropriate atmosphere. No other people were close enough to be harmed by the blast. Shifting the shoulder bag around to his chest, he reached inside arming the bomb. Hesitating only a few seconds, Terence Kelly then ended his life on his own terms.

Father Connor O'Brien received the envelope Terence Kelly mailed before departing Boston. Although what the enclosed letter suggested came as no shock, it still saddened him. O'Brien agreed with Kelly's symbolic gesture as befitting the tragedy of his life. Several days later he learned about Kelly's public suicide in Belfast. Following Kelly's identification, articles began appearing in newspapers on both sides of the Atlantic. Much of the coverage dealt with Terence Kelly's heritage through the exploits of his grandfather Liam Kelly as an IRA gunman working for Michael Collins a hundred years ago. However, O'Brien was pleased with other coverage that dealt with the modern-day tragedy of the *Troubles* in Northern Ireland that served as the backdrop of the story he would write.

Terence Kelly's letter to O'Brien appeared a year later as the forward of O'Brien's bestselling book, *Winter of Discontent.*

6 August 2025
Boston College
Office of Professor Father Connor O'Brien

Father O'Brien:

These last few months of listening to me recount my misdeeds can only have been disturbing to say the least. For me as well. Thinking it as possibly a means of expressing atonement to ease dealing with my impending death has only achieved the opposite. Revisiting in detail the cold reality only magnified my unforgivable acts of violence. While progressing toward an agonizing natural death, morphine held the pain at bay but did nothing for the mind. Nothing can ameliorate by profound feelings of guilt. Even during my more frequent morphine-induced episodes of managing acute pain, nothing eased the ever-present background of emotional distress. Why suffer a day longer? Therefore, while still capable I shall embark on my final project. An iconic end to all my suffering. A befitting act of atonement although there can never be any real atonement for the taking of lives under the guise of misplaced ideology or killing for purely selfish motives.

I recall the opening lines of the soliloquy to Shakespeare's Richard III. *Now is the winter of our discontent, made glorious summer by this son of York.* For me, *Bloody Sunday* in Derry of January 1972 began my winter of discontent as it did for the whole of Northern Ireland's Catholics. The summer that followed became anything but glorious. *Bloody Friday* in Belfast that summer day in

July began the transformation of my idealism becoming disillusionment. Now with my life ending, I recall Dylan Thomas' poem about facing death. *Do not go gentle into that good night. Old age should burn and rave at close of day. Rage, rage against the dying of the light.* I shall rage against that dying of light in my own way by delivering an iconic ending to my suffering. Perhaps this might be seen as a more fitting act of atonement rather than allowing the natural progression of cancer to dictate my death.

A terrible irony that I chose the same way to end my life as by beloved grandfather, yet for entirely different reasons. His arguably noble, mine decidedly ignoble.

Enclosed is my old British passport in the name of Terence Brendan Stewart. Another piece of documentation to bolster the factual authenticity of your manuscript.

May peace be with you, Father O'Brien.

Terence Stewart Kelly

www.ingramcontent.com/pod-product-compliance
Lightning Source LLC
Chambersburg PA
CBHW032236010726
47494CB00002B/517

9781638682257